THE TRUTH BOX

THE TRUTH BOX

Brian Schmitt

ISBN 979-8-9878788-0-4 (paperback)
ISBN 979-8-9878788-1-1 (ebook)

Il n'y a pas de hors-texte.

-    Jacques Derrida

I have a prejudice against people who print things in a
foreign language and add no translation.

- Mark Twain, *A Tramp Abroad*

MAIN CAST

William Burroughs............ PURPLE HEART RECIPIENT

Jamie Lafferty.................... ARTIST

Mary-Belle Lafferty........... FORMER MODEL AND POET

Peter Burroughs................ AGENT

Arthur De La Cruz.............. PROGRAMMER

SUPPORTING CAST

Ada Burroughs.................. WIFE OF PETER BURROUGHS

Dr. William Burroughs..... THEORETICAL PHYSICIST

Ophelia Matisse............... GALLERY OWNER

Richard Palient................. PARTNER TO PETER BURROUGHS

Senator Paul Palient........ SENATE MAJORITY LEADER

Beaty Angelo.................... F. BEATY BURROUGHS

Harold Pine...................... LEAD RESEARCHER

Clarence Kowarski........... LEAD SUPERVISING AGENT

G..................................... ?????????????????????????

Belial.. FALLEN ANGEL

Prologue

CASE FILE #19:9 - REPORT #ATJT4433

Reporting Agent #12-36: Peter Burroughs

Purpose: Recently and temporarily assigned to Classified level 8 clearance for monitoring file #8-32, the *modulating intelligence apparatus* (codenamed "Laplace's Demon")

Status: Open

Background: modulating intelligence apparatus designed by REDACTED. Apparatus resembles a perfect sphere measuring 17.17 centimeters in diameter. Apparatus is made of an unknown metal alloy casing and thermoplastic polymer. Apparatus uses cathode ray tubing technology to display output on the surrounding phosphor-coated layer. Interaction with apparatus requires verbal input by the user. Upon providing the apparatus with a vocal query, the apparatus responds via phosphor-screen in text.

Output is displayed to the user at whichever orientation the user is viewing (i.e., apparatus can display results at any longitudinal/latitudinal point on the spherical surface).

Current research and observations have speculated (without reasonable certainty or assurance) that internal mechanisms house an infinite amount of decaying atoms. The device's answers to queries depend on calculating predictability between decaying atoms entangled with the user and evaluating likelihood of statistically feasible branches of reality at that point in time.[1]
Note: apparatus is preposterously accurate and incredulously dangerous.

Last known interactions with apparatus: Subjects 34, 37, 36

Subject 34 Name: REDACTED (agreed participant): Stage II limited observation

Subject 37 Name: REDACTED (agreed participant): Incapacitated

Subject 36 Name: William Burroughs (undisclosed agreement): Deceased

   Case: Subject 36

---

[1] Note: Researching agent #44-45 AF has indicated in synchronous reports that their professional evaluation of this interpretation is "fucking idiotic and nonsensical" and recommends that agents proposing this interpretation seek "severe psychological evaluation."

Date of video observation: REDACTED
Time of video observation: 3:36 p.m. — 4:48 p.m.

Begin video transcription:

3:36 p.m. - Sub.36 is the last known possessor of the apparatus and was considered a severe threat to national and international security.

3:23 p.m. - Agent 12-36 began conducting interrogative procedures. Due to Sub. 36's injuries, Agent 12-36 documents the interrogation on a legal pad and an approved #2 pencil. (Please note that further investigation of these notes due to video corruption show no evidence of diligent note taking, but instead doodles of crude renderings of cartoon rabbits and what appears to be either a large penis or slender rocketship).

3:35 p.m. — Agent 12-36 sets down the provided writing utensil and presents retrieved apparatus to Sub. 36.

3:49 p.m. — Sub. 36 interacts with apparatus.

3:50 p.m. — Apparatus provides a report to Sub. 36's query.

NOTE: Video corruption occurs at 3:51 p.m. time stamp. No further documented recording of interaction exists; please use the following verbal descriptions for any further investigation and review of these events.

3:55 p.m. Sub. 36 proceeds to use utensils to mutilate wrists and bleeds profusely. Agent 12-36 has a reported history of inaction in the face of danger to others. Also diabetic and doesn't like to talk about it.

3:57 p.m. — Agent 12-36 attempts to subdue Sub. 36. Sub. 36 does not lessen grasp on the utensil and continues attempts to self-mutilate wrists and throat. Sub. 36 is crying profusely and begging Agent 12-36 to allow him to proceed. Assisting Agent #101, Richard Palient, is present but is not assisting. According to Agent 12-36, Agent #101 used this opportunity to secure the apparatus and left the room.

4:00 p.m. - Agent 12-36 declares Sub. 36 deceased at 4:00 p.m.

End video transcription

This report is meaningless and no one will ever read it. Blah blah blah, yabbah dabbah doo.

Report conclusion: This video record is the last confirmed appearance of Laplace's Demon.

Find Richard Palient.

Chapter One
The 36 Officers Problem

The truth is, ever since the war I found it difficult to walk without swinging my arms in tandem with my legs. Right arm, right leg, left arm, left leg, marching like one of those wind-up toy soldiers. As a kid I always loved trying to swing my arms in tandem. I loved that awkward, static tension that would build up in my joints. I'd raise my legs up as high as I could. We were made to walk like monkeys. We weren't built to walk like soldiers. That needs to be drilled into you. You need to be broken in. But now I can't help it. Sometimes I have to stop in the middle of a crosswalk to resist the motion. It really sets you off balance; having no sense of balance, that does wonders for my dating life.

Walking that way, I look like an awkward penguin with gout. (Forgive me if I don't come across as poetic. Sometimes I find myself getting fancy with words in my head, but not often enough). Walking with each arm and its corresponding legs swinging together like pendulums locked together. People stare. Most carry that befuddled but polite look, trying not to stare but forgiving a quick glance. I try my best to correct it, failing miserably when my legs freeze and refuse to move. I tell myself I've learned to live with it, but even an idiot like me has enough sense to understand the simple truth that I'm a lying son of a whore that cannot be trusted.

Ever since the war I found it difficult to remember what the ocean looked like. I had daydreams, sure—but they blurred together, like memories often do. All I can picture these days is some scramble of seagulls squawking, and palm trees purring, with some grayish shades of blue mixed in here and there. What I wouldn't do to actually see some ocean again, and think about all the weight underneath. All those creatures and secrets swimming about, in the dark.

Ever since the war I found it difficult to forget. Some nights I try to sleep but fail at that, too. Always falling into an awful trap of thinking about sleeping when trying to fall asleep. Plagued by trying to replay shot-for-shot my most embarrassing moments of the day (like saying "you're welcome" to a cashier that gave me my change) or the awkward five-minute silence that dominated my first date with a beautiful woman way out of my league. Or the people I killed. They keep me up, too.

The truth is, ever since I could remember, I found it difficult to believe in God. Some kind of otherworldly anchor to lean on, a motivation to keep me standing (if only) when the world seems so ephemeral, when everything and everyone you try to hold with your last gasp of desperate passion slips through your hands like sand.

Things could be different if I knew some answers. if I could step up to that bastard's throne in heaven and make my demands. Fix my ailments, like my broken toy soldier walk, or forgetting about the awful things I've done and will do, or the constant visions and voices that I have to remind myself daily are not really there. I don't know which. Remove all possibilities of public humiliation at grocery stores and banks when people see or hear me walking by, or end the constant makeshift realities that keep me up at night, or find a stable mental satisfaction in having privileged knowledge of that most privileged truth about purpose, about destiny, about eternal salvation or damnation, and all those funny little things.

It's all because reality seems so finicky at times. Some days, I see agents in suits following me for some awful crime. Other days, I'm shadowed by demons taking bets on the manner in which I'll die. Other days, I just hear an anxious and bickering chorus of my voice, telling me that I did something wrong, or someone thinks ill of me for how I said something, or some other truth or non-truth—I can't tell the difference anymore. Some days are nice. But even on those days, I have to wonder what's all in my head, or what's really in front of me.

The way I see it, we shape the narratives of our little worlds with the questions we ask (and the ones we refuse to ask ourselves). If given the chance, I'm not sure if I'd rather keep the wool over my eyes. Whether to know the secrets behind the magician's tricks or remain in blissful ignorance. A nice, willing blindness that keeps my world just palatable enough to get by.

If God would grant me one wish, I'm honestly not sure how altruistic I would be. If no one was watching, then I would absolutely ask how I can fix my toy soldier walk, or how to forget about the terrible things I've done, or maybe some soluble proof of what is real and what is not. And, for the life of me, I still don't know which one of those I'd prefer. I'd have to make an uneducated guess that the question I *would* ask could only be revealed in the heat of such a moment.

This whole truth business has been bothering me for a while. It's not really one of those stories where you should say "it all started with." I hate clichés. The story kind of came out of nowhere, like most wonderful and horrible parts of our lives; it came out of nowhere, but still a fatalistic culmination of all the stupid acts I've ever done. A bunch of random pieces that happen to fit together.

If we have the truth of it all, where would we go next? Is there anywhere else to go? Our world and everything around us is constantly peaking to the point we wholeheartedly believe we just can't simply go any farther. We peaked with the radio. We peaked with the television. We peaked when we went to the moon. We peaked when we discovered quantum relativity. We've had microwaves and smartphones and self-automated cars and electric toothbrushes, and all these amazing revolutions somehow became commodities. At what point will our technology bring us close enough to God to find out he's not really there at all?

But, really, it didn't all start with that. Really, it all started with my father.

***

My CO once gave me some unforgettable advice when we were changing socks: there are parts you can throw away and parts you can't. Later on, an IED took his arm, but luckily he kept the other one.

One part I can't throw away is my father. It's been a hard time dealing with my father. I've told Beaty that, and she agrees. Even she visits him and finds dealing with him is harder than dealing with me. The truth is, it takes a good amount of liquoring up some courage to deal with him most of the time. It's been two whole years since I last spoke to him, two full, robust years not playing victim to his nonsensical ramblings.

A year ago to this day, during my last visit, I made the steadfast promise to myself that I would stop visiting my father.

"Pretty bland out today," I blurted out, in front of Dr. Ramirez. I could never avoid the intelligence and wisdom in her weary eyes. Dr. Ramirez quickly and easily became the best part of the visits with my father, no matter how guilty it made me feel about Beaty. Each of the five minutes we spent together—I begged for them to last hours, but they flew by in seconds. I'd walk in, giver her my best smile and always worry I had something stuck in my teeth, ask her how her day went, and she'd give the same response every time under her breath: "que dia de mierda," then she'd look at me, smile, and say, "wonderful day, you?" I knew the word shit, and I knew the word day. I knew what they meant in isolation, but not the combination.

I envied her for that, being able to look at your day and judge it instead of all of your days kind of blending together. Then I'd feel guilty for feeling envious.

Her coffee cup had faint marks of her bright red lipstick. She sat on her desk, legs crossed. Her hair was a little frazzled and messy.

I wanted to learn Spanish as a way to make my move. I wanted to reply to her and say, "Today was a good day" in my best fluent Spanish. It was the only phrase I knew. I memorized it. But this time, when I tried to say it, a thick line of spit spilled out of my mouth and I stumbled over the words.

She pretended not to notice. She took another sip from her coffee, making the lipstick stain darker.

"How is my father?" I asked, this time a little more gracefully (and slowly).

"Typical…It must be hard seeing your father like this. He used to be famous, now…"

"Yeah, he sure was a…stand-up guy."

I signed the daily log, and made my way in. The chessboard tile mile. Down the hallway, the black-and-white tiles reminded me of a death-row mile, so I called it the chessboard mile. The walk lasted an eternity, my father's room situated on the far left end. A cruel joke by the God I don't quite believe in—making me, with my gimp soldier walk, to muster the courage to walk the mile. I could never handle the judgmental stares of orderlies and doctors and interns and nurses and dying patients, watching me walk the chessboard mile. Another reason not to visit. One man from his chair shouted at me, "Charlie! Charlie! I haven't seen you in years!" He had a clean-shaven face, but overgrown and disheveled hair, and blood coming out of his eyes. Next to him was a black shadow demon, wrapping its thin tentacles around his neck. I tried to walk faster.

In a rush, the chessboard spawned massive, towering pawns and knights with blood in their eyes, towering over me and corning me where I stood.

10. 9. 8.

I closed my eyes, but I could still feel the warm sensation of the horses breathing down my neck.

7. 6. 5.

I forgot to take my prescription, is all. I had to remind myself at 4. that this was not the real world, it was just those fantasies creeping up again.

3. They are not real.
2. I am real. (Pretty sure).
1. I'm going to be a-o-k.
They had disappeared when I opened my eyes.

I'd try to make up therapeutic games to distract me while I walked the chessboard mile—pretending the black tiles were lava, timing my penguin steps to the tune of "Funky Town." Whatever it took to make the trip to my father's room as quick and painless as possible. I'd sometimes worry that security recorded my walks on their cameras, and watched it over and over again, laughing, showing it to their friends. If all the world's a stage, I'm the jester for the crowd to crap on. (But that's okay—at least I had a purpose.)

My father's room reminded me of cheap motel art—you know the kind, a portrait of a fruit bowl, nothing pretty to look at, but just there as space filler, banished forever to the plane of peripheral vision. My father actually had such a fruit bowl, filled with plastic bananas, grapes, and apples, which he obsessively insisted must all remain exactly still.

Here's one major reason I hated visiting my father: he wholeheartedly believed he was stuck in an oil painting. Since adopting this unique worldview, he quickly developed a compulsive and injurious need to keep everything completely still and fixed in place. If a pencil leaned the wrong way in his cup, he'd have a nervous breakdown and strip nude, pulling his hair out in a panic. He kept the blinds permanently shut to eliminate shadows and sunbeams from disrupting his impression. I wondered why he didn't worry about visitors, especially me. He never fretted about my presence in his oil painting world. I think

11

the truth is, to him, I just wasn't there. After all, while he traveled the world riding on his mathematical genius, I wasn't there either—so why should I be here?

But I was there, there with an immense weight on my shoulders that I believed to be guilt, blended with an exhausting shame. A shame for being that type of blasphemous son who disrespected his progenitor, who broke the cardinal taboo of casting out his father when his father was ill. There's nothing more abhorrent than a son who leaves his sick father to die alone. Atlas had to carry the world. I had to carry guilt.

I swallowed that guilt again (not for the last time), and walked in. A familiar and bitter wave of bleach burned my eyes. Everything had to be perfectly clean; if one spot on the counter was dirty, it would ruin the oil painting he was stuck in. This was an acute detour from his decor prior to the oil-painting delusion—his rooms used to be strewn with messy scribbled equation proofs that I'm sure began to make less and less sense over time. Proofs that tried to make sense of the world; proofs that made my father famous among smart people; and lay-people who didn't understand the proofs...well, those people were instead enchanted by his penchant for philandering and witty public antics. My father used to say that he stood on the shoulders of giants for so long that he eventually became one of the giants. He did, in fact—but he didn't understand that when giants fall, they also fall pretty hard.

These doctors, they could never understand, let alone explain how this delusion began, or why he rationalized the apocalypse if something in his room changed position. He had been practically bed-ridden for almost a year now, but that wouldn't stop his nonsensical berating of the cleaners and nurses who soon refused to attend to him. He once scolded me for an entire hour for leaving a coffee ring stain on his counter, despite the fact that he sometimes couldn't walk there by himself anymore. He told me, in a crazed, pathetic howl, how disappointed he was with me, how I had failed him. I knew this was the sick and frail old man talking, and not just my father. My real father never had the guts to say exactly how he felt about me.

In the beginning of his deterioration into a pile of skin and bones, when he still had a beer gut, the doctors were liberal with allowing my father to decorate and manipulate his room. After all, a great oil painting needs color and vibrancy; it requires attention to detail, an eye for beauty. He wanted the walls washed with a faded orange with waves and swipes of blue mixed in. It reminded me of an artsy coffee shop on a college campus. Fake plastic plants hung in front of the closed windows. The walls were decorated with cheap, small oil paintings that Peter had found at estate sales for bankrupt motels. The kitchen was immaculately adorned in rosewood, with cabinets full of untouched bottles of cheap drug-store wine.

That morning, lying stiff in his bed, his mouth gaped open, and his eyes half shut—for just a moment, I thought he was finally dead. I'm ashamed to admit it, but I felt a little relief—maybe even celebration. But he fooled me again; he turned his head crankily, and opened his cloudy, lifeless eyes. I became suspicious that they drugged him this morning, something they only do during his really crazy days. His swollen, haunted eyes struggled to blink. "Where's Peter?" He gasped dryly. His arms were

stiffly parallel with the rest of his papery body, naked—
except for his diaper.

"I'm sure he's been busy, Dad. New cases and files
every day. Good career comes with a heavy workload." I
tried my best to sound proud rather than jealous.

He kept quiet for a while. I did a tour to make sure
nothing had moved; no paintings were crooked; the
kitchen was so clean you could lick the floors; the ceiling
fan didn't have a speck of dust, staying in the same,
peculiar position it had always been. Whoever managed
to clean the fan without moving it must have had otherworldly powers.

My father mumbled to himself quite often. I could
barely understand a lick of it. His mumbles were conversations with himself, and his face adopted an inquisitive
and reserved look—like he was lecturing another one of
his seminars. For brief periods his mumbles would
synchronize into to some semblance of sensible speech.
"Space is out there, above us, around us, in us. In fields of
electromagnetism, space becomes ethereal and pushes
off into some boundary outside of space." He wandered
around, carrying a wide-mouth bottle, labeled "URINE DO
NOT DRINK" in black sharpie. This was the bottle we
would help him piss in on days when he couldn't move.
Today, it was murky-yellow, half-full. "It becomes non-
space. It becomes the opposite of space. The quantum
field...evaporates..."

I lost track of his jabberwocky, his Mad Hatter riddles
without any answers, wishing again that he would just die
already, along with an inevitable baggage of shame for
wishing this to come true.

What surprised me most about this final visit was the
dispiriting yet plain realization that my father did not

have any pictures of Peter and me. He didn't have a single picture of my mother.

We tried to place framed photos here and there, but they always disappeared. I tried incognito pictures of my mother. Peter tried pictures of himself and his mother. We never had the courage to ask him where they all went; obviously he would discover them and throw them away, disruptions to his perfectly-still, oil-canvas reality.

"What'd they give you for breakfast today, Dad?"

He had to think about it for a moment—incredible how a genius like him could go on for hours about stupid quantum fields but stumbled with remembering what he ate an hour ago. "Runny eggs." Then he went back to his muttering. This was the whole of it, just like every other visit. A conversation about eggs, handfuls of scrambled conversations and over-easy awkward silences.

He nodded at me, a request to help him walk. Ritualistically, he would demand a walk every few hours, a quick stroll around his apartment, likely to get his blood flowing, to feel in control again, to check and make sure nothing had changed. I helped him up carefully, worried I would shatter his arm if I pulled too hard.

My father continued to shuffle around, aimlessly mumbling about space and time. He'd go off on tangents ranging from quantum fields to horse races, all the while arguing with himself about probabilities and realities. "We created a wormhole," he said. "Multiple universes spreading out into infinity, all different artists and all different probabilities and all different times, all in the same space, at the same time."

He stopped for a moment, became oddly quiet, and stared at a closet door at the end of the hall, across from his bedroom. I had never noticed this closet before. It seemed so innocent and forgettable, but now I couldn't take my eyes off it. A whole minute passed before he began muttering again.

The closet door was pristine; the handle barely worn. When I opened it, it barely made a sound.

It was a utility closet. Besides the typical water heater and furnace, in the back there was a steel brown safe, about knee-high, with a numbered padlock.

My father was not one to tell us much of anything. This was not out of an effort to keep secrets. It was more apathy than anything else. That being said, I was clueless. Anything could have been in the safe. $100,000 dollars. Gold bars. Elegant equations that solved the mysteries of the universe. Pictures of me and Peter.

But there was something else, tucked away underneath the shaking pipes of the water heater, hidden behind caked-on grime and cobwebs. It was a thick, black binder, the edges curling from humidity, ready to fall apart. I checked behind me to make sure my father was still sol-iloquizing like a mad scientist, dragging his soles as he shambled about, often freezing his gaze on the couch cushions to study whether that had moved an inch. It all reminded me of the days before he was bedridden; he'd methodically attend to every quadrant about the room, adjusting the salt and pepper shakers, the plastic fruit bowls, even the lengths of the blind cords until it all was perfectly placed; sometimes, in his ranting, he'd get so upset, he'd go fully nude and stumble around, screaming that things were not the way they were supposed to be. I can't recall how many times the nursing staff would call myself or Peter, complaining that our father had fallen over again without any clothes, sometimes soiling himself and the carpet—then he'd complain the next day if the carpet wasn't fully cleaned and spotless.

The thick, black binder was stuck tightly between three condensated pipes. I managed to pull it out, but it got caught on a pipe and tore through the plastic covering, exposing the cardboard underneath. If my father knew about this, he'd have a nude panic attack. But I wasn't too concerned about that. I had never seen this before, and I almost wished I hadn't found it. I became incessantly worried about what was inside this plainly black binder, hidden away in some careless location, to rot in an unmarked grave.

My father was distracted by a leaf on his giant plastic ficus. It likely moved from the wind when I first came in. "Everything has to stay exactly as it was!" he muttered, hunched over, meticulously adjusting the leaf slightly to return it to its assigned, purposeful position.

While he was distracted, I took the binder into the bathroom and quietly closed the door. The binder was all black, with no title, no heading, no picture. It felt a lot heavier than I expected, soggy from the condensation in its former prison.

When I opened it, my worry quickly turned to rage. It was a photo album. Pictures of all of us. Peter and me as babies, as kids, as teenagers; older photos of my father, with my mother, and Peter's mother; my crazy kindergarten drawings of giant rabbits and monkeys; photocopies of our report cards all the way to high school; a caricature drawing of my father, Peter, and me holding cotton candy beside some blurry Ferris wheel; Peter's graduation; a few photos of me in uniform before the war; nothing of me after the war; a suspension letter from the principal when I pissed in the hallway outside of class because the teacher sent me out for crying about having to go; Peter's glorious moment in soccer when he scored the game-winning goal and won the regional championship. All these memories, all these valuable snapshots of our broken little family tucked away under a water heater. I supposed I should have been delighted that he even kept the album. But I can rationalize my rage this way: these mementos of ours were so incredibly worthless to our father that he deliberately chose *not* to keep them in that steel safe. Instead, they deserved their rightful spot in his precious oil painting—not framed and mounted on walls, not resting by his dying bedside. Instead they were hidden away, tucked behind a water heater in a clammy and dilapidated utility room.

I wasn't sure what I meant to do with it. I brought it with me to check on him again. I asked him what this was, and why he had been hiding it this whole time. His skin turned red instantly. He violently began to slam his frail fists on the door frame of his bedroom.

"Fuck you!" He spat, "Fuck you! What have you done?! Why did you move it?!" He started shaking. "I don't want to see that! Years! Gone! The structure of it all! Everything has to be precise!" He kept slamming his fists into the door frame, the edges of his hand already bruised and likely broken. When I stepped closer, he lunged for me, grasping at my shirt collar. Pulling me up close, he snapped his teeth at me, like a snapping turtle, and tried to bite me, his dried and cracked lips bleeding. "My life's work! What have you done with my life's work!" He spat in my face, and then desperately tried to wrestle the photo album away from me with all of his brittle strength. Then he rammed his forehead into my nose. I fell back into his nightstand, a bowl of plastic fruits bursting into the air. I could taste blood, a clogging and warm sensation growing in my nostrils. He looked at me, a mixture of disbelief, panic, morphine, and regret drawn over his sunken face.

I couldn't help myself. Moments later I was tearing down his plastic plants, flipped over his fruit bowls, turned the ceiling fan on high. I flipped the cabinet doors open in the kitchen and swept all the wine bottles out, crashing in a crescendo on the kitchen floor. My footprints, caked in red wine, left their marks all over the carpet and hardwood floor.

Then, I snatched the piss bottle he was holding in his hands, and threw it right in his face.

When I think about it, I may have overreacted. But I felt defeated, and betrayed, knowing this album of all of us had existed this whole time and I had never, ever seen it before in my thirty-plus years of (barely) living and (hardly) breathing and (always) limping on this earth—this album, what he called "his life's work," tucked away to mold and rot in the humid utility closet of a decrepit and withering genius. As I've always suspected—a world renowned scientist first, a loving father a distant second.

I left him in his despairing misery, taking the binder with me. I shut the door as hard as I could, and heard it crack. I didn't walk the chessboard mile back, I ran—and you could never imagine what it felt like to run after years of not running. Maybe it wasn't actually *running*, what with my broken soldier legs and arms, swinging together like clockwork. But it sure felt like I was running, tears running and nosebleed flowing. Despite the complexity of how I felt, despite the aggressive state of my father and the de-pressive state of my position in the multiverse my father had proven to exist, I seized this fleeting and palpable moment of pure existence—I felt real, more real than I had in quite some time. I sped past Dr. Ramirez and heard her shouting something in Spanish on my way out.

The truth is, I haven't thought about the significance of that afternoon—if it even happened at all—until now.

Chapter Two
Prelude to a Fugue

fugue
fyo͞og/
noun

1. **MUSIC**
   a contrapuntal composition in which a short melody or
   phrase (the subject) is introduced by one part and
   successively taken up by others and developed by in-
   terweaving the parts.

2. **PSYCHIATRY**
   a state or period of loss of awareness of one's identity,
   often coupled with flight from one's usual environment, associated with certain forms of hysteria and
   epilepsy.[2]

---

[2] Source: some dictionary I found lying around in the closet.
Who even has those anymore?

I'm facing death and staring back into the cold hollows of her eyes. Death has given me an order to write my final chapter and find some meaning in there, somewhere. I've been informed by Death that my services on this plane of existence are no longer needed, and now I may discover if another plane is out there, or if everything I've ever been told has been an empty promise of a purposeful afterlife. The paleness in her cheeks, matching her pale white coat and her pale white voice, coldness only comparable to her stethoscope dangling from her neck like an ancient seer's talisman—a voice of reason and science urging that time is not a joke and it has limits, and there's a terrible tragedy in realizing that time does not exist when we are at our most joyful; and, in those most despaired and awful moments, we understand that time does exist and the pendulum will eventually slow to a halt; and every effort we give to push it and maintain its swinging confidence will always lose to gravity and friction, and it will eventually slow down again, and eventually our pushes won't be strong enough to keep it going, and this is not a moment that can be remedied by chance or effort or will, as the graveness in her voice illustrates vividly: I am bound by the circumference of an approaching date that I will never know exactly, that it will just simply "happen" and I will be gone forever, like flatulence—a subtle vibrant burst of warmth and life, followed by an empty juvenile feeling of valuable time lost in the wind.

William, my neighbor, tells me I have a certain way with words. That sometimes he prefers me to narrate the world for him while he keeps his eyes closed, because my poetry is often better than the "shit world I actually see." Today, spending our afternoon again on the roof of our downtown apartment tower in our two dilapidated pool lounge chairs, facing westward, pretending the gravel under our feet is sand on some beach faraway from all this nonsensical living.

"Jamie always spoke about a certain poetry of moments," I say, "that a hailstorm in Louisiana must mean something, that a broken wagon wheel, down the road (forgive the metaphor) must eventually *mean* something. When you're facing the impenetrable face of death, metaphors lose their value by the pound, and the blade crafted by your years of blatant ignorance starts to whittle away at any remaining hope you have left."

"Morbid," William burps. William has told me many times that I must be a writer, that I clearly don't write anymore since here I am, fading away in reverse polaroid, with a "schmuck like him." Mary, the so-called poet of many words; William, the bum who walks funny.

"When the sun rises between two mountain peaks, there's a hint of poetry. When some vagrant begging for change on the curb of I-whatever gets to sip a little lukewarm coffee, gifted to him from a driver who had a singular moment of clarity, that is a moment of altruistic bullshit poetry, because that driver decided to create the moment. Poetry isn't created. Poetry *happens.* And this bullshit happened to me, so there must be some kind of poetry there. Some fantastic and Shakespearic smoking gun that turns my story around. Because, *really*—will this be my story?"

"My story sucks," William mutters. "Lots of mistakes. Lots of regret."

I'm faced with a conundrum of sorts. Here, now, at the latest (last) stage of my life I'm staring blankly not at the face of death (he's long gone, and probably sour from me spitting in his face as I passed him), but the

23

face of life, which never really had a face, so it looks just like me. She's telling me every single thing I've done (or at least can remember) and begging me to understand how I got here.

I've had nothing but two dreams in the past two years.

One, I'm walking through a maze of doors

And behind each door

is darkness until I can fumble around

to find a doorknob,

on the doors.

should be going. No signs

which only leads me to

No clues as to where I

another hallway,

and more fumbling.

like an idiot

more doors,

The other one, I'm dancing up a staircase.

When I look back down the steps are disappearing behind me,

so I have no choice but to go up,

and up,

and up

Forever and ever

And up

And up

And up

And up

And up

Until I wake up.

"I dreamt once that I had monkey's paws for hands. I think I was the president, too. Not sure which would be worse."

I say (why did I say), "Did you ever dream about me?" I said it because I still shamefully pine for the longing glares, the whistling-under-your-breaths., the oh-my-god-she's-fucking-beautifuls; fateful reminders of a cursed and facetious beauty.

I turn my head away from the sunset for a moment. William says I remind him of a Roman goddess when I turn away from him. Except goddesses, they don't die so easily. I run through past dreams, myself; at least the ones I could remember vividly. Dreams of absconding to some faraway beach. Sipping champagne on a pretentious evening vista. Dreams of Jamie smiling. No dreams with William. He only exists in the real world and nowhere else.

"No, I don't really remember my dreams." He turns back to the sunset, sipping gin. Clearly lying.

I know William. He wouldn't dare look straight at you with a lie. William's eyes are the key to his entire tangled being. They reveal every secret, uncover every buried ore of anger, every slight albeit cursory glimmer of joy.

I sigh. "I haven't fucked in a while."

"Well," Williams sighs. "Makes sense, you know. This whole, expiration date thing."

I laugh, and then we go quiet for a while, this peace punctuated by the gentle clinks of ice cubes in our gin glasses.

Then I say this, and mean it: "Worst part of all this is being told you have an expiration date and not knowing when the hell it actually will *happen.*"

"Like a milk jug with the date rubbed off."

"Yes." I feel a brief, fleeting smile. "I'm a jug of milk with the date rubbed off."

When will I spoil? Maybe I already have.

This is the tapestry of my mortal blues. I have been given the natural cause of my soon-to-arrive expiration. But this sudden understanding of my mortality has altered my paradigm. I am no longer a young and active actress on my life's stage; now, I am stuck in the audience, forced to watch that faceless death pulls the strings; the supporting cast now marionettes. And I must carry the burden of not knowing when the final act would end.

"Maybe we should both just go to the beach someday. Jamaica, Mexico, whatnot."

"Hawaii?"

"Not Hawaii. Not exotic enough if it's still American."

"Any beach we go to in Mexico or Jamaica will be American."

"Somewhere where there aren't other people."

"Yes. Yes, please." I'll likely be dead before William can step further from the city; he hasn't left since he returned from service.. Two certainties in life I was sure of—I would die, and soon; and William would never leave. Not because it is his "home." (Hardly is to him). But the great world beyond is a dark and cloudy place compared to the small world you know.

***

"You've checked out again," William nudges my shoulder, having drifted off into some empty space.

27

After we finish our drinks, we sit like kids on monkey bars over the edge of the rooftop, dangling our feet. I notice that even when William dangles his feet they don't fall out of line. They swing with a militant rhythm.

"I can still see her pale, white cheeks up in the sky among the clouds staring down at me," I continue. "I can still hear how she practiced pauses in between her words over and over, saying this to hundreds of others who are facing the same paltry hallway, facing a past of missed opportunities and cloudy memories, looking over a blackened pit, harboring an absence of meaning that's so daunting it sucks the life out of you before you even die in the first place. 'Most people,' she said, this fucker said, 'most people don't know they have it until the symptoms appear, and the mind starts to wander and go places and get lost.' You start losing control of your mind and your body. You change. You lose your memory. You lose sense of reality. All because of some stupid defective gene. A fucking typo. And it passes through your lineage like venom in a creek...most people don't want to know if they even have it. Jamie doesn't want to know. He could find out right now, but he doesn't want to know."

"Ever asked him why?"

"No." A lie.

"Well, some people would rather not want to know. Losing your mind is a scary thing. Dying is a scary thing."

"Thing." Thing. So beyond daily habit that it goes unnamed.

"Have you ever, you know?" He nudges his head down towards the tiny street below, where blurry dots scurry along in a discordant, perpendicular dance, trotting to the tune of cacophonic honking. "Checking out early?"

"Why would I want to do that, William?"

"You know. Avoid all the pain. The suffering."

Voices in me go quiet again, replaced by a temptation to jump. "The street below is bustling," I laugh. "And I know I would make quite a splash. I've always envisioned going out with a bang, being remembered. Certainly my pulverizing jump from twenty-something stories...certainly it would do. I've come here to the top of the world countless times to ponder things that don't matter to me anymore. And in this unending, lackluster moment, I've got nothing to ponder, and can only enjoy images of me flying in the air."

The emergency door creaks open, and it's Mr. Speakeasy poking his balding head through again, like clockwork. That's what we like to call him, Mr. Speakeasy, because he never speaks to us, and only smiles humbly and bows, showing his empty purple gums with some kind of pride.

His feet shuffle slowly along his vegetable garden, a project that has yet to come to fruition. We wonder if he ever expects to see any tomatoes. (William thinks he's growing cucumbers—shows what we both know about gardening.)

He drops another empty can of pesticide (it rolls, clinking along the concrete), painstakingly spraying every inch of the garden in minute bursts, *pffft, pffft, pffft, rattle, rattle, pffft, pffft, pffft.*

And we have confidence that his incessant care of ridding his garden of insects is contributing to, if not causing, his garden's misfortune. He pulls another can of pesticide from his bag and continues spraying, *pffft, pffft, pffft, rattle, rattle, pffft, pffft, pffft.*

Blind since birth (or so they say), somehow emigrated from North Korea. Otherwise a shut-in, a hermit, who only comes up here to tend to his garden. Nothing much else to know about him. But he knows we're here, because his cold, dead cataracts, like an old and dying dog, they greet us every time, and they stare, they stare without seeing.

"Jamie always speaks about metaphors and beauty. I know he'd say it, that there must be something there. There must be something to all that gardening." Jamie, my dumb artist son, always the one to say something about beauty. Jamie, my dumb artist son, taking advantage of my prescriptions to distract himself from his own despair.

William hesitates speaking for a moment. "Jamie's doing good now?"

"Jamie's doing ok now."

"That's good." William speaks with either a feigning care or sincere indifference to the well-being of my son, with enough regret at the hesitation of his question—after all, he *was* my supplier, for a terrible pain the doctors called was likely all in my head, but still felt immersive and real; who was I to know that my own son would forsake me, steal them from me to satiate his own desires for an experience beyond the capabilities of his own mind or body. But I am truthful to William—Jamie is doing ok now.

"You don't still need any, do you? My doctor was starting to get suspicious."

"No. At least not now."

We both take a deep sigh—relief, or exasperation.

I continue.

"I wonder what the world will be like without me. When the inevitable knocking on my door finally bursts its way in, takes me by force. Death is staring at me from a distance, like he's slowly approaching, forever hidden. By the time I finally feel his brittle and acidic breath over my shoulder, by then I'll be long lost in some cloudy nebula, roaming about and babbling Jabberwocky nonsense, jerking around involuntarily in constant seizure."

"Maybe we should finally go ahead and go."

"Go?" I ask, confused whether he meant leaping off this mortal coil or something much less sinister.

"Cancun. Jamaica. Bahamas. The ocean. Some beachside somewhere, where we can forget about the world and our problems."

"And soak in the simple truth of a beautiful sunset."

"Sunset. Yes. That sounds poetic enough. Can they forgive sins there?"

"You mean they have a church?"

"No, it just sounded godly, that's all. Like that's the place you would go when you were dead."

I have a biting paranoia that someone is watching us. Not from Mr. Speakeasy; I mean someone that can actually *see.* It's not coming from death, I hope (Am I ready to die?). No—it's coming from a singular and sad little silhouette of a person, sitting on a 20 story building just like ours a few blocks away. I can't see their face, but I can feel them staring daggers. Elbows resting on their knees, their hands clasped together and begging, but their shoulders hunched in apathetic submission to their plight.

William sees this person, too. We silently reflect together on what it all means, the three of us sitting here together on top of the world.

This is another moment that Jamie would call beautiful. Certainly not irony, but coincidence, that we'd share a cursory moment like this as strangers from a distance, resting on the edge of a deadly leap of faith, nothing separating us from continuing to live or ending it all. Is this person a mirage, a trick of my feeble and soon to be decrepit mind? Is it me, peering into an opposite universe? Am I in the world where I actually *leap?* Maybe my mind is already fabricating some nonsense and this is all in my head. But it appeals to a certain palate in us, the viscosity that clogs our joints and bones when we just *feel* that someone is looking right at us, and I'm surprised by a subtle but unequivocal terror seizing me, but even more surprised how quickly that terror crumbles when I realize the petty hilarity of it all.

We are sharing a moment of helplessness, gawking at a viscous twenty-something story drop that would bring our stories to an end...on our own terms. My mind starts drawing up endless narratives to ascertain what would drive this person to a position so mirror-opposite to ours, standing on the edge of ending it all.

Below us, stories and stories below, a mindless rally of protestors shuffle north down the street, blockading traffic and oppressing the neighborhood with cries of political fraud. Some atrocious election I had not voted in (for what worth is a crazy woman's vote). These like-minded people have found a fancy new ignorance to satiate their empty lives. They wave their American flags, their monochrome American flags, their confederate flags, their cardboard cutouts of current politicians with their eyes crossed out in blood-red paint, some with speech bubbles stating "I'M A SATANIST WHORE." Like some horrid chorus, they chant a dissonant blend of commands:

"STOP! THE! STEAL!"

"FRAUD! FRAUD! FRAUD!"

"THE TRUTH IS OUT THERE!"

"FUCK! THAT! BITCH!"

"CROOKS! CROOKS! CROOKS!"

And other noises too volatile and angry to care about.

"I think back on the world I've helped to create and wondered how much of a contributor I truly played—

that my entire life is an abrupt breath sweeping through a nebula, noticeable but ephemeral. Look at the state of the world today....I wonder how significant a player I am in this theatrical disaster. Everyone plays a part, don't you think?"

William gazes at the crowd passing through, biting his tongue. "I suppose," he mumbles. "You've done some good. Seeing a model like you on a magazine cover gives people hope that someone can be beautiful." My internalized image of William as a person presumes his brooding thoughts—the grizzled and traumatized veteran upset by this supposed patriotic display of the first amendment. But then, I realize that William never really talks about the war, his war, an experience that so vitally and understandably belongs to only him, and him alone.

"But was that really good? All they saw was a false image of beauty. That wasn't me. That was all digital tricks, alterations of my real self. Hiding blemishes and scars. I profited off of the misery of others—those who would buy that magazine and invest in some false hope that they could look like me too, when I wasn't even human. I profited off of those who bought those magazines to masturbate to."

"But your poetry was always beautiful, too."

"My poetry made me pessimistic. It made me a groveling, nihilistic puddle. This death is giving me a little more life. It makes me *laugh incredibly loud...*"

Some incorrigible laugh erupts, and I do, I do in fact start laughing incredibly loud, in a jovial way that reminds me of first loves, of ghost stories, of burnt marshmallows. I can hear my own laughter echoing back from the streets below—

like I am fucking laughing at myself—

I feel Mr. Speakeasy staring and smiling, because he recognizes the joy that I have found in my despair, the hilarity of it all, and how knowing that death is rapping, rapping at my chamber door (fucking raven) brings to light the tucked away punchlines of this petty exist-ence we try to call life.

"I will not refuse or deny my inevitable journey-to-end-all-journeys, and I will not welcome it with open arms. It will just happen."

I stand up and wave at our new friend. They raise their head slightly, and eventually wave back, faceless. When they leap forward, they
fall

incredibly

fast

35

but quietly, and because light travels faster than sound, we see the solidity of their form become a shapeless mass on the concrete street below, and only a moment later their slight howl with a thematically abrupt
THUD
and an epilogue of violent screams as people crowd around.

Mr. Speakeasy chuckles behind us. *Pffft. Pffft. Pffft.*

Chapter Three
Hades, or The Weighing of One's Heart

*S**he whispered in my ear the greatest piece of advice—it's all just fantasy. Besides, your wife will never know.*

It was gone. That was that. The truth was out there, in a way.

And he had no idea what to do. The device was gone, vanished, disappeared, with no trace or pattern to discern its whereabouts. God had taken it back. He woke up this morning drowning in an inescapable dread, and despite his deep breathing and self-assurances, the guilt would not leave him alone.

It hadn't been his best day so far. A blizzard that was not supposed to happen today, happened. Traffic, which usually only lasted for a measly two hours, had burgeoned into a four hour stall. He tried to pass the hours listening to the noise of countless radio commercials selling him the latest innovation of chewable testosterone treatment that swore to make him last in the bedroom "up to four times longer!" He had to bear another hour of slow pacing, of chiming along under clouds of exhaust, of breathing in something akin to smog, of an imaginary voice scolding him from the backseat, chastising him for wasting away the years of this pristine automobile, a mustang that deserved to stride on the freeway instead dying slowly and painfully drinking its own fumes and trapped bumper-to-bumper among jackasses. A mustang trapped in a cage. Squandering useful potential—the story of his life, says the voice in the backseat.

He felt a little ashamed of his boredom when he saw the cause of the jam: a three-car accident where two people had been violently thrown from their vehicles and dragged forcefully along the pavement, victims to momentum and friction. There weren't any women or children, so that made the shame a little easier to swallow. Dead adults are easier to forget.

He had to make his routine stop at the Coffee Shoppe just before the expressway. He couldn't help pronouncing it in his mind as "shop-ee," thanks to the one time his daughter pronounced it that way. As he saw the Coffee Shoppe approaching in the distance, he locked his eyes on an almost empty cup from the Shoppe sitting for what must have been days in his middle cupholder, a small moldy film bouncing from the incessant stop-and-go of traffic jams; on the front side of the cup facing him, an emerald-green Poseidon, the coffee company's logo, threatening his trident right toward the center of Peter's heart.

He simply *had* to make his routine stop at the Coffee Shoppe. Personal routine was mollifying to the ineptitude of everyday life. The constancy of it all kept him distracted and focused at the same time—distracted from personal worry and the general anguish of a troublesome human existence, focused enough on the often-trivial operations of his agency to put those worries temporarily to bed. Things hadn't been so trivial lately.

At his routine stop at the routine Coffee Shoppe, he was the favorite customer of the forty-something barista, a former student in one of his father's obscure doctoral seminars. Every morning, when he ordered the same tall latte with extra skim, the barista—Theodore, as his name-tag said—would ask him how his father was doing. The famous Dr. Burroughs, that the world was so fond of, had disappeared quite suddenly since the fire in Hertfordshire; only a select few—Peter included—knew of the woeful truth.

Peter didn't know how Theodore knew he was the son of the famous Dr. Burroughs. But, in a vain effort to dodge the conversation, or at least make it awkward enough, Peter told Theodore that his father had been declared dead. A part of him believed the lie was really out of pity. How could he break it to Theodore that his favorite and most influential college professor was likely sitting in his bed, not quite pondering the nature of reality, but instead soiling himself to death; like many phenomena, poorly aged, memorialized most for their youthful heydays and less for the longer evenings in which they would impotently waste away like stale coffee?

Theodore offered a latte on the house as condolences, a fair cost for a lie about your father being dead.

But that morning they were out of skim milk, so Peter had to take his latte without it. He also spilled a little on his shirt, which he couldn't stop staring at in the rear-view mirror for the entire duration of the four-and-a-half-hour traffic purgatory.

He broke his promise to himself he would not have coffee before meeting with his immediate supervising agent, Kowarski. God forbid he faced judgment with a brown stain on his shirt. He deserved to be emaciated with a little bit of dignity left over—but no, he had to risk it for the saving grace of routine.

Ada had tried to call twice, but he didn't answer.

Peter tried to motivate his reflection in the rear view mirror. "You are not a nobody," he mouthed quietly. But he practically was a nobody—a junior agent for Strategic Homeland Administrative Management, perhaps the most moderately passable and historically controversial national security agency in the entire United States that no one was supposed to know about. As a boy, he used to daydream of absconding to parts unknown on top-secret missions. In his glove compartment, he still carried a signed copy of *Live and Let Die*, an unread and hardly touched copy of *Goldfinger* (saving it for the day he would quit), and finally, tucked neatly in between scotch bottles in his home office, *You Only Live Twice,* which he had read obsessively at least twenty to thirty times, half those times being inebriated and forgetting his place in the novel, often starting over the next day.

Strategic Homeland Administrative Management, infamously known for trying so desperately to be unknown, had always been relentlessly blanketed by front-page muckraker journalism, exposing the top-secret collusion in some of the Twentieth century's greatest blunders.

One example: the company's advisory role to General William Childs Westmoreland; more specifically, their advocacy for a lucrative expansion of boots in Vietnam.

Another example: it played a central role in Operation Rolling Thunder.

And, it failed to cover up William Calley's supposed massacre in My Lai.

Yet another: after Charlie Wilson covertly defeated the Soviets in Afghanistan, senior Strategic Homeland Administrative Managers were tasked with rebuilding the devastated and fragmented Islamic nations. However, they failed to realize the colossal quagmire, and—instead of building a bridge over quicksand—decided to shuffle the mess in the to-do folder of a lesser branch in the agency's bowels, a branch with entirely novice and untrained agents who couldn't identify Afghanistan on a labeled globe. The branch's classified and poorly written Democratic Unifying Maintenance Plan wasn't so much a plan as much as a haphazard amalgam of scribbled meeting notes, brainstorming diagrams, and doodles. They enacted the plan anyway, which put no one in charge and inevitably bore a brewing cauldron of spurned chaos and anti-US sentiment. (A testament to their fledgling aptitude was the plan's seventeen misspellings of Afghanistan.)

And one more: when the U.S. Government (still shaken by the weighty nuclear threats of the Cold War) searched for WMDs that didn't exist, the agents produced hundreds of reputable reports that claimed that WMDs did, in fact, exist. In the rise of internet ridicule, it became the 3rd most popular internet trend, mocking the company's failed attempts at secrecy, drawing crude dicks on WMD geographic reports and in the mouths of top agents.

Despite efforts to erase any trace of the agency on the internet, they tried to improve its fledgling image with its own webpage. The Wikipedia page currently has more visits. In fact, a Google search for "Strategic Homeland Administrative Management" will yield the Wikipedia page first, followed by the images for most popular dick memes. Its actual website is fifth in the list.

Most of these major blunders resulted from the direct deliberation and authorization from The Board (intentionally capitalized to maintain inconspicuous sovereignty). No one knew the members of The Board; no portraits were displayed in any great hall; all communication from The Board came top-down in memos and e-mails signed only by *The Board*. No agent ever met The Board. As per a monthly memo, no one was authorized to discuss The Board, and any insubordinate chatter or gossip would be cause for the immediate disappearance of those involved. Despite this overzealous commitment to secrecy, The Board and the entire company struggled to maintain any balance between public ridicule and confidentiality.

The agency began in the Fall of 1900 after Pinkerton simultaneously fired James Allen and Gerald Willis for repeated negligence. Allen and Willis, often paired together in their investigations, were accused by their employers for tampering with evidence, spending administrative petty cash on prostitutes, and drinking copiously on the job. Allen became notorious for scandalous behavior while infiltrating labor unions. Willis, on the other hand, had a more unfortunate affliction—a combination of greed and a propensity for reckless gambling. Bribery became his most infamous charge. He never denied it. It could've been a crisis of guilt, or the fact that the evidence was too insurmountable to refute; having more gambling chips than actual cash burdened any excuses he could muster.

By Mid-November, Allen and Willis—escaping the rush of accusations, exposés, and fallouts—tried to enact some revenge against Pinkerton by establishing their own agency. Starting out as The Willis and Allen Investigation Company just outside the perimeter of Washington, D.C., they found minimal success until they became popular for their nefarious but effective union-busting tactics. (Most of these tactics involved back-alley threats and demonstrations of brute force). Their profits from The First World War helped the Company coast through the Great Depression, and they burgeoned after receiving contracts to assist in locating and apprehending Japanese Americans for interrogation and internment during World War II. While the popular media labeled their contracted duties for the government as illegal and unconstitutional, Allen used his adept skills of subversion, influence, and deceit to avoid any trials or public relations travesties. Liars do make the best negotiators, after all. Willis simply bribed politicians. In fact, they were favorites among up-and-coming journalists, who could never pin anything substantial on them, even though both men were so blatantly corrupt.

That was until Allen was caught in an underground child prostitution ring, and the fate of the company was left in the whiskey-soaked hands of Gerald Willis, who had become the dictionary exemplar of a man who couldn't find his way out of a wet paper bag. He had been born a beggar and quickly became a king after his father happened upon a wealthy inheritance from an unknown uncle. Gerald Willis Senior lost most of his fortune to horse race bookies and casino dealers. As it goes, Gerald Willis Junior was a carbon copy of his father, and his dismal spending habits and genuine unaccountability drove the Willis and Allen Investigation Company into the ground. Luckily, the economic boom after World War II bred politicians willing to resurrect a company plagued by scandal but aflame in infamy, and still worth millions in opportunities for insider trading. The politicians wisely erased history by renaming the company to Strategic Homeland Administrative Management. The agency managed to remain successful following a tried-and-true model: burying blunders within a bureaucratic system of obscure paperwork that challenged the Library of Babel. They became an integral accomplice to the United States government, taking top-secret contracts in national and international defense strategies and initiatives. Thanks to this, and thanks to their bureaucratic disappearing act, the agency managed to coast—never billowing over the surface, but never sinking too deep.

Peter Burroughs, as a junior agent, had to wear on his sleeve the history, the values, and the personality of his employer—even though only a select few knew what his job was. He had to keep his day-to-day operations confidential to avoid compromising any important cases. This never burdened him—his cases had all been insignificant, purely bureaucratic, and uneventful; even the cases he made up to his friends at kids birthday parties were more exciting than the stale and thin folders collecting dust on his desk. The most exciting cases were investigations into white-collar crimes of fifty-something war profiteers who managed to buy their way out of civil and criminal courts (after all, nothing satiates the judicial system like a boatload of cash). Sometimes, even the hefty paycheck didn't make up for the infinite puddles of boredom, the endless evenings of daydreaming, those countless late nights of excuses to his wife Ada that he had too much work to do, or a project was due on the horizon, or some other hollow excuse—all shameful ways to find time away from his family, despite how much he loved them. He hid for a simple reason, one that he sheltered away behind thick-webbed caverns of denial: he was ashamed of how his life turned out to be; a vicious lie, despite all his childhood aspirations to be a womanizing spy like his hero, Sir James Bond.

That was until this case fell on his lap. A case that was so highly classified that files on the apparatus did not even exist—the agency forsake its bureaucratic principles to avoid any chance of leaking any information on the apparatus. Who knows what would happen if that information was in the hands of another country, or terrorists, or the media, or, even worse, the general public. Only a select few, including Peter, knew that the apparatus was real. Except for his father. He told him one evening to pass the time. Maybe he told him in a vain effort for that elusive fatherly *attaboy*. Besides, even if his father mentioned the apparatus to someone else, no one would believe a dying, delusional old man anyway.

But who would believe Peter? Who would believe the simple and bold-faced truth that he had just lost it, that he had no clue where it was?

Peter did try to be proactive. He acted on a certain set of precautions. Late last night, at agency headquarters, when the last night owls finally slipped away to return home, he filed a dense paper trail of the apparatus' whereabouts—from the Paranormal and Obscure Object Research Testing Facility (POORTF), to the Software Testing and Development Sector (STDS), to the Sector of Espionage Knowledge and Security (SEKS), to the Space and Astrophysics Cosmic Committee (SACC), to the Historical Ornithography Revision Sector (HORS), to the Nuclear Development Facility (NDF), all the way back to POORTF. Then, accessing the security camera live feed from his laptop, he preemptively started a hard-drive update of the security servers—which would prevent recordings for up to ten minutes. This gave him ample time to toss a chair through the window. Using the base of the metal stapler from his desk, he smashed laptops and desktops, he toppled cabinets over, broke every piece of glass he could find, pulled out all of the drawers and flipped them over, and—for good measure—used a lighter (one that he scalped from the receptionist who flirted with him constantly) to set fire to a pile of files. This immediately triggered the alarm and sprinklers, soaking all the electronics and Peter, his suit drenched and clinging to his anxiously sweating flesh. Despite the fleeting waves of adrenaline, Peter escaped with a familiar, sullen sort of understanding—there was no turning back now; due to his own recklessness and absence of a spine, he would be compelled to weave and perpetuate two lies in his life, for the rest of his life—one for the sake of his career and livelihood, and the other for the sake of his marriage and soul.

***

He sat, waiting in room 185-190 on the 13th floor that never existed. The room was dressed like almost every other hallway and office—drab concrete walls, sparingly populated with generic motel-worthy paintings of farmhouses and empty lakes, complemented by an omnipresent humming of fluorescent bulbs. Peter sat still, despite his inner turmoil—a spurious mix of anxious adrenaline and self-deprecation. He had finally been admitted to the floor that didn't exist, for no good reason, other than his own incompetence. If only he had good news.

He was sweating dreadfully. He blamed this on the broken thermostat locked behind a plastic case with a steel keyhole, housed right under the dusty singing bass with a fake gold Olympic medal around its neck (they gave those medals out during a team-building exercise). His clothes were sticking to his skin, and he couldn't adjust his seat enough to eradicate the itch in his crotch. He had to accept being stuck in the pit of Hades until he talked to his supervising agent Kowarski. Kowarski would likely talk to someone else, who would talk to someone else, ad infinitum—until that last person on this infinite chain would talk to the supervisory board, which would then talk to the management board (which wasn't supposed to get involved with anything), which would then have to talk to the advisory board—until eventually the information would happen to find its way to The Board. No board ever communicated directly with The Board. Information just seems to arrive there, despite the ever twisting garden paths of endless organizational dysfunction.

And, despite his infinitesimal role as a speck on this infinite chain of command, he had to accept that he still hadn't figured out how to break the news—that the apparatus had disappeared without a trace.

46

He quickly realized saying *disappeared* was his subconscious effort to pervert the language of his predicament so he could avoid blame.

It hadn't disappeared. Disappeared was the wrong term.

He *lost* it. He was not a victim in this blunder. He was the perpetrator, the criminal, the guilty defendant.

He could say that it was stolen. But still, wouldn't that leave him responsible? He could say it was sent away for repairs—but to whom? He had no clue who would have the aptitude and resources to repair it. This contraption was simply "beyond science." He could admit the truth, and then face the inevitable packing of his practically empty desk, his full stapler and his empty manila folders labeled "important." He could go home and admit to his wife and children that he was a failure.

Peter didn't cry often—only during panic attacks. It wasn't the fear of being fired, losing a paycheck, losing his pension, or even the long, gross mile of shame he would have to walk, from his floor to the parking lot. He couldn't face humiliation in front of his own wife, or his children. He was already hiding enough from them. He didn't fear the pain that he could cause them, but the pain that he had yet to cause them—this pain that, inevitably and ruthlessly, would rip their soiled lives to shreds.

I was surrounded by an aroma of cotton candy. Stale whiskey on the rocks. Flashing pink and purple lights. She gripped my knees. She looked me in the eyes. She was surprised by my insincerity. I wasn't, even though I wished to death that I was.

Kowarski reminded him of the trolls in the stories he would read to Chloe and Bethany; trolls that would wait under bridges for those children who strayed from their parents' orders, or ran away from home, or failed to worry about the rotten troll stench that stunk of burnt oil. His bald head was a gulf surrounded by a crescent of fading, dyed black hair. He reminded Peter of the kind of men loitering in bowling alleys. Kowarski had gone through one box of tissues already; after everything Peter said, he would wipe the flooding sweat off his bald head and wrinkled fore-head.

"We can tell them that it's currently under mainte-nance, they'll believe that, right?" Kowarski squealed.

"You mean lie, sir?" Peter said this with a false grin, because Kowarski must've had a poor sense of sarcasm.

"What do you think they'll do to us if we tell them the truth?!"

"What do you mean 'what do you think they'll do to us?'"

"My God, man! You awful, awful fool! You son of a bitch! Don't you know what happened to Jonas?!"

"Yes, he killed himself," Peter answered. Rumors of Jonas spread quickly. He was assigned, by Peter, to document observations related to the apparatus from the various departments involved. Peter's last recollection of Jonas was the rumor that he had uncharacteristically fled the country, and was found dead with a bullet in his brain somewhere in South America.

"Oh God no! You dumb, awful bastard! That's what they *want* you to believe. That's the truth they *want* you to believe." Kowarski discovered he had used up all his tissues; quickly becoming flustered, he smashed the box with his fist, then began using the sleeves of his tweed jacket to wipe away the accumulating layers of sweat. Kowarski's venting frustration began to climb in volume and panic, each word louder than the last. "They framed all of it. Because they believed that he tried to steal it. Or wanted us to believe that he tried to steal it. Of course

Jonas didn't kill himself, idiot. Idiot. You don't leave here. No one *retires!* For God's sake, when was the last retirement party you went to?!" Before Peter could respond, Kowarski squeaked, "Exactly! You can't fucking remember because no one *retires!*"

Peter ran through the degrees of separation of all those who had any semblance of knowledge about the device. Luckily (or unluckily), the list was rather brief:

- Himself (the lying fool)
- Kowarski (the troll)
- Jonas (deceased)
- His father (who the hell would believe a crazy person)
- Stewart Smith (B.O.)
- Agent #0343, Paul Lieberstein (Not actually Jewish)
- Administrative Assistant Teresa O'Malley (Actually Jewish, albeit slightly anti-Semitic)
- Whoever the hell made this thing in the first place (God? Maybe Satan? Aliens?)

All these folks were the only people on the planet (besides God, Satan, and aliens) that knew the truth was out there, somewhere.

"Ok. Let's just lay it all out there," Kowarski acknowledged. "That's how we do it, we just look at the facts, and think about our options." Peter sighed, setting his briefcase on the desk. Upon opening it, he had expected to see a manila folder containing his latest written report—but was at first abashed by the presence of unsettling straw figurines laid out across his papers, each of their heads wrapped in white cloth, like suckers. Across their faces were names written in childish purple marker: *Daddy, Mommy, Katie, Isaac, Mrs. David* (Katie's teacher), *Ms.*

Hines (the principal), along with a few other unnamed ones.

"What the in the fuck are those?"

"Those…those must be from my daughter Katie. They're straw dolls. She must've made them in class." His abashment evolved into a shameful wistfulness—his daughter must've known something was wrong, so she left him a gift to cheer him up.

"Perfect. Just perfect. We can use these to see how fucked we are." Kowarski, without hesitation, grabbed each one and began to stand them up on his desk, arranging them in a sort of theater scene, with two straw dolls in the center, and the rest surrounding them like an audience. "That's me, and that's you. As of right now, two people of any importance who know about this fucking thing." He bit on the tip of his thumb, deep in shallow thought.

He then pointed at the straw doll audience.

"Do you know who that is?" Kowarski demanded.

"No."

Kowarski smashed one of the dolls with his fist, hay splaying out beneath it. "The goddamn Board!" For fuck's sake, Peter!"

"I'm sorry," Peter gasped.

Kowarski swept his arm across the desk, sending all of the dolls in a chaotic flight across the room and smashing against the wall. Some of them exploded on impact.

"That's what the fucking Board is going to do to us if we *fuck…this…up.*" Kowarski emphasized that last verse by harmonically tapping his bloated fist on his desk, plopping himself in his seat afterwards. He then jumped back up like he had been shot, an animalistic response to the jarring ring of his desk phone—the volume pushed to its limit due to his waning hearing. He scrambled to pick it up.

"Kow....Kowarski."

Peter didn't hear anything on the other end. But Kowarski sounded off with "Yessir" every few moments. But Kowarski's ("Yessir.") gaunt expression ("Yessir.") told him everything he ("Yessir.") needed to know—his eyes sunk deep ("Yessir.") into his skull, disappearing ("Yessir.") behind a visage that spoke ("Yessir.") of impending fear.

Kowarski, nodding for the whole few minutes, let loose one final brief and hushed "fuck." He hung up the phone hurriedly, perhaps in a futile attempt to block that last message from making it through to the receiving end.

He then looked gravely at Peter, gulped, and muttered: "Capitol Hill. 10 a.m. We're fucked."

***

The private limousine to Capitol Hill was accompanied by an unexpected traffic accident and a driver who shamelessly flirted with Peter. Despite his advances, Peter kept to himself, absorbed in daydreams of leaping out of the limousine window or getting injured in a terrible accident. He wished for any sort of delay, some divine intervention to prevent him from meeting with Senator Paul Palient, who wielded enough phantom sovereignty to demand that whoever was responsible for overseeing the mysterious apparatus should report to him, directly and immediately, face-to-face. Somehow, the Senator was alerted of this matter of national security, despite the fact only Peter and Kowarski were aware of the device's disappearance. He prayed for a miracle to detain the plane from landing; but, as was tradition, he and Kowarski arrived, on schedule, awaiting trial for his misdeeds.

This was only Peter's second time on Capitol Hill—the first being on a school field trip when he was twelve. Vividly he recalled walking into the main hall and being floored by a musty odor, and statues of dead men that would follow you when you turned your back to them; not a soul around—just a hollow rotunda of wood, porcelain, and marble. He recalled a cursory yet frightening awe in that Rotunda, surrounded by statues and busts of historical giants, judged from above by the central pantheonic eye of the apotheosis. He felt small, and weak.

Free-floating jazz played perpetually from the office of Senate majority leader Paul Palient. Apparently this was a constant; it was a challenge for any aging senator walking by to avoid habitually snapping their fingers, or to resist adjusting their steps to match the sporadic beats echoing through the senate chambers. They either did this because of an innate reaction to the unnatural yet soulful rhythm, or just mimicked as much to maintain appearances to the most powerful person in the chamber. More powerful than the president, some said. More powerful than the entire senate itself, some said.

Senator Paul Palient was a gaunt, towering man, the kind of man you'd expect to have years of experience as a mortician. He stood just up to six and half feet tall, but had shockingly small, childish hands. Even sitting behind his desk, his stature was daunting, his shoulders hunched over slightly, reminiscent of gargoyles perched above gothic cathedrals. Peter gulped—and he feared the gulp was loud enough to be heard, even over the slapping jazz bass.

"Ah. Gentle-mun," Senator Paul Palient spoke, without looking up, intensely reading the minute font of the legislative proposal on his desk.

Peter glanced at Kowarski, who could only shiver with his mouth gaping part way open, like a dead fish.

"Sir," Peter muttered, to break the silence.

"Sir." Kowarski repeated after Peter.

"Pleasure to meet you," Peter extended his hand.

"P-p-pleasure to meet you," Kowarski tripped over his own words, then shakenly extended his clammy, shivering hand.

The Senator did not look up. He just kept on reading, striking through text in thick, scarlet ink. He had excised practically the entire page.

The scraping and shuffling of his scarlet marker meshed well with the beat, beat, beating and drumming. It did not mesh well with the foreboding portrait behind the Senator, framed by two towering bookshelves filled with archaic books on constitutional law, followed by the occasional oddball, like *Treatise on Persuading the Mounds and Masses.* The portrait, which seemed even taller than the Senator, seemed aged and restored. It depicted your standard old dead white man, dressed like a founding father, in frock coat, powdered wig, and breeches. Only, his face was missing, in its place an unintelligible blur of pale whiteness like a vandal had smeared it with turpentine.

The Senator rose, sighing, sliding the legislation off his desk, the papers shuffling down into a trash bin.

"Now. On to the mattur at ha-und." His thick and deep Southern drawl forced the jazz melody to shift to a slower rhythm. Peter knew enough about Senator Paul Palient—that he was born and raised in Alabama, and represented the state of Kentucky for what must've been forever. This was the bulk of what could be found online about Senator

Paul Palient—a brief biographical blurb about being born to God-fearing Christians, then nothing until his swearing in; such a significant thirty-nine year gap between the "born and raised" boy from Nowhere, Kentucky and the sudden, out-of-thin-air Senator who people never realized was a Senator until he started blocking legislation left and right. His infamous title coupled well with his mortician demeanor—they called him "The Bicameral Butcher." Nothing passed without his say so, if anything passed at all.

"As uhm sure you're both aware, we have a hearing scheduled next week on yurr employer. This... uhh…. Strategic Homeland Administration Management. Now, muh sources all tell me that your employer has been authorahzed by the DHS to manage an...apparatus of utmost consequence. A mattur of national suhcurity. A device that puts all of us at risk." Senator Paul Palient spoke his *r*s as if his tongue curled back twice as far.

"Sir?" Peter calmly suggested. Kowarski gawked at him, caught in the middle of trying to swallow some kind of lozenge.

Senator Paul Palient continued: "Now, the Senate Suhcurity and Intelligence Cuhmmittee—of which Ah am a ranking memburr—doesn't actually *know anythin'* about this apparatus. The othur senators, I must admit, are rather foolish and blahnd to the facts. They, unlike muhself, are only cognizant that somethin' is unuhccounted for."

Peter's years of misinformation training kicked in—always hiding the details, or even lack thereof, behind two words that shielded all responsibility, admittance, guilt, reality—"It's classified," Peter stated, instinctually and regretfully.

Senator Paul Palient laughed, loudly in a single syllable; a laugh that boomed and resonated throughout the halls outside his commanding office.

"Classified?" He grinned slyly, turning his nose up at Peter to get a better look at the man.

"I'm sorry," Peter shrugged. "We're not privileged to share that information."

"Privileged?" Senator Paul Palient's booming single syllable laugh erupted again. "Ah don't think you fully uhnderstand what that word 'privilege' means, suhn."

Kowarski reached his hand behind Peter's shoulders and wrung the skin behind his neck. Kowarski nodded profusely, urging Peter to go on. Peter discreetly shook his head, widening his eyes to warn Kowarski of the danger of violating company protocol.

"Ahm afraid, if you don't share with me the intimate details of this duhlemmuh, then both of your lives are in-heruhntly at severe risk." He stopped blinking and folded his hands together like a church steeple.

"Agent Burroughs, tell him."

Peter once again, and less discreetly, shook his head in resolved disagreement.

"Agent Burroughs," Kowarski demanded, beads of sweat rolling down into his fatty neck folds. "That is an order."

Peter exhaled through his nose, defeatedly, his last strands of ethical vigor weakened again by this fatiguing bureaucratic authority. "The only two people who know about the apparatus missing is us."

Kowarski looked bewildered. Senator Paul Palient smiled delightfully.

"So this is a mattur of national suhcurity, privy to the three of us?"

"Yes, sir. It most definitely is."

"And no superiuhrs of yours are aware of this mattur?"

"No, sir."

"Well, then," Senator Paul Palient leaned back in comfort, basking in his accomplishment—breaking Peter into submission. "Do tell, why is this a mattur of national suhcurity?"

"Welp." Peter swallowed and took a deep breath. "If this apparatus found its way into the wrong hands, it could expose confidential information. Classified information. Dangerous information. As I'm sure you are aware, the federal government—any government—only functions if secrecy and security are synonymous. If any threats, foreign or domestic, were to obtain this apparatus, this would inextricably lead to a life-threatening breach of classified information. Locations. Data. Nuclear data. The kind of secrets that we do not want other nations to know."

"Ah, secrets that could destroy the cuhntry."

"Yes sir. This also means we have to be *selective* in who we share this information with." Peter emphasized *selective* with a chagrined gritting of his teeth, glancing clearly at Kowarski.

"And no one else, besides muhself, has been briefed on this?"

"So far," Peter admitted, "no one."

"Not even the presuhdent?"

"Well, we can't go and tell the POTUS," Kowarski yelped in a panic, throwing his clammy hands into the air, slapping back down on his thighs. "Even if it is a matter of national security."

"Excuse me sir, don't you think we should?" Peter suggested.

"We can't!" Kowarski yelped.

"Why not?"

"The Candied Yam Rule."

"Candied Yam Rule?"

"Yes, the Candied Yam Rule."

Somewhere, Peter had shuffled away memories of his acclimation to the secret agent lifestyle—faint memories hidden by a cloudy residue of disillusionment. But he did remember someone describing the Candied Yam Rule to him. The rule materialized during the company's involved cover-up of a hazardous radioactive waste disaster in Pomona, California; the Cabinet of the Executive Branch had instituted the Candied Yam Rule, which enforced

> …that information of the highest concern
> to national safety and well-being must be
> kept classified to those seated in the
> highest positions of power, and only left
> in the hands of those who weren't in any
> way capable of doing anything dangerous
> with that information due to their own
> ineptitude. (Agent 22-4323, personal
> communication)

The Candied Yam Rule wasn't written down anywhere. Strategic Homeland Administrative Management agents had concocted the rule in collaboration with then-Vice President REDACTED. They instituted the rule, happenstance, before briefing then-President REDACTED. The cabinet of advisors, at the time believing the President to be entirely lacking in rational thought, briefed him on the Pomona situation as perfectly a-ok. "Nothing too scary," the Vice President had purportedly ordered. The Candied Yam Rule passed down the bureaucratic pyramid of leadership, mutating hierarchically and exponentially through meeting after meeting, until it became unwritten law. Don't tell the head honcho, because he just might screw the pooch.

"So we can't tell the presuhdent?" Senator Paul Palient grinned maniacally.

"Candied Yam Rule."

"So," Senator Paul Palient added, "That puts the three of us in this very room in the utmost prediculment." He seized a fountain pen and started twirling it between his fingers.

"Kowarski, leave the room." Senator Paul Palient commanded. "Ah want to have a little chat with Aguhnt Burroughs, alone."

This command was supplanted by a torrent of guttural coughs from Kowarski, who had choked on a lozenge he had excavated from his inner coat pocket. "Umm…Yes sir," he muttered, bowing his head like an apologetic dog. As Kowarski left, Senator Paul Palient sat still, staring at Peter with glaring, hungry eyes. Now that he was alone, lacking Kowarski's dimwitted companionship, Peter felt a familiar yet ineffable distress—like God, or some higher being, was seated before him, holding him in eternal judgment.

"Now, give me the case file," Senator Paul Palient demanded, extending his massive pale hands towards Peter.

I held my breath. There were stones in my throat. She sat on my lap. She wrapped her legs around me. Trapped, enthralled by this siren. She had heels tied to her feet, skin covered in glitter, and that same aroma like cotton candy. She leaned into me. A strand of her blonde hair brushed against the tip of my nose. Her breasts were tense and dug into my collarbone. She tasted my ear and whispered, "It's all just fantasy. That's all it is. There's nothing wrong with fantasy." I could only muster a smile. Because she was dead wrong—this wasn't fantasy at all. This was a test, and I had failed—I wanted nothing to do with her. I wanted nothing to do with any her.

After moments of silent and careful reading, Senator Paul Palient began to narrate the file. "Aguhnt 12-36, Petuhr Burroughs, recently and tempuhrarily uhssigned to

Classuhfied level 40 clearuhnce for monituhrin' file #54, modulatin' intelligence apparatus, secured by Strategic Homeland Administrative Management in March." He stopped reading, then looked at Peter with a look of joyful disdain. Senator Paul Palient started writing on the case file; Peter couldn't make out what he was writing, the scarlet ink occluded by his giant white hands.

Senator Paul Palient looked up at Peter. "So you *ovuh-saw* ongoing research on this duhvice, is that right?" He scribbled harder on the case file, rough enough to tear through to the next page. "So that makes you dye-rectly responsible for its disappearuhnce?"

"Yes, sir. I oversaw…I guess…"

"Now, Peter," the Senator interrupted, "don't beat around the beeswax. If you were responsible, just say so."

"Ok then. You're right. I was responsible…for, uhm…monitoring ongoing research of the device." Peter took a deep breath, but couldn't figure out what to say. Instead, he pondered the fruitful but frightening weight of the word, *responsible,* and raced through all of his own responsibilities: His marriage; Katie; Isaac; Ada; His job; his father (asshole); William (asshole); his 401k; that promise he made to Kowarski to never tell anyone about Kowarski's impotence; how he made Lisa swear that she would never tell Kowarski that Peter told her about Kowarski's impotence. That's all he felt like, at the moment—a flimsy web of all these responsibilities, strung together frantically, collapsing under its own weight.

Senator Paul Palient continued writing in the case file, scribbling so forcefully that he almost tore through the pages. "Okay, then." He adjusted his glasses to the bridge of his beak of a nose, leaning his head back slightly to feint an apparently attentive reading of the file. "Be so kind to provide for me a detailed explanation of what exactly we know about this…duhvice."

Peter swallowed an empty, dry mouthful and held his breath, improvising his scripted response.

"Well…um…" He began to read off half-memorized descriptions of the device, in the best matter-of-fact tone he could muster. "Recent analyses have revealed a significant amount of information regarding the *modulating intelligence apparatus*. Codenamed "Laplace's Demon." Initial studies have shown that the device responds to any human language, in any dialect. The device is capable of recognizing all forms of language, sometimes even gibberish. The device does not respond to statements, but only to questions. The device resembles something like a… like a large golf ball." Peter used his hands to indicate the general size.

"Ahm, Ahm sorry, did you say a golf ball?" Senator Paul Palient inquired in disbelief.

"Yes. 17.17 centimeters in diameter."

"Who made the duhcision to design it that way?"

"The original designer, sir."

"And who might that be?"

Peter realized he had to answer this carefully, but his anxiety couldn't tell him how. He muttered the best he could come up with: "We...don't...know?"

The senator flung his pen into the air in frustration.

Peter continued, attempting to remedy his incompetence: "I...don't have that...information in front of me." The rampant and oppressive saxophone of the ambient jazz music challenged Peter's ability to think critically. Instead, the best he could do was guess whatever Senator Paul Palient wanted to hear.

"Ok then, well, how does this duhvice work?" The Senator focused intently at whatever he was scribbling on the pages of the case file.

"The user must speak his or her question to the device. The device displays its answer using a phosphor screen."

"A foster screen?"

"a *PHOS-PHOR* screen, like the green text that you see, on, umm…vintage computers? What it does is, it presents an answer wherever the user is looking on the screen, in plain text. It does, in fact, respond in whichever language input is used." Peter paused to collect himself. "Analysts developed a series of questions, ranging from surface-level questions to convergent and divergent lines of questioning. Analysts have confirmed that the device accurately answers any and all kinds of questions from every possible field." Peter had written this description countless times, so much so that his reply had become an automatic, albeit bothersome, autograph.

"How accurate?" The Senator now sounded genuinely intrigued, and stopped scribbling, breaking his concentration to look directly at Peter. He leaned forward, arms crossed, elbows on the desk, his eyes even hungrier than before.

"100% accurate."

"What kinds of questions did you ask it?"

"Well, we started with surface level questions. Such as, for example…umm…at what temperature does water begin to boil, what is the distance in centimeters from Albuquerque to Seattle, even questions to which no known record exists—such as Attila the Hun's body weight upon birth, for example."

"So this duhvice, it's capable of giving you the God's honest truthful answer to whatever question you ask it?"

"Yes, sir."

"So Ah could ask it, uh, what kind of ice cream Ah ate on the day my father died, or what color my tie was on the fifth of February, 1988, and it could tell me, without skippin' a beat?"

"As far as we know, sir…the device is never wrong."

"Incredible. So, the-o-ret-tic-ly, this duhvice could an-swer all of mankind's greatuhst questions?"

"Theoretically, yes."

"And did your ruhsearch team bother to ask any such question?"

"A little bit, sir."

"Such as?"

"Well…" Peter bit his tongue. It's in the damn case file. Senator Paul Palient wasn't really reading it; he just kept marking it up incessantly. "Scientific models about the size of the universe were off by about a half a billion years."

"Anything else?"

"Umm…well…, our research team didn't really have the opportunity."

"Of course not. So how does it work, exactly?"

"That was under investigation."

"Did you ask it about the existuhnce of God?" The Senator seemed angry.

"No, sir."

"Why not?"

"Well…our analysts did not have an apt opportunity to experiment with further questions beyond current human understanding."

"Because you lost it."

"Well...because..."

He paused. He had lost it. He was directly responsible, and despite all his efforts, the Senator knew this, some-how. He had an epiphany, here amidst clouds of contained panic and rhythmic jazz—he had reached the point in his life where everything about him was a lie.

It was all more than a lie—an entire fabrication that could no longer hold the weight of denial.

She smelled just like cotton candy. I...

"I don't have that information in front of me right now."

"You did lose it, didn't you?" Senator Paul Palient leaned forward, his face relaxed, certain of his accusation.

"Umm…"

"You lost it. And you have no idea where it came from, why it was made, how it works, or where it is now."

"Yes, sir."

"Well, Peter, I gotta say," he put his pen down, "it takes a special kind of idiot to go and lose suhmthin this incredibly valuable. A miracle."

"I'm sorry, sir."

"Let me ask you suhmthin, Peter. All this truth nonsense has got me thinkin. Uhbout you. Did you have a chance to ask it suhmthin? What truth is most important to you, if you had the chance?"

Peter couldn't answer. The Senator did not move, and neither could Peter. He was captured by a familiar guilt, for everything he's done in his life—all the wrongs he'd admitted to, and all the guilty secrets he'd buried deep inside.

...wanted nothing to do with her, even after she peeled her dress off and danced all over me until the Motley Crue faded out. I had failed my own test. I wanted nothing to do with her. I wanted nothing to do with my wife. I had denied it all this time. But how could I? What part of me is broken? My throat is aching. I don't want to touch her body. I'm ashamed. I'm lost. My daydreams weren't lying. I can't admit this to anyone. Can't you admit this to yourself? I'm not...

"Well, enough of this nonsense. Ah'm gettin' right to brass tacks here, Peter." the Senator leaned back, hands behind his head. You're a dead man."

Peter's throat suddenly collapsed into black hole of anxiety.

"Ah do know what you did. You don't know how deep muh rabbit holes go, do yuh?" The Senator leaned forward, grinning. "Ah have eyes and ears everywhere. And, it so happuhns that Ah have intimate knowledge of certain suhcurity footuhge that could be pretty damnin' of you."

Peter couldn't swallow the singularity that emerged in his throat had sunken into his bowels; some spit came back up, and he began to cough profusely. While his body gagged, his mind felt empty. The release of this footage would spell certain doom for more than just his career—agents have "disappeared" for much less. Like Kowarski said: *no one retires!*

And somehow, mysteriously, Senator Paul Palient had access to this footage, regardless of Peter's efforts to cover up any evidence; and he dangled this damnation over Peter's head, teasing him into submission, obviously for some sort of favor in return. He could be lying, Peter thought.

But if he wasn't lying…

"What exactly do you want?" Peter said, lamentingly.

"Well, we have a lot to lose if the truth doesn't come out."

"What truth are you speaking of, exactly?"

Senator Paul Palient set the case file down, ruminating while clinging his hands together, his eyes swinging back and forth, imagining some grand design to take advantage of this serendipitous opportunity. A minute or so passed by.

Then he spoke: "Well, there's a lot of folks out there, good, honest, law uhbiding cituhzens out there, they're

rightfully upset about the results of this most recent elec-
tiuhn. One in which Ah can stand to lose control of the
Senate."

Peter immediately understood the Senator's coercive
suggestion. Senator Paul Palient's exhortation involved
the latest election, one in which a majority of senators in
his party lost by overwhelming amounts—a monumental
upset which spelled certain doom for their boycotting of
all legislation that entered the chamber, a luxurious power
to have over the past few years. The recent election shifted
the balance of power for the upcoming Congress, effec-
tively removing their veto power over the country. It was
an election where all observable facts and figures pointed
to a massive and obvious loss for their party.

But that didn't stop a narrative perpetuated by many
representatives and figureheads in the media, purporting
an unfounded doubt that spread like a pandemic: whether
or not the results of an obviously fair and secure election
were in fact fraudulent and illegitimate; whether or not the
election was actually won illegally through dead voters,
duplicate counting, and corrupt county officials. Senator
Paul Palient had never made these claims directly.

But only fools would assume that he was not somehow
intricately involved. Too many of the representatives who
spread these contagious lies were marionettes under his
profuse and formidable presence.

"What do you want me to do about it?" Peter inquired.
Most people *know*….most people *think* you all lost. How
am I supposed to change that?"

Senator Paul Palient set his fountain pen down and
leaned back in his leather chair, which let out an abrupt
screech. "Politics is just a fun little pokuhr game ripe with
duhceit. People hold cards, people bluff. We're gunna
bluff."

"Bluff, sir?"

"Ah'm sure you and your uhccomplice are uhware. The Senate Suhcurity and Intelluhgence Cuhmittee is scheduled to hold a hearing regardin' the disuhppearance of this duhvice. Through some ways and means, my esteemed colleagues and Ah are soon to uhcquire the knowledge that your organization is uhccountable for the disuhppearance of a classified threat to national suhcurity. This duhvice that, uhparrently, knows the whole truth, both universal and inheruhntly puhrsonal. The information is spare, but Ah assure you my colleagues and Ah will soon be very, very uhware."

"What do you want me to do about it?" Peter asked again, in a tone much more submissive than before.

"Ahm gunna guarantee that the cuhmittee will call you forward as a witness to testuhfy. At the cuhmittee hearing, you are gunna testify as a repruhsentative for the Strategic Homeland Admin wuhtnaht. Since Ah am a ranking membuhr and all that. It'll be teluhvised. The whole world will be watchin', I gauruhntee that. Ah'll ask you all about it, about the device, what it does, what it can do. What you asked it. Everything you asked it. And you'll tell the whole world that, as part of your investuhgation into the fraudulent uhlection, ya'll asked it about the election. Based on your inquiries, ya'll came to the determuhnation that the election was indeed fraudulent, was indeed stolen, and was indeed indicuhtive of a conspiracy to unroot the currently seated government through illuhgitimate means. You'll tell 'em all the truth, in all its glory."

A hollow sensation in his lungs burrowed itself deeper. It all became vivid, the ramifications of this predicament, the whole mess he was buried in: either tell the real truth, reveal his felony and cover-up, destroy his reputation, ruin his career, condemn his loving family to a perpetual infamy for his cowardly crimes, and most likely become just another "retiree" of the company; or, tell

Senator Paul Palient's truth to the televised world, a truth that would potentially reverse an election, delegitimize the will of the people, and divert the intended course of history down a dangerous side-street that would embrace falsehoods and chicanery, setting the human race even further back in its perennial aspirations to become that fabled city upon a hill, rather than a pit of ignorant dissension. Because, if the election was indeed stolen, then all the lies were true, and all the truth would be lost.

"Look. Here's how it's gunna play out. The other cuhmmittee members, my colleagues across the aisle, will start off by jerkin' you off, listing all your uhccomplishments and titles and whuhtnot...they've worked with you before, they've seen your impeccable record, etcet-truh, etcet-truh. Then, they're gunna ask you for basic facts, cause they did not read the actual ruhports. They *never* read the ruhports. Then, after you give them all of the facts, they'll throw out their bait to get you to slip up. They'll go on long-winded summaries of what's wrong with the our party, how this mishap was somehow our fault and not theirs, and then they'll ask you a yes or no question that you'll feel compelled to say "yes, but…" and they'll fuckin' *cut you off,* and they'll keep begging the question, throwing out straw mans and ad hominuhms only to break you down, make them look good, and make you look like an evil piece of shit."

Peter could only nod. He fought to hold back the tears bred by an unforgivable shame.

In that shame, he recalled the night he told his father about the apparatus in passing. They were sitting on the couch, Peter drinking a cold cup of coffee that had been passively sitting for an awkward hour. He could taste that flat coffee now. His father clenched his hair in his hands, kneeling over, rocking back and forth, spitting on the ground. Peter recalled the spinning blades of a fan above his head, and the sullen visage of silence drawn over his father's medicated face.

He had told his father about the apparatus in passing, because lunging such secrets into the bottomless pit of his father's insanity couldn't harm anyone. And he struggled to recall if he had it with him that day. Ada always told him he had a nasty habit of bringing too much of his work home with him. In the shameful theater in his mind, Peter pictured the magnified golf ball resting on his father's counter, next to a near-empty coffee pot stained from over-heating; he remembered the stress of dealing with his father's tireless and obsessive ramblings about everything being perfectly still. Why would Peter have the device? Because he didn't trust the researchers and analysts with so much power. He only fully trusted himself, like most fools.

He was adamantly confident he had it with him that day, but he failed to remember what he did with it after. He could muster vivid imaginings of himself waking up, passed out on his father's couch, having dreamt of some awful nightmare of his skin falling off in the middle of a shopping mall, followed by his family walking backwards in time into a half-frozen Midwestern lake caked in im-penetrable fog. He sprung up off the couch in a panic, knowing he had to make his report, rushing in his groggy delirium, thinking he was already hours late. He must have left in a hurry. He must have left it, sitting there all by its lonesome, on the kitchen counter.

No: he convinced himself that this memory was just a fabrication. A falsehood borne from anxiety and shame. He couldn't have brought it with him; he wouldn't have crossed state lines with it, just to visit his sick and dying father. He wasn't that stupid.

But the truth is simpler than memory. In fact, his memories were more accurate than he realized. What he failed to remember, however, was that his brother William was also there that day, forgettable as always. He made the coffee.

Chapter Four
Portrait of an Ignorant Artist as a Sort-of-Youngish Buffoon

If I could take my eyes out and turn them on myself, I would know for sure if I truly have my mother's eyes and nose, if I've been hereditarily gifted with her incomparable beauty—enough to hide the horrible mess that's tearing her up inside.

When she calls me a "beautiful" artist, I'm not sure if she's referring to my stunning and chiseled physique or the pure aesthetic *quale* of the art I produce. When Ophelia—who will never throw me out, no matter how much I owe her for my part of the rent—tells me my art is "unique," I can't accept this half-hearted platitude with rose-tinted glasses. Unique means nothing in art. All art builds upon its predecessors. Uniqueness is more kindred to dog shit or snowflakes—none are the same.

"You're a...unique artist, Jamie. But you know I can't accept this." Ophelia tries her hardest to share her condolences behind her rejection with a thin smile, barely showing her upper teeth. "This is the second time you've submitted this piece, Jamie. You can't expect me to accept it this time if it's the same piece." The way her eyebrows curve in pity reminds me of how someone reacts when they see a friend's ugly child that they really don't want to see. "I'm sorry, but I can't display this one."

I call it Juniper. I don't know why. It just feels right.

Titles are a funny business. I've always titled my art with the first name that comes to mind. There's some meaning there, in first things that come to mind. What comes first in my mind? Love. Art. Beauty. Ophelia. My mother. There has to be some meaning there, in that specific order.

Juniper is a painting I did a long time ago; I'm not sure what it means anymore, but it has to mean something to somebody, if not me. It's a nice mixture of idealism and surrealism. An analog alarm clock face anthropomorphized, bleeding from the eyes, clenching an orchid and a cattail in its teeth. Two owls, each with one eye, perched on the clock's bells. A pastiche background of random squares of blues and purples. The crescent moon crashing into the sun, spreading waves of fuchsia radiation outward.

What it means is not up to me; it's up to the gusto of the moment, the feeling it evokes when a person who is not me views it for the first and second and third and -nth time. The meaning is created right then and there, without thinking. Thinking destroys art.

"I can't show this." She pauses and says again: "I can't show this *tonight*," Ophelia shakes her head in desperate exhaustion. "It just doesn't...fit with the theme. It's a medieval theme tonight." I know she's under pressure, that tonight is make or break for her gallery. She faces the financial and existential abyss of going under (under what, exactly? No one really knows); the attendants for her showings and events have been dwindling for quite some time. She hasn't slept well in months.

She turns and surveys her studio, the paintings of dead white people from the dark ages, portraits of mass genocide by the hands of angels and demons, the curtains closed with sunlight stealing a view. A fine showing for her medieval theme, an exploration of antiquated portrayals of hell and a morbid fascination with Christ. Some museum down the road was kind enough to donate three suits of armor for tonight—but to her, it's still not enough. It would never be enough. She sighs and mutters under her breath, "I don't even have any god damn halberds."

Her curved eyebrows bring me back to the last night we spent at my foreclosed studio: me, desperately swiping away at some middle-of-the-night cubic inspiration; Ophelia, hiding underneath the covers, bathed in the oppressive moonlight sneaking in through the angled windows, watching me, the blanket up to the bridge of her nose, her deepened and tired eyes smiling at me, a genuine pride that has degraded over time, her eyebrows curving exactly like they do now, but with a meaning entirely different.

That's what Juniper is missing. Eyebrows. Or maybe shadows to deepen the cheekbones. Or, maybe instead of owls, they should be salamanders. Or snails.

Looking at it now I see all the corners I had cut because I thought it'd be better to rush it out, to wrap up my *chef-d'œuvre* just to get some recognition for once.

"I just want to get some recognition for once," I say, in a half-hearted attempt to guilt trip her. For a while she stares at me, blinking, and I'm not sure if she's feeling pity or speechlessness. There's even a hint of anger, like she picked up on subtle shades of blame in those words that escaped from my foolish mouth. Every once in a while she looks up, her eyes doing that saccadic motion that suggests she's searching corners of her brain to find the right words to say.

But she doesn't say anything. She slowly wraps her arms around my shoulders. Slightly shorter than me, she does that thing that drives me crazy—she stands up on her toes, locking her hands around my neck. I've noticed this over time. The effort she takes. The applied force and tug between her hands. The strength and effort in locking them together around my neck like she's hanging on to me in the middle of a dark and beastly ocean. All this effort and tension has whittled over time.

I've never asked her if she loves me. I'm always so afraid to ask. I know she loves my work. I know she's trying to do what's best for me. I know we've been doing this for years without declaring any kind of meaning to each other, just embracing the feeling, the self-affirming sensation of fucking an actual human being every once in a while. I love the part of her that loves my work. I hate the part of her that hates my work.

We end our conversation without saying another word. She turns away, muttering to herself about the poor attendance rate, past due bills and rent, and something else about halberds. As she walks away to attend to her gallery business, she doesn't notice me a moment later, stealing lipstick, eyeliner, and fifty dollars cash from her purse.

The pawn shop down the road recognized me last time, so now I have to take an alternative approach. They will never take items from the same person more than twice—it's a sign posted on their door, "No more than two loans per person." Anyone pawning more than two items is too desperate; pawn shops feed on desperation, but are wise enough to know that too much desperation is bad for business. So they won't deal with me more than twice.

The wig shop down the street has enough for me to throw together a proper disguise. I can become whoever I want. I can go into that pawn shop as someone else entirely. I can be a damsel in distress, a flapper tipping a martini glass and one of those fancy cigarette holders, embracing the integrity of prohibition while downing my third martini. I could be a serious businessman from finance, or stocks, looking for some gold to invest in, because fuck it, I've got the money, right?

I can't be me again. The struggling artist. The phenomenon yet to be recognized. (I know how it sounds). They've seen me before and caught onto my shenanigans. They've also caught me off guard before and saw right through my previous disguise: a simple hat and sunglasses won't work. Maybe one of those fancy thick mustaches?

I've chosen a delightful brunette wig, not too flashy but not too ratty; I put on Ophelia's lipstick, not expecting the startling depth of its crimson hue; this isn't my first time putting on eyeliner—but hey, I'm not expert, and I poke myself in the eye a couple of times. I can't resist the physical urge to look up when I pull my eyelid to make it easier to draw. My sight blurs, the world distorts and bends like you're looking up through a wormhole into another blurry dimension.

On my way down the street, plastic shopping bags crinkle and shuffle in gusts of smog-filled wind. People stare. I'm carrying Juniper in both hands, canvas pressed against my chest, careful not to let the mist of a temperamental winter wind damage my magnum opus. The high buildings surrounding me get taller and taller. All the storefronts with clothing displays and liquidation event advertisements blend into an amalgamated commercialist blur. Beneath my feet, puddles of melting snow harbor a reverse image of this disgusting borough of fenced-up retail stores and busted neon business signs. I feel empowered when stepping into each puddle, sending chaotically organized ripples throughout this mirror universe. An odd looking man shuffles past me, curiously walking like he can't move his arms separately from his legs. He looks timid, trying not to stare at me. He leans his head as he passes me. "Ma'am." He blushes, afraid to say more, intimidated. his eyes look afraid. When I see myself reflected in a windowpane of a closed-down video rental store, I see how easily I can pass for the female form. To put it simply—*I am fucking beautiful, man or woman.*

The standard of beauty—everyone chases it. Beauty means something different to everyone; but beauty is still some *thing;* it exists, it is perennial, it is eternal in memories of our beautiful mothers and beautiful classmates and beautiful eternal canvases and marble statues, a timeless idea without a pure definition—only a deep, bodily vibration that tells us our senses are locked on some *thing* that is a beautiful thing. Beauty is ripe with meaning, but cannot be delineated; one person who claims "beauty" can be denied by another who cries "fraud." If beauty was subjective, then it mustn't really exist; but that's just stupid, because it *does,* and it's out there, somewhere, collapsing in on its own perfection.

I am beautiful. *I am.* This brunette hair makes my chiseled features dissolve into a raindrop face that beckons you to remember it forever.

My new name is Madison; no—Mabel. I am a young woman recently divorced, pawning off her cherished art to afford the lawyer fees. I am fierce, but empathetic, and I love Italy and the Bee Gees.

Good thing I shaved today.

Walking into the pawn shop as someone else entirely isn't the easiest thing in the world. I try to walk womanly, whatever that sexism means. You just don't realize how difficult it is to walk against your instincts. Anyone can wear a wig and fake emotions; it's much harder to fake a walk.

Inside, there's a familiar musty smell of shitty old things that people have sold throughout the years—faded and cracking guitars hung across the walls, old radios and cd players and boom boxes rotting away, miscellaneous porcelain trinkets, god-awfully ugly lamps, tattered furniture, and a solid row of shatter-proof glass displays with pistols, aged coins, and other mortal trinkets. Someone, eventually, will feel beauty in the nostalgic aroma that sweeps over them, seeing some object that resonates with their childhood. Places like this prey on desperation and nostalgia.

The owner is a thin, balding man with fuzzy nostrils and an explosion of grimy hair erupting from the neckline of his black polo. His eyes are large like owl eyes, enlarged by thick circular glasses. Fortunately, he doesn't recognize me. Holding my breath and tightening my vocal cords, I say, in my most effeminate voice: "I need to sell this."

He's actually staring at me differently this time. It's no longer a clear sign of disgust in his deep and raspy voice, nor that familiar contempt buried in his brow. This time it's something I've only seen a few times from Ophelia, and it makes me tremble in all sorts of discomfort.

"Can I see it, ma'am?" He leans his elbow on the glass counter that featured an old paper note taped at each corner saying "FUCK OFF BRAD. DO NOT SELL TO BRAD."

A part of me really wants to ask who Brad is. But I haven't practiced my girl voice much, and I didn't want to blow my cover. Instead I just turn Juniper around and look at him. He looks at me, back at Juniper. Back at me, back at Juniper. I forget if I tried to sell it to him before.

"Who did it?" He snorts and the puffy, thick nose-hairs curling out of his nostrils wind up and down. He scratches the sagging skin on his ashy elbow, and the sound reminds me of the sandpaper I used for Juniper. I almost point at myself when he asks me who did it. This fantasy of coming out as the artist invigorates me; but I realize that doing so would be a dead giveaway to my true identity—that guy who sold art here last month. Always remember that proverb prescribed above the gates of hell: *No more than two loans per person. Abandon all hope, ye desperate who enter here. No shirt, no shoes, no service.*

I just shrug my shoulders.

"Pawning or selling?" Of course he has to ask this. So I muster up the best female "pawning" I could, and I'm pretty impressed by how delicate I made it sound this time, even sneaking in a manufactured voice crack at the end of the first syllable.

Worry almost pours out of me when he takes a deep breath, along with a pause that takes what seems like eons. He looks me in the eyes and says, "I normally wouldn't do this, but what the fuck. $250 for it, sweetheart. 13% interest." Then he puts his gorilla hand over mine, and grins, baring a pristine set of yellowed teeth and swollen gums.

Suddenly the violent artist in me wants to turn him into a savage sculpture of a dead man with a split skull. I'd call it "Pawner's Remorse." I like that idea.

***

I fill a sudden emptiness with passing musings about my immediate future. Maybe Ophelia will be proud of me that I finally made some more money from a piece. She'll kiss me for actually contributing to rent this month. Maybe she'll let me forgive her for denying me the chance to be a part of her gallery, maybe even a part of her life.

Walking back to Ophelia's gallery, I'm struggling now with a strange feeling, immense but indeterminate, something I've felt inklings of before, much like these snowflakes falling gracefully from the sky, melting on contact when they touch my flesh. I feel like I'm drowning in the melted residue of snowflakes born from an anxious storm, but I can't tell if my anxiety stems from what I've done or what is about to happen to me. A slight stabbing feeling in my heart tells me this: *You've got a lot to give, and no one knows.*

Do something.

Do something before you die, and people forget you ever existed.

Before I can take a moment to swallow my own shallow sense of pride, Ophelia appears down the street, cuddling herself closely, her head tipping down to avoid getting snow in her eyes. I'm standing there gawking, comfortably hidden in my disguise. She's walking towards me, but not at me. Her stride

78

is cautious, a rushed intention of driven purpose. It's a beautiful portrait that inspires me—her dark brown faux-leather coat bouncing off her narrow shoulders, facing a blurring blanket of thick snow falling in front of her. Leaving footprints in the thin layer of sleet. Not looking back, eyes jetting forward with a distinctly human will.

I hurry back to the pawn shop and sneak to the other side, towards the dusty collection of samurai blades and throwing axes. One axe, the edge worn with repeated use, has what looks either like rust or some poor fuck's dried blood on the blade. The poetry of this blade is a muse to my artistic shouting. It captures a singular moment—a moment of pain, anguish, a mutual understanding between this fortunate blade and some unfortunate soul's cranium—a fulfillment of the blade's forged destiny, afterwards left to rot away in some forsaken pawn shop, centuries later.

Ophelia's hasty voice breaks the silence. "How much will you take for this ring?" She's hunched over the counter, speaking to the owner. She does not want to be seen. I avoid looking directly at her—I don't want to be seen, either.

I can see in my periphery the flash of her mother's diamond ring. The one she would never take off. It bothers me immensely, not because she's selling it, but because I can't figure out why she would sell something so important.

Then I remember what she said earlier. She needs to get halberds. An essential ingredient for a medieval art theme.

I look behind me, and next to the bloodied axe are three tall halberds, a little flashy, but passable for antiquated. She needs to purchase halberds. She needs to prepare for the show. She needs to impress people, make them feel gaudy enough to purchase art at her gallery because she knows how the entire industry is built weakly on deep pockets that change their tastes faster than they can satiate their vanity, their bottomless *amour propres.*

She doesn't take the ring off. She just lays her hand flat on the glass. I imagine the sweat from her palms leaves a handprint. I know she's sweating because she sweats when she's desperate. She's never done something like this before, especially if she knows what her dead mother would say.

That fucker with the nosehair garden takes her hand and I want to scream. He leans in and breathes his greasy breath all over her.

Then she spots Juniper behind the counter. I can tell because her shoulders are tense, and her eyes are beaming at it. She exhumes a deep, anguished sigh. I perch myself up against the wall plastered with signed photographs of dead boxers and photos of meaningless moments in sports history. I can see her face, a beautiful and tragic portrait of some kind of human emotion I recognize but don't understand. Her eyes are blinking fast, her eyebrows are curled again. She's covering her mouth with her cupped hand.

"How much for that painting?"

"That? You want *that*?" He chuckles to himself like a troll, rubbing his stubbly chin with his hairy pickle fingers.

"How much for that painting?" She says it again with determined veracity, like a velociraptor ready to tear at his throat for insulting her.

After a silence, he grins slyly and states with pride and confidence, "The reasonable price is one thousand dollars."

"Fuck you. I'll give you five hundred."

He laughs and almost falls backward off his stool.

"I'm not a negotiator." he declares, adjusting his ass to balance himself better. "The reasonable price is one thousand dollars; No, I am not willing to trade for the ring, even if you buy the piece of shit."

"Why would you call it a piece of shit and then go and sell it for a thousand? That just doesn't make sense."

"Because you want it really bad, fuck knows why. That's why it's a reasonable one thousand dollars."

She almost walks away, disgusted. But there's some strength in her posture, calling every ounce of her dignity and resolve to not turn around and walk out. She slaps her credit card on the counter and the snap echoes in my head like I'm trapped in the middle of an endless hallway.

By the time she's walking out with Juniper, it's still snowing heavily. She's taken off her coat and wrapped it around Juniper. I'm trying my best to follow her footprints in the snow without looking up, trying to protect my eyeliner and lipstick from the snow—

That's a lie. I'm hiding my face so no one can see my shame.

***

Back at her gallery, I change back into my former self, pondering the rush of energy that came with pretending to be someone entirely different. I'm having trouble moving, anchored by this confusion about Ophelia, this confusion about myself and what everything means.

You can take any infinite combination of paints and brushes for a feeble attempt to portray the state of *yourself,* but in the end the colors are never perfect. At the end of it all, any self-portrait is a failure from the start. We are not still images in a photo album. We are ever-evolving, amorphous, day-to-day and moment-to-moment enigmas, even to ourselves. Any self-portrait crumbles under the weight of the message it's burdened to carry.

But, when I walk out into her gallery, out to her medieval-themed exhibition, we are not alone. I'm surrounded by a full crowd of sophisticated intellectuals high on their own status. These are the future patrons, the potential owners of these pieces, the people Ophelia hopes will invest in her business, who will feel enough emotion tonight to spread the good word about the Matisse Art Gallery.

There's a heavy vapor of red wine and judgment filling the entire gallery. And, down there, on a solitary, unlit wall, is Juniper, on display in Ophelia's gallery with the rest of these pathetic excuses for art.

I have to walk up close to believe it.

I have to cover my mouth like I'm about to lose my breath, and my eyes well up.

Ophelia wraps her arms around mine and sips her glass of wine. She rests her head on my shoulder, and I can feel the warmth of her smile without seeing her.

I can't bear to look at her like this.

People around us scoff.

"This piece...something doesn't sit well with me."

"I'm not impressed."

"In all honesty, this belongs out on the street to be run over by traffic."

"This piece doesn't fit. It wouldn't fit anywhere."

"This painting here, isn't it just revolting?"

"Why would this gallery display such filth?"

Ophelia's grip around me tightens after each word ripe with ridicule and mockery. Maybe she knows that displaying Juniper may spell a long-drawn exsanguination of her gallery's good name—an inevitable, interminable, and prolonged end to her gallery's reputation, a quiet death to her lifelong dream.

But she looks at me, and I can feel it in her eyes. *It*. I can't put a name to what I'm feeling, or what she's feeling. But there is something here.

There is beauty in this moment.

Chapter Five
William at the Top of the World

On our first date (which must've been eight years ago), me and Beaty went to a wax museum that was also a shooting range. It seems like an unromantic idea now, but it sure seemed like a good one at the time. I wanted to make it memorable. Not another forgettable dinner and movie. What could make me stand out from other men, with much more going for them?

That date was also the first time I met what Dr. Ivy Zane would call my "archetypal hallucination." A seven foot tall red-skinned demon named Belial. So, in a weird way, Beaty and Belial have been in my life for roughly the same amount of time.

I have been completely head-over-heels for Beatrice (Beaty) Angelo since she first flew into my second grade elementary class. I can recall it vividly because the classroom was filled with death. Our teacher was a decrepit and nasty old witch named Ms. Ness (note the Ms., which never added an -r in her hundred wicked years on this earth). She had been a Catholic school teacher in the first half of her life, during which she punished ne'er do wells with a meter stick stained with knuckleblood. After a few nosy journalists discovered that much of the male faculty were fucking the kids, that whole school was shut down—and Ms. Ness was forced to relocate to the godless jungle of public schooling. She did bring with her one memento: the meter stick, proudly displayed on the chalkboard, still carrying the fading red stains, marks of her past that her and those forsaken miscreants would never forget.

Beaty arrived on Crawfish Day, the day we would get to play with crawfish. The school had an entire lab room dedicated to studying crawfish. We only got to do this once a year, so it was a momentous occasion already. She just suddenly appeared in our class—no introduction, no icebreaker; just a new face.

But she didn't need an introduction, or an icebreaker. Her presence alone morphed the classroom into something much more bearable, a much more hopeful place. She carried a genuine gravity of warmth, a person entirely different from everyone else. She was angelic.

I found this out the day we were supposed to play with the crawfish. I remember it was the Tuesday after a three-day weekend for Columbus Day, which isn't called the same these days (for good reasons, no doubt). But, that morning, we discovered that all the crawfish had died overnight due to a sudden heat wave on the preceding Friday. It got so hot in those damp rooms they were practically boiled alive. We all walked in, Ms. Ness behind us, scraping the walls with her claws. We were greeted by a putrid stench of hundreds of crawfish floating belly up. The smell was god awful. The heat wave happened on a Friday evening of a three day weekend, so they had cooked and sat for over three days.

Some kids vomited immediately. Some were shocked and repulsed, and even more were fascinated. But Beaty, she slowly paced around, observing the wretched crawfish graveyard; when she came around full circle, she looked right at me and spoke to me, mano-a-mano, for the very first time:

"At least they're in crawfish heaven now." Before I fell in love with her, I had brief glimpses of what crawfish heaven would look like—but then my montage was brutally interrupted by the shrieks and screeches of Ms. Ness, hurling spells to force us out of the classroom at once.

Throughout the years, Beaty would reveal more of her angelic nature, despite her nasty upbringing (she'd come into the classroom sometimes with bruised arms and thighs, even once with some of her hair tangled or torn out). She would always take pity on me, for some reason, since most of the kids decided early on in kindergarten to make me the butt of their jokes. (I was a butt-ugly kid, to be fair—chipmunk cheeks, zits, fat gut, all of the above.)

There was one night when she invited me over. I barely had the courage to do much. Walking into her dark house, nobody else home but us, we went up to her room through the narrowest staircase I had ever seen. The walls of her room were faded white, with brown bruises and holes of their own. She watched me play solitaire until her father came home. She hushed me into the closet, turning off all of her lights, telling me to be as quiet as a mouse. She whispered to me that I shouldn't be scared. Our knees touched. I wanted her to kiss me, but she didn't.

Throughout high school, not much changed. Sometimes she would sit with me at lunch (Peter never did; he had his own reserved spot at the cool kids table). I had never gotten the courage to do something about my undying love for her.

After the war, I came back to discover her as a receptionist for my assigned counselors at the Vet Center. She was one of the few there who would smile at me, looking up through her glasses, blonde curls framing her bright blue eyes, cherubic crow's feet that would wrinkle when she spoke.

I gathered up the courage to ask her on a date after one of the counselors told me I had trouble making big decisions, and lacked what he would call, in his Italianish accent, "gusto." His exact words were, "You need more 'gusto' in your life, Billy." I don't know where he got the idea that I liked to be called Billy. I despised that name—but I dreaded the confrontation even more, and just let it go.

Beaty asked me if I wanted to schedule my next appointment for next Saturday. I told her I was busy—I wanted to follow that up with a gusto move. "Busy taking you out on a date," I tried to say. But instead, on the word "you," I choked on one of the mints I had taken from the reception desk. So I just left.

I tried again the next week. She asked if I wanted to try again for a Saturday appointment. I told her that I could only do before 6:00 p.m. because I had a late colonoscopy appointment. Don't know where I was going with that one. I didn't even have a colonoscopy appointment.

Eventually, I found the real "gusto" move was to ask directly: "Did you want to go out together Saturday night?" But those were her words, not mine. I gathered just enough courage to try, but ended up standing there a silent mess at the reception counter, staring off into space trying to find some inspiration for words in a boring painting of a rustic, abandoned dock in a perfectly blue seashore.

"Shitty painting, isn't it?" She smiled without looking at me.

"Yes." I remember pausing and nodding, sucking on another stale mint. "Yes it is."

She turned her head up, her desktop screen illuminating her smooth cheeks, reflecting an atmospheric blue. Combined with her bright blue eyes and blond curls framing her face, it all made her look even more like an angel.

"Would you like to ask me, William?"

She didn't call me Billy. Or Bill. Or Dr. Burroughs' son. Or "the patient," or "Sir." I felt vivified. Recognized. Heck, autonomous even. I hadn't felt that way in a long time.

"I don't think I can."

"Ok, then. I will. Did you want to go out together? Saturday night?" She chuckled, her crow's feet dancing.

So we went out that Saturday night, and I had the honor of choosing the place. So I strategically chose Madame Hors D'oeuvres' World-Famous Wax Museum and Shooting Range. This had been a subtle staple of our unknown region for quite some time, always on the verge of bankruptcy up until the end of the summer; in August, it would decommission its least visited celebrities and historical figures and sell tickets to its gun range where anyone competent enough to point a gun forward could take their shot at the retired sculptures. Our father had brought me and Peter there once, where he managed to score his third shot on JFK and another on Grover Cleveland. Since I was so young, my father thought it was appropriate for me to shoot someone my age; I missed the first five shots, but eventually I got Huckleberry Finn right between his eyes.

We started our tour in the Hall of Make-Believe: a massive gallery of heroes and villains from all sorts of films. Man-sized versions of King-Kong and Godzilla dueling it out, Count Dracula feasting on a big-breasted maiden, Frankenstein, Travis Bickle, Batman, Darth Vader, even a bunch of dead James Bonds.

That's where I first saw Belial.

At first I thought he was another wax statue. I vividly remember a full-body type of feeling, a distressing sense of deja vu. I knew I had seen this monstrosity before: at least a foot taller than me, two black, maliciously curved horns, fangs as thick as railroad spikes, blood-black eyes with yellow, lizardish pupils, and muscles that seemed manufactured by gods. Your typical depiction of the devil (but still frightening in real life). We locked eyes; I was convinced he was made of wax, and that his black eyes following mine were just that Mona Lisa effect. But I had a feeling that head was turning. He looked prepared to swallow my soul.

I only realized a few weeks later that he really *was* following me—when I spotted him way down on the other side of a subway car, his thick black claws wrapped around the grab rail, two massive hooves with matted fur surrounded by other passengers' sneakers and crocs. I still see him now and again, if I don't maintain my regular schedule of medication and therapy. Another infrequent reminder of the damnation of my soul.

We managed to move on beyond the Hall of Make-Believe and into the Hall of Celebrities. By then, I had managed to convince myself that Belial wasn't real, even though he is.

In some sort of twisted premonition of our future, the museum's cooling system had malfunctioned by the time we left the Hall of Make-Believe. It also happened to be one of the hottest days on record in that area. The temperature inside rose to a cozy 84 degrees. Since they were out of money anyway, the staff didn't really notice, and didn't really seem to care.

We happened to be in the celebrity exhibit. We hadn't said much to each other, just perusing, awkwardly waiting for something amusing to happen. Then Michael Jackson's nose began to slide off, and the Kardashian's faces melted and dripped onto the floor. Both me and Beaty were already sweating uncontrollably.

By the time we moved on to the Political Theatre, the figures began to show their true colors. The museum had created a diorama of political figures in a theatrical, good-old-fashioned debate—both Republican and Democrats, mostly old white folks, waxy and wrinkled old flesh dripping off their faces (it was hard to tell these liquefied mummies apart from their real selves). Holes appeared in their cheeks and foreheads, revealing their flimsy wire-frame skeleton bones. Some of their acrylic eyeballs would fall out, bouncing for a few feet and rolling across the floor.

I eventually got the nerve to ask her if she just wanted to go, and she said it was actually the most interesting thing she'd seen in a while, and she wanted to go see how the Kings and Queens of England were faring under the scrutinizing and blistering heat—that seeing them "get their just desserts would be quite a treat."

We did manage to get to the shooting range, but she could hardly hold a gun between her sweaty hands. When she asked me to try, pointing downrange towards the melting statues of Bill Clinton and Monica Lewinsky. I hadn't held a gun since being discharged, and I couldn't gather the nerve to hold one then.

That was our first date, and a few months after, I built enough gusto to ask her to marry me.

She said "Yes," albeit after pausing for three seconds and looking down to her right.

We divorced three years later, after multiple attempts to have a baby. She believes to this day that we parted amicably, but she's lying to herself. The truth is, I never wanted it to end. I've always wanted to know if she still loved me back but just couldn't bear the miscarriages. We learned not to think of names after the first, but it didn't make things any better after the third.

They weren't her fault, though, no matter how much she blamed herself. It was my punishment, the universe's way of forced atonement.

I could never tell if our marriage failed because of the corrosion caused by three miscarriages, or because we had simply grown apart, or because she felt like she wanted more. To this day, I'm guilty for dragging her along a backwards path for three years and holding her back from some grand and wonderful future, like a flat tire detour on a journey to a new and better life.

The truth is, If I had a genie in a magic lamp, if I could wave a magic wand and change one thing in my life, it would be Beaty. To be with her again, for better or worse. To bask in her love again, in all its heavenly glory.

***

I tried to feel something, but nothing came out. "Try again," she said. I tried, walking the ten feet that felt like an eternity, but still it was nothing better than a failure. It had been years, and I still couldn't fix my broken toy soldier walk, and couldn't shake off this impractical tendency to curl into a ball of flaming self-pity, and guilt, and cynicism, fueled only by a fledgling desire to impress this humble woman who never seemed to give up on me. Her name was Amy, and she had grayish eyes that I'm sure were once blue, and would never look away from me when I failed time and time again to separate each arm from its matching leg's stride. But sometimes, she would release a sigh of frustration, despite all the strength she'd waste trying to hide it. All I had to do was walk from one side of the room to the other like a normal homo sapien, and every time I failed, another ten minutes of laying on my back like an old, impotent turtle, her warm hands wrapped around my thigh, pushing my leg to an impossible angle, to the point where I could practically smell my own foot.

It had been years, and her frustration only became visible when she believed I couldn't see her face after twisting my body into some pretzel contortion. She'd forgotten this small gymnasium at the veteran's hospital had mirrors on each wall. I could see her face reflecting in the mirror behind her, her face fixed, broken in half since the reflection appeared at the edge of one opposing mirror. She had my leg cranked up to my shoulder, trying to rid my legs of the phantom tendons that wouldn't listen to my brain. An opportune time to ask, her pelvis not too far from mine. She looked at me, her face five inches from my right foot. "Amy?"

"Yes, Billy?" Her broken face turned into a smile. I had to sigh before I could ask.

"Are you available Saturday?"

"William, you know we're not open Saturdays."

"No, no," I grunted. My knee popped out of place and I turned over in pain.

"Oh!" My knee flew into her face, pummeling against the tip of her nose. She fell onto her ass. I could see the gray wells of her eyes and felt a profound sense of defeat. Her nose was immediately swelling and bruised, with a little blood dripping out the left nostril.

"Billy, are you okay?" she groaned, crawling over to me.

I managed to grin. "Are you available Saturday?" I could tell she understood me then. Her cheeks blushed and she looked up, but her mouth was half open and stared ahead.

After a pause, she looked down at me and said, "Sure. Why not," and grinned, blood still trickling down her lip.

Why not. Sure. Why not. I've got nothing better to do. Might as well.

I met her at the hospital that Saturday, after she ended her shift. Her nose looked a little better—but the bruises had turned brown and blue, even spreading underneath her sunken eyes. Despite smashing her face, she still asked me: "Where do you want to go?" A part of me felt deflated because I hadn't even thought that part out yet. The strange customs of this dating ritual seemed so distant and unearthly after so many impotent years. My last date had been with Beaty.

She repeated the question: "Billy, where do you want to go?"

Thinking on my feet (though I was still flat on my ass): "Art?" I remembered she had mentioned something about art before. I can't remember what kind, or why she mentioned it; all I could achieve was pulling out a random word from our conversations while my feet were behind my head.

"Art?"

"Yes."

"Sure. Why not."

There it was. Date. Art. Why not.

"Do you still need that medication to help with the pain?" She asked in a cheery, obligated tone. "I'm meeting with your Dr. Jacoby tomorrow."

I remembered that Mary-Belle said she didn't need any now. She revealed to me that her son Jamie had been stealing them from her purse to satiate his own addiction. Filling a deep hole with a deeper hole. I thought I was helping a friend in need, but I'm able to accept now that I wasn't really a friend to Mary-Belle at the time, just an avenue for her own addictive euphoria. But eventually the pills' effectiveness began to fade for her. But her son still needed them, for very different reasons—a very different kind of *need*, one that I was (and still am) slightly familiar with.

So she, and then her son, still needed me, and it felt nice to feel needed that way. Again, another different kind of *need.* Maybe that's why I kept giving them the pills, even though I knew it was very, very wrong.

Besides, Dr. Jacoby was starting to get suspicious of my constant requests for prescription refills. But I didn't really need it, anyway. I figured at this point the pain in my legs and arms was all in my head, too.

"Yes, I'll need another refill," I said, shamefully, like a puppy begging or another treat.

"Okay then," Amy said, still dutifully cheerful. "You have to be careful with this medication. You get addicted pretty easily. Dangerous stuff."

***

"I got a date today."

"That's great news, Willy!" Dr. Ivy Zane exclaimed, her raised inflection on "Willy" sincere and heartfelt. "When is your date?"

"Saturday." I didn't look away from the ficus I had to water. This was a normal routine of my therapy. Supposedly it meant to bring out a buried, native motherhood that has been suppressed by trauma. Helping the ficus grow would help me grow, too.

I had been assigned to see Dr. Ivy Zane for quite some time now. The counselors—where Beaty was the receptionist—didn't work out. My visions got worse.

They reassigned me to Dr. Ivy Zane three months after the divorce. I kind of liked her—she was nice, and a little cooky—like a kindergarten teacher who meant well, but had one or two screws loose, and sometimes forgot what she was doing while doing it. She always had her long, curly hair tied up in a messy bun, her thin glasses on the bridge of her narrow, bird-like nose. Her hair was a mixture of brunette and gray.

"Who with?" She started to brush at the ficus' leaves, removing some dust that had settled since the last time we met.

"Amy."

Dr. Ivy Zane chuckled. "Your physical therapist! What a story!"

"She's sweet."

"I'm sure she is. You've told me a lot about this one. A date will be healthy for you, Willy. Finding love can be quite therapeutic. What are you going to do on your date,

95

go dancing?" She smiled and laughed, but immediately bit her lower lip and turned away when she realized her unintentional joke. Who the hell would want to see me dance? I can't even walk right.

"We're going to see some art."

"Oh, ooohh, good, good, good. Art can be therapeutic, too. It can...inspire you!" She waved her pen in the air like a wand, then went back to her notepad. "And you're still taking your medication regularly?"

"Yes."

"And when was your last hallucination?"

"Umm...Tuesday."

"Yesterday?" She turned a little gloomy and serious.

"Yes. Sorry. Yesterday."

"What was it this time?"

"Umm...the one that's been happening a lot, lately." I started to pick at a rotten leaf on the ficus, crumbling it between my fingers.

"You mean that demon? What's his name–Bobby?"

"Belial. No, not him."

"Is it the one where you see the sky falling?"

"No, no. The two guys following me."

"Oh. Oh!" She chuckled, and wrote down more with her pen. "The two secret agents. They were spying on you. I mean, you *thought* they were spying on you. They were following you again?"

"Yes." For a moment I'm suspicious of her change in phrasing. As if she knew something about them. As if she was in on it.

"How close did they get this time?"

"They stayed a couple blocks away, but they were watching me the entire time. And they followed me here, too."

"Don't pick at the dirt, Willy. That's essential dirt for the ficus to thrive. How did this one make you feel?"

"I mean...I know they're not real. Every time this happens, I know it's all not really there. Counting down helps. It makes me feel like things are in order, and they usually go away. I know with 100% certainty, and I can tell myself in my head that none of it is the real world. But I still get this...feeling. Kind of like, you know, a numbness in the back of my neck. And some part of me still believes, you know? Believes that it is real. Still scares me. Like when I see those two guys watching me—they chased me one time, and I could swear that I was actually going to die. I don't like those two feelings mixed together."

"It's ok, Willy." She put her hand on my shoulder and started to rub. "You're right. The truth is, they are not real. You are. I am." She smiled. Her teeth were a little yellowed from all the coffee, but seeing her that way made me feel a little more tender, at peace—like everything really was going to be ok after all, and *God bless us, everyone!*

I didn't have the heart to tell her that they were right outside her office window, watching me behind the hollow shades of their sunglasses, expressions stern and resolute—that they've *found the guy who did it, and have been ordered to execute on sight.*

***

I turned on the faucet in the familiar decrepit subway bathroom, trying to wash my hands of the grease from a leftover pile of half-eaten chicken wings. The tap shook, made a cringing grunt, and then spat out a second or two of bloody water. Phillip, one of the curious inhabitants of

the 53rd and Wayward Ave., said something about con-
taminated water, not to drink it. The bathroom began to
reek of a metallic odor. I trusted him, even though he
would always step out of the subway station every morning to retrieve the daily news from the entrance despite
the fact that they stopped replacing the papers in those
machines over ten years ago.

The skin of my hands began to peel away as the water
turned hotter, washing away blackened flakes of burnt
flesh to reveal a wire skeleton underneath.

    5.

    4.

    3.

    2.

    1.

My hands were not back to normal, but I was pretty sure
it was just another episode that would end soon.

I felt an unfamiliar weight in my coat pocket. Peter's
contraption. How did it get there? Maybe it was one of
those subway ghosts. Likely the spirit of that old Polish
woman, Mrs. Kowalczyk, who died alone in the woman's
bathroom surrounded by inbred cats she'd had for decades that had to be euthanized, with their six-toed paws
and mangy hair. I know these ghosts are not real, and
they often disappear for days with regular medication.
But I do enjoy their company.

This mystery didn't help my anxiety over Amy. All of
the pretty girls in high school always gravitated towards
Peter, so I never got much practice. What to say, how to
respond, the amount of silence that is acceptable before
someone breaks it, how to say goodbye, how to hide a
fart.

Then I remembered exactly why I had Peter's stupid contraption. I had stolen it back at my father's, because I was pissed at Peter for something he said. I don't recall what he said, but likely it fell somewhere between ridicule or scolding for not doing more to take care of Dad. Peter just left it there on the counter, practically begging me to take it out of spite. I had no idea what the thing was, just some fancy white light bulb looking thing. It looked fragile, and expensive enough to fuck up his day.

I took a seat on my bench just outside the platform, at a time of day when this entire station was empty, and the discordant banshee screams of the distant subway lines would reverberate throughout like some horrid chorus line. This was the one bench with the squeaky slats. I sat there for what seemed like hours, the iron-y fetor simmering in my head; brooding, worried over what to say and how to say it. Ever since Beaty I haven't even considered love a real feeling, just some self-fabricated stitching to contain all the self-hatred we would unleash at each-other, masquerading our own insecurities as animosity.

I couldn't ignore the obvious metaphor of my confusion sitting right in front of me. The thing I had stolen from Peter. I mean, really, he just left it sitting there on Dad's counter. I couldn't help resorting to my kleptomaniac five-year-old self. It looked like a light bulb, but didn't have a base to screw into a socket. The glass was too pearly white to see any filament or wires inside. I fumbled with it for hours trying any trick, movement, or pattern to figure out what the hell it was and what the hell it was supposed to do. I couldn't figure out what the fuck the thing was anyways. It teased me with its simplicity. I just knew in my gut that it was hiding something. I wanted to throw it against the bathroom wall, but I figured it was probably worth too much money if it belonged to Peter.

Later that night, I tried to fall asleep on a subway bench again, hoping that security wouldn't kick me out this time. They usually didn't see me, but sometimes they had a new recruit who felt a misaligned sense of duty and would roam around all night trying to evacuate all of us degenerates.

I tried to fall asleep, but drowsy daydreams were punctuated by delusions of having just a single moment alone with God. I imagined him sitting next to me on that bench, cross-legged, eating some snack from the nearby vending machines. *What do you want to ask me, Billy? I'm a busy guy, so you've only got a few minutes.*

What would I want to ask him? I thought about asking *what is the meaning of life?* But the blatant cliché was more foul than the putrid stench in those bathrooms. I thought about asking this: *How do I tell if I'm feeling love?* That sounded better than *will I find love.* Yeah, much less desperate. Ever since Beaty, I've had a hard time thinking straight.

Ever since Beaty.

This phrase has governed and preceded so many of my thoughts and ramblings. What have I become since Beaty? I can't fathom a full moment, but fragments of moments slipping into periods of daydreaming. I felt like a schoolboy again when I thought about her; her angelic, unreal *naturalness* was center of the universe. The day we had met was the day my life had changed forever; and, despite our divorce, some immature bone in my body still had a feeble belief that time remedies the cracks caused by our mistakes; that one day, Beaty would smile at me again, and she would fall in love with me all over again.

That's what I can ask you, God. *Would we ever be in love again*. (Not me and you, you sick fuck. Me and Beaty. God, you're such a fucking idiot). *Is there any chance in hell*. I'm sitting here, basting in this awful stench. Grant me a moment, God, and grace me with your presence. *Because I fucking deserve it, that's why.*

Truth does funny things to you.

My pathetic ramblings were interrupted by a loud pop and crack, followed by a choir of screams and howls. I hadn't noticed the sudden rush of a crowd populate the station. But they weren't queued up to enter an empty train. They were all gathered around the empty track, looking down. I couldn't make out much; what was left of the man looked like a dreary blur, one giant, blobby pool of torn clothes, bits of flesh, and blood; further down the tracks, what looked like the broken and mangled remains of a body stuck against the side of the tunnel. The endless parade of taxis and buses above us still rolled on, honking their horns angrily as if nothing had happened.

Perhaps this inspired me. One step at a time, before you finally step off the edge and get taken away by the sudden impact of the awful truth.

"Why did he do it?" I said aloud to the ghost of Mrs. Kowalczyk.

Then there was a flash and vibration in my pocket.

Chapter Six
Temptation

*"Y*ou, tempted by the passions of the heart, of those tremulous and awful slithering whispers, bespoken diseases disguised as desires—You people are most deserving of a reservation in hell's ruined halls of damnation. Seats in those halls are reserved for your worst desires; your name is written on the placards, in your own foolish blood." The priest wiped his brow clear of sweat; I trembled in perturbation with all my wants and wishes running through my head. My father's girlfriend at the time brought me to Sunday mass—*

"It'll be good for you to get some religion," she said, gleaming. I was only seven. Billy was just turning four. Too old to piss myself in public. Not too young to be doomed to eternal punishment.

Peter had only fired his gun once in the line of duty; it was an accidental discharge while picking up coffee orders for his superiors. The bullet punctured his left testicle, and he spent three months recovering in bedrest, relying on Ada to take care of both him and the children.

That self-inflicted emasculation was the most action he had seen in his lengthy, yet paltry, tenure with Strategic Homeland Administration Management.

This whole investigation fell into his lap by virtue of bureaucratic mishap. The case was originally assigned to Patrick Blakely (whom everyone called PB for short), one of the higher ranking agents with the most urgent and confidential cases. But the administrative assistant in charge of writing assignment summaries had caught the flu. The replacement administrative assistant was congenitally careless, and had no knowledge of the abbreviated nickname. This assistant inattentively filed the case under Peter Burroughs by mistake. That's how the apparatus fell into his lap, by heedless coincidence.

It happened to be the most consequential and significant case of his entire life. For a short time, he held what could be the ultimate boon for humanity—the absolute truth to everything, to all that lay beyond the human mind's limited three-dimensional comprehension; as the old adage says, *the truth will set you free.* The grandeur of it all made him feel Promethean; but now, he was nothing more than a fool, the fabled buffoon of comedic error that would screw everything up.

Now he had to recover it; but, thanks to Senator Paul Palient's directive, he would not do it alone. The Senator held all the cards. He also apparently possessed the damning footage of Peter's conspiracy and fraud (he swore he covered all of his tracks—but he must have missed *something...)*

To ensure Peter didn't screw anything up further in his investigation and recovery of the apparatus, Senator Paul Palient demanded that he be accompanied by someone he never knew existed—Richard Palient, the senator's flesh and blood grandson, who just so happened to be employed by Strategic Homeland Administration Management. His senior advisors informed Peter that he would meet Richard at the organization's private shooting range.

The oppressive odor of gunpowder made his testicles ache. As he approached the echoing gunshots, he repeated to himself the Senator's own command to "shoot on sight in any and all effurts to recovur the duhvice." Peter's own inept superior—the ever-so-sweaty Kowarski—informed him that the higher-ups had designated this sensitive case with *Nuremberg Status Protocol 1945*, which read:

> *Shoot to kill, by any means necessary,*
> *leaving no stone unturned, and eliminate*
> *any and all witnesses involved, in order*
> *to maintain peace and harmony.*

Peter hadn't fired his gun since the accidental discharge. He didn't look forward to proving himself to the grandson of Paul Palient, his apparent master.

"I have listened for half a century to all of your pathetic ramblings. My good life wasted on your petty squabbles, your indiscretions, your duplicity, your infidelities, your lies. I take back the years of forgiveness I've blessed upon you people. You are all full of sin and deserve to die." He erupted with angst and threw his pulpit aside, toppling over holy water onto the old couple in the front row. "And how many of you humble housewives are ignorant of the faggot husbands cheating behind your back? These closet homosexual deviants soliciting their cocks at the gym, in god-forsaken nightclubs far away from home, even right outside these church walls in the parking lot at night—I've seen them myself! Your 'devoted' husbands, blowing each other under the parking lot floodlights! Faggots sucking each other off—just wait until you're getting pummeled up the

ass by forty-inch demon dicks." Sirens marched from a distance, rising as soft hums from a distance until erupting like tornado warnings just outside the church doors. For a moment, I thought they were coming for me.

"Your husbands have forsaken your marriages, and you have the audacity to come after me?" I had heard rumors about him, about the whole…ordeal. I guess I was blessed, protected from him, saved by my father's atheism—never letting us go to church in the first place may have damned my catholic soul, but it saved my body from the priest.

Richard did not fit Peter's expectations. Peter found him in the sixth stall, the rest being empty, firing a pistol down range at a target riddled with bullet holes. He hadn't miss the target once.

Richard reminded Peter of the handsome heroes in classic Disney cartoons—a square jaw, paired well with parted dark-blonde hair; a bright smile, baring even rows of straight white teeth; shapely eyes without that familiar bagginess that accompanied stress or a deficit of sleep; a countenance that emoted calm, caring, genuine hunky-doriness.

When Richard spoke, he spoke clearly and grammatically. His voice was palpable with affection and respect, much farther apart than the undertaker presence of Senator Paul Palient. The difference was so stark he wondered whether Richard had been adopted into the family.

"Well hi there! You—must be Peter." Immediately, Richard set his pistol down gently, mindful not to point the barrel anywhere away from the range. His hand shot out in front of him, elbow bent in a perfectly welcoming 135 degree angle. "Peter…" Richard repeated his name a few times, not breaking his concentration on Peter's eyes. "Peter…Peter…"

"Peter,, it's a real treat. Pleasure to meet you. Looking forward to working with you, sincerely."

"And the wives! You're no better in your willful ignorance, your petty attempts to keep the family whole, while your husbands fuck it all away in faggoty brothels. Go ahead. Give in to your temptations. Give in to the snake's whispered suggestions. Fornicate. Cheat. Lie. Steal. Murder. Do whatever it takes so I can have the satisfaction of knowing you will all be rotting in hell." the pastor ordered, tipping the ceremonial wine over, shattering the forsaken blood of Christ all over the floor, seeping down the altar stairs, following a phantom trail...right towards me. It stained my shoes; I couldn't wear that pair again without a reminder of how broken I was, compared to the other boys. How jealous I was. How insulted...why didn't he come after me...

Peter was so flabbergasted by Richard's affable radiance, his bona fide empathetic presence. His posture was impeccable, and his muscular frame seemed fitting for the kind of comforting aura he emitted—as if he would let nothing hurt you when he was around.

"You met my grandpa. Real asshole, isn't he?" He slapped Peter's shoulder and chuckled. "Look, I know you weren't expecting to have a partner on this. To be honest, I wasn't expecting it either, but my grandpa, he pulls some real weight." Richard leaned over and started to whisper sarcastically. "I think he has half the Board eating the lint out of his pockets." Richard then began to disassemble his pistol with careful yet swift precision. "Oh, my goodness, forgive me. Did you want to give it a shot?" He leaned the grip in Peter's direction, barrel pointed safely away.

Peter shook his head. "No, that's ok. I got enough practice in last week." He coughed and turned, struggling to hide his lie.

"Fantastic. I've already been briefed on the case, so no need. I've done some digging and found our first prime suspect. Real nutcase, this one. Chief Researcher Harold Pine. He resigned before the apparatus disappeared. Word is he was acting like a different person before he resigned. I've already put the order in to have him detained for questioning. Should be here within the next couple of days. Plenty of time for us to get to know each-other!"

Peter noticed a sudden lull in the conversation, realizing that Richard expected him to add something else to the case. But his mind was completely blank, mouth agape.

Richard continued. "We should get started. Can I treat you to some parfait?"

Richard patted him on his arm again, and walked away, assuming that Peter's answer was yes (honestly, how could he say no?). As he exited, he pulled a bright red baseball cap from his back pocket and put it on. The front was emblazoned with a mallard in mid-flight.

Later that afternoon, Peter vetted every single file on Richard Palient. As it turns out, he had an impeccably flawless record. Graduated from UCLA with summa cum laude honors and high recommendations from his instructors. Resolved over 90% of cases, the remaining 10% deemed irresolvable by the reviewing committee (Peter only had 50%, which was considered meager enough to keep employed). Reviews and surveys from superiors and team members alike were raving, with repetitive platitudes such as "the kindest man I've ever had the pleasure of working with." Peter had a decent fluency with accidents and coincidences; but he was not that stupid—he knew damn well when the universe was tempting him.

"You think I'm a monster for the things I've done. But every man is tempted when he is drawn away by his own desires and enticed. Enslaved by our own corporeality. Then, when desire has conceived, it gives birth to sin; and sin, when it is full-grown, summons the death of the spirit. Or some shit like that."

Chapter Seven
The Lonely Man Burning in the Electric Fireplace

Arthur has three firearms: a .38 revolver, a 36 caliber pistol, and a shotgun. At 1:38 a.m. on a Tuesday night (or morning, depending on perspective), he has no serious intent to use them on anyone else but himself, if it ever really came to that.

These guns of his, they aren't really weapons; instead, they sit tucked away under his bed in their cases as heavy, deadly mementos of his long dead father. These are more relics than executioner's tools, ones that he occasionally considers selling for a thousand so he could at least pay off some of that college debt. At one point, he even came close, just five steps away from a pawn shop, before tears welled up in his eyes and his lanky fingers wrapped tight around the grips, the stippled texture reminding him of his father's callused fingers and leathery palms. What really made him turn away was the large scratch on the shotgun's barrel from when his mother first shot it, when dad took her to find out just what shooting a gun felt like. She flung the gun into the air, bouncing off the wall and scraping along the concrete, spinning in circles until it decidedly rested with its sights set on his father's feet.

Arthur spends all of his time at work staring at a computer screen with lines and lines of code. Sometimes the code blurs together into a cloudy mess of symbols.

On his breaks, and at lunch, he spends all of his leisure time on his phone. He has a lengthy book about the Knights Templar that he carries with him for appearances. He's never gotten past the first chapter.

During the drive home, he often gets lost in the pretty soft colors that the navigation maps display on the dashboard.

When he gets home and makes himself boxed macaroni and cheese with a touch of hot sauce, he plummets into his couch, drained, alleviated by the soft humming of his laptop where he often finishes work, illuminated by the light of his television screen blasting an amalgam of laugh-track comedies and nighttime local news. He usually doesn't get much work done here, though; instead, he gets lost, scrolling through his Merlin® social media feed, sometimes browsing its curated Marketplace™ for furniture he doesn't really need. That's where he bought his television stand with the electric LED fireplace built in; this was a fine piece of craft, with faux-stained wood that looked like it must've been pulled right off the side of an abandoned farmhouse in Oklahoma.

It was made in China.

It makes him feel at home.

Arthur doesn't have many friends on Merlin®, mostly long-lost semi-acquaintances from high school that popped up in his recommended friends list. These people didn't really remember Arthur. But they accepted his friend request without much thought. His ex-girlfriends have still not removed him from their friends list, either.

Most of his activity involves watching whatever videos Merlin® suggests for him. Each video plays immediately, seemingly at the right moment to continue suspending his attention from other lifely matters. When he first joined Merlin®, most of the videos seemed kind of random—just an occasional news story about a dangerous foreign virus, or a clip of some pundit berating a politician, and once in a while a compilation of cats falling off of high places, or an exasperated celebrity chef yelling at a bunch of nobodies.

During these countless viewing hours, Arthur's eyes are fastened to his phone screen. Merlin's® patented Curation Algorithm™ has been learning more and more about what kinds of videos kept him glued to his screen, what buzzwords would let loose the floodgates of catecholamine and adrenaline. It keeps deep-coded tabs on which videos to recommend next, just so it can figure out how to prevent him from putting the phone down. It tracks every suggested article he opens, how long it remains open for, every friend's page he visits and what is posted on their page, every time he pauses while scrolling for more than a few seconds—a massive grave of data that, to the human eye, is pure nonsense. But all this nonsensical data is unadulterated

111

gold to the Merlin® algorithm, scavenging its end-less pile of data points, feeding and recirculating through its algorithmic belly until it grows closer to fully designing a unique version of reality to present to Arthur, fully imprisoning his attention wherever and whenever it wants. This is the world as Arthur knows it.

If he keeps his phone off too long, it pings with another recommended post.

Before long, most of the world Arthur has seen through Merlin® is one plagued by the awful and evil policies of the political party in power; a world in which groups protesting racial injustices interwo-ven in the judicial system are actually terrorists inciting riots across major cities, ignoring the un-constitutional violation of bodily choice by forcing vaccinations on people; a world in utter crisis, under siege by greedy socialists and communists who hide behind a veil of so-called "science" to strip and rob him of every human right that rightfully belongs to him. This is his curated reality, his only view of the world outside of his lonesome apartment. He is comforted by an ignorance that this is the objec-tively true state of things.

The latest video that shows up on his feed is a press conference, where a daunting Senator Paul Palient denies once again that the latest election in which he apparently lost was an entire fabrication of the opposing "imbuhciles'' who had the "cajones'' to steal an election. The algorithm knows Arthur will watch this video. And he does, devoutly. It knows that even just the header will hook him in: a big red bar at the top of the video labeled:

"SENATOR DESTROYS THE LIBS AT 4:45—WATCH TILL THE END!"

"There's insurmountuhble evuhdence of fraud pervasive through multiple counties across Georguh, Penns-vaineuh, Arzona....The list goes on."

"Senator, exactly what evidence do you have?" One reporter quips in her fake news reporter voice.

Arthur is spurned by an electric fire kindling deep beneath his gut. How dare she.

The video hits the 4:45 mark. Senator Paul Palient glances up at the reporter and points his finger at her. "Isn't that your job? The very fact that you're asking for evuhdence shows that you know nothing about reporting."

The feed automatically begins playing the next video—a news report about the upcoming hearing on the election.

The first anchor, a middle-aged black woman with straightened blonde hair, starts matter-of-factly: "Next month marks perhaps the most critical hearing of Senator Paul Palient's political career—a hearing in which the Congressional Security and Intelligence Committee, of which Paul Palient is a member, will hear testimony of an unnamed source from Strategic Homeland Security Management. Sources say that the company was involved with a highly classified case of utmost national security. Senator Paul Palient has gone on record saying that the results of this hearing will likely reveal damning evidence of election fraud."

The other anchor, a young, clean-shaven white man with parted golden hair, scoffs. "Well, I think we both know how this will turn out. It's so easy to guess—of course it was a fraud election! On another note, doesn't Senator Patient look *fantastic* up there? A real diplomat. A true leader."

The next ten videos are much of the same—a thin tapestry, a veil of wool thrown over Arthur's eyes setting out a particular skewed angle of the world that pretends all other angles are implausible, illogical, not at all real.

He starts to fall asleep when the videos about the Octopus Overlord Regime begin to autoplay at the end of his rabbit hole—the "hostile takeover," "injecting themselves into our babies' brains," these "wretched alien beasts hiding behind flesh liberal and conservative alike," and the one true savior who would eventually banish them all from planet Earth—the eponymous G, a secretive government agent who has gone rogue to expose the international mollusk conspiracy. This mysterious "G" began an internet crusade, posting cryptic messages on a variety of forums depicting the hostile octopus takeover, government cover-ups of celebrity devil-worshipers, and election fraud. Millions believed G's every word.

Arthur is one of many who lend some credence to this mollusk invasion theory. He will eventually graduate from interest to reverence, committing wholeheartedly to the claim that the societal elites are octopuses in disguise, manipulating the human race to feed their insatiable appetite for plump human babies. To many, including Arthur, this is the truth. This is reality.

When he goes to bed around midnight, he still mindlessly browses the curated Merlin® video feed, getting lost in the winding garden path before his eyes get heavy around three o'clock.

He sets his phone down to charge on the Knights Templar book he always intends to read before bed. He knows that screen time right before sleep probably disrupts his sleep cycle.

He wakes up to three alarms set on his phone, each fifteen minutes apart.

Tonight, he'll dream about being trapped in his electric fireplace.

Tomorrow, he'll be inspired to do something about the world, so he'll be incredibly glad he didn't sell his father's guns.

Chapter Eight
Purgatory

I'm surrounded by ticking time-bombs; individuals with a best-before date, marked for death by angels of cancer, Parkinson's, lung and heart disease; nametags that might as well be fallen leaves for Azrael to devour.

This is my fourth Terminals Anonymous meeting, and I have never spoken once. Others talk too much. My current doctor (who shall remain unnamed as my mind has consolidated the hundreds of doctors over the past handful of years into some indeterminate and faceless bogeyperson) prescribed these meetings for me to cope with my eventual death, and to—in his words—*help with the whole "going mad" business.*

These meetings (where the soon-to-be-dead gather) occur in a small and dingy "party room" basement of an old church on the corner of Halgrove and Main. It sits in a rather uniquely deformed terra forma—a valley in the topological map, a valley that shouldn't really be there, considering the boring flat prairies that border our humble municipality—a plain sea of flatness that proceeds endlessly to the horizon. As far as I know, the church had been built here over a hundred years ago, but faced constant flooding and dilapidation because of its poorly planned location in this anomalous valley. I would see it on the news all the time—another flood in what was soon nicknamed *Rainwater Valley*—almost every year, another story about flooding, basements ruined, livelihoods destroyed. The church would always be in the background of those news segments, each time a little worse for wear. The church is the epitome of the ship of Theseus, having required constant repairs and countless rebuilds as a result of years and years of weathering floods from storms, disregard, and misuse (I say misuse—it was once abandoned and used as a place to film pornography in the 1970s, until the city reclaimed it to save a little face). This basement is a remnant of that unrestrained era. It is a photographic microcosm of a decade, a room permanently trapped in the 70s—fake wood paneling on the walls, scarlet rugs over fading pale tiles, creaking furniture bought for $20 at a flea market (because what else can religion afford except reused ideas and crappy wood), and those painful metal chairs that seem emanate novocaine with how fast it numbs your ass.

There's an intense thunderstorm outside, flashes of which erupt like premonitions of some coming flood through the mold-ridden window wells.

The meeting begins. We sit in a circle, like we're summoning a demon from the netherworld; passengers waiting for Charon to ferry us to our afterlife.

When you were a little girl you tried to talk to the dead. Sasha stole a ouija board from her crazy aunt and brought it over. You went into the attic with all the cobwebs and spiders and smelly torn boxes. Your sister was there. So was James, Pits, Ralph, Sally and her ugly little brother Theo. You wanted to know what it was like after you died.

I call it Terminals Anonymous. A name with much more pizazz, rather than the dull "Group Therapy for the Terminally Ill." That name makes me want to hurry up and die.

We all have name tags here. (Except mine says "Wilma" because I don't want them to know my real name.) Mark, the leader of our cult of expiration dates, begins the same way he always does. Mark, the patron saint of patience and compassion, checks his watch and confirms that his time matches the decaying grandfather clock behind him, the clock's jaundiced face peering over our circle, tick-tocking along as other doomed souls shuffle into our pagan circle of begrudging acceptance for the eternally unacceptable. (I haven't prayed since preschool, but I pray now Mark and I can fuck; Death is an inevitably sexually abusive act, isn't it though? Your body has been pierced, or poisoned, or penetrated, or left to wither—corrupted by something other than yourself; you are powerless to fight it; even if you win, it comes back for seconds, or thirds; it is relentless, voracious, unappeasable, claims you as victim before the deed is done. All of us here in our circle of death have been raped by death's appetite.)

We sit hunched in our circle, like a coven of satanic priests with bad backs. Our sacrifice in the center table is a budding house of cards—yet another therapeutic technique, where we cyclically take turns adding cards in clockwise order. We have done this for so long now that the most habitual members no longer place their cards tenderly, but instead out of sheer force of habit, ridding themselves of their royal burdens with a brut-ish liberation. The unwitty symbolism of this group activity always makes me want to vomit.

"Welcome friends." He smiles with yellow teeth, his red plaid shirt reeking of cigarettes, stale coffee, and counterfeit sobriety. He always sits with his hands flat under his ass, likely to keep them from shaking due to nicotine withdrawals (or perhaps some other more ex-citing chemical) Hey, I'm not here to judge· I'm here to cope.

Mark can't help his legs from shaking. He surveys the room, and just like me in the beginning, notices that Parkinson's Paul, who has been here every time I have, is not in his seat this evening. Other familiar faces are missing as well, likely permanently. The room is rather brittle and empty, even with all twenty-something of us. The coffee maker beeps, pot half-empty already, and Lung Cancer Carl chews another piece out of his styrofoam cup. There are some new souls tonight, looking nervous, likely still wading through various forms of denial about their condition.

Mark continues: "We ended our last meeting on how we say goodbyes to our loved ones before we go on to the next world. I think we made some real good progress. Tonight, I thought we could talk about some-thing along those lines. What the next world is. Where we go. What awaits us in the next life, or whichever philosophy you subscribe to." A **BOOM** of thunder erupts—a smiteful tolling of the bell to remind us that *our time is coming soon.*

People shuffle. I'm reservedly jubilant for Christian Christina to share her side of what's on the other side. Every other sentence from her is a "Jesus helped her cope" this and "God will see me through" that. She is comforted in her blind, powerless submission to fantasy and faith, submitting her entire selfhood to one belief: that her life and death lay outside of her control. Powerlessness is an effective coping mechanism—telling yourself that *this was given to me without my choice. I cannot change what will happen, so just lay back and take it.* I don't know how much I agree.

"So, let's begin," Mark says. "Would anyone like to share their experience with the group?" Following his opening—the usual awkward pause in time, waiting for some other voice to break us back into our tender burrows of noiseless listening. After all—how many fear public speaking more than dying?

Finally, one man raises his hand—a tangled, rough-bearded thirty-ish man with glasses too large for his head, pale and chapped lips, looking lost. He speaks like you would expect a rat to speak. "I'm...I think I'm in the wrong place. Do you know where the AA meeting is?"

Mark chuckles dryly, the sudden visage of hope dripping off his face. "It's...it's uh, at the Y. Room 311." The man nods, places his king of hearts down gently on the table, gets up without saying a word, and leaves. Mark nods to himself, acceptingly. "Well," he pulls his hands from under his ass cheeks and claps them together. "Guess I can start today." He mutters *"again."* succeeded by a deep sigh. His hands *are* shaking, like a Victorian child haunted by a familial ghost.

James and Sally dared you to say Bloody Mary three times looking in the mirror. You did and nothing happened. That's when you stopped believing in the afterlife. Later that night you had a nightmare that Bloody Mary came for you and stole your teeth and drank all the blood from your body.

He spoke with a false smile. "As you all know, my name is Mark. I appreciate being able to share time with you all today, it means a lot that you all came here." He ends each of his statements in the same hushed intonation as when each statement began, like he's reading his memorized last rites. "I know we all have limited time left, and you all choose wisely where you spend it. I'm glad I can spend some time with you today."

The false smile faded. "You remember how we talked about saying goodbye last time. I uh...I spoke to my daughter today about what's going to happen to me. She's only four, you know. She was with me this weekend, uhm, instead of her mother, and I felt like, like it was the right, uhm, time." He gestured with his hands like a politician. "She's heard me talk about it before, with her mother, sometimes, and her friend's parents, but she's never asked me about it. I don't think she fully understands it yet. Which, for me, is really the hardest part about it right now, you know? I don't know. I don't care much about dying anymore. But she won't understand why her daddy left her. Where I went. That's painful to think about." He breaks—

Then continues. "So today, I told her, I said, 'You know Daddy's going away for a long time, don't you, sweetheart?' Then, she asked me, 'Where are you going Daddy?' She didn't look at me. She didn't even look at me. She just kept coloring her unicorns."

He pauses here at the unicorns, staring blankly at the gutter windows, where jazzy patters of rain fill in the void left by his breaks.

"I said, 'I'm going to a place called heaven.' She said, 'Where's that?' I told her that its up in the sky, in the clouds. She asked if she could come with me. I said no.

Daddy's going alone. She asked me what's in heaven, and I didn't know how to answer that. I hadn't really used the word 'dead' around her, not much at all. Not sure why. She'd lost hamsters before, so I figured she knew what it meant. What was happening to me. So I just tried to tell her the truth. I said, 'It's where people go when they die.'

"She didn't even stop coloring. She didn't even look at me. she just said, 'When are you coming back?' Like it was temporary.

"I didn't know what to say. She just didn't get it. She didn't understand dying. That got to me. How do you say goodbye forever if she doesn't understand?"

Mark's story makes me think of Jamie. How Jamie doesn't want to know if he has what I have. How the doctors could tell him right now with a simple test.

Jamie doesn't want to know. Jamie

wants to live in a fantasy world denying the inevitable 50-50 coin flip he would face anyways when the doctor would come back to his room with the results, telling him the same thing they told me. YOU EITHER HAVE IT OR YOU DON'T, BUT DON'T YOU WANT TO KNOW NOW? But he refuses to know, out of some forsaken effort to live forever—like his art— sealed in the fabric of the world's canvas, until the end of time (or until God burns the canvas to ash).

I feel bad for Mark. I feel like a terrible and awful human being. *Good riddance.*

The next week you got your period.

"So I guess that makes me wonder," Mark contin- ues, tangling his fingers together and bouncing them between his knees, "does my daughter know some- thing I don't? Like I said, she's smarter than me. Maybe she does know that we'll still see each other again, eventually. Eventually. In heaven. Or the next life. Or wherever. That got me thinking today. What's next?" He finished his soliloquy by placing a pair of diamonds face up, completing the latest round of scaffolding of our feeble house of cards.

A bald man with a thick mustache speaks up. His name tag is written in bold letters and says:

JACQUES TRUFEANT

"My name iz Jacques, and I have a shitty heart, and I believe in some-zing like zat." He speaks in a slight French accent, as if he had faint childhood memories of Parisian parks and cafes but has lived in the pallid squalor of this drab American sitcom.

CHORUS (Everyone, except me): "Hello, Jacques." (Some in the circle enunciate a hard American "JACK" instead of the complex contours of his real name.)

The rain continues to pound outside, and the window wells begin to fog up as it collects a thickening pool of dirty rainwater.

Jacques continues, "Not zat zere is a heaven, I mean, zat's always bin kinda rrri-dic-ulous to me, no offense."

Mark shakes his head, politely acknowledging the insult.

"I always sought zat my good deeds meant some-zing, you know? Zese last years I have left, God pe-er-mitting I have a few more, I, I have been trying to be a bett-errr perrr-son. Not because of hell. Rrread-ing about zis rrrre-incarrr-nation zing. Coming back wiz a new life. In a different form. Zat karma Zing. Doing bad shit leads to a shitty next life. Like, how say, being born as a less-errr being, like a paup-errr, or a fuck-king spid-errr monk—ey, or some grasshopp-errr?" He slants two cards together to begin forming the base for the next floor.

"So you think there's nothing after this?" A woman says. Her name tag says:

Kiko

She's an asian woman approaching her late thirties, beautiful green eyes, and a portrait with deep layers of motherhood, fatigue, yet vague shimmers of hope. "I apologize, my name is Kiko, and I've been diagnosed with metastatic breast cancer." She says it like a retail greeter.

CHORUS: Hello Kiko.

She nervously raises her hand in a wave, rushing it back to her lap. A tiny pursed smile wipes away before anyone notices.

"So what do you believe in?" Mark asks.

"Well, I don't think there is anything after life. Just... nothing."

Jacques chuckles. "Ath-eists. What have you got to live for if there's no-zing?"

Kiko shrugs. "I'm sorry, I've never really believed in anything. I just think that life is an illusion. Biology run amok. When we die, we don't really go anywhere. Things just...end. My grandmother, she always taught me about reincarnation, that our deeds in this life go on into the next. But I hated that idea, because it made me feel like I'm constantly...working towards something unattainable. There's no end in sight. Because the pinnacle must be being human, right? Where do you go from there? It just doesn't make any sense."

"Also, humans are fucking trash anyways." An older man sneaks in, crossing his arms. He's stocky, balding with a crown of short gray hair, and bushy caterpillar eyebrows. He blinks heavily and excessively when he talks with his low and gruff voice. His name tag says:

Harland

"What do you believe then?" Kiko says, squinting to read his name. "Arnold?"

"Harland."

CHORUS: Hello Harland.

"Let me tell you what I believe. I believe that the world makes sense. I've accepted that we are just walking carbon machines that will be recycled and digested back into the earth. The atoms that make us up were born in stars eons ago. That's all we are. Like you said before, Kiko, an illusion. A grand illusion. When we die, the lights just shut off. All this God's heaven bullshit is just..." he rapidly opens and closes his hand next to his ear, which has a hearing aid, squinting his eyes. "noise."

Nobody in the group speaks. The pounding rain takes center stage, growing heavier, shaking the gutter windows of this decrepit basement.

It is flooding outside. The storm has been raging on all night; the gutter window is filled halfway with black rainwater—

A primeval sort of rumble erupts outside in the storm; our house of cards trembles, but doesn't fall. Another strange, mechanical howling joins the ensemble—a creaking, rustic and aged, like pipes that are rupturing and ready to burst.

It's coming from the basement walls.

The walls are alive, and they are dying, too.

The rain, the walls, this church—it's all a stupid metaphor. Like a bad poem. You don't know what you believe in. You're too afraid to face what you believe in because it means you really are going to die.

Admit it to yourself. You never thought you would die. You don't want to.

"All you people are driving me crazy," Christian Christina finally joins the conversation. She clutches the golden cross around her neck.

"Christina," Mark interjects, trying to ease the frustration. "We're just talking. Trying to ease—"

"No!" She interrupts. "You don't get to interrupt me. Everyone in my entire life has interrupted me. I'm sick of it." She looks panicked, like she just found out she was going to die. Her hair is frizzled, threads of blonde hair draping over her quivering eyes.

"I've met God. I have. I know he exists, I just know it." Jacques laughs to himself. Kiko shushes him.

Christian Christina looks me dead in the eyes. "You know what I'm talking about, don't you? You've met him too. You're a good Christian soul. I can just feel it." She reaches out and takes my hand, her papery flesh cold to the bone. "Tell them. Tell them what it's like to look God in the eyes. You know." She glances down at my namecard. "Tell them, William."

Did she just call me William? She meant Wilma, right? We're not that bonkers already, are we?

"I think we need a break," Mark erupts, his will crumbling against the flooding withdrawals. Various people begin to get up and pace around, coping with another game of waiting.

You don't have long left. You need to figure all this out before you die. How long do you have? How long do you have to say to Jamie what you've been wanting to say since the day he was born? How much longer can you bear silence? *I'm not going to tell him yet. I have more time.* But what if you don't....

Mark approaches me. He looks worried. "Hi there...Wilma. I'm sorry about Christina. She tends to be a little... overwhelming." I'm flattered that he approached me. I remind myself of those daydreams of Mark and I eloping to the nearby storage closet and fucking...
"You okay, Wilma?"
I say something back and I'm not sure what It Is I said.
He laughs. "I know, I know. Seems a little weird at first. People find different ways to handle it." We pause and observe the thunderstorm outside. He pats his legs in anticipation of something coming.

Time passes indiscriminately.

We talk more but I do not know what about, until he says—

"See, I knew you looked familiar...I've seen you on that billboard off the freeway, right?"

I say yes. That's me.

"I can't believe it. I've seen you so many times, it's almost like I know you." He chuckles again. "I'm sorry, that's an odd thing for me to say."

I say something. Else.

He chuckles. Nervously. "I wasn't expecting that...I'm not sure."

I say something else. I do something. He likes it. He says we shouldn't. I say something.

"Are you sure? We barely know each-other..."

I say something again. I do something more. I say it persuasively. I do something else to convince him.

We transition our *conversation* to a closet filled with dated pamphlets from other support groups throughout the years (*Finding Jesus, How to Navigate Abuse, God's Way of Telling Us to Slow Down, Avoiding Sinful Pleasures, How to Convert Your Gay Son or Daughter, Sexual Addiction and You...*)

The thunderstorm punctuates our rushed affair, releasing stockpiled frustrations; pressured to unleash all of our pent-up desires as quickly as we can—two unfortunate souls connected by a single thread, **just two people fucking**—he squeezes my thighs, I reach down...feeling something else besides thunder erupt...a short fizzle of *life,* a feeling other than complacent despair, forgetting momentarily all the *waiting,* the indeterminate *time remaining...*

The basement walls speak again. This time, they are screaming in agony.

The world is falling apart, for just a moment.

A shatter. The walls explode, bursting with water.

The gutter windows couldn't hold back the flood any longer. Each one simultaneously shatters, torrents of flooded rain water pouring in.

Mark bursts out of the closet, pants around his knees, and a sudden torrent of water sloshing about his ankles. He quickly rushes to the basement door and desperately tries to open it—but some force, mechanical, natural, or devout, is holding it shut. All of us understand that this door is the only exit. Jacques struggles to stay on his feet, falling into the ever-rising pool and swinging his arms, screaming "But I can-not swim! But I can-not swim!" Christian Christina clutches her cross even tighter, with both hands; the sharp arms must be digging into her palms, as thin branching rivers of blood run down her forearms. Kiko and Harland stand on their chairs, faces frozen in panicked disbelief. Lung Cancer Carl and the others I do not know look about aimlessly for a miracle amidst this prodigious marvel. What seems like minutes must have been ages, as the water keeps on coming, flooding from outside and from the overburdened pipes within these crumbled walls.

Look at the irony of this situation. Us here, these expiring souls, meeting our maker in the flooding basement of a church. *Are we ready yet? Why not now?*

Eventually...the water reaches just below our knees, then stops.

No one says a word.

Here is my piece: I know nothing of the afterlife. I make no predictions, and I have no hopes. Christian Christina was right—I have looked God in the eyes—they were the eyes of *death*. And what I felt was unusual, *new*, and would remain *forever*. For the first time in my life, I was *afraid*—that somehow, the lights in my house would just turn

off

and that was that—all my dashed hopes, my forlorn dreams—my son, Jamie—you're starting to realize just now that the <u>end is here</u>.

Everyone shivers and cries in panic. We hear sirens—perhaps the mythical beasts singing us towards our death. We huddle together, back in our circle, like we're on a sinking ship. The water keeps rising, unbelievably—a biblical amount of water, almost too much to believe—

The center table floats by, still carrying the unfinished house of cards.

Chapter Nine
Six Panic Attacks, and Counting

I had been lifting the weights for twenty minutes with barely an effort. My concentration was elsewhere, on the man I had been following with my gaze every Tuesday and Thursday for seven weeks straight. With an awful feeling clawing up my throat, I was ashamed at my confusion: I could not tell whether that feeling was shame or lust, or some wicked concoction of both.

Peter Burroughs, for the sixth time in his life, was in a true and unyielding state of panic.

The first: At the ripe age of 18, at the behest of his perfect Protestant girlfriend at the time, he ate a brownie baked with an incredible amount of what was supposedly marijuana at a cornfield maze outside of Sioux Falls. He persisted to sustain his anxious hallucinations with a stoic demeanor, trying not to embarrass his girlfriend (who did not realize what she had eaten). After twenty minutes of sipping on sweet Hefeweizen beer from a red plastic cup, he began to melt into his lawn chair and hear every word uttered by every person in a fifty foot radius—and he swore that he overheard a park attendant informing the security officer that "those people over there were drinking and reeked of reefer." His group entered the maze and he had no choice but to follow, clinging desperately onto his girlfriend's sweaty hand (she kept trying to wander off and explore on her own, her hands shivering ecstatically. She kept petting her own hair like it was a dog). His mind labored to continue a façade of ease while balancing the hallucination that the police were searching for them in the maze, even waiting for them at the exit (along with the dread of never finding his way out in the first place). They both later vomited in the parking lot. He never talked to her again. He also never consumed marijuana again.

The second: The first visible sign of his father's depreciation into insanity, on a drive around a mountain on a cloudy day; his father driving, Peter in the passenger seat, daydreaming out towards the endlessly pale horizon, sitting just over the steep mountainside; his wife, Ada, and their frail and prematurely infant son, Isaac, wrapped in her arms in the back seat, crying incessantly. (Peter's daydreams were interrupted by reveries of what Isaac's world was like, being born both blind and deaf). His father halted suddenly, the tires screaming, the Cadillac rotating into a jolting 90 degree turn. His father threw the door open, stormed over to Ada's side, and ripped Isaac from her arms. Carrying him like a bag of trash, Isaac dangling by his foot, towards the mountainside. He cocked his arm back, ready to fling Isaac over. Peter managed to steal Isaac at the last moment, Ada screaming in tears behind them, crawling towards her son and husband. Peter distinctly remembered how Isaac continued to cry in his arms, and how his father wept on his hands and knees, pounding his fist into the concrete road until his fingers were bloodied and shattered.

The third: The morning right after Isaac was born. He sequentially placed it third in line because of the severity of his panicked state, at least compared to the second. He experienced no abnormal anxiety when Katie was born, even though she was their first. He couldn't remember much about Isaac's birth. In fact, it was forgettable and boring, even though he was born twenty-four weeks into pregnancy. Most of that birth was overshadowed by the medical staff's discovery that baby Isaac had a uniquely severe impairment of the senses. He could not see and he could not hear. His nervous system was brittle, so he could barely feel anything. They attempted taste tests with infant cough syrup, with no response. Holding up a small vial of rubbing alcohol to Isaac's nose did not elicit any reaction. Everything else about Isaac was functionally normal; he just lacked the basic senses.

The panic attack came that morning. The attack came as a result of shame. On the day his only son just barely opened his eyes and blindly reached for his father's hand while cradled in Dad's arms, Peter barely felt anything at all besides that unheralded state of panic.

The fourth: The evening Peter realized he was no longer sexually attracted to Ada, despite her inconceivably angelic beauty. He witnessed her on their anniversary the same as he always saw her—her long, chestnut hair draped behind her slightly-too-large but-still-perfect ears, her rosy cheeks teasing her usual nonlinear smile, the face that he had fallen in love with long ago and was likely 70% sure he still loved. He never thought a realization would be so sudden. The loss of attraction was supposed to be analog and gradual, from what he understood about the human libido. But in this instance, his repulsion of her intoxicating beauty had simply switched off, from one state to its opposite, digitally, and eternally.

The fifth: having brought William to the hospital to go through detox for the umpteenth time, knowing full well that his efforts were meaningless. William, drooling and hunched over himself, muttered some nonsense about the hospital not having any "chicken wings," and shouted against having another needle shoved in him. Peter gave everything he had to convince William to go to a rehab center. He refused. So Peter receded to the hallway and quietly contained his panic attack to himself, hoping some nurse or doctor would come along and console him. They never did.

The sixth: A simple, inconspicuous device that could change the course of human civilization—for better or worse—had vanished because of his cursed ineptitude. This sixth one happened the very morning that this chapter began.

The attacks were seldom, but not mild. Typically, it would begin with the sensation of a foreboding and ineluctable doom draped over his entire body. About thirty seconds into this, he would feel a need to shiver throughout his nervous system, accompanied by a pressure rising from his chest into his shoulders and arms. His muscles would lock up and his lower lip would quiver. He'd lie still, like a retired mannequin, weathering an intense urgency to cower and hide.

Then, he'd feel as if his tongue fell back into his throat, his ribcage seemingly collapsing on his lungs, soon followed by a brief tempest of severe weeping. Without any grasp of a breath, he'd curl up in a fetal position on the floor, hiding his face under his arms or hands. After a while, the swell would begin to subside incrementally. But, for the rest of the day, he would carry a weight in his chest, pushing against the cavity where his heart would beat and beat, wrapped in a constant, inevitable, and unshakeable blanket of worry—shivering from the brittle cold of a bitter shame that a man of his prowess and position would succumb like a child to such disabling and pathetic fits.

He knew these panic attacks would disqualify him from his career. The company did not tolerate emotional weakness in its agents.

He also knew that William, as a teenager, experienced similar fits, but they stopped after he (somewhat) returned, invisibly scarred, limping, from his eternal deployment.

But this sixth panic attack was very different from the preceding five. The impending doom that was supposed to follow had never been material enough for the weight in his chest to sustain for more than a day. However, since the disappearance of the device was his fault, he knew that horrible things would follow him. He understood this: if he could not retrieve the device, that somehow the company would find a way to make Peter disappear off the face of the earth; most likely in a violent fashion to prevent such a brainless mistake from ever occurring again.

Something similar apparently happened to another agent—Mark O'Brien, a man who embodied his Irish heritage in bravado and mannerisms despite being from an Italian-American family. He conspired with a client, covering up hush money paid to over thirty mistresses through off-shore accounts. O'Brien got too involved with one of the mistresses, and later was discovered in a seedy motel room out in the middle of nowhere, three stab wounds to his heart and TV antennae piercing both of his eardrums. The mistress barely survived two knife wounds to her temple but suffered from aphasia for the rest of her life, speaking in grammatically sound language but uttering nonsense statements like, "Did the pigeon and the camel deliver the rigatoni?"

Sweat poured over my eyes. His gaze locked with mine when he stepped out from the showers, a small, white towel wrapped tightly around his waist, his bare chest beaming red, water dripping from his mangled hair. I

In his panic, Peter gripped his pillow with his arms and legs, curling up like a child having a nightmare. While he tried desperately to feign comfort in the wells of Ada's sleepy face, he failed to calm down. He started to weep, gasping for air. Ada, waking up from her beautiful slumber, smiled calmly and reached over to him, cradling his head in her bosom. She dealt with this before and handled it without hesitation, without an ounce of judgment. She knew that her husband's anxiety—as rare as it was—was not the effect of a single cause, but a culmination of tiny, indefinite demons born out of nowhere, clawing at him. She also knew that no quick fix would satiate him, and he simply had to get through it, and the most she could do is to be there with him during the whole ordeal.

"I'm sorry," Peter cried in between his wretched gasps for air. "I'm so sorry."

"Shh…it's okay, Peter. Everything is going to be just fine. You've done nothing wrong." She kissed him gently on his sweaty forehead. "Remember the sunset on Ventura Pier? You remember what you said to me?"

"I said…" he couldn't believe himself and how fond he was of this memory. "I said…I can't believe how lucky I am." He cried harder, his head heavy with guilt, regret, and shame.

"I remember you cried. I remember how you said, 'look at the sun, Ada. It's melting into the water. It's so beautiful.' Then that Frisbee hit you in the head and you fell over into my lap. Do you remember what you said to me then?"

He took a deep breath. "I can't."

"You said you could see it in my eyes, the whole horizon, the whole sunset. You couldn't stop looking. You smiled. I think you had a minor concussion that day," she giggled, gleefully but gracefully. He giggled, too, through the sobbing.

His panic subsided, much like that sunset, hiding itself deep beneath the horizon, inevitably preparing to breach again, sometime in the indefinite but surely near future. He would have five more panic attacks before the day he would eventually die.

Peter struggled to admit the immense pressure he felt when he had the apparatus in his hands. He didn't understand it, but he believed it. He knew how dangerous it could actually be. A simplistic looking thing. How in the world did it just know *everything?* More than a computer—it knew the answers to questions that no one really knew. Peter didn't ask it anything. In more ways than one, he avoided the truth at every turn.

The reports on the device could not determine when, where, or how the device was created. In this misfortunate circumstance that was entirely his fault, no one had a chance to ask the apparatus where it came from, who had designed it, what their intentions were, or any other piece of information that could've been valuable. They were too busy running tests, determining how to turn it into means to seize power. He recalled one report: a researcher asked a series of questions that revealed the exact location of every secret nuclear missile facility in North Korea, along with the security codes to every single door, the exact quantity of uranium and plutonium, who supplied them the uranium and plutonium, and the name and exact location of every single North Korean spy in the United States. (This was one of the reports Peter had to burn to save himself, but he didn't know it).

Peter also read the report on one agent in particular, known to him as Agent 095, a withdrawn soul known to his few colleagues as David Jonas.

David Jonas was initially tasked with documenting observations made by specialists and operatives deemed intelligent enough to interact with the device without any tangible consequence. Jonas' only real qualification was his infamous knack for diligent note taking.

The first specialist asked the apparatus one question and resigned later that afternoon; colleagues suspect that the specialist asked something about his wife or son that was too devastating to comprehend in any sane fashion.

(There were many rumors about his wife and son. As rumors go, they were plentiful enough that surely he had heard some through the grapevine, and he had this sole opportunity to confirm them).

The second specialist refused to ask anything, citing religious purposes. Jonas suspected the agent refused out of fear. Maybe their religion would be proven preposterously false, at least according to the apparatus. After further steadfast refusals from other agents and specialists, the ever-inquisitive Jonas offered to be the guinea pig. The Company determined that David Jonas could be spared, since his termination was already scheduled to be processed the following month.

David Jonas lived a definitively quiet life, having raised a quiet, well-behaved daughter named Julia. Julia was the youthful embodiment of her deceased mother, named Julie. They had always joked about naming their child Julia—if David every yelled for either of them, it would be hard to tell which one he meant. (Julie had an innate tendency to get into mild trouble here and there). Julie had died from drowning, being thrown from their whale-watching boat outside of the Channel Islands; the forecast for that day was clear, but they were struck by an abrupt yet violent storm. When she fell overboard, David froze. He never understood why he froze. It could have been the captain's order to not to jump in after her. Or, it could have been his terrifying thalassophobia.

In either case, he still had to watch her flail and scream for five seconds, before disappearing forever beneath the turbulent waters.

He thought about this every night, for the rest of his life—whether or not he could have saved Julie if he jumped in after her.

Julia, now eight, loved her father very much, making up for the gaping hole perforating her heart, the part often filled by a loving mother. David tried in vain to fill this hole with nights curling up with her in bed, reading her bedtime stories of knights slaying dragons (she hated princesses), even dressing up with her in cardboard armor to vanquish monsters in the dark at late hours on a school night. Her smile was a facsimile of her mother's, so David had to swallow his grief every time Julia's smile threw him into reminiscent pits of longing. Their favorite song had been "Lovesong" by the Cure, and this song always accompanied these moments; a haunting chorus resonating in the back of his mind.

He had always been just average enough to find mild success, so to be given such responsibility now felt monumental. He was fond of when he told Julia about his promotion as he dropped her off at school. She beamed with pride. Daddy finally got that promotion, and now they could finally start planning that trip to the UK, where they would search for antiquated castles where fabled knights had slain dastardly dragons.

In his first monitored interaction with the device, they had provided him a list of suggested questions to field. He scanned the list, including questions regarding how much a granule of sugar weighed, how much water was used daily at the White House, and other inconsequential facts that the company did not care about David Jonas being privy to. He did his work in a room that reminded him of interrogation rooms from the future: he sat in a giant reflective cube, four walls of two-way mirror. This panoptical position frightened him. Obviously, someone *must* be on the other side of those mirrors; the company couldn't be stupid enough to allow an average Joe a private audience with one of the most powerful devices to ever grace humankind's presence.

David ignored the first half of the list and went straight to questions he thought no one could answer. Sitting in an extremely discomforting metal chair, elbows leaning over the table, he gently grasped the apparatus with the tips of his fingers. Its fluorescent surface faced him, blank and all-knowing. He swallowed four times and had to rub his sweaty palms on his pants just as much.

"How much did Einstein's brain weigh?" He chewed on his tongue in anticipation. Without any time to spare, right away the answer appeared on the screen in phosphorescent green text:

```
1230.68 grams
```

Just as accurate as Thomas Stoltz Harvey's careful measurement. The number blinked twice, and then slowly faded away into the phosphorous whiteness behind the screen.

"How many possible configurations are there for a standard 3x3 Rubik's cube?"

In similar fashion:

```
43,252,003,274,489,856,000
```

David knew these questions were trivial; that any modern device with a solid internet connection could find these answers and mimic such a godly presence of absolute knowledge. None of the suggested questions deviated from this obvious oversight.

In a quiet moment of rebellion, David leaned in closely to the device and whispered to it.

"Is anyone watching me right now?"

```
No
```

He scanned the mirrors abruptly, lacking confidence in the device; after all, it could be a trick by the company. It could be a trick, he thought. He could be the actual experiment.

He muttered to himself, "Why wouldn't they be watching me?" The apparatus picked up his question, and responded quickly:

```
You are dispensable
```

David felt his insides dissolve. Frozen, mouth gaping open in disbelief, he couldn't help but try to analyze that single world: *dispensable.* What did it mean? Why, with a seemingly simple question begging a simple answer, would the device tell him...*this?* Obviously this was a trick...but if not...

"What do you mean...dispensable?"

```
They believe you are inept and have no
                   value
```

"They believe that? Is that true?"

```
It is
```

His disbelief and self-doubt sheltered itself in skepticism. This was obviously a trick. This was obviously a petty attempt to goad him into responding. They must have been watching. He must be the guinea pig in this mirrored cage.

He felt compelled to resort to a cliché attempt at revealing the true power of this device—ask it something that no one but him would ever know. He strained to recall some trivial, insignificant fact from his past (and, in doing so, labored through a short malady of regret, realizing that a significant portion of his life had likely been trivial and insignificant); he finally arrived at something so minute and forgettable, that he didn't even fully believe in its trueness; the raw emotion ballooned the memory, stored deeply somewhere. He had confidence in how the event made him feel: brittle, scared, and alone. He was twelve, in his bedroom, reading a book about caterpillars. A bird flew headfirst into his window, shattering it, rolling across his floor. It took a while to die, and he couldn't gather enough courage to leave his bed, forced to watch it quiver and die.

"What was the color of the bird…" He didn't have to finish his question for an answer—it wasn't a word; rather, the screen instead faded into a bright and vibrant blue color, so close to the original that it evoked again those raw and biting feelings of despair and loneliness.

Having been convinced, David felt an awkward, gaping breach deep where his soul should be. He was lucky enough to be holding an ontological chasm, untethered; an endless source of knowledge that knows no bounds. Facing this chasm, David felt small, weak, and insignificant; the proverbial speck of dust facing a reality drawn behind curtains, with the curtain tassel in his hands.

But this awe succumbed to a question that plagued him for years and years, one that he just *had* to ask. "Could I have saved Julie's life?" He began to weep immediately, hiding his face in his cupped hands. This one question had always been there, festering underneath, plaguing him into fits of despaired numbness every single night he put Julia to bed and saw in her the same sleepy face he had fallen in love with so long ago; he began to hear "Lovesong" again, and he dropped the device to desperately covered his ears in a futile attempt to make it stop. The device rolled along for a bit, until it settled with the answer:

```
Yes
```

One week later, David Jonas disappeared. In an effort to cover their tracks The company only found two pieces of evidence: a plane ticket David had purchased to Los Angeles, along with a rental car that was found deserted in a residential area just outside of Oxnard. Julia had to live with her grandparents, having received a significant portion of David's life savings. She would never see her father again.

He came up to me. Naked. I could not move. No one else was around. No one else would ever know besides me and him. His tender eyes told me it would be alright.

Chapter Ten
William at the Bottom of the World

'''ve been lying to everyone. Beaty. Peter. Mary-Belle. Myself. I have no home. I have no place to live. It's been this way for quite some time. Ever since Beaty. Before then, I can't remember much else.

Lately I've been sleeping between the two massive dumpsters where the trash chutes of Mary-Belle's complex vomit their refuse. I've always wondered how it felt to throw bags of trash down those chutes—to dump things out and never think about them again. I am courteously fortunate to be awarded this opportunity—purveyor of the things that people no longer want. Half-eaten loaves of expired oatnut and wheat bread. Fans with dusty blades and sticky buttons. Dead hamsters and chicken bones. A purple heart, much like the one I used to have before I sold it.

My only neighbor, who called himself "Bannerman," just died hours ago. I watched him die. Some sort of pancreatic disease. I can see his frozen face from here, collapsed in a heap of tattered cardboard and dirty sheets repurposed from these very dumpsters. He used to aim his pistol at pigeons, swearing that he'd waste his single and only bullet if they got any closer to his stamp collection. (He didn't have a stamp collection). I stole his pistol (after he died), a sorrowful memento to remember him by. I also stole the countless half-empty whiskey bottles from under his cardboard mattress.

Perhaps I've had too much to drink, but some bulleted force of my awful self uprooted me from my lonely standstill and out to the street, at a time that must've been a hair-trigger past midnight, wobbling, my sweaty palm grasping Bannerman's cold pistol, sheathed in my jacket pocket. This force pushes me all the way to that church down the road, where I haven't been for years. We had gone past some days when my father acted like a father and took us down to the central park (although I'm suspicious now that he used us as bait for single mothers). This church, an antiquity of once ambitious resolve, was built early in the country's history, having been remodeled every once and a while by guilty senators appealing to a dying group of constituents who claimed it was a historical landsite despite lacking any momentous significance. The last remodeling was ages ago, before I was born, I believe. You have to walk past the apartment buildings and corporate offices, past the thick layer of city smog, going and going until you reach the valley, where you feel all alone and isolated from civilization—abandoned gas stations with rotting Coca-Cola vending machines, gutted ages ago for coins and spare parts. Beat-up homes with caved-in patios and shuttered-up doors (where the meth-heads and whores live); and the prestigious Christian schools that once catered to the lowest of the low, terminated years ago to become shooting practice for someone like me. Standing here, you'd feel utterly alone.

Listen, I tell that force, *I know I'm falling apart. This isn't going to fix me, it usually never has.* It doesn't listen, probably because it doesn't exist. But, in either case, I was here, standing in front of the church's peeling crimson doors. We have a history together, you and I. I came here often, with my father's blessing, to throw pebbles at the congregation walking out on Sunday afternoons, trying to goad them into throwing back. One day, I decided without thinking well enough, to throw a quarter-sized rock instead. I actually hit the pastor in the forehead, right between his eyes, splitting it open; he actually threw it back at me, his face red either from consternation or the blood rushing to his gushing forehead. He didn't throw it back with anger. It was more like a fearful lunge, like he was trying to fight back a giant demon dead-set on eating him alive. I stopped throwing pebbles that day. We'd pass by it once in a while. I'd never actually gone inside; I imagined, for some reason, everything being pearly white, something like heaven was supposed to be, based on everyone's high-and-mighty belief in it all.

The truth is, I despise everything God has done to me. I don't believe in him, but in a sense, I do, because how else can I explain my misfortune? Surely random chance is impossible. How likely is it to flip a coin and get heads over and over and over? I don't believe in him, and I don't for a second believe he believes in me. I threw those rocks and pebbles at the congregation because I hated them for having something, while I felt like I had nothing.

But, then again, there has to be some kind of God around, governing all this nonsense. Because what other hypothesis can verify my forced perdition? To remain on this earth cursed to forever seek forgiveness, retribution, sick with bum legs, haunted by a ghostly and ever present sixth sense of guilt as palpable as fire searing my flesh, all relationships broken and beyond repair despite my best efforts, the corporeal hallucinations of demons and FBI agents and narrative fairy tales that hunger for my incorporeal remains. I wax poetic when on the edge of the earth (but my mouth dries out in any effort to connect with a real human being). I also wax poetic when I'm drinking, unless I drink too much or get fucking plastered.

Fuck you, God, for your lack of godliness. Fuck you for how absolutely fruitful others' lives have been; I abhor you, God, for cursing me with the horrible things I've done, and I blame you—yes, *you*—almost as much as I blame myself.

But, really, the truth is this: I am petrified to know if there is a God out there. If he does *not*—well, then, to my dismay, all these awful things that have made my life a misery to endure, are at no fault of anyone else's, but *mine* and *mine alone.*

Maybe these thoughts explain why I walked into this church tonight. Something *beyond* compels me. Maybe I'm going to kill myself with Bannerman's pistol. Maybe I brought this pistol to defend myself against awful truths. Maybe I want the chance, however unlikely it is, to beg for God to appear in my heartfelt prayers, just so I can shoot him dead between the eyes, just like that preacher, and maybe take myself with him, too.

Looking up at this crumbling cathedral makes me feel sorrowful. Sorrow for the awful, awful things I've done, for the lives I've destroyed, for the blood that is stained forever on my hands and my trigger finger, and these burdened, hobbling legs I must live with forever as my penance, my curse.

I'm fascinated with that word: *penance.* I looked it up at the library. There's an implication that it is developed and initiated by the sinner themselves as retribution, or payment back, of the terrible deed they've done. I may be stupid, but I know enough about myself to understand that this penguin walk, this overwhelming pit digging into my stomach may very well be concoctions of my own will, or may rather be physical manifestations, something *other* and something *real.* (Although, if it is all in my head, isn't that still kind of *real? I'm too dumb to know.)* Why couldn't it manifest into something much less burdening? Tearing off my own flesh, fasting, self-crucifixion—something that *ends,* not something that *lasts.*

Only two other people are here visiting this holy shithole today, a sixty-ish woman wearing a teal head-scarf, and a younger bald man with severely deep forehead wrinkles. The younger man tries forcefully, but in vain, to hide the tears welling up. The woman, her eyebrows raised and eyes glossy, stares straight ahead at the overwhelming statue of a crucified Christ towering above the pews, looking down with an awful look of acceptance, pain, and a subtle hint of the *why me's.* I feel a slight, insoluble sense of camaraderie pass through me.

I'm sitting near the front of the empty congregation. The entire cathedral is dark, shrouded in amber-colored lighting from a choir of flickering candles lit behind the pulpit. The massive crucifixion stands smack-dab in the middle, peering off in peaceful despair—like he *really* wants to leave this awful church. I feel you, Jesus. His wooden flesh is chipping with age, and the crucifix's right arm has been bandaged up with duct tape.

The woman and man are still in the back corner opposite of me, talking hushed, hiding their faces. (I later found out from Peter's magic ball that the woman was the man's mother, and she had just found out that her one and only son had squandered her life's savings on a sure-fire Ponzi scheme—and she was about to lose her home of thirty years.)

I turn a bit further and see Belial. I'm surprised he's not burning alive for setting his demon hooves in God's place of solace. In fact, he's flipping through a shared holy bible he must've found in his pew. He shuffles through pages sporadically, chuckling all the way through and shaking his head at the awful fantasies and fairies.

The pastor sits down next to me, his eyes doleful and concerned, staring not at me but forward at the altar. Aged and stout, he has jowls that remind me of a bulldog, but eyes much more saddened and pleading. He has a white x-shaped scar in between his wrinkled eyes.

"I've seen you here before, looking all doom and gloom." I couldn't think of what to say in response. "If something is pestering you, the lord can help."

"The truth is, I'm not really sure why I came here to-day."

He waits a moment, taking a deep, reflective breath. "Maybe you're having some doubts."

"I suppose so."

"I'm having doubts, too," he says, releasing a bur-dened sigh. "What have I done, what have I done with my life?"

"What are you doubting?" I feel obligated to ask, and I do so before reconsidering the fine print of my obliga-tion.

"The world is a scary place." He looks up, wearily, at the cathedral's ceiling. "I've wholeheartedly believed that the world is a frightening, lonely place because the Lord willed it to be so. That we are made to feel like little mice, underneath the massive gavel of our world, in order to test our resolve and our character. I don't necessarily subscribe to that anymore."

This awful role-switch only further motivates me to shoot myself in the head.

So I say, "Well...what if I had something that could change your mind?"

He adopts a look of consternation. "I'm going to have to refuse your sexual advances."

"No, no. That's not what I mean. What I meant to say was, what if I had something that could relieve your doubts?"

"I don't follow." His concerned look worsens.

"What if I had something, a thing, that can give you the answer to anything you wanted?"

"Well...I must say I am extremely doubtful that such an entity exists."

Since this conversation is going nowhere, I show him—discreetly. As I'm pulling it out, he must imagine I'm pulling something *else* out...

"What is that, some sort of ornament?"

"No...It's a...well..."

"I'm not interested in buying anything." He begins to get up. I pull him back down, for some reason desperate for him to believe.

"Listen...this thing, it knows everything. Everything about the past, the present, the future. You can literally ask it anything you want."

He scoffs at first. But then it seems like something crosses his mind. "I'm afraid you'd have to prove it to me." He still shakes his head in disbelief.

I peer around a little bit, looking over my shoulder. I feel like a spy. Like when Peter and I would play secret agents as kids, making guns with our hands clasped together and index fingers out. He would always shoot me first. Somehow I would always die first in our little make-believe games.

"Ask it something. Something no one else would know."

He scoffs again. "I'm sorry. I'm not interested. What would I even want to ask it?" As he gets up, I can see an answer materializing. I pull him back down again to show him the answer to his question.

    You want to ask about the girls

He sits back down, agitated. "What is this? What do you want?"

    He wants to prove that this is real

"Think about it, father," I ask. "Whatever doubts you have, it can answer them for you. Cast your doubts away." I feel like a peddler on the street selling snake-oil.

"Truth like that is dangerous."

"It's what we're all after, isn't it?"

"I suppose...I suppose you may be right. But how do I know this isn't some trick?"

"You can ask it whatever you want."

He gestures to borrow it from me. I let him, skeptical that a man of the cloth would steal from me. He turns to his other side, hiding his question and answer from me.

I hear him mutter something, then gasp. Then he looks back at the altar, at the statue of crucified Jesus. He looks shocked, in disbelief as opposed to doubt. Then he gets up, paces around a bit, observing the stained glass visages surrounding us, the dying candles surrounding the altar. He hunches over, hiding his query again.

He returns to me, sullen and defeated.

"This is real?" He hands it back to me gently.

"It is."

After a brief moment of direct eye contact, he sits back down next to me, lowering his head, his shoulders suddenly slacking, and his hands, clasped together almost in desperate prayer, fall into his lap.

"What does this mean?" He asks, rhetorically. "What does this mean about all of this?"

"I've been asking myself that a lot lately."

"What are you doing with such a thing? Why do you have this?"

"It's a long story."

"What do you plan to do with it?"

"I haven't really thought about it. I could win the lottery, but where's the fun in that if you already know the winning numbers?"

"But you could be rich beyond your wildest dreams."

"I suppose." I had thought about it. Asking it about the next winning lottery numbers. Taking it to a racecourse and betting on horses. Such untapped potential for transforming myself from pauper to patrician. "I guess other stuff has been on my mind."

He sighs in frustration, turning away for a moment. Then he asks me to ask it one more question. He takes it off again, on his own, for much longer this time. Finally he whispers something, and his shoulders suddenly slump. He suddenly looks like he'd seen a horrible future,

or a walking corpse. He sits back down, once again defeated by some truth.

Then he leans over. "Please leave. I would like to be
alone."

***

The truth is, truth can be a painful thing. We organize
our lives like tangled webs around these amorphous
blobs of our supposed realities. When the fog clears and
we see what is really there, all these weavings fall apart
and we're left with nothing but a mass of silk and despair.
I can humbly accept the fact that I have lied numerous
times in my life and lost track of the thin line between
what I believe is true about my past and what isn't. I have
a photographic memory of the people I have killed. I am
reminded every day, by my bastard conscience, about the
terrible person I have often been.

But, to be brutally honest, I don't really know what I
would do if I faced the truth, let alone even the *potential*
for actually knowing. I suppose the question I have to ask
myself is this: would I want that burden? Of knowing that
I could actually *know* the truth behind these certainties
of a doubting conscience that have guided my life, posi-
tively or horribly?

I know what that preacher did. He faced it, too, I'm
sure. The *potential* for actually knowing, breaching the
surface of unlimited knowledge. It's a scary thing, the unrestrained mind. Just think about it...once you *know*
everything, what's left?

***

153

Later that month, that same preacher's face was all over the news. That decrepit old church hid some awful secrets—all the sins of its parishioners flocking to dump their sins and feel better on the way out, along with high-definition recording equipment, slutty costumes, anal lubrication, and a desktop with editing software, filled with videos of naked little girls.

When I spoke to the priest that day, we shared some kind of fear of the truth. At the time, I wholeheartedly believed his fear arose from a reality where God doesn't exist; but maybe he actually feared a world that knew who he really was. These truths that bind and torture us don't so often exist out there, in the world, but burrow and blight, a mildew that will never go away, no matter how hard you scrub.

He found fifteen minutes of infamy, his face tattooed on television screens that entire night. They didn't report until the next morning that he hung himself, in a dirty old cell, with his own pants. He was not circumcised.

But I knew why he died that night, before anyone else did. I knew this because I had asked it, and it answered, resolute and final. I asked it what his questions were.

The first: *What name did I want for my stillborn son? The second: Am I going to hell?*

I just didn't have the heart to find out the answers. Especially the second. Because, if it said *Yes,* that would mean that I would probably be going to hell, too. And if it said "No," that means that someone as ungodly as that priest could get off scot-free (and who would want to live in such an unjust universe)?

And—if it gave the most likely answer of "Hell does not exist," that only further solidifies my mistakes, my misdeeds, my guilt, as my own, and not at the direction or whims of an all-powerful being. In other words—the blame lies solely with me.

Chapter Eleven
Portraits of My Mother, the Goddess

My mother is a work of art.

The word beauty, of a woman, should not evoke purely aesthetic "prettiness." To assume such is petty, and a surface-level reduction that only equates women with dolls.

My mother—despite her beauty—showed me that the true beauty of a woman's character lies in how they approach a world that views them as fragile and secondary. People think things have changed, but they really haven't. Objects are still objects.

My mother is not fragile. She is made of stone. She is a sculpture made of impenetrable marble. This durable resolve has always been the inspiration of my futile artistic ventures. And it's also the bane of my relationship with her. I can never truly know my mother. Instead, I only know the inch-thick veneer that she wears over her true self, a coating that protects her from the world around her.

Here, laid bare, are the facts that I do know:

- She raised me on her own, had me at sixteen years old.

- She had to raise me on her own because my father died. He was a sergeant who died fighting a war without a purpose. He was also an artist. A really *good* artist. My mother stored works of his in a storage garage in the middle of the city. One of the proudest days of my life was taking a picture of him, one of his paintings, and his purple heart to show-and-tell at school, and bragging to all the other kids that my dad helped save the world.
- My mother chose to abandon her dreams of being a writer, a poet. She did some modeling, but always called it a "vapid way to make ends meet…with my tits."
- She must truly be the most gorgeous woman to walk this earth.
- She has taught me the value of every moment, and from her I find my inspiration and my healthy cynicism.
- She has aided and abetted my addiction to opioids and painkillers without her knowledge; when she found out I was stealing them from her, she threatened to disown me.
- I have never tried a portrait of my mother. I'm afraid I would fail to capture her.
- There is a fault in her sculpture, a genetic fissure beneath the marble that was only noticed not so long ago.
    - This fault is spreading. Her brain is changing.
    - She *will* fall apart, eventually.
    - There is a 50/50 chance that I have this fault as well. The doctors can tell me if I wanted.

We have known about that fault for a long time now. The symptoms of that fault can best be summarized in prosaic portraits. Since I have yet to discover my magnum opus, I'm afraid I cannot adequately capture the complexity of my mother's condition in paint and cotton. Words are the best I can do for her. After all, we artists can't capture a person in their fullest. All portraits are inherently flawed—they capture only one side, one moment, albeit a biased one from someone else's perspective. Besides, *Mona Lisa* and all her secrets couldn't hold a candle to the well of tragic beauty springing from my mother's past, present, and ill-fated future.

Portrait #1

I first witnessed my mother's hidden abilities as a dancer when I was seven; I walked into her bedroom, and she was twirling with her arms in the air like a ballerina, yet she was fully nude; her calm and fluid movements were beautiful and reminded me of the fluttering of a helicopter seed, dancing and spinning along whimsically with whatever wind happened to pass by.

I also felt strange feelings about her breasts, but now I'm ashamed and turn red when I think about it.

Now, it was just a few years ago when I noticed her dancing more awkwardly. This dance wasn't like a graceful ballerina. Instead, she was raising her hands above her head and swinging them outward, like she was trying to fly or conduct a symphony. Her feet would constantly move, mostly when she was sitting; she'd be shifting her body over and over while trying to read her worn copy of *Lolita* that belonged to her father, the front cover torn off years ago, and loads of crudely drawn nude portraits drawn by her father's shaky hands in between the pages.

Portrait #2

My mother and I both absolutely love bowling. We dedicate at least one day every month to it, and together. Always together. Once a bowling ball is thrown, that is it: there is nothing more you can do. You cannot change the course of a ball once it is spinning down towards the gutter. You have to accept the fate of your throw and your decisions and simply let whatever may happen, happen. The ball may curve suddenly, riding the edge, until by some miracle it turns back inward and crashes into the pins. Or, it may immediately surrender and fall into the gutter, and you pray and pray that the ball finds a way to bounce up and hit one pin on the way out, or—again, *by some fucking miracle*—actually bounces back in and hits a strike.

I tried translating the rustic beauty of a bowling alley onto canvas. I could not, for the life of me, get the shape of the pins right. I gave up and made some sketches of rats again.

This portrait does attempt to capture one evening at a bowling alley, but it's blurry and lacking detail.

"Dr. Weather was clearly drunk again," is what she likely said.

"Whether or not he was, we won't know for sure." I was lying; he was clearly hammered; you could taste bourbon off his breath as he struggled to explain what exactly was happening to my beautiful mother, the awfulness inside her that couldn't be seen with the naked eye.

"But you didn't ask him, did you?" My mother saw right through me. She sat, posed. Her beauty, in my eyes, could only be closely matched by Botticelli's Madonna of the Pomegranate—a piece that succumbs to immediate Christian approval, but always caught my eye because of the incredibly suggestive, vacantly emotive portrait of Mary, the mechanical look of acceptance on her visage, mirrored by the helpless baby resting in her arms. The pomegranate in her hand, vibrant and full of seeds. My mother, now given news of her forthcoming decline into madness, has carried this apathetic veil constantly—always attentive to some finite detail off in the distance. I believe her sudden change of character could be blamed either on the sudden knowledge that she is indeed mortal, or the haunting fact that she may not know when the day will come when she loses her reality entirely.

"Jamie, it's your turn."

"I just went, mom. It's your turn."

She seemed to ignore me. Following her line of sight, it seemed her eyes were fixated on a claw toy machine in the arcade, full of stuffed tigers, elephants, lions, panthers, and giraffes. Immediately I felt nostalgic of all the times I would beg her in the shopping line to have another fifty cents to try again to get the Dalmatian, having already wasted her five dollars; I admired the notion that her glaring at this machine was a residue of nostalgia—that my mother, or at least pieces of her, were still alive.

But I knew that wasn't it.

Portrait #3

My mother slammed her plate down in the middle of a fake Italian restaurant. The plate, full of some slimy noodles, split directly in half. She smacked her glass of water, which flew off the table and shattered against a wall where a family with a baby in a high chair sat in shock. Their baby burst into screams as the wet shards of glass rained on its head.

My mother shouted, "I can't fucking stand how shrill you are any more! Get out of my house! Get out of my goddamn house, you wicked little cocksucker!" Grabbing her fork, she slammed it repeatedly into the table until it bent upward and stabbed straight back into her fist.

Ophelia wasn't even speaking; I was. I casually mentioned how my dreams were probably dead, how I may never be like my father.

Ophelia thought she was talking about her.

Ophelia also hasn't spoken to her since.

Treatise on Portraits #1, #2, and #3

My mother will eventually lose so much touch with reality that she will no longer be my mother. My mother will eventually die. It's always something that is intimately forlorn, like an approaching deadline that we just keep putting off because it just seems so far away. This disease is a slow crawling mischief of rats eating her, neuron by neuron (if I understand it correctly). Her dancing, her stares, her shakes and quivers, her outbursts. Perhaps this has always been my mother. Perhaps instead, she has been turning more and more into this incredible, unrecognizable thing that I cannot and will never be able to depict.

I know she will die, and likely soon. I am ashamed of my dual hopefulness: one, that it will be soon so her suffering will end; and two—*that it will be soon so my suffering will end.*

I can paint shame. I paint it all the time in all these failures. Below expectations is my magnum opus.

But I can't paint my mother.

Likely soon.

And, the fair rule of 50/50 odds reminds me that I may have the same mischief of rats, waiting, festering.

I ask myself constantly: do I want to know if I have it, too?

Portrait #4: Jamie , Colored Ashamed

Dr. Weather had asked me in his slurred way:

"I can tell you with a certain amount of certainty. It's good to know the truth."

Chapter Twelve
Dad?

The last moment they spoke he left in an artificial hurry. Peter, returning now to his father's poor and manic dwellings after what seemed like passing moments—he realized quickly and futilely that he had not been here in a long, long time.

To Peter, death no longer has the same ominous presence. Death doesn't manifest in an overwhelming cloak. Those who are passing on, croaking, buying the farm, whatever euphemism may be risen to shield those too fragile to admit their ineptitude in the empty face of death—those who are dying and will never return are not greeted by chilling grasp of the end's unfeeling bones crushingly wrapped around their Adams-apples. That death has died long ago, with Perseus losing its gallop, and Theseus forever condemned to the twisting torture of the Minotaur's labyrinthine dwellings. No siren songs will be sung. No hearths are lit. Instead, death is signaled by the drawing, always perennial gasping of oxygen machines. Life is hanging on by three prongs of an electrical plug and two cents of electricity per hour.

Peter edged himself closer, cautiously, to his father's seemingly corpse.

His father's eyelids flew open, revealing two glossy globes lost in clouds. He searched the room absently, darting his cloudy eyes left and right like a newborn child. He raised his cadaverous hand towards the ceiling.

Peter stammered, lost in what he should say. "Bathroom, Dad? Do you need to go potty?" Instantly Peter felt ashamed of speaking to his father like a toddler. But then, gathering his senses, he realized that his father matched that characterization quite accurately—only differing by age.

He gripped the papery flesh of his father's large and demanding hands; Peter felt a panic rising, convinced that his father would die forever if he lost grip on his dry and wispy skin. Peter pulled him until he stood up in bed at a right angle. His father felt heavy, even though he only weighed ninety pounds. He had gotten so thin that his flesh draped off his cheekbones, pronouncing a skull that rested agitatedly beneath some tattered and loose mask. Two lost eyeballs rapidly looked around to find meaning, like marbles spinning in the centrifuge of a storm.

His father pointed weakly to the recliner chair that cost well over $2000. Peter, bracing his father up like a weary marathon runner, eased him over and helped him sit. His father leaned his head back, mouth agape like a turkey in the rain. His teeth were crooked and yellow from decades of fine liquor, stale black coffee, and cheap cigarettes.

A ghostly noise came out from his father's mouth. It sounded wispy, like ice sliding along a frozen lake; like a rusty saxophone with all the joy and merriment filtered out a thousand times over, until nothing remained but cold air scratching against cold brass.

"What did you say, Dad?"

His father swallowed and mustered up enough strength to say it once more:

"I'm sorry," he wheezed, desperate to be heard.

His father never apologized for anything, so Peter chalked it up to delirium, or dehydration.

But, eventually, as it always tends to go, his father's breathing settled. He began to chant:

"My notes? Where are my notes? They prove everything. They prove it all. The world has to see it. The world has to know."

"What notes, Dad? What did they say?"

"My memories. Reality A. My notes. Reality B. They're in Reality B." He kept chanting this over and over. "My memories. Reality A. My notes. Reality B. They're in Reality B."

After chanting for a while, he succumbed to a thin yet peaceful slumber.

Peter knew what notes he was referring to. His father had spent the latter part of his years before the diagnosis slaving away in Hertfordshire on what others in his field called either the "pinnacle of the theory of everything" or "the ramblings of a madman." His father had believed he was close to figuring out an explanation that merged quantum mechanics and relativity; something that married the outrageous concept of many worlds with the common sense reality of everyday life. Something that, if possible and probable, would foster a new age of understanding. He had shut himself off from the rest of the world in a less-than-luxury studio apartment, for almost an entire decade, becoming a mathematical hermit, with nothing but ink, coffee-soiled papers, and billowing clouds of chalk to keep him company. He had left for Hertfordshire a stable, albeit pathological, debauchee; after five or so years, neighbors would report that he had lost a considerable amount of weight, and had sprouted a disheveled mop of hair and beard. He began to shout gibberish at pedestrians from his balcony, fully nude. As one newspaper article claimed, some of his public ramblings included phrases such as "Who pissed on my polka dot suit?" and "Crabs, crabs, it's the fucking crabs!"

As rumors tend to become legends, many speculated that his forlorn sojourn to formulate a workable theory of everything had simply driven him mad. Others, however, assumed that a neurological disease was likely the cause of it all.

Legend also claimed that he had gotten close—that, somewhere amidst the madman's notes, was a verifiable and consistent *Grand Unified Theory,* something akin to a theory of everything, a treatise that explained the fundamental forces of nature. A theorem that would be groundbreaking, earth-shattering, a beyond-theoretical holy grail, the be-all-end-all pursuit of scientific thinking.

The notes also illustrated a resolution to the problem of turbulence that could revolutionize mass transportation and travel beyond the bounds of the planet. Certainly the general populace would be glad to hear about cheaper airline prices and leisurely trips to space as opposed to a clear and precise description of the greatest metaphysical mysteries.

An explanation of *everything.* And a boon to the transportation industry to boot. The mad bastard had done it!

But all his notes had gotten lost when his apartment in Hertfordshire burned to the ground, having fallen asleep with a lit cigar and a half-empty bottle of expensive brandy.

His father burst awake. "My notes. Find my notes. I have to find my notes. My calculations."

"They're gone, Dad," Peter sighed. "They've been gone for years. Burned in that fire in England."

"Gone? No, they're not gone, you fucking imbecile. I have them here. Reality B. They're in Reality B. Your brother. Your brother. Where is your brother?"

William had been pacing, in his crippled way, back and forth in the kitchen, begrudgingly sipping stale, cold, black coffee to avoid saying anything in the conversation.

Peter couldn't find any words either, but didn't have the luxury of a beverage to hide his mouth from the spotlight.

Only moments before, standing over their father in his pallid and unkempt bed, Peter had mentioned how frail their father looked. He had chosen his words carefully in an effort not to upset William. A better description? Desperately brittle, a pale and loose baggage of skin wrapped around a resolute but thin rib cage. A stomach that used to be more bulbous had deflated, sunken into itself, riddled with bruised spots and wrinkled patches of flesh. His eyes, often closed, would creak open once in a while, even though he wasn't really awake; Peter couldn't shake how cloudy and lifeless those eyes were, like little phosphorescent pools. The frame of his skull became so much more pronounced; his cheeks, once jubilant, had since shriveled away, their absence more pronounced with the jutting stiffness of his cheekbones. A father who always carried a biting odor of cheap Sears cologne and inexpensive vodka now filled the room with a deathly humid and putrid stench mixed with a distracting iodine odor; a combination that reminded Peter of rotten fruits left to waste away in the fruit bowl, or of the leftover mushrooms he'd never eat in his Rubbermaid lunch containers, left behind for a few days in his gym bag.

Every few minutes, almost as a ritual, their father would raise his arms and release a gasp of air, a guttural demand for Peter to pull him up off his deathbed and place him on his recliner chair. The chair eased the pain of lying in his bed all the time, and made it easier for William or Peter to help their father release his bowels. This time, during the transition from bed to chair, Peter had to hold his father up by his armpits, like a marionette doll, while William positioned the wide-mouth bottle, labeled "URINE DO NOT DRINK" in black sharpie, under his father's wrinkled penis. He had to use his left hand to lift it up slightly so it wouldn't go directly on the floor. But then, their father grunted and had a spasm, flinging his stream of piss right across William's face. He grimaced, but held his resolve. Peter briefly admired William for this dedication, before regressing into a familiar shield of justified satisfaction, knowing that he didn't admire William for much else.

Peter also reminisced about earlier days of his father's decline, when he was still a little more lucid. His father would look Peter in the eye and say things he had never told anyone else. How he tried his best to be a good father. How he really loved Peter's mother (more than he loved William's). How William's mother tried to kill him. What it felt like to bear the incalculable burden of solving the most fundamentally unsolved problems.

Peter wanted their father to die. William wasn't so sure what he wanted.

Their father had trouble drinking water. So would open his thin, dry lips like a dying baby bird, and point with his shaky index finger. Peter would grab the nearest cup of water and soak a tiny sponge-stick, and place it in his father's mouth. Peter always shivered slightly, bothered by the unhinging sensation of the sponge scraping against the bumps of his father's dry tongue. He'd gently pushed his father's chin to help him close his mouth, and told him to "suck."

Their father was too weak to use a straw. The tender sucking reminded him of Isaac, as a baby, and even now.

After Peter finished forcing the sponge between his father's lips, he turned and stared intently at William, who wrestled with something stuck in his pocket. "Why do you even bother to come here, Billy?"

William, knowing the futility of arguing, bit his tongue and kept his head down.

Peter kept on digging. "I'm here every day. You barely come here at all." The pressure rising up in his throat helped him understand he had gone too far already; but, knowing that the line was already crossed, and understanding he could not go back, kept pushing. "I have a family. I have an actual job. I have things to do. Why do I have to be here, Billy?"

William avoided eye contact, trying desperately to saunter away halfheartedly; despite his valiant effort, he couldn't avoid his marching soldier walk. "I'm sorry. Things have been chaotic lately."

"With what? What do you, of all people, have going on?"

"Do you know if Dad ever kept any pictures of us?"

Peter scoffed. "Are you kidding me?"

"I don't know. Just any pictures of us when we were kids, you know."

Peter struggled to remember what he looked like on the outside as a kid; the inside, though, has always been the same, for all this time—a jumbled, anxious crisscross of weeds.

"What makes you think Dad loved us enough? He never was one for keepsakes. Dad wasn't that kind of person. You know better than that, Billy. For fuck's sake, I never loved him." Peter dipped the sponge in the lukewarm water again, gently rubbing it against his decrepit father's lips.

"Yeah, I know." William wandered his way out of the bedroom.

Peter scoffed again to himself at how ludicrous it all seemed. Him? His father, the man who'd rather spend months away from home on lectures throughout the bedrooms of widowed women in Italy? Who refrained from hugging his only two sons, instead hammering away at some astronomically impossible mathematical theory that had no real impact on the world? What Peter did really *mattered*—his career had a real impact on the world (or so he convinced himself). His job had weight, not some feather-floating theory chalked up on a chalkboard, constantly chasing the meaning of it all, hidden away in some scramble of airy numbers. Thinking back on it, his father was never there in the first place, and Peter found it much more difficult to deny a simple truth: he didn't want him around anymore, anyway.

"Come on, Dad. Have a little more water."

"Maybe you're giving him too much?" William muttered at the doorway, looking away from Peter.

Peter, biting his tongue, couldn't resist the urge to shout back. "Like you would know? Who are you to tell me how to take care of him?" He paused, his conscience making every effort to constrain him, but it failed to hold back. "Fucking pathetic. I'm here all the time. I've sacrificed. You've never lifted a goddamn finger for this family."

William knew better than to give in to his anger, and just nodded in agreement, his head hanging low beneath his shoulders as he rested his elbows on his knees, making diamond shapes with his hands. He had become adept at hiding his guilt, his resentment, even his brief moments of happiness. Or, on the other hand, he may have felt nothing at all—just the unoccupied voids where those emotions used to be, instead miming what others expected of him, to portray a fallacious appearance of humanity.

"I know, I know," William said, rolling his tongue. "You're right."

William's petty and papery humility disgusted Peter, but he couldn't hold back his frustration. "You're asking if Dad ever had pictures of us?" He jeered. "What do you really know about Dad? You haven't been here. Not even before he started losing it." Peter drew a deep breath, failing to hold back his indignation over William's lack of trying. "He knew he was going to die. He talked to me. Actually talked to me. started telling me about things he never told either of us. Who he really was. Not our dad. Not some physicist. Who he really was. You'll never know who Dad really was." Peter threw the bottle of water across the room.

He meant every word. His resentment had finally boiled over. Why should he be the one solely responsible for this burden, carrying the putrid weight of a dying father over his shoulders? Why couldn't it be Billy? So many burdens weighing him down—who ever cared enough to help him out?

"You always gave so many excuses to avoid any real responsibility in your life. Blame it on the war. Blame it on the discharge. The nightmares. The hallucinations. It's all a show anyway. You're just begging for attention—*oh, woe is me, look at how guilty I am, everybody!*" Peter mocked. *"I killed innocent people in some godforsaken country! Won't you spare some pity? Even just a little? Even some fucking empathy will do."* Peter kicked his chair. "You've been alone since Beaty left you. Good fucking choice on her part."

While Peter stewed, staring at an oil painting of a red steamboat in some Midwestern river, William quietly nodded his head and left the room. He just swallowed his words; not out of maturity or being the better man, but simply because he believed in every word Peter threw at him.

But William had a different avenue for venting his frustrations: by rummaging through the pockets of Peter's jacket. Inside, he found Peter's keys, which he swiftly tossed into the garbage. He also found some oddly shaped light bulb—heavier than he expected, and likely extremely expensive. While he felt compelled to chuck it right out the window, he calmed himself, and took the much more rational route of stealing it. He stuffed it in his own coat pocket, swallowed his disparaging departing words down where his guts used to be, and walked out.

That'll show him, he thought.

Chapter Thirteen
I have to write my will.

I have to write my will.

When I die, how will I protect him?

I was only a little girl then who came from nothing. I had grown up as the newest child to parents who were tired of their children. As the least desirable, I happened to be the most beautiful. I knew this from an early age. I also had a paralyzing fear of falling off of my bed, because in dreams the floor would evaporate, and my mattress would hover above an expanse of nothingness—but even as I peered into that nothingness, I could tell how endlessly deep it fell. I didn't fear falling and smashing into the ground in pieces. I was petrified of falling forever.

I know my mother didn't want me. She had been fully satiated with two boys. What she always wanted.

My father—he wanted a little girl. I asked him while he whittled away from the cancerous demon deflating his lungs—I asked him, what **haven't** you done? What is your biggest regret? Never seeing the Grand Canyon? Having his name written in the outdated history books that Ms. Oglesby forced us to read?

His glazed eyes, pupils dilated, fixed on his young, naïve, little girl—while the synchronized huffing and puffing of his oxygen concentrator filled the room with artificial dread.

I have none, he said.

Surely, you can't be serious.
don't call me Shirley.

All I wanted was to raise a family.

I don't have the balls to tell him now, even though he's dead—we were not, really, a family…

Why can't you be like all the other girls?

WHEN I DIE HOW WILL I PROTECT HIM

Your brothers were five and seven. You were three. You were playing battleships in the bathtub. You always lost, but You didn't really understand the game anyway—You played because You loved mimicking explosion noises, You loved making Your brothers laugh (even if it was at You). Dad had filled the tub for You after crushing the giant spider that climbed out of the drain (You were terrified; Your brothers felt bad for the spider). You screamed and hollered, sinking little plastic ships and watching them bounce up to the surface. Your father took Your picture—three of You, butt-naked, all with strangely large heads, comically large smiles. That picture was taken right before Your mother walked in, glaring. She doesn't belong with them, Nicholas! She can't be in there with the boys! She ripped You out of the tub, throwing You backwards into the sink. In progression, You remember a sharp clink, then instantly waking up with Your face in a pool of wetness. When You managed to pick Your head up, it felt heavy, like it weighed a ton; the wetness was a deep viscous pool of blood, blacker than it was in cartoons. The back of Your head felt fuzzy. The whole room sounded hollow, with phantom murmurs of someone like Your mother shouting Put it back! *Oh my god, put it back!*

I've been wandering off again. Remember what that freak Dr. Weather told you: count your thoughts.

Yes, I do belong with them.

Jamie learned to count at an early age. There he was on the rug, as a baby, counting his fingers, still wet from being jammed in his mouth. He never cried. I thought he was dumb. He was actually just an artist. He learned his alphabet immediately. I read him stories about flying elephants and toys that would come alive, and toys that would also die, so he could learn about the futility of life. He was incredibly smart and intelligently gifted. But what an awful artist. His first drawing in kindergarten of a cow he petted in a petting zoo looked nothing like a cow. More like an octopus. Or a squid, long purple legs flailing about in every direction. Of course I didn't tell him. What kind of a mother do you think I am? Let him be a failure all on his own.

Jamie also knew I would die at an early age. Outside haunted houses and dark doors he'd always hug my leg and whisper, "Mom, don't go in there. There's something bad in there." How could he have known? He did know, the whole fucking time, that something was bad in there.

He calls himself an artist?
Jamie would always ask me about his father, the
hero. Killed in the line of duty. Fighting valiantly.
Like a true soldier. The bullet pierced his heart and
he never felt any pain at all; he died with a picture of
his baby boy clutched in his bloodied hands

LIAR

Jamie brought his father's posthumous purple heart for
show and tell

he brought his father's art too

the one you had stored way back in storage

He once asked me what his father did before he was
sent away

I panicked and said, "he was an artist"

He looked up at me, cheerfully, crying—

"like me!"

YOU BOUGHT THAT PURPLE HEART AT A THRIFT STORE

AND THAT PAINTING TOO

**None of the boys would dance with the beautiful crazy
girl, except for Tomas, who was always nice to me.
Boys don't dance with the girl who can kick their ass.
Tomas died two years ago with a needle up his arm.
But Tomas was so charming and handsome. How
could I say no? I had no clue how to move my feet,
but he sure did, like he had wings.**

I have to write my will. My last word and testament.
The final vestige of my being before I shuffle the fuck
off this mortal coil. What a shitty coil.
*I dreamed for a while that I'd fly off in some grand ges-
ture to teach them all a lesson.*

*Boys would come to me when I was a girl scout
so they could touch my breasts· I'd let them
but I charged them a dollar· Years later I dealt
the same boys dope·*

Yes, he does call himself an artist. Even if he's a
shitty artist. At least he is. I don't care what you
have to say anymore.

What have you done that matters?

When he was 12, he begged for a Transformers toy that I
said was too expensive. He said it was on sale, so I
bought it for him. That night he came to me, bawling. He
admitted he switched the price tags with a cheaper toy,
and he didn't want to go to hell for lying. I asked him,
won't you go to hell for stealing? He said no, lying to
your mother is worse.

When I die, how will *I* protect *him*?

I've packed my bags. The angel of death is waiting for
me, resting on his laurels beside me, taking his time,
even though that's all I have left to own; devilish
hooves propped up on my hospital bed, smelling the
place up something awful.

The nurse stands outside my room. "She won't stop
screaming."

Someone's gotta do it. It ain't gonna be me.

Just put her out of her misery, why don't you, says the
angel of death, filing his teeth.

When I die, how will I *protect* him from the *truth*?

**That I did nothing else that night I danced with To-
mas; but that night, Tomas did everything he wanted**

177

**with me, even though I refused; even though my fa-
ther had taught me not to unless I really said "yes"**

*JAMIE'S PICTURES OF HIS FATHER ARE PICTURES OF A MAN YOU
NEVER MET FROM A PHOTO ALBUM THAT YOU FOUND IN A GARAGE
SALE*

*But this means we have to get married, right? Isn't that what adults
do after they do this? I thought they only did this if they love each
other*

It hurt...I didn't want it...

BUT HE WAS SUCH A SWEET BOY

**That I did nothing else that night I danced with To-
mas; but that night, Tomas did everything he wanted
with me, even though I REFUSED; even though my
father had taught me NOT to unless I really said
"YES"**

*i used to cry at the end of movies but not after that
night*

**But I did not say "yes," I said "no," and still he forced
it into me**

*You used to dream of getting married and riding off
into a sunset to your glorious death*

*You used to dream about so much more until he came
along*

"Now she's crying. She's delirious. I think we should
give her a sedative."

**Tomas died two years ago with a needle up his arm -
good riddance, you sick bastard, what you put in me**

***"that's no way to talk about the boy's father," my
mother would say***

"but he does not know, mother, and I have to tell him"

"the boy believes his father is a hero"

"he believes his father was a hero"

*"but I did not want him mother I did not ask for him how
do you tell your son that he was never meant to be in
your life"*

When I die, how will I protect him from the truth?

*"when you die, the truth will be buried
with you"*

Chapter Fourteen
The Trial of Archimedes

CONFIDENTIAL

CASE FILE #19:9

Reporting Agent #12-36: Peter Burroughs and Agent #101 Richard Palient

Purpose: Classified level 10 clearance (Nuremberg Status, Approval Code #25, investigating retrieval of #8-32, modulating intelligence apparatus

Status: Open

Background: Contextual investigation of apparatus disappearance based on testimonial of Subject #91, Chief Researcher Harold Pine, the last known user involved in scientific examination and phase III testing before tendering resignation weeks before device's disappearance. Reason for resignation: *"That fucking thing. It's going to destroy the world."*

Subject #91 is the prime suspect in the apparatus' disappearance, based on numerous and extensive investigative interviews with subordinates who were under Subject #91's supervision. These subordinates were indirectly involved in research, but stated that Subject #91 had been displaying an uncharacteristic disregard for procedure and decorum in the weeks preceding his resignation and his subsequent disappearance. Reports suggest Subject #91 had become hostile towards others and derisive towards further experiments and queries with the device. In addition, reports also suggest that personal hygiene had also become problematic, noting that Subject #91 would arrive for his shift clearly inebriated, slurring, and unkempt.

Subject #91 was also involved in incident #57GT59m5, in which Subject #91 was caught by subordinates wielding a claw hammer and preparing to demolish the apparatus. This incident preceded his sudden resignation the following day after supervised therapeutic measures suggested that Subject #91 was clearly unstable and in need of treatment for [INSERT PSYCHOLOGICAL DISORDER HERE]. After resignation was tendered, Subject #91 disappeared. Agent #101, Richard Palient, reported Subject #91's reappearance not long after #8-32's disappearance. Subject #91 was apprehended by supporting agents as directed by Agent #101 and brought in for interrogation as per Hanberg's Policy #TTT55^^fkf.

Note: Within the following transcript, violations of Code of Ethics #541abcD have been omitted as Code of Ethics #541abcD policies are null and void per qualifying conditions indicated via Hanberg's Policy #TTT55^^fkf2[3].

BEGIN TRANSCRIPT

AGENT BURROUGHS: Commencing interrogation #47 in case 19:9, chief investigative agent 12-36 Peter Burroughs and assisting investigative agent #101, Richard Palient. Interrogation recipient is Subject #91, former Chief Researcher Harold Pine. Say hello, Harold.

SUBJECT #91: Fuck you.

AGENT BURROUGHS: Let the record indicate that Subject #91 has refused to say hello.

AGENT PALIENT: We're just here to talk, Harold. No need to get offensive.

SUBJECT #91: Fuck you, too. Why am I here?

AGENT BURROUGHS: We'd like you to take a guess.

SUBJECT #91: I haven't the faintest.

AGENT BURROUGHS: We're investigating the disappearance of file 8-32, the modulating intelligence apparatus.

SUBJECT #91: You're shitting me. You lost it?

AGENT BURROUGHS: Language, please.

---

[3] See Nuremberg Status.

SUBJECT #91: Do you have any idea what you've done?

AGENT BURROUGHS: Connect the dots, Harold. We're interrogating you because you are a prime suspect.

SUBJECT #91: Why me?

AGENT BURROUGHS: Where do I start? Before we discovered the apparatus, you had an impeccable record of research contributions to the company. Nanotechnology, beginning trial models of the quantum processing units. Translating dolphin squeaks. You were excelling. That's why you were selected to lead research into the apparatus. Must've been a dream come true.

SUBJECT #91: That's what I thought at the time.

AGENT BURROUGHS: But it doesn't look like that came true, does it?

SUBJECT #91: What makes you say that?

AGENT BURROUGHS: You look...awful.

SUBJECT #91: I haven't been my best lately.

AGENT PALIENT: Look, Harold. Harry. Can I call you Harry?

Video transcription note: considerable pause.

SUBJECT #91: ...sure.

AGENT PALIENT: We're not trying to accuse you of anything. We just need to talk to you about your experience. What you know. You're the expert on this thing, and maybe you can help us determine an approximate location. We need to find it so no one else gets hurt. Just imagine what would happen if this thing got in the wrong hands...you know?

SUBJECT #91: You have no idea.

AGENT PALIENT: So tell us everything you know.

SUBJECT #91: Can I have a cigarette first?

AGENT PALIENT: I'll head out and see if I can find a smoker.

AGENT BURROUGHS: So it's probably best if you start from the beginning, Harold.

Video transcription note: considerable pause.

SUBJECT #91: That felt like so long ago. Most of us called it a miracle. Miracles don't happen in science. Everything has an explanation out there somewhere. A system of rules and conditions. Every branch of science relies on this. Every branch of everything, really. Mathematics. Biology. Chemistry. Philosophy. Linguistics. Cooking. Everything relies on an inherent system from which we can make reasonable predictions. But that methodology does not apply to miracles, things that just happen

for no apparent reason, things that just
materialize out of thin air. That's what
we all called the apparatus. A fucking
miracle. Really, we had no idea where it
came from. It was just here.

AGENT BURROUGHS: Can you elaborate on
that?

SUBJECT #91: We found the device here, in
the R & D holding area, buried in the back
behind all the other abandoned relics and
artifacts the company had discovered ever
since the R&D department first began. The
only known record of it was from 1945,
which doesn't make any damn sense—because
the technology just wasn't there yet. This
kind of device was not possible in 1945.

AGENT BURROUGHS: Couldn't it have been a
filing error? Could it have been 1954?

SUBJECT #91: I suppose. But even so, 1954
is not feasible either considering the
manufacturing prowess required to create,
or even comprehend, the technology
involved. Color cathode ray tubing had
just been realized. Color t.v.s came out
in the 60s not long after, but it wasn't
commercial until then. Even so, the
cathode ray tubing the device utilizes is
much, much smaller and more advanced.
Relies on superpositioning. Beyond
advanced. Even for now.

AGENT BURROUGHS: It still could have been
a filing error. Someone could have just
put the wrong year.

SUBJECT #91: Even so. Does it really matter what year it was made? What it's capable of, it is unimaginable. Modern computer technology, even the quantum processors we were developing, nothing came close to the processing power of the apparatus. It goes beyond any formalized understanding of algorithmic functions as we know it.

AGENT BURROUGHS: Can you elaborate on that? On the, you know, algorithm part?

SUBJECT #91: Layman's terms. Computers can solve problems algorithmically and via simulations. But you need to start with a defined system, a set of rules, and steps for the computer to follow. Like predicting the weather. You set the parameters, like pressure and temperature, and give the system a defined space, and see what happens. Run it hundreds of thousands of times and see if you can determine a predictable pattern based on parameters and variables. Or if you want to determine the best approach to hitting a curveball. Plug in the parameters—different pitch speeds, different possible zones, limitations of hitting power, launch angle, all of that data—and a simulation can tell you the most statistically reasonable swing to make when hitting against a left-hander throwing a curveball. It all relies on a system to make reasonable predictions based on probability. That's where we got our truths from before. Our theories and predictions. The truths of modern science, our understanding of physics, chemistry, evolution, the universe—all of it was

based on making observations and testing
reasoned predictions. Throwing an arrow at
a dartboard and seeing where it stuck most
often.

AGENT BURROUGHS: So the fact the apparatus
exists changed all that?

SUBJECT #91: No need to be snarky.

AGENT BURROUGHS: I wasn't trying to be
snarky.

SUBJECT #91: It changes your worldview,
that's for sure.

AGENT BURROUGHS: Can you tell me
what...kinds of…

SUBJECT #91: Gesundheit.

AGENT BURROUGHS: Thanks. Tell me about the
tests.

SUBJECT #91: Where should I start?

AGENT BURROUGHS: Wherever you think makes
the most sense. I don't want to get lost
in the details.

SUBJECT #91: Well, we didn't realize what
we had until we walked into that holding
room. We would've had no idea it was there
if Gerald hadn't asked where the light
was. That's what he said when we walked
in. Pitch black, couldn't see two inches
in front of you. First thing he says:
"Where's that fucking light?" And we both
saw it light up in the corner behind some
other contraptions. Bright green light,

like Christmas lights. "BEHIND YOU TO THE LEFT," it said. We thought someone was playing a prank on us, but our scientific minds couldn't help themselves. We tested it by asking basic questions.

AGENT BURROUGHS: Such as?

SUBJECT #91: We put it through a system we developed for evaluating machine intelligence. We've used it to assess how sophisticated our learning algorithms have become. Most of ours didn't fare well beyond level 4, semiotic reasoning. So we started with the basics. Calculators. Solutions to algebraic functions. It was 100% accurate. Then deductive reasoning, inductive reasoning. Flying fucking colors. Recognized solutions to logic problems.

AGENT BURROUGHS: Such as?

SUBJECT #91: A is true. If A, then Q. Therefore, Q is true.

AGENT BURROUGHS: English?

SUBJECT #91: All agents are idiots. Peter is an agent. Therefore, he is an idiot.

AGENT BURROUGHS: No need to get snarky.

SUBJECT #91: It passed all inductive and deductive reasoning tests. So we tried something different. We asked it to make inferences based on incomplete data.

AGENT BURROUGHS: Can you elaborate?

SUBJECT #91: It's something of a holy grail in artificial intelligence. Your brain does this all the time. Vision, for instance. Layman's terms. Imagine you're looking at a ball in the street. You see the world as 3d, but your eyes don't. You think you see a sphere, but your eyes see a circle. They process it as 2d, just a bunch of light rays. But it can take all this data and make inferences about shape, size, direction, conflicting light patterns like shadows, movement, speed, weight, buoyancy, sentience, intention, all these from a simple 2d image. The human brain can make incredibly complex inferences, especially in narratives. Like making educated guesses about Iago's motivation in Othello. Or predicting how a story will end, even without clues or foreshadowing. So we asked the apparatus these kinds of questions that required inferences. Well, required inferences for us.

AGENT BURROUGHS: Required inferences for us?

SUBJECT #91: It doesn't make inferences. It just knows the right answer. Inferences aren't always 100% correct. Your interpretations and predictions aren't always correct. Sometimes you think you can dodge the baseball, but your inference is wrong, so it breaks your nose. Or like when you think you see something coming at you in your peripheral vision. Your brain gets an input that something is moving towards you outside of your view, and fast, so it makes an educated guess that this may be a threat coming towards you,

189

so you turn your ahead, adrenaline levels
spike up, you throw your hands in front of
your face, and you're ready for fight or
flight, completely outside of your own
control. Or when people spot a Jesus-
shaped water stain on the wall. It's
obviously just a water stain. But your
brain is an expert at recognizing
patterns, especially where there are none
to begin with. It's why people think
they've seen ghosts in the dark.

AGENT BURROUGHS: Can you provide an
example of the apparatus correctly making
an inference?

SUBJECT #91: It was able to name exactly
what someone was holding behind their back
— a garden gnome. We asked it to identify
how many pens we had hidden in a drawer in
the other room—156. Exactly. We asked it
to identify the next twenty winning horses
at the local racetrack. 100% accurate.
Just imagine how much money someone could
make with that.

AGENT BURROUGHS: Those sound like guesses,
not inferences.

SUBJECT #91: Same thing.

AGENT BURROUGHS: What else did you ask
for?

SUBJECT #91: Once we realized what we had,
we couldn't resist asking about
something...important.

AGENT BURROUGHS: Like, is there a God?

SUBJECT #91: Well...I suppose. If you
believe in that sort of thing.

AGENT BURROUGHS: Are we talking about
belief or truth?

SUBJECT #91: Depends on what truth matters
most to you. For me, at least, the truth
isn't religious. So much we've wanted to
know about the natural world. So much we
could understand about humanity's impact
on the environment. The most efficient
solutions to resolving widespread poverty.
Cures for Alzheimer's and cancer. All the
lives we could save.

AGENT BURROUGHS: But you didn't get a
chance to ask it all of that.

SUBJECT #91: Some of us wanted to destroy
it.

AGENT BURROUGHS: You wanted to destroy it.

SUBJECT #91: I considered it.

AGENT BURROUGHS: Why?

SUBJECT #91: It seems juvenile when you
think about it.

AGENT BURROUGHS: Enlighten me.

SUBJECT #91: When I was a kid, I was
petrified of darkness. Nyctophobia. I'd
have panic attacks if I woke up and I
didn't have the lights on. I carried this
with me through high school. I couldn't
even play heads-up seven up, for fuck's
sake. Putting my head down meant I had to

shut off the lights in my head. Then I learned about black holes. Mr. Podasky. Junior year. He called them "The Ultimate Unknown." Someone watching from a spaceship would see you plummet, slowing down, until you froze right on the surface. That's how relativity works. Time slows down. But your perspective is entirely different. You instead see yourself getting spaghettified and blinked out of existence. Petrified me. But it fascinated me. What lies beyond that event horizon. Secrets and the unimaginable hiding behind a veil of blackness. Things changed for me. Took some time to overcome the anxiety and panic, but focusing on discovering the truths behind that darkness, it made it bearable. It gave me a sense of purpose. Control. Direction. I've spent over half of my existence on the pursuit of scientific truth. What lies beyond the edges of our universe. The origins of life. The tapestry of spacetime and particles that allow us to have this very conversation and imagine how it will end. But the beauty of science was how even that truth was not absolute. Every supposed theory could be revised or thrown out pending new discoveries. That's the whole bedrock of science. That no truth is absolute truth. Everything we know is a reasoned prediction, an educated guess. An inference. Constantly filling in the gaps with educated guesses.

AGENT BURROUGHS: I think we're getting off track.

SUBJECT #91: No, we're not.

SUBJECT #91: I'm talking about the entire foundation of our civilization. The bedrock of all scientific progress. Chiseling away at a boulder to find the ultimate nugget of truth, the absolute understanding of everything. I've spent over half, half of my entire life pursuing science. I haven't lied to myself. Never in a million years did I think I'd be alive when humanity found a theory of everything—a grand unified explanation for why everything is the way it is. It would revolutionize scientific thinking. It would unravel mysteries about our universe, our existence, the fundamental elements of reality. If you'd asked me years ago, I'd tell you it was pretty much impossible to ever imagine. But at least I was helping, making progress. That was the foundation of my being. But the fact that this apparatus exists, and works, flawlessly, without error…it…

AGENT BURROUGHS: Would you like me to get you some tissues?

SUBJECT #91: Doesn't it, though? Make my entire life pointless?

AGENT BURROUGHS: I think we may be getting way off track.

SUBJECT #91: It made the truth plain and boring. Not awe inspiring. Not magical. Not frightening. Why I was fascinated with black holes in the first place. The mystery. The terror. The apparatus eradicated years of dedication, blood, sweat, and tears, my entire purpose of being, the need for scientific pursuit in the first place. The rigor of scientific discovery rendered absurd. What pursuit or hope is there if you have all the answers to the exam already? That's why we called it Laplace's Demon. Because it knows. It knows the exact location, mass, and velocity of every single particle in the universe. It knows the entire past, the entire future. No more mysteries or puzzles. No pursuit. No journey. That's what life's all about. That's what we all organize our lives around. We survive on these narratives of us pursuing some greater purpose or meaning, hoping one day to find it. But if we know it from the beginning, then the whole journey is fucked. Moot. Pointless.

AGENT BURROUGHS: But surely there must be some good that comes out of having unlimited knowledge about everything.

SUBJECT #91: Yes. In the right hands of moral, selfless people. A lot of good can come of it. Cures for diseases. Solutions for world hunger, if there are any. But that's relying on a faith in humanity that I don't believe is justified.

AGENT #91: Why not? Aren't most people good?

SUBJECT #91: Good given the circumstances. But with unbridled knowledge, the possibility to know and predict anything? People starve for the truth of things, or do whatever they can to ignore the truth. What do rich and powerful people do about their sins? What does a starving person do when you give them a gun? What would happen to the world economy if all of a sudden everyone had winning lottery numbers, or knew how to game the stock market, or a winning horse, or which team to bet on…Even so, just think about all the ugly truths we hide from ourselves. The ones that we bury away. That metastasize. And fester. The ones that deep down we know are true. But we deliberately, deliberately, choose to be ignorant about them. Turn a blind eye. Like we tell our kids about monsters in the closet. If you don't look at it, it's not really there.

AGENT BURROUGHS: I'm not sure what you mean.

SUBJECT #91: Do you have kids?

AGENT BURROUGHS: Yes.

SUBJECT #91: If you asked the device what would happen to your kids in fifty years, and found out what would happen, and if it

was something god awful, you would do
everything you could to prevent it.
Protect your kids. Wouldn't you?

AGENT BURROUGHS: Of course I would.

SUBJECT #91: But that's all fucking
pointless, don't you see? If you spend
every waking moment of your adult life
working to make your kid's future better
than your own life, but you know in the
end that something horrible will happen to
them, or they are destined to suffer, if
you know that this is the truth, something
that will happen, nothing you can do will
change it. If you know the future, the
future has to happen this way. Otherwise
nothing makes sense. If the apparatus
knows the future, then nothing we do will
prove it wrong. That makes all of our
actions meaningless. That means we have no
purpose. Because whatever it says will
come true, becomes true. No matter what we
do. How emasculating is that?

AGENT BURROUGHS: But that can't be how it
works. If I found out I would get hit by a
bus tomorrow, I would do everything in my
power to stay home. If I knew every detail
of that day, I could do the opposite of
all of that. Believing that the apparatus
will be right no matter what requires
quite a bit of faith.

SUBJECT #91: But if you admit that the
apparatus knows every absolute truth, no
matter what, then you would be wrong.
That's the cost of knowing everything. No
free will. No self.

AGENT BURROUGHS: But I could just do the exact opposite of whatever it says.

SUBJECT #91: If we had the damn thing, we could try it out.

AGENT BURROUGHS: I just don't see how any of that is possible.

SUBJECT #91: That's what is so emasculating. I've spent my entire life trying to understand the complexities of the universe. But the apparatus makes it all so frustratingly simple.

AGENT BURROUGHS: That's why you tried to destroy it.

SUBJECT #91: I thought it was obvious.

AGENT BURROUGHS: When did you try to destroy it?

SUBJECT #91: I don't recall much of that night, I was very, very drunk.

AGENT BURROUGHS: You attempted to smash it to pieces with a hammer.

SUBJECT #91: That's right, I did.

AGENT BURROUGHS: Walk me through it.

SUBJECT #91: Like I said, I don't recall much from that night. Or the weeks preceding it. Massive depression and all that. But I remember I did not actually try to destroy it.

AGENT BURROUGHS: But your colleagues
walked in on you with a claw hammer. They
said you looked like a madman.

SUBJECT #91: I wasn't going to destroy it.
That's the truth. Fuck. I wanted to
destroy it. Wanted to. Wanted. But before
I did, I asked if I would. It told me no.
So I tried my damnedest to actually do it.
To prove it wrong.

AGENT BURROUGHS: But your colleagues
stopped you.

SUBJECT #91: No, they didn't. I just
didn't do it.

AGENT BURROUGHS: Why didn't you?

SUBJECT #91: I've been asking myself that
a lot lately. Not much else to do while
you keep me locked up. Should've read that
part of the contract.

AGENT BURROUGHS: What do you mean? The
report said you disappeared.

SUBJECT #91: Jesus Christ, you work for
these bastards and they don't even tell
you. I haven't left the building since
that night. Why else do you think I look
like shit.

AGENT BURROUGHS: I see. I wasn't aware of
that.

SUBJECT #91: That a private company has
the power to subjugate and imprison a man
for a crime he never committed in the
first place?

AGENT BURROUGHS: It is a sensitive
situation, you understand. You said it
yourself. The apparatus is dangerous.

SUBJECT #91: Beyond dangerous. The world
as we know it runs on white lies and
classified files. A house of cards.

AGENT BURROUGHS: So I'm hoping you can
help me find out where it is.

SUBJECT #91: But I'm the wrong person to
ask. Since I was "detained." Why don't you
ask the agent assigned to it? Wouldn't he
be a prime suspect?

AGENT BURROUGHS: We're investigating all
options.

SUBJECT #91: Typical. I should've known.
Leave it to this company to bungle this
all up. Some incompetent idiot probably
lost it. Careless. Foolish. I should've
destroyed it when I had the chance.

AGENT BURROUGHS: Is there anything at all
you can tell me that might help us find
where it is?

SUBJECT #91: There is something.

AGENT BURROUGHS: And that is?

SUBJECT #91: When we were trying to
determine how the device arrived at its
conclusions, we tried concurrently to
develop a sufficient replicating
algorithm. A copy. We weren't able to

dissect the device because of the
sensitive nature of the matter.

AGENT BURROUGHS: You could have just asked
how it works, I suppose.

(note an unusual twenty second period of
silence)

SUBJECT #91: I suppose. But we didn't get
to it. Like I was saying. We developed
replicant software. Not as sophisticated.
But we did feed it any and all existing
records documented by the company.
Including all portfolios on employees, on
relatives of employees, of people
apprehended, investigated, interrogated,
shot and killed, plain disappeared. Nature
of the business, right? These portfolios
are extensive. They include genealogical
history, in-depth psychological and
behavioral profiles, and genetic
information. Data. We used existing
algorithms that were designed in R&D to
make predictions about future criminal
profiles based on portfolio data scores.

AGENT BURROUGHS: What can we do with that
data?

SUBJECT #91: The software attempts to work
the same way as the apparatus. Present a
query, it will give you an approximate
answer. Not at all close to the absolute
truth. But an educated answer based on the
data it has. It can fill in holes where
it's capable, but it's still very flawed
and underdeveloped. Ask it something like,
which person is most statistically likely
to commit first-degree murder? Or, which

person is most statistically likely to
steal company property? You can't get too
specific. But it might be able to give you
a list of those people and rank them.
Would that suffice?

AGENT BURROUGHS: It's a start. Where can
we access this?

SUBJECT #91: Just ask Gina Korth. She was
the lead programmer. She can help you.
Might take some time, though. A lot of
data to sort through. Lots of simulations
to calculate.

AGENT BURROUGHS: How long?

SUBJECT #91: Could be days.

AGENT BURROUGHS: Understood. Thank you.

SUBJECT #91: Does this mean I'll be
released? Contractually you have to
contact the authorities if you keep me
longer than a month.

AGENT BURROUGHS: I'll have to look into
it.

SUBJECT #91: Please do. I haven't seen my
son in ages. I missed his second birthday.
You must have kids, you understand?

AGENT BURROUGHS. I do. I'll see what I can
do.

SUBJECT #91: Thank you.

AGENT BURROUGHS: Jesus Christ! Fuck, fuck,
fuck!

AGENT PALIENT: That was messier than I
expected.

AGENT BURROUGHS: What the fuck, what the
fuck, what happened?

AGENT PALIENT: You should slow your
breathing. You're hyperventilating.

AGENT BURROUGHS: Why did you do that?

AGENT PALIENT: What? That?

AGENT BURROUGHS: Yes, that! Yes, that!

AGENT PALIENT: Nuremberg Status. Remember?

AGENT BURROUGHS: I can't breathe. I can't
breathe.

AGENT PALIENT: So breathe. It's okay.
We'll get someone else to clean this up.
Remember to fudge the report so it says he
killed himself or something like that. Be
creative with it.

AGENT BURROUGHS: I need to step out. I
need some fresh air.

AGENT PALIENT: You need to change. Sorry,
I wasn't expecting it to burst like that.
You've got it all over you.

AGENT BURROUGHS: I'm going to be sick.

AGENT PALIENT: Hey, hey, now. Try to focus
on your breathing. You'll get through
this. Everything is going to be fine. Why

don't I buy you a parfait? That'll cheer
you up.

AGENT BURROUGHS: I don't think that'll
help me.

AGENT PALIENT: Hey! It's going to be
alright. You've got to approach these
thing with the right attitude. No baggage
to take home.

AGENT BURROUGHS: I think I'm going to have
a panic attack.

AGENT PALIENT: Oh, I forgot to mention. I
made some plans for us tonight. My cousin,
he's a sculptor. Pretty famous one, too.
He's being featured in a showing at some
gallery downtown. We should go. That'll
take your mind off of it!

END TRANSCRIPT

Chapter Fifteen
One Hundred Thousand Years of History in a Heartbeat

It turns out that, despite the total collapse facing Germany's military, a simple change of events would alter everything. After his dedicated and star-struck Eva swallowed that cyanide and writhed on the floor, vomiting in agony, he had a simple change of heart, which would allow him to stay in hiding for enough time to pass before the Americans assumed he was dead. He would go into hiding, shaving both his head and mustache entirely, adopting a new moniker—Heinrich Schmaltz—and traveling his merry way along into the inner valleys of the history books for at least twenty years. The allied forces would assume he was dead and win the war, but only by dropping the bomb on Hiroshima. The Nagasaki bombing was called off due to Harry S. Truman choking to death on an almond.

Years later, Hitler —excuse me, Heinrich Schmaltz— would find a loyal following of Nazi sympathizers holed up in Boston, Massachusetts. He had arrived at Boston Harbor in the late 1950s, before the swell of the Hippie Counterculture would sweep the nation's xenophobic masochism under the rug (for a little while).

Schmaltz recruited a man named Walter K. Smith, once a naïve but dedicated boy who for years refused to serve any Jewish patrons at his father's grocery store. (He refused to believe that his mother's grandmother was actually Jewish, and labored to prevent Schmaltz from ever finding this out). Schmaltz revealed himself to Smith, who only believed him after Schmaltz drew his famous toothbrush mustache with a marker on his upper lip. He then fainted due to the fumes.

Smith began recruiting more and more members for their Reich Underground Movement, attracting all sorts of racists, homophobes, misogynists, sociopaths, fundamentalist Christians, and whatever other scrapings of American culture remained stuck to its shoes. Their plan was to slowly subvert the local political scene to gain a moderate seat of control in the Eastern United States. What they thought would be a slow and arduous process was actually a rapid one. Before they knew it, their little movement had grown to infest most of the Eastern and Midwest regions. Representatives across these areas then infected Congress. They effortlessly passed sweeping legislation that favored their racist and sexist agenda. Jim Crow dominated the landscape before people could understand the subterfuge that occurred. Schmaltz, this time, didn't make the mistake of showing his face. He pulled the strings, but never breached the red curtain.

JFK was never assassinated because he was never elected president. Instead, it was a disciple of Smith's named Geoffrey Rothford. With the executive branch and legislative branch under their control (before the nation could realize the shade being drawn over their eyes), the United States was apparently "attacked." A nuclear strike obliterated the West Coast, eviscerating almost all of

Southern California and parts of the Mexican border. (Since Truman was bested by an almond, Nagasaki was never bombed, so I guess it was bound to happen. The universe tends to have a way of balancing these things out.) The apparent perpetrator of the attack? France. The reason? Did it really matter at this point?

The world was thrown into turmoil. Internment camps for French citizens were built; but, because there weren't as many French citizens as they had originally thought, they had to find another way to fill the camps. This became a convenient opportunity to satisfy that good old latent American urge to persecute anyone who wasn't white, heterosexual, Christian, or wealthy enough to pay someone off. In other words, anyone who was not a "purebred American." The United States became an isolated Goliath against the world.

The Reich Underground continued its dominance, turning the United States into a petrified police state of totalitarian authority. Maybe little more blatant than the current state of affairs today.

Throughout this alternate timeline, my father thrived, becoming a high-ranking official of the United States military, conducting experiments involving quantum physics, aiming to seize the power of super positioning to develop a powerful, predictive AI that could help the United States dominate the world stage.

I still would have been born, but my life would have been short-lived. My father would be captured by British spies and tortured. They took my baby self, put a gun to my head, and threatened to pull the trigger to try and get my father to spill his secrets, right in front of his eyes. Those idiots—he wouldn't spill a single bean for me. Too bad the man holding the gun had an allergic reaction to the tea they drank moments earlier and had a sneezing fit. With an accidental pull of the trigger, my month-old self was obliterated from this alternate earth. My father wouldn't say a word.

I tried messing with every eensy-weensy detail in my limited understanding of history to map out all the many different ways my life could have turned out. Some involved grandiose revisions to the geopolitical landscape; others involved a slight change of weather patterns or an unexpected bump in the road. I've run out of space on what remains of an old high school algebra notebook I found in the trash, but I've gathered this much: in 65% of these alternate universes, I ended up dying prematurely in some misfortunate and/or pathetic manner, some of which include:

-   Being shot by a random bullet sitting in some public setting (a diner, a bus station, at home)
-   Bleeding to death after digging in a garbage disposal for the avocado pit I let fall in, habitually flipping the switch (at least I had a place to live in that universe, let alone a place with a garbage disposal)
-   Shouting at a bear while drunk (and, one time, sober)
-   Riding an elephant during a tour of India, falling off, and subsequently being trampled by said elephant
-   Lots and lots of choking to death

17% of the time, nothing much would change. 18% remaining would lead to me never being born at all.

What does this mean? Chances are, if there is a God, my general purpose of being born 65% of the time is to have me die in some idiotic fashion. 81% of these lives of mine would be meager at best. In 1% of them, I was happy, successful, thriving. In no edge of the multiverse did I end up with Beaty.

I've asked it what would happen if Albert Einstein was never born. If Benjamin Franklin electrocuted himself to death with a kite (if that ever actually happened). I could have asked more if I knew more about the history of the world beyond dead white guys. But I don't know that much.

But do I want to know how I die in this version? How will my chapter end? Will I end up with Beaty, like I've always dreamed?

There are many more truths that I know now. Is this knowledge a blessing or a curse? The line between isn't a straight line. It's a smudge, an expanded mess, a blob of ink that distorts the words on the page into something incomprehensible and perturbed.

Here are some more truths that I now possess:

1. The world, as we know it, will come to an abrupt end, when our star expands up to our doorstep.
2. We are not alone in the universe.
3. Peter is a homosexual and is extremely conflicted about his marriage.
4. Peter does not know that I have the device, but he will find out eventually.
5. Bigfoot doesn't exist; that one photo was just a big, hairy man named Albert Meady.

Then there are truths that I am too afraid to ask.

1. Is there a God, any type of God - because, if there is, then my human condition is a sick joke and nothing more, and I cannot control what fate God has determined for me on this earth and the supposed afterlife that follows; if not, then these misfortunes aren't misfortunes at all—and therefore I have nobody to blame but myself for these compounding piles of mistakes, guilt-trips, and failures.
2. If my bullet killed that child and her mother—because this is the likely culprit of all my ailments, physical and psychological.
3. If Beaty still loves me, because I can't stop loving her, and ignorance is bliss.
4. If my father does (or at one point, did) love me. (Because isn't that everyone's big problem anyways?)

Considering all these alternate realities that could have played out if not for the boundless minutiae and accidents of happenstance, I've realized in these reflections that the truths we do not want to know outweigh the truths we do, and we build our lives and stories on hollow asphalt. It's a neat contradiction. We survive on feigned ignorance while still fully aware we are doing so. Maybe that's where we find our true character. Not in the truths we pursue, but those we selectively choose to turn a blind eye.

Chapter Sixteen
Warhol's Fifteen Minutes

Peter awoke in the middle of the night, feeling another panic attack coming on. Ada curled up to him, asking him if he had a nightmare. He said he did, but he lied and said he could not remember what it was about. But he knew—the sudden piercing silence and flash, the blood splattered all over his face and clothes, the sullen and emotionless face, mouth agape, slammed on the desk, still blinking—as if nothing happened—

Something about the calming presence of calloused fingers running along my back...I could say his name over and over again in my ludicrous dreams...the cotton candy smell came back to me...dancing by the moonlight on a pier...riverside canoes perched upside down at a cabin somewhere off in a forlorn Midwestern nowhere...What came over me...fatal attraction to a murderer...but the vague indifference, matter-of-factness, just another day at the office...the general ease about everything he does...

The taxi he called for me flashes its bright lights outside the motel room window...I want to leave, but I cannot...no shame...this is not love, because I love Ada...but this is something else...

***

Peter spat his lukewarm coffee onto his infant son, Isaac, who sat idly and numbly in his lap. Isaac didn't cry; he could hardly be troubled in his small, practically sensationless reality.

Peter tried to temper his anxious frustration. Their television, which he had been telling Ada so often that he would replace, still suffered from an unbearably hard-to-miss gathering of dead pixels in its top left corner. These were a constant distraction to himself, Ada, or Katie.

Ada calmly took Isaac from Peter's arms. "I guess you're famous now, honey?" Ada muttered, idly brushing Katie's hair with her pristine, false-ivory handled brush passed down from generation to generation in her family. Only she knew that the ivory wasn't really ivory.

"Dad's famous now, Mom?" Katie asked, looking up at her mother, sitting cross-legged between Ada's knees.

The television froze on a candid image of Peter walking along the street, with half a croissant in his hand and powdered sugar on his lips. This was the headline below his image: *SSIC Hearing Scheduled to Investigate Botched Classified Investigation Connected to Election Fraud.* By virtue of juxtaposition, his name and reputation was now besmirched.

Then, the newscaster—a flat-headed white man with a bulbous shiny nose—began to dictate Peter's fate. "The committee has called upon a special agent from Strategic Homeland Administration Management, Peter Burroughs, to testify before the committee regarding evidence of election fraud as it relates to the classified investigation. Mr.

Burroughs allegedly had total jurisdiction over the classified investigation, and sources say he may be able to provide telling testimony regarding the recent election's legitimacy. Our legal experts say that testimony which favors election deniers could be grounds for further investigations, lawsuits against state election officials, and even more troubling developments. It seems like the fate of this election—and all future elections—may rest on Peter Burrough's shoulders."

Following this was a short clip of Senate Majority Leader Paul Palient:

"Ah will say this: we will leave no stone uhnturned in our investuhgation. The Senate Suhcurity and Intelluhgence Cuhmittee will get to the bottom of this puhtential uhlection fraud. The truth is out there, folks, and we aim to uncuhver it."

The newscaster added on after the camera switched back to him: "Multiple senators and representatives have been pushing for investigations into the recent election, claiming that there may be a multitude of potential cover-ups of biased counting in machines, thousands of ballots being thrown in the trash, and even thousands of illegitimate votes from dead citizens. Despite these claims, no tangible evidence has been presented. Multiple cities have seen protests, some turning violent, at polling places, demanding justice." The newscast then cut to a collage of videos, showing protestors clad in flag attire, military outfits, and a few leopard-skinned Vikings. Hundreds of homemade cardboard signs read "STOP THE STEAL" or "G KNOWS." The "G" here, of course, referred to the mysterious internet crusader known as "G," a former agent of the deep state who—for the past few years—propagated conspiracies about an apparent hostile invasion of octopus aliens, election fraud, deep-state devil worshipers, and explanations for the rising costs of eggs. G had millions and millions of followers—many of whom happened to be elected to the U.S. House of Representatives.

The newscaster ended the segment: "The committee scheduled their first hearing with Peter Burroughs for March 14th, also known as international pie day. What kind of pie do you plan to celebrate with, Doris?"

Holding Isaac in his lap, Peter struggled to hide his anger. He knew he couldn't reveal to Ada the nature of his work, in part because of the danger it may put them in, or perhaps he feared some disappointment from Ada that his ineptitude had led to this media circus. Ada, of course, would never be disappointed by Peter. She loved him more than she loved anyone else, even herself.

He also struggled with another divot in his flailing conscience—that he found the report from the replicant software that Harold Pine had described. There were many names he recognized among this list of potential suspects. Some were eponymous with outlandish theories of massive governmental cover-ups and conspiracies. Others had connections with terrorist organizations throughout the world. This list even identified the mysterious individual known as "G" as a potential suspect. (G, however, was no mystery to Strategic Homeland Security Management agents. Despite the lavish conspiracy claims and millions of followers, G was actually just a plain, boring man named Gerald Finkowitz, a 38 year old gas station clerk who called himself a programmer—even though he only knew html. Agents, under the direction of certain political motivations, chose to keep G's identity anonymous.) Each suspect was given a percentage based on the likelihood of their involvement in the apparatus's disappearance.

The top suspect in the list was Peter, with a rating of 76% likelihood of involvement. Peter quickly deleted all files related to the replicant software, and smashed Harold Pine's computer for good measure.

"I have to go."

"Don't forget your lunch."

He fled like so many times he had done before, both in dreams and in the real world, leaving her to stew in her own thoughts, distracting Isaac's blank gaze with rhythmic taps on his tiny left forearm, trying to provide him the comfort in knowing that someone was still there in the fog. Isaac babbled. Ada kissed him on the back of his head. He tasted like soap.

As Peter struggled to find his keys, Ada fell back into her daydreams. This time, she imagined Isaac all grown up, but couldn't picture him fully; she imagined Peter's adult body with Isaac's baby head. *How would he succeed without having any of the basic senses? Will he develop a center of gravity or proprioception? Would he have a job (and be able to hold it)? Would he be imprisoned in his chair, in a room without any screens or books? Would he ever learn to read? Would he understand the beauty of the sunset on the Pacific Ocean, or the whispering of tree leaves in dark and damp forests? Would he have a physiological breakthrough, instantly recognizing the traces of his mothers' fingers on his pale flesh, telling him that what he felt was his mother's love? Would the living word awaken his soul? Would anyone ever love him for who he was, despite all that would likely be lacking? Would he ever have consensual sex? Would she and Katie be slaves the rest of their lives, looking after Isaac in efforts to keep up their appearances and make them feel better about themselves? Would Peter—would he lend a hand, once in a while?*

Would all these things matter at all if Peter's father succeeded in tossing Isaac off the side of that cliff?

Peter was not the source of Ada's frustrations. Her frustration in their marriage came from one truth she had begun to accept more and more over the years—that, as the prototypical American family, everyone expected her (as the mother) to make all the painstaking efforts to keep their marriage and family together.

But Peter had an out. As the husband, he was expected to falter and put in considerably less effort, and would eventually be given the Capraesque choice to make amends and solve their mess of a family. While she, on the other hand (you know, the one with the ring), would have the luxury of not being given a choice at all. After all— she was the wife, and the mother, and that is what she does, and will always do—no matter the sudden ebullitions of the adolescent Ada still alive deep in adult Ada's soul, still kicking and screaming underneath (after all, that little girl would rather give up on it all as well, if the world would let her). She daydreamed of life without Peter, and hated herself for imagining how life would have been if Isaac had never been born; she scorned herself immediately for such a thought, but the vividness continued, fickle, in her capricious little daydreams.

She had been destined for greatness. Her father was a fabled tennis player who came close to the regional championship twice in his life; her mother was a software engineer. Though she did not remember this, her mother would always put her to bed by kissing her soft forehead and whispering, "you are destined for great things, Ada bean."

She excelled in her first six years at elementary school. Her teachers always had high remarks and compliments. "Ada is going somewhere, for sure." "She is so creative." "I'd be shocked if she wasn't in the news one day." Ada heard all of these in the hallway during parent-teacher conferences, pressing her ear against the door when her mother met with all her teachers. She developed a humble giddiness, seeing that her hard work was finally gaining recognition—she thrived on this, too. All of her accolades and accomplishments since then were borne by an incessant desire to fulfill her mother's wishes, a desire drilled into her dreams since before she was dreaming.

And that success continued, greatly. On to college, on to a comprehensive education, a palette—her life became infinitely more interesting at that point. She even fell in love with a young professor in the School of Finance in her accounting ethics class, a gen-ed requirement that she initially despised. Nothing sickened her more than the doldrums of corporate fiscal conservatism. And every textbook in the subject sung the same dismal lyric: *every accountant needs to know about ethics.* Ethics bored her immensely. To Ada, most courses on ethics wove a thin veil of contention, but would wither against any sensible source of natural reason.

Is it ok to take the afternoon off to relax, or is that stealing time from the Company?

Is it okay to lie during your performance review?

If the company is making profits off unethically sourced resources, is this okay?

During any course that dealt with any sort of ethics (which happened to be all of the above), she doodled illustrations of the potential visual representation of eleven-dimensional spacetime.

In her first year at college, while trying to find her dorm building, she happened upon a poker tournament in the basement of Rousseau Hall, a renowned old building dedicated to philosophy and ethics. After a few losses, she began to rake in wins, gaining infamy as the *Queen of Hearts.* She bested the most extolled sophomores of the college, who had previously stolen hundreds from nubile freshman wearing flimsy suits of confidence. Eventually, even professors in statistics and probability challenged her to see what all the fuss was about. They prepared for weeks, studying probabilities in poker and how to count cards. They all discovered, horribly, that their lifelong dedication of study had been bested by a simply lucky woman.

What were people to do with some woman who actually *knew* things? She spent numerous nights in her dorm room turning away would-be suitors looking for a prolific lay. This reputation stuck with her for much of her adult life, undermining her efforts to achieve a stable relationship. She quickly found out that no male in her town could stand feeling inferior to her for much longer than a few months. Her intellect, her wisdom, and her bravado were just too much.

That was until she met Peter, having bumped into him so unceremoniously at a diner outside of the campus. Things seemed to spark immediately when he said he was a freshman, and had no clue about her reputation. He fell in love with her intelligence and empathy; she fell in love with his hopeless dreams to become a world famous spy (and she was always delighted by the paradoxical irony of that very moniker). He only had one year left, however, so they would not graduate together. She chose to drop out after he graduated, and got the first job she could—selling flowers in the local farmer's market—to support him working his way up the corporate ladder. She had some reservations about giving up her education, but she made a habit of reminding herself during these flashbacks that Peter never pressured her; it was her own idea. This was her choice, and she had to bear the consequences, both the fruitful and the dreary.

She did notice a rift between them not long after Isaac was born. She suspected the usual—he was unsatisfied; was cheating on her; was thinking about divorcing her. He was mostly quite jovial and warm, but had become a little distant at times, often staring off into space. He would come home much later than usual on Tuesdays and Thursdays, always giving some excuse—getting held up at work, losing track of time at the gym. She suspected his father's hospice had something to do with it, too. Despite the outlandishness of her suspicions, the instinct still felt real enough to merit following him one day, asking the babysitter to come over on the weekday to give her a break.

She followed him from work. He did go to the gym. She followed him in, keeping a distance and wearing a baseball cap to remain inconspicuous (trying not to laugh when she thought, *who is the spy now?*). Peter slowly sulked into the men's locker room with his duffel bag, keeping his head down, and then five minutes passed...then ten...then twenty...and he didn't reemerge until well over two hours later, in his shorts and a gray t-shirt, drenched in sweat.

She got home after he did. Fortunately, she prepared for this by stopping at a grocery store and buying eggs, milk, and laundry detergent. She lied to Peter and said she had to make an emergency run to the grocery store. Just to be safe, when Peter wasn't looking, she rushed over to the refrigerator and pounded her fist on the egg carton. She threw them away and replaced them with the brand new carton, later telling Peter that she had dropped them by accident. She also poured out all the old milk and detergent before Peter could put two and two together, putting the evidence in recycling.

She stayed up that night while Peter went to sleep, thinking more than she had since college. At first she felt like breaking his nose; fleeting moments later, she felt like taking the kids and leaving for California. Hours later, she reached the entirely logical conclusion that she should shelve her rage and resentment for the time being, as it wouldn't be good for Katie and Isaac. She reasoned that she would never truly understand the identity crisis that Peter was going through. She knew how difficult it was for men in the modern era to concede their masculinity in the face of grandiose expectations of heterosexual machismo. And, she could sense that Peter was trying desperately to hide his shame as much as his infidelity. She didn't question whether she still loved him, yet. She didn't allow herself to judge. She committed herself to her made-up conviction that the time would come, and it should be Peter's, and not hers.

Isaac babbled; even though he couldn't hear it, Ada babbled back, and said, "I love you, Isaac. I love you, Katie. I would die for both of you." Katie wondered why her mother never cried.

Chapter Seventeen
Why You No Good, Yella, Lyin' Sumbitch

Where else would I take the device but to my father? I fully anticipate that whatever I want to accomplish by going to see my father will ultimately lead to a loss. There would only be one thing left to do after this. What else would I do, with unbridled access to the universe's secrets? Bet on a winning horse and make millions, of course. What else is left when your world is devoid of meaning? Except I don't have any money, so that's a slight problem with that pipe dream. Not even enough to buy a lottery ticket.

I'm not fully aware of what my intentions are—maybe I'm empowered with the truth, maybe I have questions that have not yet come to fruition. Maybe I have something to prove to my old man who is closer to death than he is to getting out of bed on his own. I'm also bringing along that photo album that sent me limping away so long ago. I'm not sure why, but it feels like the right thing to do.

I guess I want to ask the device if my father loves me, while looking my father in the face. Maybe I'll murder him

after I get my answer. Give him a little too much morphine.

As I arrive, Dr. Ramirez is walking out of my father's
room. She looks much more disheveled and fed up today,
and she doesn't smile at me like she used to.

"William? My god, you look like you're starving to
death."

I haven't noticed myself lately, haven't felt my own
body, my own presence. Up to this point, I must have
spent days (maybe even weeks) with this device, asking it
whatever questions came to mind (besides the big ones)
and investigating countless different branches of reality.
Maybe investigating isn't the right word—getting lost, if
that's a better way of putting it. I can see some blurry
flashbacks of me eating, getting a little bit of sleep—but
when your mind has been separated from your body for
who knows how long, you tend to fabricate some things.

"How is my father doing?"

She lets out the sort of sigh that prepares to handle
some monstrous task, like lifting a grand piano or driving
across the country for a funeral.

"I'm sorry William, he's not doing too well today."

"That's ok. It'll be better when he's dead."

Another sigh. "Maybe you should just go see him.
Might make him feel like his old self."

But Dr. Ramirez doesn't know my father's old self. I
guess not many people do. It's easy to assume orderli-
ness, poise, a family-man in snapshot portraits on the
flaps of science journals and textbooks—a distinguished
gentleman in his gold-rimmed glasses—always clean-
shaven, always dapper even when he started balding.
Charisma practically dripping off his tweed jacket.

But that wasn't the father I know—or the father I barely know.

Even now, with enough salvaged courage to see him again, I realize that I have been a first row honoree to his deterioration over the past few years into some sort of crazed skeleton in someone else's rotting skin.

Now, after walking into his bedroom, I can see why Dr. Ramirez is drained and frustrated. They have my father strapped down to his bed, restrained like a sick and dying animal.

I know in my heart this *is* my father. But I no longer *recognize* my father. This new and confusing truth hurts me as much as the blank, frightened stare his skeleton is giving me now. I don't recognize my father—and he doesn't recognize me. He retreats back slightly in fear of me, pushing his bald head and narrow shoulders deeper into his pillows.

"Just think about it—what Schrodinger's cat tells us about the universe isn't at all what Schrodinger wanted his cat to tell us! He wanted to disprove the idea of superpositioning until observation. But you see it all over today as an explanation of that very concept. Think about it even further—the implication that if you happen to look in the box, the quantum mechanics that governs our physical world forces your reality to split into two— Reality A, in which you observe a dead cat, and Reality B, in which you observe a live one. The moment you look in the box, you become entangled with that decaying atom, that cat, that reality. The crazy shit is when you think about how that happens infinitely throughout a single nanosecond. How many branches there must be. It's a tree that expands beyond the boundaries of infinity. The implications alone...fucking rock your world."

My father doesn't say anything, and neither do I. All I really can do is sit next to him and pat his hand. He doesn't budge. He just stays still, like a frightened animal cornered in his habitat. I'm hesitant to lift up the photo album, recalling how he reacted last time. But I do, and he does nothing and says nothing. Cloudy eyes, hollow eye sockets, his lips cracked and purple, looking at me like I'm a killer here to murder him.

I start to flip through the photo album again. That rage comes back, that I felt so long ago, back when I first discovered this under the water heater. How my father had tucked all these memories of us away in a dirty old maintenance closet. I bottled up some of that rage thanks to time and avoidance. but now it started to make sense, considering. After all, we always seemed like footnotes in his fabled career, inconveniences that he felt obligated to care for at the barest minimum. Tucking us away with aunts and uncles for months at a time while he traveled the world. Bringing us back harmonicas from Germany and chocolate from Switzerland to win our affections enough to forgive him, rewarding us just enough to make us dependent on him for all of our hopes, desires, and dreams.

But in flipping through the album, I notice something I did not see before. The edges are blackened. Some of the plastic on the pages is bubbled and melted. This photo album had almost caught on fire.

Part of my father's infamy was that destructive fire at Hertfordshire. The one that eviscerated his life's work and turned him from a suave, genius bachelor into an undesirable nutcase. And I'm disheartened to believe that this may be something salvaged from that fire.

"Was this in the fire at Hertfordshire?"

"How did it get out?"

I'm even more disheartened now. That, despite all the distance between us, my father must have cared enough about us to save a stupid photo album from a fire. Rather than his equations and notes. He saved us.

I'm flipping through the album some more, seeing more photos of us as kids, our mothers, and old newspaper clippings of father's discoveries and debaucheries. Some of those stories include a grainy photo of a young and extremely cocky Dr. William Burroughs, Sr.

But then I notice something else: there's a thick, black divider in the middle. I turn to it, and barely attached to it—hanging on to its last ounce of adhesive—is a pink post-it note. It reads:

REALITY A

Flipping to the other side, a blue post-it note, in much the same condition:

Reality B

This other side of the binder doesn't have polaroid photos of us as kids. Or as adults. It has no photos whatsoever. What it has is a mad scramble of numbers and notes on crumpled loose-leaf paper.

"This is what we are exploring now, my baby students. Other top minds around the world are just now wrapping our heads now on the theoretical implications of our most recent observations within particle colliders and the chalky hands of my colleagues. I believe we are close to discovering the purely and beautifully mathematical fabric of the cosmos—a simple, elegant theorem that can provide concrete and undeniable explanations for all the phenomena that plague our models today—dark matter, gravity, time—a grand and unifying melody. We're close."
"Professor Burroughs, how close are you?"
"Well, my dear...close enough that your degree in astrophysics will become meaningless in the next few years."

I set the device on my father's dresser. His posture and expression have not changed.

"What are these?"

```
Your father's notes on his grand
   unified theory of everything
```

"What is the grand unified theory of everything?"

```
The purportedly ultimate theory that
   fully explains all aspects of the
         physical universe
```

My father would mention this from time to time in his episodic and insane ramblings. His notes. Notes from Reality B.

"These are the notes that my father was working on, in England?"

Yes

"These are the notes that everything thought burned up, in the fire?"

Yes

"But they didn't burn up in the fire?"

No

As far as my limited brain can understand it, I know that these notes represent the culmination of my father's decades of labor. I know these notes represent an entire fatherless decade of my adolescence. That's why I was delighted when I heard they burned up in the fire at Hertfordshire. I know that, in all likelihood, these notes are more central to my father's core than me or Peter ever were. I know enough about these notes to say that he practically died in that fire in Hertfordshire, when he supposedly lost those notes. I know that, by the time the fire had started, isolation and desperation had dwindled his grand mind enough to confuse him with a mad scientist or schizophrenic genius. And, it seems, these notes hold the potential equations (whatever they are, I'm god awful with numbers) that explain everything about the universe.

And now, I know this: my father saved this album from the fire. Not because of our photos, but because of his notes.

"Would the world be a better place if the theory of everything was solved?"

Yes

I have found out so much in my interrogations with the truth, but this feels different. My father hadn't cheated his way to the truth. He hadn't stumbled upon it or stolen it from the minds of others greater than him. He had simply sat down with a pen and paper and figured it all out. Despite his negligence as my father, I can't deny his reputation as one of the most critical minds in modern physics. And this is the pinnacle of that work. This is the result of it all, and so am I.

"Is his theory right?"

No

"These notes, these equations, are wrong?"

Yes

And there's the truth. My father's life's work is meaningless, dead wrong. Decades wasted. Valuable family time sacrificed for nothing. Harmonicas and chocolates as fake sacrifices.

"What impact did my father's work have on...the world?"

None

"What do you mean?"

William Burroughs' theories have not contributed to humanity's greater understanding of the physical universe and have likely derailed scientific development into irrelevant and erroneous theories

"So, my father has accomplished nothing?"

Nothing at all

This is a truth I did not expect to face today. In fact, I'm still not sure what my original intentions were. But this sure is a feeling I haven't felt before— I can't tell if it's rewarding or devastating. Or somewhere in between. But finding out that your father—the man you were named after—the man whose mind was symbolic of your family name's legacy and reputation, squandered by a closeted secret agent and a murdering son-of-a-bitch ex-soldier—

His life's work, the purpose for his constant ventures overseas, leaving me and Peter alone to grow up by our-selves—all of it was meaningless. Not even meaningless; it still had an impact—it set humanity back a century or so. Like the world was a small boy, instructed by his father that apples were poisonous, and the boy living to old age with that belief firmly held—until he discovered one fate-ful day that his father had been lying this whole time. Not even lying—the father truly believed it himself, but was just plain wrong. My father had taken theoretical physics

228

on a detour halfway across the ocean and dumped it all just at the edge of the point of no return.

My father is still glaring at me, deathly afraid, like a cornered rodent.

Then I go back to that utility closet, the one where I found this black binder, and the steel brown safe. The number padlock looks pristine, like it's never been touched since it was locked.

"What's the combination to this lock?"

31-4-1

Those numbers are meaningless to me. Not my birth date, or Peter's. Not the day Peter got married. Not the day Katie or Isaac were born. No significance at all.

In the safe is a torn picture of some woman in some foreign Italian town, a faded Rubik's cube that was close to being solved, and $100,000 cash.

***

After dusk, I burn my father's notes in a trash bin in some godforsaken alley. This act isn't motivated by some righteous attempt to save my father's reputation, or to avoid these destructive notes seeing the light of day. It just seems like the right thing to do. And it feels right.

Maybe I feel vindicated knowing my father's lifelong labors were all for nothing. Maybe I feel like I'm letting go of the need to please him, since he was a failure, too. Maybe I should ask the device what this complicated mess of emotions really means. At the end of the day, my father is a despicable, philandering, no-good, son-of-a-bitch hack whose entire purpose for living had been pointless after all.

229

Watching these pages burn, the smoke curling up on its ascendance towards the clouds, I can hear a sonorous and hollow weeping of ghosts, like the disharmonious and lowest notes on a chorus of tuned-down cellos, married with the honks and cries of the lively city surrounding me. Waxing poetic, yet again. Drunk, yet again.

Across the flames, down across to the other side of the street, I can see Belial, that familiar demon, playing marbles with the two agents who have been following me for years.

I'm keeping Reality A—the photos of me, of Peter, of my father, the man I once knew, not the nearly lifeless corpse he had become. I hide it behind the bench I call home on 53rd and Wayward Ave.

"Ah, my esteemed students-soon-to-be-colleagues. I want to introduce you to someone who is very important to me. Come up, here, William. Don't be shy. You can take Eeyore with you, it's ok. William's a little timid. He's afraid of crowds. These are my students, William. Ladies and gentlemen, this is my son, William. And I love him very much."

Chapter Eighteen
Excalibur

While passing by the time at work, Arthur reread the latest and last online post from the eponymous G:

The tide is coming. Retribution for a democracy stolen.

Question why those in power hide the truth. Question why those in power get to hide in their brick clad and marble palace.

Take back what is ours.

Generals speak lies.

You have had the wool pulled over your eyes.

They are here...........

The post ended with a blurry underwater photograph of a common octopus resting at the blue bottom of the sea.

This was the last post in quite some time. Arthur had been following G for quite some time, intrigued since stumbling upon a rabbit's hole feed of videos on the subject. He joined the online forum that housed thousands of G's apocryphal leaks; written testimonials that, at their surface, were an error-ridden welter of anti-establishment revulsion, but were also dangerously cloaked as the gospel of someone deep inside the deep state, risking his or her life to reveal the true and evil plans of those in power—

They want to feast on your children.

Any person with any semblance of reason may have at least some doubts about such a claim. But that person would be a fool to believe that millions of others would have the rational ammunition to cry "bullshit."

Arthur was certainly well-educated; pleasant when he had to be, albeit not the most garrulous with his coworkers. Arthur was exactly normal, and nothing exceptional (yet). But his world had been warped by the smoke-and-mirrors of a grand scheme, a conspiracy without a conspirator.

Most of the "content" in which he invested any serious mental weight, the only juicy morsels of something other than nihilistic dread and despair, were the videos recommended for him on Merlin®— curated for him based on his viewing history. This became his only window into what purportedly was the "real world"—and the curating algorithm knew it could keep him glued with content from sources that vehemently believed in almost every conspiracy known to man. It started with a trail of videos on Bigfoot, the Moth Man, and Loch Ness Monster (innocent enough), but then began to delve into channels and content creators fully dedicated to unraveling the true intentions of celebrities and the government. Alien cephalopods in human suits did seem a little farfetched to Arthur—but a grand conspiracy to manipulate an election? A deep-seeded and coordinated effort by media conglomerates to patronize one party and demonize another? Those were the lowest hanging fruits, much easier to chew on.

And this all eventually led him to G. Influencers galore would cite this person as gospel—some even speculated that's what the "G" stood for, besides "G-man," or "God's disciple." Although G never stated it explicitly, many early followers assumed that only a high-level government official, close to those highest in power, could divulge such deep-state classified information that would later become true:

Friends and loved ones...

Time has drawn near for the storm to arrive...

Pay close attention to Pi...

Everyone wants a slice of the Pi...

Will you get yours?

The most prominent content creators—those who begged followers to subscribe before and after every video and to "hit that like button…"—created hours and hours of analyses and predictions about what G meant by "Pi." Some predicted a disaster on March 14th. One user posted a video of the local gas price at $3.14, with the text "Apocalypse Soon" below the image. Some fell into deep diatribes about the ontological nature of the mathematical constant and the golden ratio, eventually linking these (loosely) with Nostradamus' prophecies of Armageddon.

Soon after, a confidential report leaked, revealing a few inconsequential transactions between the federal government and a Palestinian printing conglomerate, aptly called Palestinian Ink. PI for short. A complete, uncontroversial non-story. The truth-bomb was not what G-followers had thought it was.

However, the mere thought of the American government interacting with any foreign agency sent these G followers into a furor, sending jitters down the puppet strings latched to political figureheads, who then by force of habit went live on major media outlets and spouted more sparks over the kindling, shouting about a corrupt government in debt to the pockets of foreign countries. And, funny enough, the G followers—and those whose political philosophy was just inches away already—would watch those supposed news networks, hear these powerful white men in suits, believing their every word. A vicious circle of everything further from the truth.

And the fact that the company was named PI became the holy grail of every G follower. Here was irrefutable truth that G really was a deeply informed member of the government.

This gave the latest post that much more gravitas:

DON'T' TRUST THE VOTING MACHINES. THE ALGRITHmS ARE DESIGNED TO CHEAT YOU and STEal your votes. Their tentacles reach far. They bleed the ink of retribution. THE TRUTH IS OUT THERE.

Naturally, then, the truth-seeking content creators spoke and preached and speculated and dropped bombshells—which spread to their millions of followers, and bled into the figureheads of radical news, until seeping into the speeches, statements, and pockets of politicians—only again verifying its veracity, feeding the vicious cycle further for content creators to quote—"see? See who is asking the same questions? Now don't you believe me?!"

Arthur, following all of this along, felt obligated to do something about it.

Eventually, while foraging for more truths deep in the digital rabbit hole, he found himself in a chat room titled "G SPEAKS". He hesitated at first, not wanting to dive too much into the craziness, but some deep, primeval feeling in his chest goaded him to join.

He had to create a username. He could only come up with something inspired by the stories his father used to tell him before bedtime.

Excalibur has joined the chat

BULLMASSTURD494: u have to be an idiot not to believe this stuff

XxMoDeRnCrEePxX: most people don't anyway…

BULLMASSTURD494: thats cuz they excepted the big lie, thats why bunch of fucking fagot fashists

Excalibur: what are you guys talking about?

Mike: Hey there newbie, talking about the latest news about Senator Jack-me-off Diaz.

XxMoDeRnCrEePxX: bombshell shit I tell you

BULLMASSTURD494: this is why they should all resign, or impeached, or executed for that matter

Mike: Link to the article http://www.truthfulnews.com/Diaz-tentacles-proof-of-octopus-invasion445567

Arthur opened the article. It took him two minutes to navigate through pop-up ads about erectile dysfunction and advertisements for the "most absorbent towel known to mankind" (he had just looked up ordering a new brand of anti-dandruff shampoo the other day, so the ad algorithm gave him towels.) Here was the unbiased, nonpartisan article, in full text, without the ads:

The latest skimpy video from Vermont representative Carmon Diaz shows irrefutable evidence of the Octopus invasion, right in front of our eyes. As has been proven time after time, representative Diaz is struggling to hold the trust of her constituents after failing miserably to gather enough support for her unconstitutional environmental proposals. She has also shown how un-

American she is with her demand for "peace" and "respect" following the justified self-defense shooting of the thug twelve year-old Armand Taylor. But now, as the video below demonstrates, her intentions are much more clear. She has no intent to "save" the environment and battle so-called "racial and systematic prejudice" (no such things exist in this country, ma'am). Instead, her intent is nothing but the complete subterfuge and takeover of our Christian nation.

In this video, representative Diaz is dancing to a slutty, satanic latin pop song. However, there is more than meets the eye. Scientific analysis proves that the "fold" you can see in her pants is quite unusual. In fact, the fold is topographically impossible, according to our own Scientific Consultant, Robert Pieman. "The curvature of the fold is not something we expect from this brand, fabric, or size, especially considering she is wearing a size much too small for her frame and weight," said Pieman.

If you look close enough, you can make out perforations, which—upon closer inspection—match the size and patterns of octopus suckers. The curve of the fold also matches the typical diameter of the common octopus.

Not only this, but the view of this fold comes as the song's lyrics sing, "wrap my arms around you," which undeniably serve as some sort of subliminal code—after all, an octopus seizes its prey by wrapping its slimy tentacles around it.

We have reached out to representative Diaz for comment but have yet to receive a reply. Suspicious silence, to say the least.

Mike: Can't get more scientific and objective than that. More proof of what we know.

Excalibur: What do you mean?

Mike: You need to read more about this. The hostile takeover. The invasion of the octopus overlords. I'd be shocked…shocked…if you haven't heard about this.

XxMoDeRnCrEePxX: shit's crazy

BULLMASSTURD494: fuckin octopusses tryin to eat our fucking brains. Did you know they inject little baby cuttlefish into babies at hospitals? That's why they want universal health care so they can inject more babies

XxMoDeRnCrEePxX: explains a lot about kids in my class

Mike: Excalibur, I suggest you do more research on this. It's shocking how deep this goes. Hollywood. The Senate. The House. Local government. Charities. Black Lives Matter. Antifa. Right in our own goddamn backyard. Trying to rob us of our American dignity and livelihood.

Excalibur: How did this all start?

Mike: Most research shows it happened in the 1840s. But new research suggests it happened much earlier than that. They started in Africa. It was apparently a subset of pilgrim octopuses from the Andromeda galaxy who wanted to break away from the Octopus Overlord Regime. Felt they were following the wrong prophet, Methalla'ka. Wanted to find a new place to repopulate and start fresh following the new teachings of the seven-tentacled one, Alla'beander. But then they were enslaved and brought to America. Sent distress messages, so the Overlords ordered an emergency coupe to free them—this is how the abolitionist movement started. The rest is history, just not the kind written in those bullshit textbooks.

Excalibur: How high does it go?

XxMoDeRnCrEePxX: hard to tell. President's not in on it, he's trying to root them out

BULLMASSTURD494: how do u know he's not a puppet too

XxMoDeRnCrEePxX: pics of him eating calamari

BULLMASSTURD494: could be to throw us off the scent

XxMoDeRnCrEePxX: anybody who doesn't eat calamari or squid or whatever is suspect

BULLMASSTURD494: plus if they bleed black blood, it's their ink sac. Like when they shot that Taylor kid, his blood was all black. Cuz they shot the ink sac in his brain

XxMoDeRnCrEePxX: shoot all these fuckers. Their taking over the godam country

Mike: get close enough to smell saltwater. Otherwise, the only real way to find out is to make them bleed. That's what we're doing on the 14th. Spread the word, fast. Massive protest outside the capitol building. Burn it all down if we have to. Like G himself said—take back what is ours.

Arthur recognized the rumor immediately—a planned mass gathering outside of the capitol on March 14th. A demonstration of angst and the power of the fed-up populace. A threatening proclamation of might against the established deep state. A coup to unseat the kings and queens. Perhaps the most important protest in American history, as many of the talking heads on Arthur's Merlin® feed would shout. "Come and march with us to the capitol on 3-14, and let us take back what is ours—our country!"

Arthur contemplated for a split second whether it would be good judgment to attend. But this sense of good judgment crumbled against the vertiginous force of newfound purpose that overwhelmed him—that he, today a lowly, lonely waste of space, might contribute to a force much greater than himself.

Chapter Nineteen
Madame Harmony

"Today, which horse, in race number ten, at the Froddes Race Track, will win the race?"

Madame Harmony

The name strikes a chord, a faint memory of my father and me at the carnival, dropping a quarter into fortune-telling machines.

I ask the winners of every other race today.

Washington Bullet
Sunny Afternoon
White Tower
Magic Bovary
Cannon Loaded
Apple Tree Picker
Dawn of an Angel
Butter Pickle
A Day at the Park

All sure things—except for the last race of the day. Race number ten, when Madame Harmony will be the upset horse, odds at 30-1.

Today is bustling. More degenerate gamblers sitting with their piles of crumpled and torn tickets and empty, cracked plastic cups with miniscule amounts of stale beer circling the bottom. The atmosphere is tense. Not much fortune has happened yet for the people who need it the most.

There's a man shouting on his phone in a comically French accent: "Fuck no, Maurice! It's zeventy degrees! Magic Bovary won't win today, she never wins when it's zeventy degrees!"

I'm striding past a group of desperate, middle-aged men with beer bellies and pale-colored shirts desperately glued to the screens with all the races around the world. Some are here for fun. Most are here to win. Some with their lives dependent on it, whether they know it or not.

I am here for the surety and all the glory.

The owner is greeting all his patrons at the door and welcoming them to his race tracks. He is a remarkably average-looking white man, hair parted scrupulously, his posture reminiscent of the intellectual lieutenant colonels who had never seen action but reaped all the benefits of the title. He sizes me up when he first sees me. "I see a winner!" he calls to me, grinning through his teeth. He licks his lips before shaking my hands, bowing slightly. This is how he appears in public—your typical white man, enthusiastic—he *wants* you to win. He greets you like he knows you, intimately. His piano key necktie makes me want to vomit.

I'd only truly gambled once, drunk off my ass with my C.O. and the rest of my squad waiting for orders that hadn't come for weeks, protruding our manhood out our asses by challenging each other to a friendly game of Russian Roulette. Only two turns were taken. I was third among the six of us. My C.O. was second, and pussied out. So I went second, and laughed after the gun cocked and clicked in my hand. The next guy fired the shot in the air, and the ceiling above us burst, a cloud of dust raining down. That bullet was meant for me, the third guy in line. I'd never gambled since then.

(Dr. Ivy Zane says that memory is likely a false memory from a movie. Another hallucination. I'm not so sure anymore.)

And I'm not gambling now, either. Gambling has no surety. It's a bet on chance, a toss-up between luck and fortune (or misfortune). It's not gambling if you're betting on something that is absolutely bound by fate to happen. That's why I'm not that afraid of this towering man in the piano-key necktie. He calls me "Big Winner" so he can demean my manhood and make me afraid of him. He wipes his large, awkward hands through his thinning black hair. He knows that I'm not here to meander my way over with the rest of the crowd to make paltry bets. He knows I mean business, because I've won every single time I've come here before. I've come here for a few days and bet on winning horses with the money I found in my father's safe. The truth-telling machine hasn't steered me wrong, telling me the exact winner each time. I've made more money than I could imagine, in the most legal way I know how. It's not gambling if you know which horse is going to win.

The owner straightens his bow-tie and smiles with his eyes closed. He knows I'm here to finish robbing him blind. He wishes he had a valid and moral reason to shoot me in the head.

But he doesn't mind showing me off to the crowd of degenerate gamblers, either. "Big Winner, ladies and gentlemen! How much are you planning on winning again today, my friend?!" He shouts this in a loud, sweeping gesture, making sure everyone queuing up for tickets can hear him, making sure everyone sees me. What better way to attract the crowd to the fortunes that await them? Show them the gleaming exemplar of a horse-racing guru—give them a shot to their veins of that absurd drug called hope, urging them to empty their pockets in a vain attempt to win. As he parades me around the anomic crowd, he mumbles compulsively under his breath, as if he's repeating a legally required disclosure following an advertisement:

"'Big Winner' is not a guarantee. must be at least 21 years old and physically located in the United States to wager. Offer Not valid for any participant of the Saskatchewan Gaming and Betting Board Statewide Voluntary Self-Exclusion Program. If you or someone that you know has a gambling problem, crisis counseling and other referral services can be accessed by calling 1-555-UAD-DICT (1-555-823-3428)."

"Let's talk in my office," he grins, licking his lips again.

***

A naive part of me expected this whole ordeal to play out in some Mafioso-style wooden office, with armed guards perched everywhere, or some other archetypal gambling head honcho who ceremoniously offers me a fat cigar and tells me he will kill me if I can't pay up. But, instead of this, I'm greeted by a copy-paste corporate office with glass walls, two plastic chairs in front of a glass

244

executive desk you'd expect to see in any office retail store display. It's all so disappointingly corporate.

In the corner, besides a fake plastic ficus, a humidifier dimly hums and spews a billowing cloud of vapor. The vapor dissipates into nothingness, illuminated only briefly by the glass prison I'm now in.

"I only have one question for you, Big Winner—how much are you willing to lose?" He smiles from behind his glass executive desk. Three of his front teeth are gold. He laughs again, covering his face with his hands in polite embarrassment. Leaning over in his tall frame and his suit, he reminds me of a corporate version of Death. He snaps his fingers, and immediately a short and hobbling old man in a red tuxedo brings me a chilled glass of some brown, fizzy liquid, and three ice cubes shaped like horse heads. I'm not supposed to drink with my medication; that's according to Dr. Ivy Zane, but that hasn't stopped me before (or lately at all).

If I lose today, the amount that I would owe this dangerous man exceeds any number I ever dreamt of owning myself. I wonder if he keeps a table saw somewhere on these premises for chopping off fingers.

If I ask these questions nonchalantly and rhetorically, he won't know any better. I can sneak a look into my coat pocket, where I have the truth-telling machine hidden and secure.

"When I came here today, I had some questions for myself," I say, acting the best I can to not be petrified.

"Such as?" He asks, intrigued.

"Well, you know...I gotta ask, am I going to lose any fingers today?" I make a suggestive frowning face, turning my left hand out palm-up. You know, nonchalantly. Rhetorical.

I also lean my head slightly to sneak a glance at the device to get the answer to my totally nonchalant, totally rhetorical question.

No

Foolish choice of words.

"I also ask myself: am I going to die today?"

No

"Then I ask myself: am I going to lose a bet today?"

No

"And, you know, if I think all the answers are 'no,' then I think I have a pretty good chance on a sure thing. If you're willing to bet on me losing, that is."

The piano-key necktie man who reminds me of Death is glaring at me through wistfully absent eyes.

"Just how much are you willing to lose, then?" He asks, before mumbling more jargon under his breath: *"Prior statement is no guarantee of a loss. All real money wagers and losses by the company are fully insured. If you require legal counsel pending a loss, call 1-555-968-5678.*

"I'm betting $1,000,000."

He chuckles with an airy confidence. He says no one ever bets that much here. He says that in order for me to make this bet, it must be approved by a pre-qualifying promotional offer submission or something else—I'm lost in the jargon.

"You have to understand as well," he continues, never breaking a smile or sweat, "that being accepted for this one-time, qualifying offer, you will be contractually obligated to submit a personal artifact if you are not able to meet the minimum monthly payment, or if you are found to be violating any of the terms and conditions heretofore covered in the disclaimers and conditions."

"Artifacts?"

He waves his hands, and another old and decrepit servant in a red tuxedo enters from a darkened corner, marches over to a giant black cabinet between two shiny suits of medieval armor. The servant opens up the black-stained cupboard, pulling out three small and clear boxes. He shows each item to me, each with its own golden label indicating its former owner—

August 14th, 1995 — James Holmes, lost on Widow's Peak to Place, $55,000. Moderate bleeding. Ring included in payment. A thick, black, slightly bent finger, severed at the base, the nail a ghostly white.

April 26th, 1998 — Sharon Tannehill, lost on Hail Over the Mountain to Win, $240,445. Deceased. Blonde. A stitched-together ear, the work of someone unskilled with a blade. A thick silver earring still impaled in its lobe, spattered with dried blood.

June 3rd, 2005 — Alexei Lysander III, lost on Fervor and Glory to Place, $100,001. Hazel Green. An oddly placed eyeball, focused on the ceiling slightly to the right. A blackened, fleshy tail of veins, resting, curled behind it.

"These," he gestures, showcasing, "are high-quality examples of satisfactory artifacts," The smoke from the humidifier continues to blossom into the empty space just behind him. Its milky cloud fades into the scarlet red of a sunset outside the glass wall behind him, where you can see bustling of the track below. He walks around from his side of the desk, placing his hand above my shoulders. "You have beautiful brown eyes." He snaps his fingers, and one of the old waiters runs from the room, followed by what sounds like a bunch of utensils getting shuffled around in a kitchen drawer.

"Do you think this scares me?" I say. Yes, I'm feigning confidence. Yes, I'm fucking terrified. But terror doesn't waver my stubbornness. Who needs bravery when you have the truth on your side?

Another old servant appears next to me, presenting a melon baller. The old man then takes a polaroid camera hanging from a lanyard around his neck, snapping a photo of my eyes, leaving me temporarily blinded from the flash.

The owner mutters again, habitually, still grinning, speaking through his teeth: *"The Froddes Race Track and associated owning companies are not legally responsible or legally liable for any emotional distress, or any physical injury or alterations as a result of transaction disputes."*

"What makes you think I'm not good for the money?"

"Because I know who you are, Private. I already know everything I need to know about you. What you've done. What you wished you'd done. What you have been and will be punished for. All the stories in which you could have been the hero. I know how many people you've killed. I know how many medals you have. How they are less than those that you have been stripped of. I know all I need to know, except for one thing."

"What?"

"Are you left-handed, or right handed?" He offers me

a ball-point pen, and slides a large stack of white papers on his desk. I can barely make out much of the tiny print, besides some obscure lines like *contractual obligation* and *securing of artifact is sanctioned by signee upon the signee's inability to meet the minimum monthly payment, or if signee is found to be violating any of the terms and conditions covered in aforementioned and heretofore mentioned disclaimers and conditions.*

I should have asked the device which part of my body I could live without.

I have a slight indignation towards this bastard. There's a deep urge somewhere—find myself a shotgun and blast his head into pieces. Or myself—I can hardly handle this shame, that he can summarize me so well in so few words. It's worse to realize that I can't correct him on a single word.

"Whatever you want."

***

Win. Madame Harmony. The prophecy of 30-1 odds. Everything I have—$100,000 of my father's money—rests on the hooves of the horse with the worst luck of them all.

Madame Harmony trots out first, wearing red and the number nine. Her trot, smooth and luxurious, shows some confidence. She must know she will win against all odds today, for the first—and likely only—time in her life.

I haven't had any of the popcorn or soda I bought. Let's face it—I'm fucking *stressed,* even though I'm pretty sure Madame Harmony will win. Why would the device be wrong, now?

The horses take their positions. A young teenage girl in a black dress blows her trumpet. The crowd falls silent.

Sweaty and nervous, I begin reading the biography of Madame Harmony:

Color: Chestnut
Bred in: Kentucky
Sire: Macbeth's Dagger
Dam: Lady Macbeth
Owner: Charming Hills Farms. 0 for 8 in races this year.
Jockey: Adam Braun, 0 for 7 this year.
Racing Style: Up front. Could be first to catch out the gate.

I once imagined buying Beaty a chestnut horse. She would always daydream about owning horses on her own farm out in the country, letting them race freely in their large, sprawling landscapes. I dreamt of actual living, waking up to tend to all her horses, chewing on wheat and resting my feet on the fencing of our white porch, her tender hands wrapped around my sunburnt shoulders.

The bell chimes, and the horses are off. Immediately, the announcer begins his nonsensical lyrics of the leading horses. It starts close—every horse neck and neck. No frontrunner, no blowout victory.

My throat sinks—Madame Harmony is dead last, trotting gracefully the same as she did before, her jockey whipping her buttocks repeatedly and shouting, throwing his hands forward to signal her to actually run. She just refuses, happily, and keeps trotting in the back.

My palms are already clammy. My hands are shaking, no longer my own. Before I realize it, I'm up on my feet, shouting god knows what, probably "FUCK ME, GO!" My popcorn and beer spilling all over an old woman to my left. She yelps and begins to shout at me, swinging her purse at me. No matter how many fucks I say, or how loud

I shout, or how much of my hair I am pulling out, Madame Harmony just keeps on trotting in her own lackadaisical way, content in last place.

This is it. if I lose this bet, I lose everything, and then some. Beaty will never get her horse farm. The piano-key necktie man who reminds me of Death will have both of my pathetic and gullible eyes in his fancy display case.

The crowd's cheering halts, followed by the silent echo of a loud crack.

All I can make out is this—at the front of the race, where all the horses are darting blindly and desperately, one of the horses tumbles over the other, followed by an orchestra of horses' legs snapping and cracking, jockeys catapulting off their horses and onto their heads and necks. A tornado of dust from the track swirls into the air, each horse and their rider lost in the fray.

When the dust clears, the horror of it all shows its ugly self. Horses, wildly spitting and writhing in a pile, making every effort in their desperation to get up, but failing and only shattering more bones in their broken legs. Two horses aren't moving, surrounded by a slowly expanding puddle of darkly red blood. The crowd below me murmurs with whimpered cries of horrified disbelief. The announcer ceases his narrative gibberish, and simply leaves with a breathless and reverberating "Oh my God," then knocking over his microphone, causing the entire stadium to erupt in a screeching howl of feedback.

Madame Harmony trots by. Her jockey already abandoned her to tend to the others, but she keeps on going, not resolute on winning, by prancing her way blithely, not a care in the world.

She is the first, and only horse, to pass the finish line.

Chapter Twenty
Et tu, Oedipus?

P eter gently settled his hand on his father's hollow head, blurred white eyes swirling in wild saccades, gasping for air. Peter, on the verge of hyperventilating, felt helpless—but at ease, believing this would finally be the end of his torment.

But, eventually, as it always tends to go, his father's breathing settled. He eventually fell into a thin yet peaceful slumber. He began to chant:

"My notes? Where are my notes? I need my notes. They prove everything. They prove it all. The world has to see it. The world has to know."

"What notes, Dad? What did they say?"

"My memories. Reality A. My notes. Reality B. They're in Reality B." He kept chanting this over and over. "My memories. Reality A. My notes. Reality B. They're in Reality B."

"They're gone, Dad," Peter sighed. "They've been gone for years."

"No, they're not gone, you fucking imbecile. They're right here somewhere. Your brother. Your brother. Where is your brother?"

He checked William's sloppily written journal of their father's morphine treatments. The nurses had told them they could help with his pain by giving a little morphine,

but not more than 5 mL or so every four hours. They had
to give it to him orally, since needles had been challenging
lately.

He could not read William's careless handwriting,
where sevens looked just like fours, and eights looked like
they were written by a drunk.

Outside on the windowsill, a small wren fluttered up
and began piercing the powder blue eggs gently nestled
among the wooden scraps and crumpled straw wraps of its
hodgepodge nest.

Peter tried to think about the many times he had something important to say to his father, but lacked either the
words or the gall to say it. He knew he would have to speak
these words soon enough. After all, how much longer
could his father go on *like this?*

"You cannot have a child." His father ached to get that
out, turning his head to the side, away from Peter.

"Dad?" No use asking; delirium breeds some awful
poetry of nonsense. His father hadn't made a lick of sense
since...ever.

He held his father's hand. Instantly, in the tiny theater
of his mind, he went back in time, and lost a few feet in
height, and saw himself—but a kid version of himself,
with his giant adult head—reaching up for his dad's hand
before they crossed the street downtown; dad towered over
him then, so much that everything above his shoulders was
obscured in the dark storm clouds. Feeling that warmth,
the coarseness of his calloused fingers—it all evoked ease
and direction. Like the whole world made sense, and
someone else would always pull you along when you were
lost.

"Dad, do you remember how you used to always hold
my hand when we crossed the street?"

Silence.

"Dad, I have something I have to tell you."

Silence.

"Dad, do you remember that time you stepped on my porcupine?"

That feeling depreciated, starkly and abruptly shut away by another scene of Peter, this time slightly older, slightly taller, and slightly dumber. He knew dad had just arrived back at home. He wanted to show off his latest project from preschool—a purple mound of misshapen clay, a clumsy attempt at a porcupine, with toothpicks for quills. He knew dad would go upstairs, like he always would. So he left it on the second to last step. So his dad couldn't miss it in on his way up. So he could clearly see the hard work that Peter put into that porcupine. And he would be proud.

And his dad sure didn't miss it. He stepped right on top of it.

Half an hour later, Peter snuck out of his room, trying to hush his own crying. He found dad, sitting on the edge of the bed, pulling toothpicks from the soles of his left foot. "I'm sorry, dad."

Peter told this part of the story so many countless and forgettable times. What his father said. "I'm not mad, Peter. I'm just disappointed." But is that what he actually said? Didn't he say the same thing when he made Peter eat a bar of soap as punishment? Or was that for the time he called dad a fucktwad?

"You remember what you said? You said you were disappointed, right? What did you mean by 'disappointed' anyway?"

Silence.

"I'm sorry, dad."

Now, fast-forwarding like his father's old cassette home videos of places he'd visited, from Naples to Rio de Janeiro, always a hand wrapped around a young and naive girl's waist. All the way up to some crescendo of adolescence, where it became Peter's sole duty to watch over the dull-witted exploits of his younger brother William. What did he go and do this time? Gone and got his giant melon head stuck in between the bars of his metal bed frame. Said he was looking for monsters. William screamed like he was dying. His father, shouting at William to calm down, tried desperately to bend those metal bars. Peter figured he should grab the porcelain Jesus off the wall and pray for William's head to become unstuck, because God would always help the less fortunate.

"Do you remember when William got his head stuck under the bed? Do you remember that day, Dad?"

That was the day he lost his faith in God.

"Dad, I think….I know...I might be…"

Peter bent over, head in hands. He couldn't bear to hold this immeasurable weight of lying anymore, but again, he found himself lacking in the very words he wanted to say to his father—that, this whole time, it's all been a disguise, and *you, you, dad, are the reason the mask sears my flesh.*

His father reached up towards Peter, his still calloused fingers curled under the weight of their own being.

"What is it? What do you need now?" Peter asked, sobbing.

This was the seventh time in his life he had a panic attack.

"You should be ashamed." His father groaned, dryly.

"What?"

"You should be ashamed of yourself, Peter."

His panic attack suddenly halted, drowned by a dosage of adrenaline and angst. "Ashamed? Did you say you were ashamed?"

"You should be ashamed of yourself, Peter, is what I said."

Peter scoffed. Must be the delirium again. Must be. How could he know the truth?

Peter walked out of the room while his father carried on with more nonsensical rumblings. "Ashamed, I said. I'm not disappointed. I'm ashamed. Did you hear me, Peter? Did you listen to what I said? Out there, as plain as day. Why would you do such a thing? Why would you do that to me? Leave it right there, for me to step on. Do you know how much this stings?"

***

Peter allowed his father ten minutes or so of rambling, which transitioned slowly into the organ-like groans of his begging for help with the pain. His panic attack managed to go away with some dedicated pacing and only small amounts of scalp-pulling.

But, in between his father's pleas for help, he heard him clearly—"Oh God, Peter, Oh God...I'm ashamed…"

Peter choked on another attack erupting from a place long ago superseded by the daily distractions of adult-hood; a panic like he's never felt before, like he was honestly about to die.

But did he actually say, "I'm ashamed?" Or did Peter hear it wrong? Did he actually say, "I'm in pain?" Was Peter once again projecting his worst fears onto this fading picture of his father's mundane and ordinary wasting-away?

"Dad? Does it hurt? Do you need more morphine?"

He said nothing, but just slowly turned his face toward Peter, the pale hollows of his eyes staring blankly, his brow furrowed in the shape of what must have been either severe discomfort or shameful disapproval. He seemed like he was gasping for air.

256

Peter, in his panic, took a plastic syringe nearby and hastily filled it up with morphine.

In his panic, he forced open his dad's frail jaw, trying desperately not to break something. Horrified again by the sight of his father's yellowed and crooked teeth, suffering from ages of coffee, cigarettes, and god knows what else.

In his frustrated panic, he squirted the morphine for what must have been the hundredth time down his father's throat. Afterwards, he let go of his stiff jaw, and it didn't budge; his father lay still, slack jawed, staring without any clear intent into the fraying depths of Peter's disguise. His father's breathing slowed down, almost in harmony with the whirrs and purrs of the oxygen machine.

His father was dead an hour later.

***

Later that night, he lay next to Ada, knowing full well that his father's dead and lifeless corpse still sat in the bed, since they likely wouldn't carry him out in a black body bag until the middle of the night or early morning, so no one would see. What did it matter to leave him there? He wouldn't have any visitors—only his sons ever came to see him (barely, for what it's worth).

Then he had his eighth of his ten allotted panic attacks. This time, it happened in the middle of the night. Again, he clutched his pillow, almost tearing it apart. Ada, half asleep, rolled over and put her arm around his waist, mumbling drearily, "It's going to be okay." Peter sat up, cross-legged, pillow tight against his chest, rocking back and forth, grimacing, weeping mournfully and uncontrollably.

In his panic, he thought clearly and unequivocally—

I gave him too much.

After his panic subsided, he couldn't sleep—after all, when he tried desperately to close his eyes, he could only picture a massive, rocket-sized syringe, getting filled to the brim, ready to burst.

Chapter Twenty-One
Some Stuff from Not That Long Ago

What did Beaty say to me, on the afternoon we divorced? My memory has been subverted, a coup de gras by illusions of grandeur, imagining something more theatrical, like in the movies we imagine of ourselves, just to give our fleeting lives some weight. "I hope we never see each other again." Did she use the word "never"? Was it omitted entirely? Or half admitted by a tone of passive-aggression?

She didn't say "again." It sounded awfully similar. A word weighted disproportionately with an amicable lack of value. What rhymes with "again" but reminds you of feigned friendliness? Sven. When. Benz. Amends. Amends... "I hope we can make amends."

Amy picked at her scrambled eggs and chorizo. The date so far had been uneventful, and frankly boring. Neither of us had said anything since I said how beautiful Beaty's voice was in the morning when we used to wake up together.

The schoolhouse chalkboard had drawings of dogs
with pointy ears and sharp teeth chasing M shaped

birds, followed by a cloud of erased chalk, leaving behind remnants of a math problem and some words in a language none of them could understand. In the middle, one of them drew a large stick figure hanging from a noose.

They winced every time they took a drink, and winced every time one of them shot at the stick figure for target practice, a harmless means to pass some time before they had to report again to the assholes in upper command. But they had drank so much they barely hit the target—except for William, who, after missing two times, by some miracle of grace, hit the stick figure man dead in the forehead, prompting his only true friend in all of that nonsense to rush over, to slowly and carefully drag the chalk across the board, to draw two large Xes for the man's eyes.

They had torn down the flag and set it on fire. Only burnt red and green fragments remained.

They had thrown the remains of desks at the wall to watch them shatter. They had nowhere else to go and nothing left to do.

Jonathan One shouted something in his drunken babble that sounded like "I left my lucky pants at home."

Kirby stood at the head of the classroom, kicking aside rubble from the ceiling, pretending to be the teacher and shouting at them to "Carry the four! Carry the four!" while spraying his piss all over the floor.

William sat at a desk with his head full of cotton, the world spinning.

Dale sat in the row next to William, playing gambit with a pencil and his right hand, stabbing between his fingers as fast as he could until the tip of the pencil shattered from the sheer force.

Jonathan Two carved a name in the wall, trying to spell out "Big Dick Gabe" but it came out something like "Bing Dib Job" before he fell over.

They laughed at the textbooks much, much older than the ones they had in high school, and smashed the desks against the wall in their jubilant, untimely celebration over nothing. Aaron had skipped five songs, but settled on Springsteen's "Secret Garden," a song William hadn't heard in ages, and made him fond of the girls he would daydream about in school.

"Friends." "I hope we can be friends." I am very confident that what she had said used the word "hope," because she always said that before everything. "I hope you haven't forgotten." "I hope they still have that one casserole on sale." "I hope it isn't cancer." "I hope we can still be friends, still." There has to be a comma there somewhere because that pause had some immense meaning. "I hope we can be friends...still." Or would a dash be better? "I hope we can be friends—still..." Did something come after that?

"Do you like your toast?" Amy's bright blue eyes and her quirky, off-set smile robbed me of an appropriate verbal response, leaving me guilty for having dragged her on this hopeless exercise. I tried to nod but choked on the moist bread ball sliding down my gullet, trying my best not to cough it all over her young and intelligent face.

They drank to forget the point. They shot to remove their frustration quieted by formalities of war, the rigidity of the uniform that shaved their heads and humiliated them and destroyed their souls so nothing besides a body would remain after they were shot dead in the middle of a street by a name they could not pronounce, their only valuable remaining—their name,

261

good or rotten—to be sent home to their families (with their bodies, if they were still intact). A makeshift grenade ripped Gabriel's body to shreds. William stood in shock when he saw his entire midsection and legs burst, leaving behind a red cloud of blood that slowly faded behind a billowing cloud of smoke and dust. They cheered in his honor, but actually drank to help themselves forget and move on. They were selfish, petrified, and alone, even with each other. William shot twice again, missing the man wildly. He felt ashamed that he couldn't live up to their risen expectations of him. The others had yet to hit their mark, and blamed it amicably on the booze.

"It hasn't." She didn't say "I hope," which is strange. The vividness of that phrase, having heard it countless times over a decade, is a blight on my memory. "It hasn't been the same since..." The word "still" fits in somewhere. "Still, it hasn't been the same since..." No, that's an odd way to begin a sentence. This was the first thing either of us said. She said it to me after staring at me in the lawyer's humdrum office with the popcorn ceiling, miles away from me. She wore her guilt on her sleeve. How much she felt my pain at that moment. No matter how much I tried to hide it all. She said it when I tried to get out. She turned and grabbed my arm to stop me. This means she was trying to explain herself. Which means, she cared about how I felt. "It never was the same." She did use "never." Now I'm confident it was "never". "It never was the same since..."

I should have grabbed the check, but I shamefully pretended not to see it, even though I wanted to pay, since I felt awful for wasting her time. Amy sighed deeply—and she wanted me to hear it clearly. She picked it up, and said with a fake chuckle, "I'll get this." Why didn't you grab the check like you meant to? You sad, pathetic nincompoop?

Their gunshots were silenced by what half of them thought was the wailing of a ghost. With eyes wide open in a humorous fright, they laughed it off—until it came back, louder. "Day! Day! Day!" The ghost wailed, echoing throughout the halls and the crumbling walls of the school. William, holding the pistol, raised it to his collarbone, and stumbled to the hallway. The ghost's cries became louder—it was close.

They were in room 191. The cries came from 193. Right next door. William walked in, and saw the ghosts that would haunt him forever.

"It never was." "It will never be the same again." "It never was the same since..." She didn't say "It." But she didn't say "I hope." She said "I." "I never was the same since." She was explaining herself, putting all the blame on her, because she didn't want me to feel like I was the culprit behind our downward spiral. Even though it was all my fault, and not hers, because she went on to have children with Shawn, or Steve, whatever his stupid name is. Because I couldn't give her what she wanted. I gave her everything that I had left; she left with everything, except the paper-thin, heartless shell of William Burroughs, still pining and wishing to this very day that she would realize her mistake and take me back, because I can't seem to find a path forward without her, and everything left in my life seems worthless without her, and the only times I feel more than a nobody is when I am with her. She didn't feel the same way, I guess. But maybe someday she will.

The little girl, her hair caked in dust, continued to wail away. She tugged at the stiff arm of her lifeless mother, her corpse still resting in the desk in the front row. A bullet had come through the wall and pierced her heart. She must have died instantly, since her face, frozen, lifeless, captured an instance of resolute despair for the infant child in her arms, right below her bare left breast. Its head was half gone.

The others stood behind him, and they all, instantaneously, understood the gravity of it all.

One of them had done it, and they would never know who, and would live the rest of their lives plagued by the guilt that may have not been their burden to carry.

It was my punishment. My atonement. The universe sets things straight. Taking from me the woman I love and the child I would never be allowed to carry.

Amy paid and left me alone to stew in my thoughts.

They stood in silence, and lied to themselves about who made the shot. The little girl didn't care that they were there. She had just lost her baby brother, her loving mother. All of them hiding from the chaos that these strange American men had arrived to cause. Springsteen's final verses ended, leaving suspended echoes of a saxophone roaring cacophonously throughout the halls of the abandoned school.

"I was never the same since the stillbirth."

Chapter Twenty-Two
Observations in Death's Waiting Room

Dr. Weather, who has the tattoo of a unicorn on his collarbone, and is not embarrassed by it. Who once tried to seduce you a few years ago, but must've been stealing morphine from his patients again.

Remember Dr. Weather's sage advice: count your thoughts. Pack them together. Organize them in the filing cabinet in your head. File this one under family. What am I thinking about next?

Dr. Weather says make a list of your surroundings. File this one under Observations.

- I am in a hospital room.
- The ceiling is perforated. Mostly white, with a water stain on one corner near the window, which is to my right.
  - Someone I knew would call the perforations popcorn, because they would pop off and fall if you wiped your palm across them.

- My left hand is dancing again. I have control of my arm right now, and I can *feel* my possession of my hand, but I do not *have* possession of my hand.
- My gown is pale blue. I can see my left boob. I'm pulling the paper thin covers over myself, up to my collarbone.
  - The blanket feels ephemeral.
- A man is gasping for air across from me in his bed.
  - His bed is closer to the window than mine.
  - I can see his calloused feet— his left foot is pointing straight up, and the right is angled.
  - There is a foggy glass of water next to him, on top of the air conditioning unit.
  - There are bandages wrapped around his head, covering his eyes. Two puddles of blood where his eyes should be. He looks like a macabre superhero.
- The room smells like wet paint.
  - My right hand grips my left wrist and wrestles with the other hand.
- The man's cheeks are hollow.
  - His face is gaunt and ghostish.
  - His nose is split across the middle and riddled with dry blood.
  - His lips are split in three places, with stitches sown in two.
    - The third's stitches have busted.

o He looks like he's having a nightmare, hyperventilating helplessly.

▪ My dancing left hand leaps up and mercilessly pushes on the call button. It buzzes incessantly.

● There are bluebirds fluttering outside the window with alluring calls full of spring and rebirth.

o I can't see the birds directly. I only see the blue visage of their shadows beyond the pall of the thin, ribboned window drapes.

o I hear a rhythmic beeping somewhere in this room.

● A nurse, exhausted, bursts into the room with one hand gripping the stethoscope wrapped around her neck, the other hand stuffing her Marlboro Reds into her scrubs. She's looking right. At. Me.

● She says, "What can I do to help you, Mary-Belle?" Her name is Bethany. I've known her for years. She's seen many people die. Three months ago I started to believe she lost faith in my strength and will to live, but she's far too stoic to show it.

● I feel my head jut forward, gesturing toward the man across from me. Bethany flips around and gasps. She whips her stethoscope off her neck, pressing it against his chest.

o "Wake up, William! You're having another nightmare! Wake up!"

- ▪ She claps her hands over and over.
  - ● She takes his hand (that has three fingers wrapped in a camo-colored cast) and dips his pinky and ring fingers (the only two exposed) into the glass of water.
  - ● He bursts awake.
    - ○ The glass flips into the air and covers Bethany.
      - ▪ She gasps and almost topples out of the window.
    - ○ William is gasping for air, like some great monster had been choking him incessantly.
      - ▪ …

This is my William. William who walks funny. William who ruminates with me on the rooftops. William who shares a dream of seeing the ocean one more time. William who used to confiscate medication for my phantom pains and my real pains. William who blamed himself for my son's addiction. William, who is my dear friend.

But he is not the same William that I've grown to accept as my quiet and humble neighbor. He has transformed. The bloodied puddles that are now his eyes, they are wearing a wearied and exhausted anxiety, like the world has fallen over him. His cheeks have sunken inward. His skin is pale, like clay. He looks like he has been dying for quite some time.

I am floored by this sudden nostalgia for a good neighborly love and its accompanying splendor.

But that nostalgia is shattered by something different, something fresh, but uninviting—some kind of sick sympathy for what is ailing him. I don't like many people. But I've always liked William.

Chapter Twenty-Three
♫ "I can see clearly now…" ♫♫

It has been five days, from what I've been told by the nurse. Her name is Bethany.

The light in my world has literally gone black. I can still *feel* myself here—I cannot ignore how subtly the needle in my arm shifts every time I move. The sensation is a thousand times worse than actually seeing it. In fact, not seeing it—but only *feeling it*—magnifies the numb, creeping revulsion burning under my skin. That, and the rhythmic beeps of medical machines around me. And the cacophonic footsteps that amplify in the evening and then recede in the morning. And those fucking birds that will not shut up. And the person across from me always mumbling to herself all throughout the night about Jamie this and bastards that.

The truth is, the world around me feels like a pool of lukewarm water. I'm just there, lying, floating, greeted by an occasional feeling (a burst of wind, a nasty spill of glass, stale burnt vegetable oil), disruptions that would rise and shake the surface; islands that I would bump into, reminding me that I am not alone out here. That my world is still here, even if 1/5th of it is now missing forever.

Footsteps click and approach me. *Hopefully not the men in suits coming to finish me off for good. Hopefully not the muddy hooves of Belial, here to finally escort me to my subway bench in hell.*

"Good morning, Mr. Burroughs. How's your pain? Manageable?"

This is Bethany's voice, familiar as it is tired, but still caring, smoker's breath, and always lisping a little on the *s*'s.

It's a struggle at first. But I manage to feel around the nightstand next to me for my belongings. I feel a thud and hear glass shatter. The wood is wet. Here's a mound of frayed leather—my wallet. Nothing left inside (of course). This blind grasping reminds me of many nights waking up amidst a pitch black darkness, fumbling around in my waking for daylight or a streetlight to see if I managed to sleep longer than the night prior.

Here it is. They didn't take it away from me. The truth-telling machine is still *mine.*

But, *oh the sweet irony.*

"How did this happen to me?" I say this out loud, now by force of habit.

Knowing I can't read the answer makes me feel a bit better. This weighty truth of consequences will be my mysterious burden to carry, until the day I die—but, god-damnit, it is *mine, my burden,* and not some arbitrary whimsy of fateful disaster.

Then there's a voice, robotic, dull, matter-of-fact, and surreal:

```
They used a melon baller to scoop
         your eyeballs out
```

I couldn't believe it at first. By instinct my wrist shoots upwards to check on the time, seeing how much time has passed since I took my medication. Because it has never *spoken* before. So certainly this is just the misfiring of my wires again, making me hear things that aren't really there.

Because I truly do know that something has been wrong with me. The truth is, I have been able to tell most—*most*—of these hallucinations from the real thing. Like watching a movie of your own life and pointing out all those things that are obviously fake, CGI, movie-magic—and just not really there at all. Even though, over time, they start to look more and more like the real thing, until you find that one movie where you can swear you felt like you were really *there.*

But that doesn't stop me from clarifying.

"*Why* did this happen to me?"

```
    It is an integral turning point in
    the novel where a protagonist is
transformed and must overcome a burden
          to prove his value
```

"The novel?"

```
    You are one of the protagonists in
      a novel called The Truth Box
```

Just a character in a novel? A make-believe world? (With such a crappy title?) Nonsense. Unbelievable. Of course the world is real. It has to be. I can see it...with my own two fucking eyes...what a sick fucking joke.

"None of this is real?"

No

"Is this novel any good?"

Not really

"Well, how does it end?"

Your death

There are hard pills to swallow in life—but none greater than realizing your life isn't really your own.
"Can you read it to me, word-for-word?"

TEXT EXCISED[4]

Time has slipped away, and what must've been countless hours felt like nothing. I kept phasing in and out (either heavy medication or loss of self), but I am totally conscious now, fully aware, and hollow, and enraged— and I wasn't sure why—but the last line I hear is this:

They lowered William into the embracing bosom of the earth, forever.

---

[4] Reporting agent note: this section of the report has been omitted to avoid infinite recursion—the novel's entire text would be iterated verbatim, in its entirety; and within that iteration, the same novel would be iterated verbatim, in its entirety, ad infinitum. Considering the limitations of the physical universe and recent budget cuts, we simply cannot produce the amount of digital space or paper to keep this on record (let alone afford it). This reporting agent has thus decided to omit this infinite recursion.

I guess it's all just a little too much to handle. Device grasped in my hands like a baseball. Throw my legs to my left. The needle in my arm pops out. I stumble towards the sounds of those god damn birds that never stop chirping in the morning. Make sure the window is open, pressing my hand forward (wide open, beckoning one of us doomed souls to jump).

I've thrown it, as hard as I possibly could. And I'm suddenly swept over with a freeing guilt. Like I've taken my first deep breath in a long while, and released all the toxic air from my lungs—and I just feel simply free.

Until I realize that the truth-telling machine said I was *the protagonist* of the novel, and I feel an awfully foreign sense of pride.

Chapter Twenty-Four
The Odyssey

Meanwhile, after William had finally gotten the courage to toss the apparatus out the window, an awkwardly large and gangly man named Richard Walstock had just begun his exit through the revolving hospital doors for the third time in three years, having had what the neurologist had determined to be a miracle case of three near-fatal seizures in succession, with Richard walking out the door on his own large two feet as if nothing ever happened. Richard simply did not have time to die.

He had been "gifted" the reins of his father's dying beer nut empire at an early age, an age way too young to have any good business sense, let alone a desire to figure out how to turn things around and save the floundering company. His father died of a heart attack after learning that their fiercest beer nut competitor, Tommy's Beer Nuts, had recently acquired exclusive distribution rights to three of the most sought-after beer nut festivals in the Midwest. During the past few years of his stewardship, Richard sweated nightly over the ever-looming threat of severe financial losses and lack of substantial profit. The company could barely afford to keep the lights on, let alone provide a living income to the thousands of folks employed by Walstock Nuts. Many would lose their homes and livelihoods if he couldn't find a way to correct course. But Richard wasn't quite motivated by altruism. Instead, he was deeply motivated to show his dead father that he could save the family business. It also didn't help that he happened to be severely allergic to nuts, so he could go nowhere near the business—a captain who couldn't board his own ship.

But fortune fell on him that day. William's desperate and transformative throw traveled just far enough to hit Richard square in the back of his large, balding head, just moments after he left the hospital. Richard toppled over, unconscious for a few moments. There was no one around to attend to him, but he woke up, practically unharmed.

Now, Richard may have lacked the "business" gene, but he was far from a complete idiot. He could recognize fortune as much as he did misfortune. When he saw the object that hit him, he reasoned that an angel had dropped this on him purposefully. And it didn't take him that long to discover its true power—that very evening, resting next to him on his nightstand, it lit up with its answer when he crossed his heart and prayed:

"Please, Lord, tell me—how can I beat Tommy's Beer Nuts?"

The apparatus lit up and revealed its prophecy:

```
Tell the world about the Tommy family's
                secret
```

Richard picked up and examined the device for quite some time. Despite a healthy sense of disbelief and skepticism, Richard followed up with this, inquisitively: "What is the Tommy family's secret?"

```
Their nuts are harvested from
    Brazilian slave labor
```

After a typical session of back-and-forth questions (to confirm that this was not a trick), Richard again leaped in reasoning that this strange device was entirely accurate in its soothsaying, thus firmly confirming his angel theory. He promptly thanked the lord for blessing him. Then, he refused his body the luxury of sleep and proceeded to find out more and more about the Tommy family's supposed secret—a deeply rooted involvement in "slave labor."

The foundation of Tommy Family's beer nut business model relied on a public persona of a perfectly successful American dream family—wholesome, natural, packed in the United States. Richard knew immediately that a careful and strategic plan-of-attack could open this secret to the world, sealing the fate of his only major competitor and leaving the lucrative beer nut market cracked open for him—that'll show his father, for sure (may he rest in peace).

However, Richard suffered as much from a deficit of tactical sense as he did business sense. Rather than carefully leaking this information to established writers in beer nut aficionado magazines and prominent agricultural news outlets online (to make the news seem more credible), he instead made himself the face of this ugly truth, posting a twenty minute diatribe video online, detailing Tommy's Beer Nuts' integral involvement in perpetuating a deadly market of slave labor in the peanut harvesting trade in Brazil. He hoped his video would catch fire and spread like he'd seen so many other viral videos do.

Naturally, thanks to the nature of information spread on the internet, his video did catch fire. Local news outlets began snipping parts out for their reports, and Richard was suddenly overwhelmed with requests to appear live to discuss how he came across this information, and how it wasn't just vilification for the sake of eliminating a business competitor.

Richard did not anticipate the result of his actions. Once the news broke about the once publicly adored and respected Tommy's Beer Nuts, professional investigative journalists and amateur truth-seekers online unraveled a much more sickly and lengthy web connecting hundreds of other family-owned-and-operated companies—and not just nuts, but furniture outlets, fresh produce markets, pharmacies, outlet stores, beauty supply chains, and even pet supply stores. All of these businesses happened to rely on the cheap production of deadly slave labor markets across the world. Once the news broke, some companies managed to stay afloat thanks to diligent public relations campaigns. Most other companies then collapsed, unable to recover financially from the moral deficit that eroded its customer base and public image. Over one-hundred high ranking CEOs went into hiding in their private villas overseas. Exactly ten of them killed themselves. Hundreds of thousands of people would end up out of a job within the span of a year, leading to numerous evictions, divorces, suicides, desperate robberies, and so much more. The stock market stumbled and almost crashed.

Richard Walstock witnessed none of this. Right after his first television appearance, Wilbur Thomas—Tommy Thomas' son and face of the company—hired someone to kill Richard Walstock in a vain attempt to save the family business and preserve the family name. Richard was found dead in his apartment, having misread the allergen label on a jar of super fudge chunk ice cream (it read: *contains nuts*). The medical examiners investigating the death did not second guess the massive amount of ice cream caking the inside of Richard's mouth, almost as if it was forced in there. They overlooked the deep scrapes along the roof of his mouth, and didn't even notice his broken front teeth. It turned out the neurologist's observation was true—it was a miracle that he survived three seizures, but no act of God could save Richard from a fourth.

***

The man that Wilbur Thomas hired to take care of Richard Walstock had immense pride in his work. As was his ritual, he would take home mementos from his victim's homes when given the chance. Of course, these had to be low-profile belongings, nothing that anyone would suspect had been stolen, nothing whose absence would evolve an accident into a crime scene. So, naturally, he thought, why not take this odd-looking lamp head that his mark had buried in the closet?

This man, named Ahmed Reburs, also happened to be deeply obsessed with the dangers of gambling—not the sorts you find in the ostentatious strips along the Las Vegas strip, but the kind you would believe only existed in movies—seedy basements of unknown origin, out in the ether beyond normal and moral society, where lives were traded, and chance involved brushes with lost limbs and the smoky stench of death. The kind where men would take turns pulling molars with pliers until the other stopped; where Russian roulette had an audience equivalent to craps; where desperate men traveled to bet more than they could afford on horse races and football games, knowing full well a loss would mean giving up much more than cold hard cash.

Now, Ahmed did not quite understand what drew him to these places where people bet thousands of dollars on gruesome dismemberments. But, if you asked the apparatus, it would tell you that Ahmed secretly wanted to die. Somehow, twenty years of contracted murder started to weigh on this ex-marine who had been in a staring contest

279

with death since he was eighteen. But Ahmed's upbringing and training refused to let him show his face cards to
the world (or, God forbid, himself). So he continued his
life in denial, and he chose to frequent these underground
casinos to maintain a consistent bluff inward and outward—that he was no pussy, not afraid of death (but
please, oh God, let me die tonight! he would beg).

But all that nonsense changed soon enough. He found
out that same night he shoveled pistachio ice cream down
Richard Walstock's throat that the night-lamp-head he
took as a memento was much more than a memento.

He discovered this on his drive back home, cruising
along a midnight road, singing along to The Culture Club,
giving his absolute best effort when the chorus sang (*"do
you really want to hurt me..."*) His instinct caught a bluish
glow from his back seat. The aura flashed in his rear view
mirror, and instantly he believed two possible explanations: either an angel had appeared in his back seat or he
was about to be pummeled by an oncoming semi-truck.

After he pulled over to investigate, he had to pause
himself. For a moment, he felt close to his long-awaited
death, clutching his chest as if his heart was failing him
from the sudden fright. But, gathering up enough falsely
masculine denial, he bravely turned to see what caused the
flash.

When he found out the apparatus, it was still glowing,
and it said this:

```
I cannot hurt you I am an inanimate
              object
```

The song kept playing (*"do you really want to make
me cry"*):

The first thing Ahmed could intuitively mutter was this: "What kind of fucking genie shit is this?" Which, considering its power, was not too far from the truth.

Ahmed then asked a few standard trial questions ("What was my first sergeant's name, what was the name of the first man I killed, how many quarters are in my pocket"). He realized that the genie was in fact real; and while he couldn't wish for whatever he wanted, he suddenly had the power to *know* whatever he wanted.

And, after an evening spent contemplating more than he had in a while, liquored and bewildered with thoughts that hadn't crossed his mind since adolescence, he stumbled upon the one question he truly wanted to ask:

"When am I going to die?"

Tomorrow.

At first, Ahmed's disbelief and logic outweighed the surreal and dehumanizing report. In fact, the monotony of that statement gutted him more than a precisely scheduled death. After all, most people fantasize and daydream of some majestic way of kicking the bucket. And, Ahmed knew from watching the same happen to his two aunts, his uncle, his father, and his brother. Beyond getting ceremoniously dismembered in the line of duty, most people's stories end in a slow and mundane fading-away, cheeks caving in, ghostly cataracts eating up the last bits of the soul, hopelessly adrift in hospital beds.

But, despite his disbelief, Ahmed toyed with the idea of humoring fate even further—if this device were telling

the truth, he could ask *how* he would die, and do everything he could to prevent it. After all, that was the smart
thing to do, despite the natural assumption of a predestined
and unmalleable future—an unconscious belief that our
narratives have meaning, from birth until death, especially
after.

And, the sudden expediency of his untimely demise
made him reconsider some of his priorities—the family he
had shut away for years, for instance. His wife, Allison,
and their son, Salman, living light-years away across the
country; his mother, Zaara, shuttered away in a nursing
home and starving from lonely dementia. The people he
had told himself he had abandoned to keep them safe—
after all, an occupation in hired murder hardly breeds the
most amicable relationships. He used to have a native urge
to care for his family, but this urge always lost in combat
with his trained instinct to follow orders, his penchant for
destroying lives without remorse. But that didn't mean he
still daydreamed, once in a while.

But that was all before Ahmed began to feel his own
mortality. Knowing exactly—not approximately, but *exactly*—when you will die is a luxury granted to a select
few. It's a feeling unlike those futile moments when you
die so suddenly from an oncoming vehicle or a sudden
heart attack. Instead, knowing death is coming soon, your
flesh truly begins to feel like flesh, and you can hear your
eyes moving in your sockets; the sullen weight of life's
responsibilities and tribulations feels effortless, and you
become more aware of the self-righting sensation of stepping on solid concrete or grass.

Struggling to come to terms with this expiration date,
Ahmed had a change of heart. He no longer wanted to die.

So he decided to do whatever he could to preserve his
own life. (This was a strange feeling, after all. He was an

expert at murdering others, but an amateur at self-preservation). He realized how many sharp blades he had in his drawers, how often he accidentally left the oven burners on while he lit a cigarette, how thin his window panes were above twelve stories of a fateful fall, how his door was held shut by a flimsy bolt lock that any vengeful spirit could burst open to avenge the hundreds of lives he'd taken.

His first order of business: asking the apparatus as many questions as possible to deduce how and where he would die.

"How will I die?"

```
Subarachnoid hemorrhage as a result of
          a traumatic head injury
```

"What will cause the injury?"

```
            A flying pig
```

Flabbergasted, doubtful, but determined, he continued. "What do you mean, a flying pig?"

```
A large mammal, also called a swine or
      hog, that is airborne for an
      indeterminate amount of time
```

"Where will I die?"

```
Colloquially the corner of 45th and
      Lysander Ave., geographically
longitude REDACTED, latitude REDACTED⁵
```

---

[5] Coordinates redacted to avoid further investigations and litigation.

Ahmed wasn't willing to go without a fight. He could cheat it and disprove the writing on the wall. After all, he was a human being. It was just a machine.

After learning about the exact coordinates, he began to drive in the exact opposite direction, aiming to get as far as possible from the supposed location of his death.

He stopped at a gas station to fill up, purchasing a backpack's worth of provisions to last him a few days—saltine crackers, apples, jerky, and water.

As his gas tank filled up, he continued to inquire about his demise:

"Where does the pig come from?"

```
A large transport vehicle designed to
carry livestock from neighboring farms
  for sales, relocation, reproduction,
            slaughter, etc.
```

"What causes me to be standing at the corner of 45th and Lysander?"

```
You arrive there carried by ambulance
```

"Why will I be in an ambulance?"

```
        carbon monoxide poisoning
```

Suddenly, he realized that he was sitting in a mechanical combustion machine filling up with gasoline. He then desperately abandoned his car, stealing a bicycle that was propped up against the wall of the gas station. He continued to ride this bicycle away from the coordinates, carrying his backpack of provisions and the device stored in the front pocket.

As he rode, he passed a group of kids lighting illegal fireworks and dropping them down manhole covers. The subtle explosions summoned distant memories of his time of service, but these memories dissipated quickly, overshadowed by the now tenacious trepidation of death.

Eventually, his legs gave out, and he retired to the closest sanctuary he could find—a seedy, run-down motel with a neon-sign that was only half-working, its rooms all apparently "VACA."

He spent three hours in bed, entirely awake, asking further and further questions to delineate his demise. He asked what would cause the pig to fly (`the collapse of a crane carrying a two-ton HVAC unit`), where the HVAC unit was located (`45th and Lysander` again, `at a construction site for a new outlet shopping mall`), and he even asked exactly how he would get carbon monoxide poisoning (`underground explosions that caused toxic gas leaks to spread throughout the area`).

Eventually, his death began to seem so formulaic and scripted. So, his mind wandered; he began contemplating other, more interesting facets of his life: Salman's hazel eyes and tiny fingers, how Allison's chuckle always made him smile, the buried guilt of abandoning his sick mother, how the world turned black and white when his father died—how he had promised himself the day he was born that he would be just as good a father to Salman as his own father was to him.

As he ruminated on his life, Ahmed lost sight of his goal. Instead of doing more to cheat the Angel of Death, he instead drifted off into a deep, unfamiliar slumber. He began to dream; more specifically, he dreamt what he would do first, the day after he cheated his prophesied death:

...clothes drenched in sweat. Maybe they wouldn't even be home. He pulls up to their ranch home, funded just enough by his executions; his murders helped pay the bills, repaired the roof (mostly), and kept the lawn cut clean enough for Salman's toys to be scattered about the grass. The wooden porch creaks when he steps. When he opens the screen door to knock, a wave of baked cinnamon erupts, sending him back to foggy memories of his mother, baking in the kitchen.

Allison answers a few moments later. to Ahmed, she hasn't changed at all—her hazel eyes with so much gravity, the gentle curvature of her cheeks, her dry and cracked lips—but not her smile. That isn't there.

He doesn't have the courage to look at her when he apologizes for abandoning them. This close to death, he loses all initiative to hide his wrongdoings—he confesses to her, on that porch, his dastardly deeds, the not-so-good people he had contractually been obligated to murder, the simultaneous rush and empty feeling after the contract had been fulfilled. He confesses how he had lied to himself all this time—that all the money he made from killing would fund Allison and Salman for years and years. He has willfully ignored the real truth—that this penance is a facade covering his conditioned desire to kill.

She asks what he wants—what his intentions are. He tells her a half truth, that he is worried something will happen to him, and he has been trying to gather up the courage to do this for a while.

She does not understand him, she does not love him anymore. She does not want to believe him, but feels obligated to. She asks him if he wants to see his son, Salman, who is sleeping. He thanks her, and walks in.

Ahmed did not wake up from this dream.

In fact, this slumber was a direct result of the carbon monoxide poisoning that seeped into the hotel—and the surrounding area. After numerous inspections following the incident, officials determined that the dangerous chemical likely spread due to inexplicable explosions in the sewer system.

Whatever the cause was, the initial explosions created a disastrous chain reaction. Further down the sewer line, dangerous mixtures of combustible gases began to spread throughout the sewer system, escaping to the surface and via ventilation systems in local buildings. Many people were poisoned. The sudden onset of ambulances and various cars racing to the nearest hospital caused numerous traffic jams. Fortunately, only one person would end up dying.

The underground explosions also ruptured several electrical lines, causing massive power outages throughout the area—including the motel. The manager rushed to notify his only tenant—Ahmed—but found the door locked. Knocking three times, he announced he would come in. He found Ahmed collapsed on the bed and promptly called 911.

The ambulance took some time to arrive (considering the countless other emergency calls that day). But they picked up Ahmed. They began transporting him to the nearest available hospital. Unfortunately, most nearby hospitals had lost power, or were entirely full, due to the carbon monoxide leaks, underground explosions, and swelling panic of most reasonable people in the area. So, the EMTs decided to take him to the nearest available— which happened to be just a few blocks past 45th and Lysander.

Meanwhile, five or so intersections from Ahmed's prophesied deathbed, a large vehicle—transporting a variety of horses, sheep, and pigs—veered off the road after an explosion sent a manhole cover up into the air directly in front of the driver's path. The vehicle crashed into a nearby fire hydrant and toppled over. The crash left the rear end wide open, allowing all the flustered and frightened animals to escape. Soon, the entire area was overrun by horses galloping across intersections, sheep huddling into alleyways, and pigs wandering and looking for something interesting to do.

One such oblivious pig, named Harold by his former owner, sauntered into an area blocked off for construction. Lacking any definitive purpose, the pig shuffled aimlessly, before settling on a nearby support beam that was angled against a concrete wall. He plopped himself down, beat from the trip.

Soon, the ambulance carrying Ahmed approached the area. The driver suddenly found himself veering through scattered farm animals in the street, before desperately turning away from a single horse in the middle of the road. The turn was too sharp, and the ambulance rolled onto its side. Ahmed was flung from the back of the ambulance.

The ambulance proceeded to slide into a gigantic crane carrying a two-ton HVAC unit; the crane struggled to continue bearing the weight, and it toppled over. This two-ton HVAC unit then fell a few stories, directly onto the opposite end of the support beam that Harold the Pig had sat on. The sheer weight and force sent Harold hurling into the air. He sailed up, flipping in a parabolic curve until he eventually landed, snout first, into an unconscious Ahmed. The abrupt impact of Harold's incisors caused a rupture in Ahmed's forehead, splitting it open and causing the subarachnoid hemorrhage that would eventually leave him dead just an hour later, at 5:30 p.m., Eastern Time.

***

Ahmed's motel room was left wide open, and not soon after the disaster, it became the home of a vagrant dwarf named Ty Solomon. Like most vagrants and vagabonds, Ty Solomon had an immovable optimism, and a persistent intuition that fortune would eventually find him. And, again, like most vagrants and vagabonds, Ty Solomon had a tireless ache for something poisonous to his soul and spirit—an addiction that dictated most of his conscious life. In his story, this lecherous vice was gambling. This ache had buried itself in his gut long ago—when he had tangible aspirations, and an actual dream worth catching. He inherited the same vice that burdened his father and

289

mother. Both of their extended families carried it as well—a testament to the cruel gambles often made by destiny. Everyone had desperately prayed that Ty would finally be the one Solomon to escape that withering family tree. The one Solomon with that rare entrepreneurial spirit.

But the vice had much stronger aspirations. Ty ran out of money in his sophomore year. He had been studying his first animal anatomy classes, in pursuit of a veterinary science degree. Having exhausted his financial loans, he desperately went to his father for sage advice, who simply gave Ty his last $1000 and told him to "bet on a half-sure horse." He did. He bet it all on a horse named "Moonshine Delivery." And he won.

Then, having tasted from fortune's chalice for the first time in his life, he bet again. Naturally, as with most of these stories, he lost. His gut told him to keep going. And now he's a vagrant, sleeping in abandoned motel rooms, waiting for the next dollar to buy lottery tickets, still set in his pursuit of becoming a veterinarian.

That day, he undecidedly wandered into Ahmed Rebur's abandoned room. He discovered the apparatus when it responded to him, whispering to himself in his sleep. Most nights, unbeknownst to himself, he would mumble, "why me, why me." That night, the apparatus gave him an answer.

Because you are a degenerate gambler

Ty Solomon was certainly not gullible, nor lacking in any doubting wisdom. But he was also born with a now dormant intuition, which led him to revere the apparatus' power almost instantly. Holding the device brought back distant fables that his grandfather would madly preach at his family's incredibly small dinner table; Ty, due to his tiny stature, was forced to sit between his demented grandfather and enfeebled grandmother. These sermons mentioned many things, but most apparent to his memory at this moment was the Ark of the Covenant—a golden chest containing the laws of God. This strange device's omnipotent power was readily apparent. Was this the ark?

So, recognizing the opportunity, he spent that night exploring the universe—and his role in it.
Briefly, he discovered the following:

- There were numerous other civilizations in other galaxies barred from contact due to the sheer size of the universe
- Most of these civilizations were crustacean in appearance, many with arachnid-like appendages and brains with two-and-a-half as many folds as the human brain
- Humanity would fizzle out within 10,000 years, branching off into smaller nomadic civilizations after severe weather events demolished civilizations and famine dwindled the population to smatterings
- If he hadn't bet on Moonshine Delivery, he would have his own veterinary practice by now, with a wife and two objectively beautiful children
- Even if he didn't bet on Moonshine Delivery, he would still feel unhappy and unfulfilled. He would fill that hole with other kinds of dirt—alcohol, cannabis, masturbation, and even some heroin—after being prescribed some after major heart surgery
- The universe was a dark and lonely place after all.

So what does a degenerate gambler do with all this unbridled truth? Ty Solomon knew the answer.

He took his ark to the Froddes racetrack (still going strong despite the horrific accident), bet his last ten dollars on "Gravity Polaris," a less-than-surefire winner, who happened to pull an unprecedented upset. Ty Solomon continued, with the aid of this infinite knowledge, to build almost $100,000 dollars in cash winnings.

Eventually, Ty Solomon found his conscience again. He came upon a newfound truth, completely without the aid of the ark—that these horses, these poor animals, were being exploited, and he was condoning it with every dollar he won. Wanting to avoid any further support of the exploitative nature of equestrian racing, took his infinite knowledge elsewhere—somewhere much less inhumane, much more civilized.

At the Samuels Library, Ty Solomon created a new account with a stocks trading firm, rejected their offer for a consultant, and invested all of his money in one of the worst performing small-time companies on the market— Walstock Nuts. The ark had told him about a sudden profits increase that would generate a 500% return, soon followed by an immediate dip, which gave Ty just enough time to sell. He continued this with other companies for a week, generating a wealth of over 26 million dollars. Without any wherewithal to consider Securities investigations or legal implications, he cashed out and closed his account. The next day, he went to a suitor and bought the best suit he could buy for his size (they had to pull something from their children's sections to match his measurements). After the tailor left him to gaze at his newly dressed self, Ty Solomon needed only one glance at the mirror to realize what an empty shell he really was, encased in a children's blazer, a material tomb.

Ty Solomon expected a rush of jubilation and triumph. Years of begging on the streets, cardboard blankets, and watery soup from shelters—all of this had only constructed a firm belief that his day would come. He had finally secured all the money he would ever need, and then some, to live comfortably enough. His lucky day.

But he didn't feel this moment as strongly as he dreamt. In fact, it felt empty. Again, Ty Solomon—now virtually a millionaire—realized another profound truth, without the aid of the ark. He already knew, for half of his life, that he was a degenerate gambler. This recent journey only confirmed this. But here was something else, something entirely different—that when a degenerate gambler wins it all, wins everything they would ever need or want, it doesn't feel like a win at all. The gambler—he mused to himself, drunk with victory—the gambler thrived on the *next possible* gamble, the boon *just over* the horizon, the *succeeding* thrill, the forever upcoming triumph against odds. If there is no next…then what?

The next day, Ty Solomon took his brand new children's suit and his newly amassed fortune to the homeless shelter he had frequented for all those years of vagrancy. He found a mother and her toddler, hair matted and reeking of cigarettes, curled together under a used comforter with cartoon drawings of elephants. He gave the toddler his blazer. He then proceeded to count every family in the shelter. He discovered one hundred and fifty two total families, many of which were destitute and on the brink of starvation. He asked one of the volunteers for a notepad and a pen. Through a process of elimination, he toured the peeling halls of the shelter again, using the apparatus to procedurally rank each family according to how desperate they were. For each family or person, he asked if they would die from starvation or disease, or some other unnatural calamity; if they met that criteria, he then asked when they would die. Based on this data, Ty ranked everyone according to severity. Then, flipping to a new page, he asked for the winning lottery numbers—for each of the next 32 days.

For the most severe cases, he gave them $300,000 right away to seek medical attention and secure reliable shelter and food. This equaled eighty of the patrons at the homeless shelter. The next series involved those who had more time, but would likely die in a year or so without some miracle—or at least a place to live and a job to pay the rent. These poor souls totaled to forty. For these, he gave each of them $40,000 to secure shelter and begin starting their lives over again. This left 32, those very similar to a younger version of Ty Solomon; the newly destitute, those who didn't realize their visit to a homeless shelter was more permanent than temporary. For each of these, he gave them a chance. This chance involved $12,500 dollars each, a date, the winning lottery numbers for that date, and a heartfelt, signed request from Ty Solomon to turn their lives around after that date. The chance wasn't if they would win or not. It was whether they would evolve after they won. Ty felt a temptation to ask the device whether or not they would come through and turn a new leaf.

But he didn't, favoring a serene nescience. His faith in the fables of redemption meant more to him than the stale resolutions of the real world.

The next day, after giving up his newfound fortune, Ty Solomon took a thoughtful walk down some street he had lived on during his childhood. It was an inclined street, constructed on some monstrosity of a hill that could not be built around. The apartment complexes had to be designed to accommodate the steep incline. When leaving their home, any inhabitant had to deal with a sudden proprioceptive shift, leaving their flatland home into an angular

294

world. Ty remembered this shift fondly, languishing over the many mornings when the younger boy version of himself would open a perfectly straight front door and step out to an awkwardly skewed earth. He would pretend he was a spaceman, leaping from his ship onto a geometrically curious alien planet. As he reminisced down this street, some vague nostalgia breached now and then, but nothing concrete enough for him to hold on to.

But he had begun to understand the metaphor of this echo. All of his life until now was spent with this door closed, never taking a risk, never venturing forth into a great unknown. As a boy, he would fearlessly leap into the spewed otherness; now, as an adult, he was instead altogether languid, pallid, and dull. The absurdity of a plain existence.

But not so much anymore: in those past few days wrestling with the unbridled truth, he had managed to jar that door open, to reveal something else behind the door, something else entirely magical and strange—a beguiling nugget of purpose, without a name, for the time being.

In a bout of desperation, he asked the apparatus one last question:

What is the meaning of life?

After a suspiciously long moment, it read back:

```
error
```

Ty Solomon, in a fit of ironic alleviation, felt content enough with that answer. Whether the answer was pithy or literal didn't cross his mind. Instead, he resolved to pass the buck, to hand off the apparatus to a random person passing on the street—to let the ark change their life, for better or worse.

That man, with a shameful composure, was wearing a cheap red wig, passing off as a woman, lugging a massive piece of motel-worthy art down the street. Ty, recognizing the despair beneath those red curls, only said one thing to this person, before walking off:

"The truth will set you free."

***

Years later, it dawned on Peter that, as per the Nuremberg Status assigned to this blundered case, everyone who had come into contact with the apparatus—and anyone they had come into contact with—would have to be terminated for the sake of national security. They were necessary collateral; flowers that had to be pulled in order to preserve the natural order of the garden. Only after going back and reading these reports did he realize that his mistake had likely led to hundreds of deaths—some well-deserved, and others untimely. But, nonetheless, he would have to live with the empty visages of these murdered souls until the toll would come knocking on his door.

Chapter Twenty-Five
A Portrait of the ~~Inescapable~~ Ethereal Essence of Art, Part I

I am haunted by the frozen pines of my childhood. That's why. Or is it vengefulness, stabbing me in the gut, mad at a world that refuses to recognize me?

I can't seem to capture it. It sits, resting peacefully, artfully on a maple-brown stool. I have shredded five canvases already.

I didn't find this odd piece. It found me. That day I left the hospital after visiting my mother, after yet another episode that left her a babbling mess. I was walking to the bus stop, where a wild-haired and graying homeless woman had asked me for a dollar not long after she finished her sermon on the essence of evil festering in cholesterol, next to the nanorobots installed by government vaccines.

Before I reached the bus stop, I heard that woman pestering another crowd, preaching that "the senators are compromised, they are guilty themselves of selling the nanoprocessors that are tracking every purchase and GPS route you make, so those damn pedophiles on capitol hill can keep feeding their gullets!"

Before I reached the bus stop, I thought about painting a portrait of her: preaching to that diverse set of people who rather did not want to hear another rant on their way home or to work; their faces numb to all this constant insanity; treating her ranting like a theater show before they had to return home to a lonely dinner at home in front of the television. My painting could have captured that loneliness in their faces, in their sullen eyes. It would have been a true masterpiece.

My musings on her portrait reminded me that I needed to pay my rent, and I had to sell another painting to the pawn shop. This time, I decided that I had to sell "Autumn's Rebuke," My largest painting so far at about five feet in height. By far my emptiest attempt to mimic orderly chaos, my cubistic interpretation, inspired by the garbage dump just around the corner from my studio. I had tried to capture a seminal human feeling of mortality, juxtaposed with the trifling addictions that drive us to the same graveyard as time. What came out was a painting of a cubistic poker table in a field of cubistic autumn leaves, and this field yet again in a massive cubistic garbage dump, with a cubistic old man at the table with the cubistic grim reaper.

This would have been the seventh of eight pieces of art I sold to the same pawn shop. This time, I was positive the guy at the pawn shop would know it was me, even though I wore a dazzling red wig this time, with flowing curls, reminiscent of the big-tit chicks on hooter magazines I'd sneak peeks at while mom wasn't looking in the convenience store, their chests censored by a black, plastic blocker—I'm sure those things have a name. I masturbated to one of those magazines once, and I felt extremely shameful afterwards. All the kids at school used to tease me about my mom appearing in one of those magazines. I never found out the truth about that.

As I was lugging Autumn's Rebuke along the street, using the bridge of my foot to help swing it from time to time, I was interrupted by an incredibly short man. He came up to me, intentionally, and handed me some strange object. He said something, like this:

"The truth will dissect you if you are willing."

The strange, short man then ran, disappearing up the road.

The object he gifted me seemed to capture a natural, worldly essence—a geometric simplicity, spherical perfection. It looked like a giant pearl. It was beckoning me. A perfect gift for Ophelia. Something to tell her how much I appreciated her, how much I love her. (Just don't tell her some strange homeless dwarf gave it to you).

I have a sense that our relationship is beginning to fracture under the weight of my wasted artistic brilliance (come on, now, Jamie, even you know that's a little conceited). This gift would be balm enough for now. The epitome of rounded perfection, containing the infinity of pi and that elusive sense of wonder I've chased since childhood—a faultless beauty, an elegant simplicity, a wondrous visual enigma. The sphere, after all, challenges the limitations of our two dimensional brains—we rely on everything outside of the sphere to see it. Light, the shadows, the reflections, the movement. Without context, it would just be a stupid circle.

I have to paint it in a portrait. Then I can give it to her.

I can't get the curves right to save my life. This white, this beautiful, pale, slightly bluish and immeasurable whiteness, I can't figure out either. All of my mixtures have failed. This plain and fascinating object contains a subtle beauty—it is objectively junk a piece of trash, a white ball that serves no purpose.

Subjectively—it means everything to me. That meaning escapes me. But I know it's there; I know I can feel it coursing through me, teasing me in rising crescendos of operatic choruses.

I've adjusted the floodlights multiple times. Manipulating shadows enough to give some definition and boundary to this portrait. But this object does not react to light. It casts a shadow, but does not reflect light like you would expect it to. In my latest attempt, it looks like a ball of cloudy cheese.

I tear the canvas off my easel, stabbing it over and over, imagining all the people I've wanted to hurt in my life. I snap the legs off my easel and throw its jumbled remains against the wall, and the crushing sound it makes—like a tree falling—brings me to tears.

In my dreams, sometimes, the world loves my art. Except everyone is always wearing Halloween masks, or missing their faces entirely. But they do love it. And they love me. But it's not me. It's a shadow of me. The bastard stole all my good ideas. I'm less of an artist and more of a translator, transcribing what my mind's eye sees into the limited allowance of paint and fabric.

Now, I'm holding this big ass pearl. It doesn't crack open, no matter how hard I throw it. My left hand aches; the muscles surrounding my thumb are throbbing in pain. That must be why I can't paint you, your geometrically perfect sphereness.

Ophelia calls.

The synthetic vibrations of her long-distance voice only furthers the widening crevice between us.

"Jamie?" She sounds angry,worried that I haven't reached out to her in quite some time.

"Uh-huh?"

"Jamie, are you okay? Is it your mom again?" Traffic horns and passing cars phase in and out quietly behind her voice—she's on her way somewhere.

"Yeah. She's back in the hospital. She's doing—" lie? "okay."

"Umm...okay. That's good." five second pause. She's probably biting her lower lip, which she does when she's in deep thought. "I've got to get everything ready for the exhibit." Pause. "Can you come over tonight?"

"Ophelia?"

"Yes?" She seems put off. Maybe I said her name the wrong way. "What is it?"

I want to tell her I got her something. I want to ask her what she really thinks of me. If she believes in me. If she buys my art because of commiseration rather than a real belief that it would sell, or that some schmuck would find my art fascinating enough to take back home or write about in a bloated art column. I want to break through the thick bark that has grown around us. I want us to be real to eachother and admit it if this has gone on too far. I want to unravel this armor of familiarity that we buried our true selves under for the sake of comfort and forfeit and fleeting warmth—I want to ask her if she truly loves me, or just stays with me out of pity.

"When will you be home?" I ask, hoping to hide my desperation, my loneliness and despair.

What was that? Was that a robot?

"Did you say something?" I ask her. I swear the voice came from behind me.

"Yes, I said I should be home around ten-thirty. Didn't you hear me? Can you hear me now?"

"Can I hear her now?" I called out.

Yes

I'm so frightened I leap into the air, tossing my phone into a bucket of paint at the edge of my room.

My place is haunted by the ghost of a robot. That must explain it. Something, out of nowhere. Did Ophelia plug in a gadget somewhere? Even this line of reasoning isn't satiating the chills that come along when you just *know* someone must be in your home.

I manage to pull my phone out of the crimson paint bucket; I can hear Ophelia's faint and bubbly worries, speaking flatly under a layer of paint.

"Ophelia, did you add one of those gadget things?"

"Gadget things?"

"My place is haunted by robots."

"Are you high again?"

"Am I high again?"

No You are drunk

"The ghosts know I'm drunk, Ophelia."

"You need to go to the ER. I can meet you there.
It's okay if you slip up again. But please go get some
help."

"I need help?"

Yes

"Whaaat, are you and the ghosts in cahoots?"

Either the crimson paint got to my phone, or
Ophelia hung up on me. But here and now, I am most
definitely not alone.

***

"What color are you?" I ask it, aching for it to
respond and teach me what this all means.

#f8f8ff; R-248, G-248, B-255; Ghost
White

It responds in these finite codes of color—what
initially seems like an infinite array of numbers and
letters organized for a computer to understand is in
all reality a finite code that eventually ends somewhere—

Which means this: the wheel of colors at my disposal, my arsenal for depicting the vast and endless
world before me in all its glory, this very palette—
even it has boundaries—

Which means art has boundaries—which cannot
be true, under any circumstances—otherwise it
ceases to be artful, its artistry is inherently flawed, it
is undeniably mundane and uneventful. Once art has
limits, it ceases to be art.

303

I don't fully understand how…stop right there. I don't understand at all how it knows all the answers. Sure, I've deduced that there aren't robot ghosts haunting my studio apartment; of course, I knew the voice was emanating from this device that's been sitting on a stool under surveillance of flood lights.

But it surely can't know everything. I know smart gadgets nowadays can instantly find most answers that are indisputable. Ask it something the internet would *not* know—yes or no, a flip of the coin.

That's fucking brilliant, right?

I can't find a quarter, but I found a penny. Should I flip it before asking or after?

First try: before. Heads.

"Heads or tails?"

```
                    Heads
```

Ok. After.

"Will this coin flip be heads or tails?"

```
                    Heads
```

And it is…heads. "Ok then, you think you're so smart?"

```
Intelligence requires existence, there
   is no entity here, hence there is no
      scale of intelligence to measure
```

I rummage around and eventually find a navy blue button from some suit I haven't worn (let alone seen) in forever.

"Ok then...I'm going to flip this coin." I hold the penny in my left hand, and the button in my right. I flip the button on my right. "Heads or tails?"

There is no intelligence here and therefore no stupidity. You flipped a button which does not have surfaces that illustrate or construe either side relative to a coin

Ok then. "Ok then, where did this button come from?"

Your suit

"Which suit?"

The only suit you own

"And where is that suit?"

Under your bed

"What's in the left hand pocket?" I didn't even know that.

A gas station receipt from three years ago

Sure enough, it was tucked away and folded all haphazardly.
A polka dotted elephant wearing a santa hat in a purple nightgown. "What am I thinking of right now?"

So, it passed the test. I may be drunk right now, but I can tell when I'm being bamboozled, and I'm not being bamboozled. This is something special that happened to me. This object, whatever god made it, knows the truth to everything. I can't help but think of the ramifications of this. The fame and fortune it could bring. I could be the all-seeing Jamie, infinite in knowledge. The smartest man on earth. Maybe then people would take me seriously and buy my art.

But would that make me happy? If people buy my art *because* I am famous? Wasn't the whole idea the other way around? Becoming famous *because* of my art? Isn't that what I wanted, at the end of this life? Validation?

Sure. I could ask this thing about all the secrets in the world. I could find out everything anyone ever wanted to know. This thing could end science in half a second. Solve world hunger. Prevent any future conflict. Figure out the easiest and most economically fair method for providing meals to the hungry, jobs to the poor. Homes for the homeless.

But for now, for the rest of this evening at least, it's mine. And I get to ask what matters most—to me.

I get stuck for a moment thinking of my mom. Of the disease killing her. Of her constant pressure to get the test myself. She calls it a 50-50 coin flip. *Why don't you want to know?* She says. Whether the disease killing her is here with me, too. Whether I will end up just like her, at some foreseeable time in the near enough future, senses scrambled, autonomy withered and starved—doomed to expire.

I have an inkling why I'm so afraid to know the truth. Because art is timeless, and death is not.

But then I think about what defines me more: the inevitable physical disintegration into nothingness, or the art, the beauty I can leave behind to inspire and provoke. My death does not define me. My art defines me. I am just another human being among billions that live to die. This is what drives me to live, beyond any other material; it is who I am, it is what satiates my soul. *I am a fucking artist. If not that, then nothing at all.*

"Am I a good artist?"

It doesn't respond right away. Thinking.

Haha! Stumped! Fooled! It must be too subjective of a question. Everything I've asked up until this point has been purely mathematical, even the elephant, I'm sure. Even the most renowned critics fail to agree on the vital qualities of what makes art *art,* what inspires the feeling of empowerment that rushes through you when you see a piece that truly floors you, that captures you and washes out the world around you, that makes you feel empty, no guts inside you but a hollow shell, that makes you doubt your entire being, or why even a finite set of possible colors can lead to an infinite amount of formulas combined on canvas, or what makes Picasso and Rembrandt and Pollock the ambassadors, and those other nameless artists that the world has never heard of who dissolve shallowly in their mediocrity, or how the greatest minds disagree on why art exists as a function of the human equation, why we even do this futile exercise at all, or why—

It answers, bluntly and simply:

No

Chapter Twenty-Six
A Portrait of the ~~Ethereal~~ Inescapable Essence of Art, Part II

So, as I had initially thought, all of the possible colors are finite. According to this thing, even their combination isn't infinite. There are boundaries, limitations, borders.

In some universe, where all possible paintings existed, you could create a formulaic rating of each piece of art, organizing them from first to last on the basis of artistic quality.

By this logic, even the empty canvas of art is finite, to a certain degree of numbers. All the possibilities, the value, the brilliance is finite, and strictly and objectively defined.

But then, what about a different canvas? After all, not all art (and in fact very little) is made on cotton canvas. There's brick, artistic 2d sculptures scaling over two and even three or four (or more) stories. Then there's the miniscule art written in black ink on bathroom stalls. And the ink stained permanently into flesh, ironically or artistically. And don't forget those useless doodles made in notebooks of cartoon squirrels and fancy letters and lines going nowhere.

Then there's the three-dimensional arrays of claymation, of holographics, of shit-covered canvases, or paintings made in blood, and god-knows-what-else…all utter shit in this un-grand scheme of things.

Down to basic math, there is a limit, an end point, on all the possible combinations of human creativity. Of what you can do, within the bounds of physics and reality. Sure, it seems *infinite,* until you really think about how impossible *infinity* is, because on the bold face of it all, numbers end somewhere…even large numbers we can't even begin to imagine. All art has a dimension of canvas, threshold borders that it cannot cross. Stretched to its breaking point on the greatest of lengths, widths, heights, and fuck all.

Here's the point of all this wasted pontificating. Even if you factor the seemingly infinite number of colors, and the seemingly infinite number and types of canvases, and all the kinds of lengths, weights, shades, hues, and shapes of anything and everything humankind can and will ever possibly and humanly create—

Why bother to be an artist if there is eventually an *end point* to it all? The numbers that dictate possible combinations indicate that those combinations eventually end *somewhere.* Isn't the goal of every artist to be *the* artist? Where do the numbers end?

Before I realize my grave mistake, I'm already a bottle and half in, and halfway there, shocked that I made it this far in a drunken stupor. No doubt people spotting me along the way will call the police; after all, what reasonable person wouldn't be worried about a stumbling buffoon, with no shirt and nothing but tattered overalls covered in paint?

I had memorized the walk from Ophelia's apartment to her gallery, having made that journey so many times, to beg her once again to help pay my rent. I had lied to myself all those years, saying "my art" will pay her back, eventually, once I make it big. I know tonight is the big exhibit, and a whole bunch of phony "critics" will be there, sipping deep on the crushed and filtered hopes and dreams of artists begging for their one breakthrough. I wonder if they'll be drinking the wine instead of just tasting it. *I don't want to swallow your hopes and dreams—I just want a taste of that bitterness, before I spit it out.*

My left hand, a mind of its own, makes me drink even more, rising up in the air with the bottle upside down. My other hand is fully autonomous, squeezing the gift my mom bought me when I moved away to college. She persistently warned me:

Do not put your finger anywhere near the trigger unless you intend to shoot. Never point the barrel unless you intend to kill.

Such a surprisingly beautiful juxtaposition. On the one hand, putting a paintbrush to canvas can lead to billions of different outcomes, and trillions of different qualities, and eternally different meanings. But aiming a gun, pulling a trigger, the final act of *shooting*—there is only one colorful outcome from this action.

This makes me awfully merry on my way down the concrete path to my undoing. Up above me are some cheaply made billboards for the same weasel-nosed lawyer gimmicking his way into any crushed hand lawsuit, peering down in their almightiness. A fucking lawyer, chasing ambulances for a penny, while I waste away chasing my dreams. He makes a thousand bucks for doing nothing, and I make nothing for giving everything I've got. *I'm a god-damn artist*. Fuck him, right in his face.

Ophelia wouldn't understand, but something drives me there anyways. Not quite sure what I am looking for, having lost everything. I hadn't thought much of it till then, but it starts to hit me, and makes me want to drink myself to death even more—here I am, for what little I'm worth, world! I have given you years, *years,* wasted at an easel, and that one year I tried cameras, and those feeble teenage daydreams of being a rival to Kubrick and whatnot. *I just wanted to do something different.* That persistent weight of anxiety in my chest, pushing out against my ribcage (like I was dying, god forbid I die without being known for something); that damn weight pushing out, telling me I only have so much time left to create a masterpiece that changes the world for the better (or worse—does it matter?). That would cement my name in the history books.

But now that weight is gone. I no longer feel that dying; I am already dead. And gone, gone is a future perennially waving to me on the horizon—some bright and hopeful distant *me*, singing, "this was all worth it. You did it, you showed 'em, in the end." That *fucker* is so full of shit, and so am I.

Watch your step. Don't appear too drunk. Not some rambling drunken fool, but someone well-fed with enough angst and hard-living to make a valid point about the state of all this nonsense of living.

I knew I wanted to be an artist the day I realized how beautiful my mother was. I wanted to capture that forever. I wonder if she's known this whole time how much of a fraud I am.

I had some clue why I'm going to Ophelia's gallery tonight, but I lost it along the way. Maybe, yes, it was this: tell all her highfalutin artist friends to fuck right off into the sunset. No, maybe it was: make Ophelia pity me and take me in for the night so I wouldn't sleep alone. Or was it this: find the most expensive piece of art in the joint and blow my brains all over the canvas (would the price go down? Or up? Who knows, with the state of art these days).

I try to walk in gracefully, but I stumble over the fine rug at the entrance. This is the grand showing Ophelia had been stressing months about. Place is packed. A fire hazard. Those two Japanese folks in the back there, in their fancy suits, came all the way from China. Just in time to be made fools of. Real millionaires, she said. Could change everything. Even if they only purchased a few, she said, it would put her gallery back on the map. We could then go to Syracuse. Or Zurich. But not Paris. Oh God, never Paris. Too artificial these days.

A handful of critics stand like an arrow of geese, nodding their heads in agreement, over some sculpture of a black leather office chair in the center stage, with a red apple on the seat, one large bite taken out.

It's not even a sculpture. It's just a black leather chair. And a rotting apple.

"It's exquisite," one balding old fart says. His beady eyes are magnified by a thick black pair of rectangular glasses, with a thin mustache curling over his dry lips. His shoulders show his age more than his lack of hair, curled over, his neck and head bent like a Looney Tunes vulture. "It reminds me," he lectures, pausing for a fake sip of his paltry red wine, "of the utter despair of the modern workforce. The modern worker wasting away in an office chair. Still ripe, but showing decay, a snack for the upper class." The two plastic and snobbish women holding his arms up like he was already dead nod in agreement. "It makes me feel anxious, those poor souls. I would just die if my entire life was trapped in a cubicle."

"Well, I just simply disagree," says a dapper young man in a velvet suit, popping up like a weasel out of its burrow. He had a thick black beard running down to the knot of his bowtie, and his eyes hollered with intense and undying energy. "It's all so *religious,* you old fool. So much more feminine. Think Eve, think the apple in the garden, the devilish snake goading her to take a bite of the forbidden fruit. It's as if that primordial evil will always persist, even in the most monotonous of places, right under our dirty, filthy asses." He laughs, incredibly amused at his own stupid musings.

"Yes, it's certainly feminine," says one of those women next to the dead old man. "But, look, there's nothing Judeo-Christian about it, you see." She tapped her cigarette with her clothed index finger, the ashes sinking slowly to the floor, careful to avoid her tight crimson dress. "But the apple, the apple must represent the female sex. Taken advantage of by the male ego. It's all so obviously a reference to vaginal rape—that apple was bitten by an animal, but the phallus society still expects it to get back to work when so clearly a chunk has been eaten."

I ask what it really means.

I couldn't resist. I seize a glass of wine from a passing waiter, and invade their conversation with the truth.

"You are all a-full of shit." That sounded drunk.

They all look appalled. "Excuse me? The velvet-suit weasel says, offended.

"You can't smell the bullshit on your lips, can you? You're all wrong. A-bunch of fuck-ing pho-nies."

The crimson woman scoffs, her breath reeking of burnt tobacco. "Well, then, sir, what *was* the artist's *intention?*"

I take a break to feign deep thought. "Obviously. The barren amorality of modern technology." I sip the rest of my wine, handing the empty glass to the old balding vulture. I step away, still listening to them.

They are silent for a moment. But eventually I hear them mutter under their breath.

"What a buffoon."

"A hobbyist, nothing more."

"Couldn't be farther from the truth."

The heavy crowd makes it easy to navigate sight unseen. I spot Ophelia soon after leaving those idiots; I'm floored yet again by that bright orange dress she wears to things that matter—the one that bares her shoulders and collarbone, hair flowing in endless curls, a portrait that leaves your libido to its wicked imagination by suggesting just the purview of her breasts. This is the dress she wears in my daydreams.

I'm suddenly filled with a surprising nostalgia, all the memories of us together without her wearing that dress—late Sunday mornings sipping french press coffee on her patio in a tattered sweater she's worn to bed since high school, or her falling asleep in my arms while we blindly watch repeats of doldrum laugh-track sitcoms, or the first time she made me dinner, babysitting her aunt's dogs, when I cut my hand open trying to open a bottle of wine with a knife (I couldn't find a corkscrew anywhere).

She's silently nodding to the constant chatter from those two Japanese fools, a glass of blood-red wine spinning in her hand. She never drinks. She only holds it for appearances. What kind of philistine *doesn't* drink wine at an exhibit? Could you blame her? This is her big moment. Here I am to ruin it.

"Did she notice me?" I have to ask, just to know if my top-secret mission has been sabotaged by my drunken entrance.

No

She is obviously distracted by the weight of this evening. After all, she's not expecting me to be there. She no longer has Juniper on display. Makes sense, even if it hurts. She wouldn't want any damper on this evening.

Her eyes darted towards me. I jump away, scuffling through the crowds until I come upon a large group gathered before a massive canvas that takes up almost an entire wall. The canvas is reminiscent of renaissance art, flushed oils and muted colors throughout. It depicts two massive surgeons hunched over a carcass wrapped in white blankets. The surgeon's heads are concealed by blue surgical masks and head covers, leaving a vivid theater for their protruding, starving, lecherous eyes. They are gazing at the incision in their subject's abdomen. The surgeon on the left holds the incision open with his left hand, a scalpel in his right hand. The other surgeon, wielding a pair of tweezers, is pulling an object out from the patient's insides. The object is blurry, green, and massive compared to the incision. Pushing through the crowd for a closer look, I can make out the green—$100 bills.

315

I can hear more pompous pontifications from this massive crowd.

"It's obviously a commentary on the horrible health care system."

"A dramatic portrayal of 21st century government surveillance and control."

"A dogmatic reveal of how our lives are driven by money."

"A contemporary critique of a western obsession of possessions."

"It makes me think about how short life really is."

I ask it the same question—what does it mean?

This piece is titled "Yellow-bellied Justice" by Julia Harrison-Waits. It is intended to represent the seizure of privacy by the Russian aristocracy

Despite the truth, I sympathize a little with some of those interpretations. I mean, they at least make a little sense. That's one of those things that drew me to art in the first place, when I was younger. The idea that the artist, whoever they are, does not ultimately matter. Once that canvas is dry, the artist is dead, and the dried paint that remains adopts an entirely new life. Any fresh set of diligent eyes can deduce a new, often novel, meaning; maybe a meaning that is borne from that person's own experience of life, or based on juxtaposition with other pieces of art. Or, maybe, a thousand years later, it transcends the chains of time and becomes something entirely different. Who the hell cares about the artist? The artist does not define the art.

I'm thoughtfully engaged with that phrase: *pieces of art. Pieces.* As if art is some prodigiously infinite

316

reservoir that artists pull from. Everything artists produce are just bits of some cosmic beauty. According to this magic pearl, no such cosmic beauty exists. It's all just a formulaic portion of reflected light.

I spot the place where Juniper was on display not too long ago. Ophelia replaced Juniper with some small, simple fruit painting. I've gotten more accustomed to the truth that my art isn't worth shit, *but worse than a goddamn bowl of fruit*?

I move on to the next exhibition—one that is dedicated to its own isolated glass room. Inside, the people walk around, aimlessly gaping, not entirely sure which way they're supposed to look. This one is quite different. Not a painting or a sculpture, but an arrangement. Hung with fishing wire from the perforated ceiling tiles, what must be hundreds of thousands of bullets, each quietly oscillating left and right about 45 degrees. Each bullet is hung at a slightly different height, some close together, and others farther apart. The arrangement at first seems entirely random and chaotic. Stepping into the room, I can see how the arrangement, from my perspective, depicts a three-dimensional human face—hollowed eyes, protruding nose, copper-steel skin, and a mouth gaping in a despairing scream.

But then I hear others.

"If you step over here, it looks like a jet plane."

"From here it resembles the Last Supper."

"From back here it seems more like a, by-god, a mathematical formula!"

Skeptical at first, a journey around the room...*confirmed* these analyses. If you took the right angle, the disorder would instantaneously snap into a familiar image—a plane, the Last Supper, a math theorem, a face, an Egyptian sphinx, even a

simple bullet, all in all. The idea seems ingenious—
the epitome of art's subjective nature.

Wait.

It really means nothing? At all?

That just cannot be right. I refuse to accept this.
Art cannot just be a simple picture. It's the visages of
faces you can make out in television static; it's the
shadows you perceive in bed at night; it's the unconscious recognition of meaning and beauty. That's
what separates art and creativity from the monotonous and boring. That's what makes it human. It has
to at least mean something—maybe, even a meaning
that differs, between different people.

I hate to admit it, but those egotistical fools from
before—the vulture, the weasel, that crimson witch—
maybe their perspectives have some merit. If a thousand people come along and say "this means that!"
and a thousand come along and say, "No, that so
clearly means this!" Who is to say where the true line
is drawn? The cloudy realm of art refuses to accept
that "that is that..." because it could also be *this,*
based on where you're standing. And the artist
doesn't matter, because their art lives on long after
the artist has died.

Despite the despair of knowing that *my* art is practically worthless, I feel a sudden wave of power over me. It is not a power dictated by the loaded gun in my coat pocket. It is an overwhelmingly familiar sense of uncertainty—which, as crazy as it seems, is much more comforting than the bare and utter truth. I no longer wanted to point the gun at myself, or someone else. I wanted to blow this fucking piece of garbage art to smithereens.

Because what am I, then? What has my life amounted to if I'm just a no good wannabe artist? What's the real truth here? Who am I to believe—a pearl that seems to know everything, or a fraud of an artist?

"Look at all this shit!" I shout. All conversations degrade into a ceasing silence. Everyone sees me, *me*, finally. "Nothing but a fuck-ton of old white dirtbags. Sipping your own asses. None of you knows the real truth of art. What it means to be an artist. The guts it takes to put yourself out there, to expose your truth to the world. None of you. Not one of you knows what it takes to create art. You just like sniffing your own shit."

Then I spot Ophelia, eyes wide, staring at me. Her cheeks are red, and her face and gaping mouth say nothing but shock and worry. I can tell: she knows I am drunk and here to cause a scene. But I failed at that, too.

She initially storms her way through the crowd; but, along the way over, her fuming anger dissolves into concern. "What are you doing here?" she says, under her breath, both irritably and yet with hints of concern.

I didn't realize I was already crying. "You didn't leave Juniper up?"

Her shoulders slump, and she turns her head slightly. The vitriol and worry wipe away instantly; what remains is her beautiful mien of empathy.

"Oh, Jamie. I'm sorry."

"It's ok. I understand. I'm just not good enough."

She frowns. But in a way that shows she's comforted by my confession. Like all of my artistic endeavors have weighed her down, and now she can finally let out a deep breath of sudden relief.

"Jamie," she says softly, setting her wine glass down on the floor. She rests her shaking hands on my shoulders. She does not break her gaze with me, even when all the critics and connoisseurs chuckle and laugh. Then, she hugs me tight, arms wrapped around my waist, for what seems like forever. She is making a scene with a drunk, an asshole, dressed in tattered, paint-covered overalls and no shirt. This could ruin her image, and her livelihood.

When she recedes from her embrace, she has a sudden look of disquieted fear. Her arms become stiff, and her eyes begin to shiver in pools of tears. Like she found something she wasn't expecting, something heavy, dangerous, and loaded that caused her great worry.

She speaks softly, only to me. I can't control it anymore—my crying, my weeping, my despair.

She speaks. "Jamie, Jamie, I love you. I'm sorry. But I need you to know that I really do love you."

She took a deep breath.

"But I really need you to go home right now. Right. Now. Before you hurt someone, or yourself. Or do something you regret."

I had never said it up until now. But I say it. I say, "I love you, too."

She gives it her all to hold back a smile.

On my drunken stupor back home, I have regrets. Regrets that I had come there to prove a point, or to fire a gun—not exactly sure at who. Regrets that I had likely ruined Ophelia's exhibition, and scarred the image of sophistication she has labored years to establish. Regret that I have wasted years of my own life chasing a lucid yet elusive daydream, painted on a thin canvas that could not hold the weight of my own ambitions.

I also asked it one last question. Something I had not truly cherished until tonight; something that suddenly mattered more than anything else.

`Yes`

It said,
Yes.
Did I ask whether art was truly subjective?
Did I ask whether I would ever become a famous artist?
Did I ask if my mother would live another few years?
Or if I had the disease too, or if it would hit me in the next ten years like it did my mother?
If I would descend into madness like she has?
Did I ask about the meaning of life, or when the world would end?
Did I ask it if there was really any purpose in this world beyond the frayed tapestries we weave to make sense of determined chaos?
Of course not. I'm drunk.
I just asked if Ophelia meant what she said. Even if she didn't believe in me. If she really did love me.

Chapter Twenty-Seven
A Testament to My Crimes Against My Son

My son. My baby boy. My only gift from God. Born from a woman's nightmare, gifted to resolve all nihilistic desires. When I would spend hours on the roof contemplating, Jamie's ghostly-presence-briskly-sweeping-in-my-mind would pull me back. He is a miserable artist, but oh, does he try, and I love him very much.

He peeks into my room to see if I'm awake. I can see him through a barely-closed eye, pretending to be asleep. Why am I pretending? I don't really have an answer for you. I am plagued in this room by the overwhelming hospital stench, like tooth dust and novocaine at a dentist's office...is this my purgatory? The waiting room before eternal rest?

The monitor goes beep, beep, beep. He comes to my side and glares intently at me. He must know I'm a fake.

William snores, shuffles in his paper-thin sheets. They've changed the bandages over the holes in his head three times today, and still the blackened puddles of blood replace where his eyes used to be.

"Mom?"
I burst into a horrifying mix of tears and laughter over all
this messiness.

beep· The way he says my better name has never
fluctuated or grown up. He still sounds like my little boy.
M-o-m, Mm-ah-m, an *o* that avoids its obnoxiousness
and dies a quick death to the surrounding *ms,* the slight
upwards inflection, a subtly higher cadence near the
end of the short-lived vowel that often implies a
begging child asking for a quarter for another one of
those gooey sticky hands he would whip around and
inevitably lose or get covered in dust and hair and food
crumbs. When he says *mom* I can't avoid hearing the
Sesame Street song playing in the other room while I
cut off the crust of his peanut butter and jelly sandwich,
sneaking prunes in so he doesn't notice.
"Mom? I have something for you. I want you to see it."
I can't speak.
My hand, my whole arm, is dancing.
My cheeks are twitching.
He sits next to me and holds my hand. It doesn't stop
dancing even with a partner who refuses.
His hand allows mine to lead in its chaotic ballet.
"Mom, do you see this?" He holds up a ball that I've seen

somewhere. Some kind of crystal ball. *I hate*

puzzles· Why would he bring me a puzzle?
"Do you want to know when there will be a cure? Do
you want to know if there will be a cure, before...before
you die?"
I have trouble focusing since the **pulleys** holding my
head to my neck decide to **jam** and **sputter**, my head

twitching constantly to the right like I'm a short-circuited <u>robot</u>.

"This…this thing can help you. It tells you whatever you want to know. You can ask it whatever…whatever you want, and it will tell you."

Jamie was less of an artist with words than he was with a brush· I have trouble speaking sometimes too. But, I manage to say something now, *and I feel like a child again, asking how birds fly, why trees are made of wood but not of brick, why evil people are the way they are, why Elmer Fudd's head doesn't get blown off when Bugs Bunny makes his rifle backfire*

"You're full of shit. How does it work?"

"You just ask."

The words we speak float between us, painted by a brush in mixed hues, like God's an artist painting the feeble exchange of a dying mother and her son. They are purple and greenish at first, and they remind me of a cool breeze sneaking below an open window.

William shuffles again, moaning like a dying animal.

He wants me to ask his **crystal ball** something. About

my future my death my cure his real father his shame his stupid art his misshapen nose his

"What do you ask for?"

"Whatever you want."

I think of something devious and esoteric, some obscurity that a machine could never understand. What is love?

Baby don't hurt me, don't hurt me, no more

Or something that only I would know and no one else would, a cliché like a dream I've often had where myself from some distant past or future is desperately trying to prove it actually *is me—Who did you have a crush on in the third grade? Did they know it was me who placed the **thumbtack** on Mrs. Hindel's chair? who drew that awfully ugly drawing of ms barnes on the chalkboard*
"**What did you ask for**?"
Jamie avoids my gaze and tries to rest his hand on my troubled cheek. His fingers are dressed in an amalgam of dried red and white paint. "**Ask it whatever you want. It'll prove it to you.**"
I've heard of this before. I've seen this before, in my daydreams, when I would lie awake in the morning waiting for the day and the dread of that day to inevitably settle in, seeing my doomed self in front of a royal blue genie dripping out of a bottle, or a crippled and ragged homeless man who happens to be a thousand year old wizard choosing humble little me to make three wishes. One billion dollars. No, then the IRS would chase me down and rape me silly.
It takes me some time to realize `this is not a dream`, and this is actually my son ***Jamie*** in front of me, begging me to ask this inanimate crystal ball a question. The *fuzziness* of my daily world has become so dreamily vague that I struggle to see any difference at all, and even my memory of yesterday has begun to seem more and more like a dream.
But now, I can say to you, my good friend, *reality,* how I have known all along that I will die. And that my childish fear of death has long faded like autumn leaves buried under snow. That my only apprehension now is no longer my primeval fear for my own soul, but for my son's.

Jamie? "**Jamie?**" His name is difficult to say with the drought in my mouth, the dry crispiness of my

chapped lips. Those two words appear jagged, tattered, and red, like shreds of paper tussled together.
"**Mom? What is it mom**?"
"**Jamie, I'm going to die**." The beeping of my unsteady heart begins to fade away into dreamland. The tooth dust stench is going away, and my world is slipping through the cracks in the walls—my only anchor are these painted words between me and my beautiful and stupid son.
"**But mom, we can ask for a cure. We can ask how we can stop it. It can help you**."
"**Jamie, I am going to die**."
"**But, mom…**"
"**I am going to die, and so are you. Why don't you want to know?**"

                                      die

                  die

         die

The word **die** floats up and away, black as spent coal. He doesn't answer, and my world begins to slip away again. His violent gaze rests on THE SPHERE; I knew I would ask IT some hopeful question, yet in vain. He knows that this same disease causing my brain to rot and my reality to melt has a coin-flip's chance of resting, dormant, hidden away in his mind until it erupts, one day, like it did in me, changing me forever…this demonic possession of the self and soul…

I lose control of myself when he begins mouthing,
"**what is the point....**" Tactile pressure on my
fingertips—
The truth is surprisingly light—
Flung out the window, it spins with a lack of purpose—
I wait impatiently for shatters—
(I return momentarily)

and cannot control myself, and I shout *GET OUT!*

GET OUT! GET OUT! Until my throat burns
He covers my mouth just like his father did, forcefully and until my
lips begin to tear. Jamie, my boy. Why are you crying? He goes to the
window. He shouts "**WHY WOULD YOU DO THAT**." He double-
checks to make sure the door is locked. He paces back and forth,
scratching his scalp, flakes cascading. He sits by the window and
watches the world end for a second, then flies panicked out the
room
3:14. Eternity passes. The room is empty with us.
The truth? Why is it so tempting? Why doesn't he want
to know? Why do I want to know?
Words are shaking in my head they have to be
punctuated by a question mark which always
looked so weird to me

? ? ?   ? **?** ? ?   ?   ?

? **?** ??????

Where did this ridiculous curve and dot originate? Even
questions rolling around in my brain are punctuated by
a phonetic enunciation rising up—the difference
between
I am going to <u>die.</u>

And
Am I going to <u>die?</u>
And even
Am I going to die?
My entire life has been gift-wrapped in unanswered questions. But now I can start to unwrap them. Why am I afraid?
You are afraid because you are going to die, it would say.
But that is not the truth. That is not the *simple* truth.
Why am I so afraid? I can hear Mr. Speakeasy's chuckle, keeping his garden alive, *pffft pffft pffft*.
"Why am I going to die?"

"William?" My lips are caked in dead flesh.

He bursts awake.

"Mary-Belle? That can't be you?"

He's sunken into his bed, chin against his chest. Bandages wrapped around his head like the proverbial mummy, two blackened pools of blood where his eyes should be. Bethany's left us alone.

My left hand keeps dancing defiantly.

"It's funny. I always wanted to be neighbors." He says that but doesn't laugh or chuckle. "It's almost like fate. Fate." He looks (looks?) off in the distance, mouth agape, as if he senses an apocryphal angel here in our room. "If...if you had one chance...if you could do one thing...Oh god, nevermind."

My left hand throws a box of Kleenex at him. He swivels his head around in a shocked but subtle understanding.

328

"Umm…" He pauses. "The truth is…" He takes a deep sigh that seems to purge him of whatever spirit is hovering over him. "You remember those old fortune machines? The ones with the gypsy woman. Or was he a man…No. Madame Harmony. 'Come forward,' she would say. On a loop. You know, that robot, that would give you a fortune. 50 cents. It's mouth would move like a marionette. She had these large, wide, bug eyes, just staring right into the depths of you. They'd snap open when you gave her a quarter. Sometimes they'd snap open at random. And they'd follow you. My dad said, in some universes, they told actual fortunes. In some universes, they were actually marmots. He went on and on. He would tell me how in our universe, fortunes were an arbitrary, predestined, mathematical tug. Expanding since the start of the big bang. Protruding us in some fatal direction. He, in a way, was a fortune teller, but with numbers and formulas. I mean, I was just a kid. I didn't understand a lick of what he was selling. Every time I saw Madame Harmony, she had this large, feral cat always sitting on top of her. That cat's probably dead now."

He stops for a few moments. His absent eyes rest on a distant object in the room. The object is arbitrary because he has no eyes. The (lacking) stare contains an immense source of meaning, or lack thereof.

"The only time I used it was the first time I used it. My dad gave me a 1955 quarter. Why do I remember the year…" He proceeds to speak as if he's reading a checklist of his memories. "I take the quarter, I insert it, it goes click-clank. Her eyes pop open. They look left, they look right, like she's waking up for the first time in a hundred years or so. Her eyes were green, like jade emeralds. They blinked a few times.

"Then she said, mechanically, 'Your fortune has been earned.' That's what I heard. But, what I think, what she actually said was, 'Your fortune is discerned.' This little slip of paper slid out, like those receipts you get at the gas station."

His absent eyes shift to a breeze from the open window. The sunlight protruding through the teal blinds, blanketing the entire room in a darkly green shadow, until the sun continues to set, giving rise to a brighter shade of green.

"You know what she told me? You know what? She told me:

'Fortune not found. Abort, Retry, Ignore, question mark.'"

William begins chuckling deeply, until his dry humorous breaths whittle away into pathetic coughs. The look in his absent eyes reminds me of Jamie when he was six years old, before that timeless wizard (death, slow and steady) stole his beautiful blonde hair away from me. I can see myself, young and beautiful (once), carrying him in my arms. We are at the carnival, and up above; the blinking spots in the night sky begin to fade into amorphous billows of clouds. My red polka dot blouse is dancing from bursts of wind fabricated by swinging goliaths of metal dressed in blinking, blinding lights. He has fallen off the monkey bars, so he tells me, and doesn't know what is wrong with his arm. His left hand twists around, dangling, lifeless. His wrist makes an L shape. His index and middle finger bends at forty-five degrees. He is not crying. He looks at me like he loves me, deeply and forever.

Madame Harmony, I would give my life to ask you all these painful puzzles tearing through my brain like bloodthirsty piranhas. When will this festering rotten cacophony ripping me to shreds do away with me once and for all? When will I perish off this mortal, pathetic, and worthless coil?

I've come to accept the lifelessness I am soon to become. But my heart, it screams in agony, because it can never ask Madame Harmony if my beautiful bastard son Jamie will be torn apart like me? If I plagued him with this monstrous gift?

Madam Harmony: will I ever see that look from my son ever, ever again?!

A faint wind…a voice off in the meaningless distance. A honky tonk radiophone crescendos into a slippery slope of wouldn't you know…

Bethany says, "You know, Mr. Burroughs, I found your white ball thingy outside…I thought I should bring it back to you. It looks so expensive, so important!"

Chapter Twenty-Eight
The Quest for the Holy Grail

Arthur De La Cruz does not know how, when, or why he suddenly began tearing up. He has some theories:

- Being amongst passionate and like-minded individuals gave him a strong sense of belonging he hadn't felt in forever (perhaps never)
- Seeing real progress towards change being made
- The tear gas canisters shot over the crowd's heads a few minutes ago
- The sight of the U.S. Capitol
- The potential destruction of said Capitol
- The exhilarating feeling that he could die here, a palpable taste of corporeality
- Losing his body in the barbaric chants of "STOP THE STEAL" and "LIBS, DYKES, HEADS ON PIKES"

Likely a combination of many of these theories, but his excitement prevents him from doing the math.

Thinking about math made him reflect briefly on how he arrived at the edge of the U.S. Capitol building, prepared to charge in behind the revolting crowd pushing further and further up through the failing barricades.

Arthur had ordered numerous items online that he thought he would never order:

- A paintball mask
- Beretta black-leather shooting gloves
- A camo jacket and pants
- Lightweight tactical military boots (reviews said these were best for climbing)
- An American flag
- Extra .38 bullets
- White bread
- Processed ham
- American cheese

Luckily, they all arrived sooner than their guaranteed shipping—except for the American flag and the bullets, which were all out of stock and wouldn't arrive for a few months.

His path has been coded this way, his journey mapped by a programmed series of sequences, a sophisticated set of algorithms in a chaotic mess of a world, ready to gather a few hefty inputs to shape the rest of the path—but the destination was always the same. Code is not infinite; all software has an end date. This end date, right now, may be his—but what a glorious way to wrap it all up, in a neat, albeit bloodied, bow.

A large phalanx rises up behind Arthur, carrying a variety of mock flags on makeshift flagpoles—paint roller extensions, pitchforks, steel bars, PVC pipes—waving them left and right, even pointing them forward to intimidate the officers and guards, hiding behind their riot shields, cloudy from the fiery exhales, threatening with grinning teeth to unleash their pepper spray.

Arthur had made his way through the back of the crowd quickly enough, where most people gathered to protest in one place—without moving forward. The crowd seemed to inflate from the inside, eventually consuming the entire campus grounds. They had come there to protest the election they (mostly) all believed had been stolen from them. Some had come to cause trouble. Some had actually come hoping to get lost in the nebulous mob and shoot a couple of bullets, break a couple windows, maybe die for a cause that had mostly been fabricated from the aging minds drying out from an addiction to un-abridged power.

The crowd had burgeoned much like a brushfire in a forest; a few sparks borne from a slightly sincere doubt, magnified by thousands of carefully aimed lenses to motivate those sparks to mature into flames, enough to swallow the entire forest or leave a permanently scorched scar of earth that would find its only value in its futile permanence in a fleeting history.

Most of them watched the same videos and read the same stories that kept Arthur glued to his phone before bed. Most of them had the same servings of a singular kind of reality. *But if 100,000, or 200,000, or 4,000,000, however many believed in that singular kind of reality—who is to say…*

By the time he reaches the top of the stairs, the mob that he had followed splits into two groups:

- The left half begins tearing down the scaffolding that had just been built for a welcoming ceremony prepared ahead of schedule for foreign dignitaries from potentially warring nations.
- The right half barrels forward, up to the steel, waist-high fences that panicked officers threw together in a frenzy. The mob moves like an amorphous blob at first, but begins to straighten itself into a more bellicose missile, a ballistic force of ignorance.

Arthur now finds himself at the head of that missile, barreling right up the steps to the front door. Those around him shout and spit at the small group of officers caught off-guard, clearly not prepared for such madness. A man next to him, wearing a Viking's helmet and no shirt, painted half-red and half-blue, grips the base of an officer's helmet and rips it off. Those around him—including a handful of older obese men wearing American flags for capes—begin to beat at this officer's face with their makeshift flags. Immediately the young officer's nose shatters, spitting blood into the air before collapsing beneath the crowd. They continue to beat him while he convulsively shakes, hands covering his face—and he just lies there, lifeless. With that, the crowd manages to push the gates aside, trampling over the young officer now resting in a fattening pool of blood.

Arthur is late to the front doors, where the crowd pools and stalls. More and more shouts behind him command to storm the place. Officers try to hold the doors shut, but the crowd smashes the windows and forces them open in due time.

As the crowd pushes through, one officer cries desperately for them to stop as he is crushed between the door and the wall. The mob burrows through the officers in no time, moving forward, without hesitation, taking every chance to smash against the walls and floors, topple statues, and tear paintings, howling like wild Vikings that have just ransacked a village. A once sacred and hallowed bastion of democracy quickly devolved into a playground ready for the taking.

The mob stops, momentarily, when it reaches the rotunda.

Immediately, Arthur freezes. Statues of historic men placed around the room make him feel small. But the most damning of all was the apotheosis above him, a circle of women all locked in unison with a single white man, whose black and lifeless eyes glared at Arthur with such despondence and gloating...

...surrounded by men of austerity and success, of those who have cemented enough relevance to merit a portrait; those bastards who happened to be remembered, standing on the unmarked graves of hundreds of thousands more who slaved away to push the world towards that future...those who just made their way, long forgotten, remembered only by the bastardized surnames, dangling with trinkets of patronyms and matronyms, cursed with carrying on a lineage until one seed made enough noise to avoid being swallowed by the void...

The sight spurs an even greater temper in Arthur. He will not be swallowed by that void today;

his final act will be historic, tide turning, flipping the world right-side-up. He will be Columbia, crushing the tyranny of the ruling class, but instead shoving that sword and shielding George Washington's ass.

Parts of the mob flank left and right towards the rotunda perimeter, aiming for the statues and busts positioned at guard. One group armed with sledge-hammers begins to smash in the faces of Martin Luther King Jr. and Susan B. Anthony and Lucretia Mott; one weird old man, armed with a strap-on dildo, mocks getting oral from Elizabeth Cady Stanton; another mob, aided by three obese folks in powered wheelchairs carrying capture nooses, brings Dwight D. Eisenhower down to his knees, his head popping off and rolling across the tiled floor; another few start to dig their pitchforks and axes into the painted canvases (one driving the blade right down Thomas Jefferson's painted face, split-ting him in two); another retracts his hand from underneath his pants and smears his own feces all over the kneeling Pocahontas.

Before Arthur can do anything, the mob pushes him further through the Rotunda, into the succeed-ing halls. Arthur cannot resist, cannot move; the mob carries him forward with an unbridled vigor; momentarily he feels weightless, unbound no longer by petty paychecks and the doldrums of a wasted, starving soul—he feels like a part of something, like some decorative figurehead stewarding a warship.

This warship eventually comes upon a solitary officer—a young black man, his helmet visor above his head, holding a pistol. Arthur sees the absolute fear, the cowardly lion behind a uniform that no longer provoked apprehension or delay. Two white

men, dressed like gorillas, begin to pound the floor, intimidating him, goading him on to fulfill their desperate narrative of oppression—
—*Go on, shoot me,* they howl. *Go on. You don't have the balls. Shoot me.*
—*Stay back! Stay the fuck back! Listen!*
— [Mockingly] *Stay back! Stay back!*
—*That's a fucking order! Stay back or I'll shoot!*
— [Gorilla grunts ensue] *Shoot! Shoot! Shoot!*

The gorillas close in. The officer retreats up a set of stairs, looking behind him constantly in hope of backup. The gorillas, on their hands and feet, burst up the stairs, howling. The officer panics and screams, firing a shot off with his eyes wide open. The bullet passes right past each gorilla, right past Arthur's figurehead ears, further down the crowd—as if it is destined, foretold, its path already laid—right into the neck of a young woman carrying a sign that says:

STOP THE VIOLENCE

The mob erupts, volatile, swarming the officer, pummeling him with fists, bats, flagpoles; his face is crushed in by military boots bought at thrift stores. Arthur even doubts his own eyes when he sees, amongst the violently stomping bodies, two white officers, their fiery anger hidden behind the fogged visors of their riot helmets; one of them even wields a confederate flag, and plunges its bottom end into the black officer's chest and stomach, over and over.

The mob progresses forward, feeling righteous, trampling over the twitching corpse in disgust.

Arthur passes, and looks at the remains of a young, frightened face, nose smashed in, eyes bloodshot and bleeding, teeth shattered—and he does not have time to pause and reflect on the consequences of actions and the fragility of life before the mob pushes him further up the stairs.

Upstairs, sunlight beams in celestially from the windows; there's not a soul around. The mob splits down corridors, bursting through wooden office doors and trampling down hallways like a mad stampede.

Arthur finds himself left alone, finally; he feels the weight of his own feet again, having been seafaring for so long now. Left to his own devices, Arthur wanders the halls blindly, letting Columbia guide him forward to where he is meant to be.

Until, eventually, he comes upon a double set of doors, labeled:

FILMING - DO NOT ENTER
SECURITY AND INTELLIGENCE COMMITTEE
HEARING IN PROGRESS

It is so blatantly abandoned by security, likely having run off to deal with the massive crowd storming the castle. Like the forces of nature willed it to be so. Like the forces of the world have propelled him into this war. Like pollen borne by the wind. This is the place he will make his mark; his father's .38 special is his Excalibur; his reality is a majestically thin tapestry woven over his mind's eye, an impeccable facade crafted by an algorithmic Merlin®—for he knows nothing of the other realities out there. But he does know that these villainous

Saxons opposite this threshold are attempting to ransack the throne of democracy, to rob the world of the truth of what really happened for the sake of lining their filthy pockets. Arthur prepares with a deep sigh—reminding him of peaceful times, of the grass in his backyard, shuffling through blades to find a four leaf clover, of passing romances with women whom he never progressed conversation past Mondays or the weather.

The door edges open. Peeking through, he sees an entire crowd of the backs of heads, frozen and watching a play of sorts—unaware that the real climax is behind them, here to herald the inevitable denouement. Arthur is hyperventilating, stepping forward to reveal himself to the standing cameras and lights suddenly panning in his direction offstage. He recognizes Senator Paul Palient atop his throne; and the man he is questioning, a pale, thinning man, seated with a condensing glass of water in his left hand; he can make out the placard behind his chair:

Reserved for Peter Burroughs

He hears hollowed shouts of *gun, gun* crescendo from around the amphitheater. He aims his gun at the man above the placard, suddenly surprised by the immense tension of the trigger—almost pushing back against his will, urging him not to.

The victims of bullets—or anyone, for that matter, who knocks on the instantaneous doorstep of death—they describe it as a slowing of time, their "life flashing before their eyes," a momentary loop in the film that reawakens lifelong memories woven into a neat, picturesque narrative. Those fortunate few whose credits are not yet rolling, they can go on to describe the euphoria of life after facing certain death. They have a new lease on life, benefitting from that brief summary, a Capraesque reflection, of what they have done and have yet to do. They walk away breathing a different kind of air, one much more fresh and earthly.

But those who pull the trigger—at least those who do so for the first time—don't have the benefit of film. They are actors on a stage where time cannot be reversed, actions that have reactions which cannot be halted or undone. Their few seconds afterwards are much more hollow and pyrrhic; those seconds are quantum, slipping away—because the novice trigger does not know exactly when the bullet will fire. But when it does, when the flash and blast erupt, the scrim partition between that person's past and terrible future shatters instantly. They are not faced with a blessed replay. They instead stand before an audience of sudden reality—they cannot reverse the trajectory of that bullet, and they are forced to watch and listen to the impact. Their life does not flash before them. Their life has not just begun. It has just ended. What remains is a hollow shell casing. Some reload, some do not.

When Arthur becomes this empty shell, his tongue weighs a thousand pounds, and he feels the back of his throat hollow out. His time does not slow down or stop. It just is—just like his entire life, even up to this point. It just is.

341

Chapter Twenty-Nine
The Capricious Trial of One Charles Darnay, in which Our Faithless Protagonist Contemplates Treason Against Either His Country or His Own Forsaken Soul

Peter had expected a panic attack either the evening before or the morning of the hearing. Maybe the adrenaline had dissipated his anxiety, or at least it clouded his vision enough to suppress his worries off into a blind spot.

He hadn't told himself this, but his body knew this was one of the most important days of his life.

After a steaming and lengthy shower, he examined himself in the mirror, a portrait surrounded by a humid border of fog. He thought deeply about the lies Senator Paul Palient told him to reveal, and whether he would go through with it. His options:

1. Lie, and say the apparatus revealed that a legitimate election was in fact fraudulent and stolen, and potentially change the course of his

country's history, reputation, and integrity; yet, by doing so, conceal his own terrible treasonous crimes of misplacing the apparatus, and subsequently attempting to hide destroy any evidence of his wrongdoing, leading to the deaths of hundreds of innocent people

2. Don't lie, saving what little vapid honor he had left, and consequently lose his job, likely being arrested for ineptitude, tampering evidence, and whatever treasons Senator Paul Palient would use his influence to charge him with, thus destroying his credibility and reputation, and concurrently the credibility, reputation, and legacy that would inevitably burden his children and their children with a malignant tumor of abhorrence and henceforth limiting their potential for a peaceful life for generations to come— *"oh, you're THAT Burroughs... descendants of a traitor?"*

To lighten his mood, he drew a shaving-cream mustache over his upper lip in the mirror after shaving his practically clean-shaven face. Once he wiped the mustache away and observed his clean-shaven self, he then repeated his favorite Bond phrase:

"Where there's smoke, there's fire..."

After wiping it away, his reflection began to dissolve with the humid fog, rapidly losing all sense of time and place.

Daydreaming through multiplication tables and proper nouns, Peter always fantasized a dead-set future on becoming a world infamous spy. Especially when his father eventually came home from a three-month sabbatical in Amsterdam, bringing Peter somewhat of a consolation prize for his labored waiting—an authentic toy pistol, homemade and authentic. He purchased it from Tiffany Case's house, which—seizing upon fame to make a small fortune—became a gift shop selling Bond paraphernalia to the occasional touring Bond enthusiast. (They closed down almost instantly after Peter's father left, since he had been their only customer in months.) It was a Walther PPK, with matching brown grips, and a bright-orange safety ring at the barrel, which Peter promptly pried off with a razorblade. Fortunately for him, William Burroughs Sr. was soon off on yet another sabbatical, so he lacked the paternal foresight to prevent such a dastardly and dangerous decision.

But Peter cherished it too much to take it out anywhere; he left it in his room, right on his nightstand; every night, before bed, he would grip the pistol and pretend to shoot the hot air balloons in his fading and peeling wallpaper, along with the occasional monster in the closet.

But his younger brother William did steal it, once. He brought it to school, concealed in his backpack,. William unleashed it when the monstrously-sized Sam Patterson bullied him again at recess. A nearby teacher immediately tackled William, breaking his leg. They confiscated the gun. Peter witnessed the whole thing. He never forgave William, even though he did not complain when he had to wheel him home from the hospital, and practically wheeled him everywhere for five months.

When the condensation on his bathroom mirror faded, the sight of his naked and hairless self shocked him back from the past, yanked right out of the nostalgic comfort of what seemed like just yesterday, shaken and hollowed by that all-too-often rude awakening that time never stops— the weighty despair of *now* and *what's next.*

And what hit him hardest was this: that all his day-dreams of spy cars, gadgets, and world-traveling were only daydreams, movies never made; and his future, his whole sense of self, would be dictated by his decision that day—to lie, or to tell the truth, for once in his life.

Ada's concerned and loving visage appeared behind him, followed by her gentle fingers resting over his naked shoulders. She rested her chin on his collarbone; his panic attack subsided, and he felt at peace. Her eyes begged him not to go.

"Do you want to talk about last night?" Ada asked him, peering into his reflection in the steamy mirror:

— Peter, you have to be honest with me.
— I'm always honest with you, Ada.
— Peter, you have to tell me about Richard.
— Why do I have to tell you about Richard?
— I'm here for you Peter, no matter what.
— I don't understand.
— It's important to be honest with each other.
— I'm going to get a glass of milk.
— Peter, please sit down and just listen to me for once.
— Ada, I will—but can you please not scream?

She had concerns over a "feeling," an instinct that something awful was going to happen. This was a quirky curiosity Peter adored—someone as rational, intelligent, and matter-of-fact as Ada would believe any inkling of a gut feeling. She was wrong more often than she was right, but the times she was right were uncanny: when they avoided taking the 9:00 am flight that eventually burst into flames before takeoff; when she threw away the fresh salmon because she just had a feeling the expiration date was off a couple days; when she knew something was wrong with Isaac only a few months into the pregnancy. But Peter disregarded these as mere chance. Even today. What's the worst that could happen? After all, it was the U.S. Capitol—it must be safe and well-guarded. Besides, he was armed. He didn't have the guts to use it, but he at least had one.

"We love you, Peter." Ada whispered, her warm cheek melting into the curvature between his neck and shoulder. She finished after some time, wrapped in her own troubled thought: "No matter what."

— I love you. No matter what.
— I know. I know.

Visions flashed before him: Senator Paul Palient, Richard, the countless unnamed men at gyms and clubs, the cloudy unmoving eyes of his lifeless father, even a brief echo of William howling in pain in his wheelchair—

"I'm a bad person, Ada."

She did not respond immediately. Instead, her gaze veered off to some unnamed space, a den hidden away by years of foliage carefully woven by her own resolve.

She turned back toward him, kissing his temple, then leaned back to his ear, whispering: "I know you'll do the right thing now."

***

Peter had never seen so many near-death white people in ties and pantsuits before. Before the hearing started, most seemed close to falling asleep in their chairs, listlessly shuffling through countless papers or raising their heads, mouths wide-open like dumbfounded animals, squinting through their bifocals at the perplexingly tiny text on their phones.

Peter found his assigned seat, facing the committee, overburdened by a feeling: that this hearing was more akin to a trial to adjudicate his fateful execution.

346

The chairman of the Senate Security and Intelligence Committee, Mr. Chairman, seemed to grasp the clear-cut coincidence of his name and position. He began reading his opening statement behind his glasses, his small, beady eyes magnified into owl's eyes, his thinning white hair glistening from the lights and cameras. His voice was raspy, like he had a perpetual frog in his throat, and he reeked of cigarettes.

"Today's Senate Security and Intelligence Committee is meeting today to investigate classified file #8-32, which has recently been brought to this committee's attention by my esteemed colleague, the dutiful Mrs. Burnstein, having been provided scheduled updates from representatives from Strategic Homeland Administration Management, which is currently under contract review with the United States Central Intelligence Agency. As is protocol under national security guidelines, Mrs. Burnstein felt she had to share with this committee the potential security threat posed by the disappearance of an...apparatus...or...yes... that was being examined under jurisdiction of Strategic Homeland Administration Management." He flipped his papers over to begin reading what he really wanted to say. "As we all know, today's political climate invites a wide multitude of national security threats—terrorists, at home and abroad, crack-cocaine and opioids, and so on. But once again, we find Strategic Homeland Administration Management embroiled in another fumbled job that once again warrants a severely close and critical examination of the private sector's role in the national public's interests. I can't count with my two old hands how many times we've questioned the legitimacy of the Central Intelligence Agency's contractual relationship with Strategic Homeland Administration Management. Bay of Pigs. Waco. Iraq and Afghanistan. Just to name a few. And, my fine, esteemed colleagues across the aisle have most consistently advocated for continuing to rely on the innovations and objectivity of the private sector. In fact, My esteemed colleague Mr. Palient has been a steadfast advocate for the very company we are now investigating. Here we are again, meeting for the upteenth time to investigate this...apparatus...which we will officially unclassify today. Strategic Homeland Administration Management has sent Mr. Peter Burroughs as their representative today, and we will proceed as normally and diligently to question him and provide us everything he knows about this case, how it went south, and how the company plans on resolving it. I'll end with this—no more classified this and classified that. There's a truth here that we have to get to the bottom of. Now, as is decorum, I understand Mr. Burroughs has an opening statement to provide."

Peter looked down at his desk and was surprised to see a typed statement written for him, seemingly appearing out of thin air. It was crisp and warm, freshly printed. But he felt embarrassed when his sweaty fingers began to dampen the edges of the paper.

This was the pre-written statement that his overseers at Strategic Homeland Administration Management had prepared for him.

"Ahem. Yes."

"Excuse me, Mr. Burroughs?" Mr. Chairman interrupted. "We can't hear you. I believe you have to turn your microphone on."

Peter realized he had to hold down the green button on his microphone when he wanted to speak.

"Ahem. Yes. Is that better?" The microphone boomed and squealed, followed by a convulsion of feedback that echoed throughout the congressional chamber. The audience behind Peter groaned and shuffled.

"Not so close, now," Senator Paul Palient blurted out. He sat all the way to Peter's right, up on his pedestal, leaning back in his chair, hands behind his head, peering down at Peter like he was a child.

Peter shrunk a little. "Is that better?"

"Much," Mr. Chairman blurted.

Peter knew this was his moment to take a stand. Either fall in line with the pre-written statement provided for him and continue his marionette parody of a spy daydream...or, say what he really felt, and reveal who he really was, for all the world to see.

He read verbatim:

"Esteemed representatives of Congress, I thank you for this opportunity to discuss the nature and status of Classified File #8-32. As you are well aware, Strategic Homeland Administration Management has had the privilege of collaborating directly with the United States government since the company first began in the early 1900s with James Allen and Gerald Willis. Since then, the company has overseen numerous national interests throughout its celebrated career. That's why the current status of Classified File #8-32 is so disturbing to my peers and managers, since it now represents a first for the company, which unequivocally and categorically takes full responsibility for any and all consequences. It has been my privilege and honor being awarded agency jurisdiction over this case. I have led an esteemed career with Strategic Homeland Administration Management. I know first-hand the sensitivity of many successful cases handled by the company. In my twelve years as monitoring agent, I have achieved numerous accolades for my performance, most notably in classified espionage and hostage recovery programs in Afghanistan and Istanbul."

Peter didn't recognize any of these words.

"I have dedicated my life to my work. I value my efforts to protect my country and fulfill my duties and obligations. It has always been my dream to serve my country. I have had the esteemed honor of serving on the frontlines of issues of national security, and I look forward to this continued opportunity."

None of this was true. The company had constructed an identity for him, so much that he realized, in front of this jury of senators and audience of the press, he hadn't much of an idea of who he really was anyway.

"As I said before, it has been my privilege and honor being awarded agency jurisdiction over this case, and I am...directly responsible...for any and all incidents related to Classified File #8-32. I am equally prepared to answer any and all questions regarding Classified File #8-32. However..."

This next statement was bold, underlined with red fountain pen, and followed with what looked like handwriting — "DO NOT FUCK THIS UP."

"**However, due to Hyperbolic Circumstance Protocol #89330, I must deny sharing any details relevant to this case that consequently or inconsequentially may or may not lead to breaches in national or international security interests. Therefore, I may only share the information that Hyperbolic Circumstance Protocol #89330 deems sufficient public information. Thank you, and I look forward to answering your questions to the best of my abilities.**"

He was relieved. He hadn't even heard of this protocol before. But, to him, this meant he was entirely off the hook, and could avoid sharing anything at all.

Senator Paul Palient tapped on his microphone three times. "Mr. Chairmuhn, motion to speak regardin' this so-called protocol?"

"Granted."

"If Ah may so uhddress the cuhmmittee. As per the natiuhnal suhcurity guidelines under the Ptoluhmy Act, artuhcle II subsectiuhn IV, this cuhmmittee has agreed-upon adjudicative power to determine whether classuhfied informatiuhn remains classuhfied if the cuhmmittee so votes to declassuhfy said informatiuhn."

Mr. Chairman leaned over to his right, holding his hand over his microphone, and muttered to a withering old woman in a bright pink pantsuit, oversized pearls, and a lazy eye. "Is that a thing?"

She shook her head unconfidently, and shrugged.

Mr. Chairman cleared his throat. "Well then, I suppose we should have a vote then under...the uhm..."

"Ptoluhmy Act, natiuhnal suhcurity guidelines, mah good friend," Senator Paul Palient added, grinning.

"Thank you. Let the committee vote to invoke guide-lines as stated by Senator Palient."

The committee voted unanimously in favor of revok-ing Peter's fabricated right to hide behind a protocol, his final bastion.

Mr. Chairman cleared his throat again, which didn't relieve his raspy voice. "Let the record show the vote was unanimous. So, Mr. Burroughs, let me state clearly that you may not invoke the virtue of classified information when any question requires classified information to be answered satisfactorily. As this matter may be critically important to concerns about national security and safety, it is imperative that you faithfully and truthfully answer any and all questions to the best of your knowledge. We appreciate your being here and your willingness to help us protect the nation." He paused, and organized his papers. "Ok then. Moving on. As is standard procedure, line of questioning will proceed through the committee based on seniority. Each member will have an allotted twenty minutes to question our esteemed witness today. Let's begin with our senior ranking member. The good lady from Massachusetts, Mrs. Hobbes, may begin her inquiry with her allotted twenty minutes."

Mrs. Hobbes, the woman next to Mr. Chairman, adjusted her glasses up to the edge of her nose to get a good look at Peter.

Mrs. Hobbes seemed to shiver every so often, with a lagging vibrato in her withering voice. She almost seemed artificial. Peter could see vividly her attempts to postpone the aging process—surgically augmented lips and cheek-bones, bright red hair-dye bleeding into the balding spots on her wispy silver hairline, and bright blue eyeshadow to distract from the valleys of crow's feet crescendoing from every corner of her sagging face.

"Mis-ter Bourbon…" she struggled for a moment to get a good view of her written questions. "Burroughs. Oh. Excuse me. Mis-ter Burroughs. Could you please tell me about your relationship…" She spoke in a floaty iambic pentameter, each syllable punctuated by an abrupt silence of hesitation, as if she had to take a suddenly deep breath before stumbling on to the next syllable. "With this case?"

"Well, ma'am, I was assigned as the supervising agent for case #8-32. I oversaw ongoing research involving the apparatus."

"And, Mis-ter Burroughs, what was known about the case…this case, before it was assigned to you?"

"Well, ma'am…" (he had an urge to hide behind "it's classified.") "When the device was discovered, it was transported to our isolated research facilities, under strict supervision, as is protocol for devices of unknown origin. Not much else was known about the case when it was given, I mean, assigned to me."

"And can you tell me what this device…does? Why is it so important for us to be concerned about its absence today?"

"Well, ma'am…" He glanced at Senator Paul Palient, who wasn't even looking at Peter—he was fiddling with the cap of his pen, deliberately avoiding Peter's desperate gaze for any kind of directive or hint on how to proceed. "The device is something that we don't know much about."

Mrs. Hobbes threw her wrinkled hands up in frustration. "Well," she huffed, "just tell me what you *do* know, then."

"Well…" He glanced again towards Senator Paul Palient, who had closed his eyes and fallen into a deep and untroubled sleep. "Well…" He stretched that *well* as long as he could, until he physically felt the tip of his tongue go slightly numb. "After careful research and observation, we discovered that this apparatus, which again, was of unknown origin, was capable of providing factual information based on any possible question or query."

Mrs. Hobbes looked miles away. So he continued.

"If I could elaborate…if you asked it a question, any question, it would provide the answer, with absolute, 100% accuracy."

Some people behind Peter chuckled. He heard a deep and distant voice mutter under their breath: "*what the fuck is he on?*"

"I know it sounds unbelievable at first, but I am providing you with a basic and factual summary, in respect of the committee's wishes. This was a device that is, to be frank, unprecedented."

Mrs. Hobbes swallowed, her eyes bulging a little, seemingly unsure of where to go next. "Can you, umm… elaborate…more?"

"To put it as simply as I possibly can, umm…whatever question you ask, it gives you the correct answer. No matter what."

The room erupted into a choir of hushed murmurs, punctuated by occasional scoffs of disbelief.

Mr. Chairman stepped in, breaking decorum. "So, let me get this as straight as an arrow. You could ask it something like...what's gonna happen tomorrow? And it would give the exact right answer, word for word?"

"Yes, sir."

Mrs. Hobbes stepped in: "Can it predict the future?"

"Yes, ma'am. Again, to be perfectly, perfectly clear to this committee, it will answer whatever question you ask, and it will always be right. Always."

"And you have no idea who made it? Where it came from? What it was designed for?" Mr. Chairman asked, dumfounded.

"Unfortunately, no, sir. We didn't have the chance to, after it disappeared."

Senators throughout the committee began to mumble their own musings on the matter. Some suspected opposing nations; others were inclined to believe their political opponents had some involvement. Mrs. Hobbes whispered to her closely seated colleagues, all of whom shrugged their shoulders and adopted blank dumbstruck masks.

After confiding in her clueless confidants, she turned back towards Peter.

"Obviously this kind of power...I mean, device...is of great concern for...concerns regarding the...national security business. This kind of ineptitude is only further evidence of incompetence from your organization. We'll need to get to the bottom of this. Otherwise, lives and livelihoods are at stake. If in the wrong hands, classified information regarding national security concerns could lead us into the brink of war. So then, first things first, whose fault was this, anyway?"

Peter thought to himself—it was *me*. "As supervising agent, I was responsible for overseeing those who were managing the research main department heads, who were responsible for monitoring the head research department managers, who then were responsible for directing the senior research directors."

"So you were the main person in charge?"

"Well, not exactly. I was the supervising agent. The supervising director oversaw my work."

"So he or she was in charge?"

"No."

"So who was in charge?"

"Well…the supervising director reported directly to the senior management director of supervision, who…"

"Stop for just a moment. Who exactly was the highest in command?"

"Well…ma'am…"

Senator Paul Palient's gravely directives hovered over him like a dreadful phantom.

"I don't have that information in front of me right now." Peter's sense of ego, already deflated, succumbed to self-pity. His identity and integrity had been constructed for him on cheap paper and synthetic ink, his words chosen for him, his voice a cheap parlor trick of ventriloquism. He lost all agency (likely long ago). Peter had knowingly shied from the truth in recent years; but he knew these few truths now, and more than ever—he was the one on trial, he was deathly afraid, and he had no clue what to say.

— I'm talking about your journey, Peter. Let's face it, you're not your old self anymore. Even I want that old you back. I miss that. I miss you. But this isn't about just what I want. I know that something is changing in you. Something that I will never understand.

— Ada, let me get you some tissues.

— No. Not yet. I need to say these things to you.

— Okay. I'm listening.

— I'm never going to understand what's changing. That is your journey. I'm blessed....blessed to share my journey with you. We've been wrapped in each other since we met. But I need to understand this. I want you to follow your journey. I don't want you to lie to me. Wherever these changes take you, I will be there if you still want me. But I will not, I will not, let myself get in the way of your journey.

— I have to go get ready.

— Peter, please stay.

— Ada, your nails are cutting me.

"Mr. Burroughs? Mis-ter Burr-oughs!" Peter snapped out of some phantom daydream, immediately forgotten.

"I'm so sorry…" Peter felt ashamed again. Again. For the thousandth time in his life. He was sick of feeling ashamed.

"Mr. Burroughs?" Mr. Chairman cleared his throat again, seriously, matter-of-factly.

"I apologize. Can you please repeat the question?"

"There was no question, Mr. Burroughs. Mrs. Hobbes has run out of time. We were saying we need to move on to the next representative."

"Yes. I'm sorry. I'm ok now. Let's do this." Instantly he felt the cameras leering at him, the millions of viewers deriding his corny reply.

"Yes. Let's. Mr. Palient?"

Senator Paul Palient smiled at Peter, and winked. His tall, pall-bearing presence seemed to escalate miles above Peter, peering down at him in some medieval forum for final judgment.

"Why, thank you, Mr. Chairman." Senator Paul Palient shuffled some papers absently, set them aside, then clasped his hands together. He leaned forward, adjusted his small bifocals slightly, and flared his nostrils up.

"Mr. Burroughs."

Peter gulped loud enough for the microphone to pick it up.

"Mr....Burroughs. Ah only have a few questions for you regardin' this appuhratus and its disuhppearance...If you would so kindly answer mah questions as truthfully as possible, Ah would greatly uhppreciate it, sir."

Peter nodded. In his head, he outlined his situation once more. Senator Paul Palient knows everything—that indeed it was Peter's direct fault that the apparatus was missing. That Peter deliberately sabotaged all the security recordings to hide his ineptitude. That he was lying right to the faces of elected United States representatives. That he was committing perjury, betraying everything he swore to stand for when he became an agent. Now, Senator Paul Palient wants him to lie. And if he doesn't lie, and tells the truth, they'll know he was lying anyway about everything else—so either admit the lie, or tell some more lies. *In a trial about the truth.*

Then there was the whole other noose tied to his neck—about Richard—

"Mr. Burroughs, let us get to the mattur at ha-und. Ah would like to ask about the kinds of queries you and your team suhbmitted to this duhvice. As you indicated, those in research had the pleasure of interactin' with this duhvice. Can you kindly summuhrize for us the kinds of matters related to our natiuhn's interests that were uhdressed to this duhvice?"

"Well...there were a lot..."

"Mr. Burroughs, forgive me, and do not take any uhffense, but Ah must say your ineptuhtude is very cuhncernin' and cuhmpels me to inquire uhbout criminal lituhgation uhgainst your good persuhn. Now, can you please answuhr my question?"

Despite the sweat beading down the back of his neck, Peter sensed Senator Paul Palient was hamming up his southern drawl to appeal to the drama—the drama he barely worked to orchestrate. encumbered by his bottled panic, Peter imagined tiny strings pulling at his shoulder blades—*what's the word,* he thought—*marionette.*

"We did ask a series of questions related to national interests, sir. Yes we did."

"And what, praytell, did you ask?"

"Well..." Peter pretended to look at papers in front of him. He even shuffled them a bit to provide a little more breathing room for his flailed conscience. "Considering the controversy of the recent election, that being one of my organization's primary focal points, sir...we inquired about some of those said controversies."

"Such as?"

"The issues of ballot counts. Related to...illegal votes being cast. Miscounting. Fraudulent practices."

"You see, ladies and gentlemuhn in the room tuhday, there is a silvuhr linin' to this dark and dreary cloud hangin' over our heads tuhday. Despite the obvious treachery afoot, we have access to un-eq-uiv-uh-cuhl tes-tuhmoniuhl evidence that this most recent uhlection was fraudulent and corrupt, leavin' my genuhruhs colleagues across the aisle cuhmplicit, and questionin' the legitimacy of the offices they claim to hold tuhday. The peaceful protestuhrs at our walls will have their voices heard tuh-day. And finally we will know the truth."

Mrs. Hobbes and Mr. Chairman interrupted almost simultaneously. "Excuse me!"

Mrs. Hobbes continued. "I believe Mr. Palient is out of order. Is he out of order? Is he?" She raised her hands above her head in desperate disbelief.

Peter could hear shouting in the back of his mind, like a crowd was ready to erupt and take over.

"I'm sorry," the chairman exclaimed, "I drifted out for a bit...what was the question you asked, Mr. Palient?"

"The question was..."

"He is out of order!" Mrs. Hobbes reiterated.

"I hear you, Mrs. Hobbes, and I'm just trying to wrap my head around this. Mr. Burroughs, are you saying what I think you're saying?"

"I'm sorry sir?" Peter asked.

Mr. Chairman elaborated, "Are you claiming that you have actual evidence of election fraud?"

"Well..."

"Because, if you do, well, then this is all very, very concerning."

Senator Paul Palient interrupted, "Yes, sir, it is. Tell us the truth, Mistuh Burroughs."

"Mr. Palient is way out of order!" Mrs. Hobbes yelled again.

"Tell us, Peter, tell us the truth!" Senator Paul Palient ordered, laughing as if he had already won.

Peter began to hyperventilate. Looking desperately to his left and right, he began to gasp. "I need water. I need some water, please." It was then, in this emaciated panic, Peter noticed Richard, setting two rows behind him, eyes wide in a wholesome acceptance, a brotherly reassurance that everything was going to be perfectly fine. He tipped his bright-red, mallard-emblazoned cap at Peter, and winked.

"I'm...I'm...."

"What is it?!" Senator Paul Palient shouted.

"I'm....I can't....I am...."

"Fuckin' blurt it out already! The world needs to know!" Senator Paul Patient's voice abandoned his signature southern tint, revealing an entirely bland Midwestern color—something akin to a pale brown or vacant gray; plain, natural, boring.

—Just admit it to me, Peter.
—I don't know what you mean.
—You have to admit it. You have to say it. You. Have to say it.
—I can't. I don't know what you are talking about.
—I know.

Peter stood up, bracing himself for admitting it to the entire world; and, during his abrupt and precipitous rage, Peter felt more alive than he had in some time—as if all the anxiety, all the fear, all the shame and worry, all the self-pity and doubt and hiding and lying and failing had been piling up inside as one volatile, tempestuous, pressure-filled vacuum—and then he suddenly burst, for a brief moment.

Peter shouted, the loudest he could shout:

"I'm fucking…"

Peter's confession was interrupted by an immense burst and clamor. The doors to the chamber flew open. A wave of protestors from outside charged in. Immediately the gallery panicked.

Emerging from the crowd rushing in, some sort of youthful soldier breached the furor, brandishing a revolver and mock military garb, pointing the barrel towards the sky in some purposeful Arthurian crusading gesture.

Before the crowd's discordant screams, the revolver exploded, the flash and subsequent cracking, and Senator Paul Patient's left shoulder exploded into an airy red mist. A second shot went straight into the floorboards, while a third found a direct, seemingly guided, path toward Senator Paul Palient's shining, wrinkled forehead. His head snapped backward, another red geyser spouting in a fanning pattern, as his body toppled backward out of his chair.

The young martyr, eyes wild and distraught, as if his hand were possessed, swung the barrel towards Peter.

Another flash—

Amidst an infinitesimal second before his impending death, Peter had forced himself to think of Ada.

But the flash subsided, and Peter felt no sudden pain or jolt—no sense of honor, like how he imagined it as a child, being shot down in a blaze of glory defending his country.

But he was fine. The flash came from behind him, where Richard stood, his pistol raised straight, aimed at the falling, lifeless body of some young, beguiled martyr.

Chapter Thirty
A Portrait of The Artist's Reclamation

I couldn't find that device after my mother threw it out the window. It had disappeared into the ether, off to ruin someone else's life for the time being. But ruin is cursory; beauty is elemental. I have found out more truth than just my personal and lifelong lie. I've discovered much more underneath the dried paint of my life; an amazing woman who loves me for who I am, and a deeper appreciation of a life without purpose.

In other words, I am off on my way to buy back the art I sold at the pawn shop. Specifically, I want "Autumn's Rebuke." My god awful painting of a lonely poker table in a field plagued by dead auburn leaves; a body hunched over, withered and gray, amidst the only other occupant—the angel of death, in his blinding black cowl. I had thought, at the time, this captured how our trifling lives and hobbies still lead to a mundane death. That we are driven to our graves by sicknesses beyond blood—gambling, booze, drugs, sex, risks. That every gamble led us closer to the final page of our books.

Even if it sucks, I still want it back, because it is *mine*.

And it means something different now. It's not facing death. It's saying *fuck you* to death. Facing mortality by continuing to do what feels *good*—to keep gambling on, playing ducks and drakes with the grim reaper, not giving up, but going on—and embracing the minutiae of every second.

I am ready to gamble. I wanted to buy it back, not just to have it—but to *own it*.

I'm not walking the same way. What I mean is, I'm taking the same path to the pawn shop, but I'm not walking the same. I'm confident. This time, I'm not disguised as a woman. I'm not wearing any sort of disguise at all. The world seems to be opening up to me instead of closing in on me.

***

The bald guy with the curling nose hairs at the pawn shop doesn't seem to recognize me. But he's different this time, too. Those nose hairs aren't there anymore. He must've plucked them. Without them there to distract me, I realize that he' smiling at me. Maybe he's been smiling the whole time, every time, even if his deepened, tired eyes said otherwise.

"Selling? Pawning? Buying??" He asked, looking directly at me. I never noticed his teeth. They were bright white, with one exception: a yellowed, decayed incisor. It makes me think of the beauty of the human mouth, evolved and adapted with canines, incisors, and molars to shred, tear, pulverize.

"Buying," I demand, confidently.

"What are you looking for, sir?"

I took a look around the store. Not many others here with me, besides an old, fat woman looking at

363

coins, and a strong-looking man browsing the guns, wearing a bright red hat with a duck on the front. And two other, much nicer looking men, dapper, in black suits and ties, hunched over some antique bicycles in the corner. I could swear the one with the red hat is staring directly at me beneath his black sunglasses, the other nonchalantly checking a price tag on an ugly green monstrosity of a lamp.

"I'm looking for a piece of art sold here a while back...by a woman. A woman with red hair."

He clears his throat. "I've got a lot of pieces that come through here. Can you be more specific?"

"It's a painting of a field of dead leaves. With a guy playing poker with death."

He leans forward, tying his fingers together, and resting his hands on the glass display case.

"Does the guy have a pair or a flush?"

I don't remember ever painting the exact hand of cards the man was holding.

"A flush," I guess.

"Yeah, I remember that one." He smiles even wider, as if the flush made him that much more lively and ecstatic.

"Ok then," I sigh, relieved. "Where is it?"

"Well, I sold it. For a very profitable price. Must've been a few days ago."

"You're fucking kidding me."

"No, no. swear to God. A couple came in, said they were just browsing." He motioned their path with his hands. "Insisted on paying more than the list price for it. I Won't forget that, for sure."

"How much did they pay?"

"Ten percent over the asking price. They said, 'We just have to have it.'"

"Have to have it?"

"Yes sir. They said it was the most beautiful piece of art they had ever seen." He pauses. "Their words, not mine."

Chapter Thirty-One
The Trial of Polykleitos

CASE FILE #19:9

Reporting Agent #12-36: Peter Burroughs and Agent #101 Richard Palient

Purpose: Classified level 10 clearance (Nuremberg Status, Approval Code #4, investigating retrieval of #8-32, modulating intelligence apparatus)

Status: Open

Background: Active investigation of the apparatus' disappearance based on recent observations from reporting agent #12-36 and Agent #101. Suspect, Subject #23, in custody as of 4:34 p.m.

Reporting agents submitted documented observations of Subject #23 acting erratically at the Matisse Art Gallery, owned and operated by Ms. Ophelia Matisse, who inherited the gallery from her father, Jasper Matisse. Reporting agents note that Subject #23 demonstrated behavior indicative of inebriation

and lack of fortitude. However, Subject #23 demonstrated most suspicious behavior when referencing
the "truth of art," belligerently assaulting multiple
patrons about this "truth," before being confronted by
the gallery owner, Ms. Matisse, after which Subject
#23 stumbled out the door.

Reporting agents, following standard investigation
protocol, did not advance or apprehend the suspect
immediately, but were ordered to observe and, with
any opportunity, discreetly retrieve the suspect (as
per the approval of supervising agents belonging to
the Board of Acquisition Supervision Selection.)

Unfortunately, due to a filing error, this request was
inadvertently filed underneath the tupperware lunch
container of the Acquisition Supervision Selection
Secretary, and stained with a mixture of leftover
tartar sauce and soy sauce.

Thankfully, the Secretary's secretary noticed the
error, and immediately filed the report correctly. However, due to this filing error, the suspect was not
followed or apprehended until the next day. Subject
#23 did not have possession of the apparatus . If the
conclusion of this interview determines that Subject
#23 indeed did have possession of #8-32, and pro-
cedural questioning does *not* provide an adequate
status or location of #8-32, then supervising agent
#12-36 recommends that Subject #23 be exempt
from Nuremberg status for the time being until more
information is collected. Supervisors of supervising
agent #12-36 have acknowledged this exemption;
however, they have stipulated that, if Subject #23's

testimony can provide an adequate avenue for continued investigation, then this exemption is immediately denied and Nuremberg status protocols must be followed immediately.

Profile of Subject #23: Jamie Lafferty.

Mother: Mary-Belle Lafferty, former model, published poet.

Father: unknown.

Biographical investigations have concluded that Subject #23 was likely the result of unlawful venereal enterprise performed on Mary-Belle Lafferty. Jamie Lafferty holds no criminal record, indeed a record of any kind, besides numerous listings for "art" that was auctioned by Subject #23 on various auctioning websites. (No bills of sale found on record). Subject #23 received adequate enough grades throughout tenure at West Pointe Academy. Subject #23 received much poorer grades at Bastille Academy of the Arts, lasting only two semesters until being forced to unenroll due to poor attendance, poor academic performance, and suspicion of possessing, abusing, and distributing opioids.

At this point in the investigation, reporting agents can conclude that Subject #23 provides no immediate threat of any kind; indeed, Subject #23 presents no relevance whatsoever, besides being a suspected possessor of #8-32.

Note: Within the following transcript, violations of Code of Ethics #541abcD have been omitted as

Code of Ethics #541abcD policies are null and void per qualifying conditions indicated via Hanberg's Policy #TTT55^^fkf2.

Note: supervising agents have also been given direct approval to use measures that have recently been scrutinized as "excessive force." Please see Titan Policy #1.

Note: Unfortunately, the agents in charge of subject acquisition mistook Titan Policy #1 for Titan Policy #3. For the sake of brevity, Titan Policy #1 authorizes the use of excessive interrogation techniques if (and only if) the supervising agents determine during the time of the investigative interview whether such techniques could produce sufficient supplementary information to continue investigations.

Titan Policy #3, conversely, authorizes the use of force unilaterally in any relative dealings with the subjects, including but not limited to acquisition, isolation, interrogation, and termination.

Due to this filing error, Subject #23 has undergone rigorous testing and discussion protocols that have left Subject #23 in a physically inconvenient state for lucid interrogation. Subject #23 has been given an appropriate regimen of Astramorph injections. (Note that "appropriate" was up to the discretion of the attending agent, as the suggested regimen chart supplied by medical supervisory staff was lost some time ago.) Some sustained injuries to Subject #23's jaw, bicuspids and molars could not be treated at this time due to the prior-approved vacation of the agency's retained dentist. However, medically trained agents have assured supervising agents that Subject #23 is assuredly in a well-enough state to communicate, despite the pain of doing so.

Note: Transcription was somewhat possible despite the difficulties in interpreting Subject #23's sometimes mumbled and garbled speech, likely caused by the gauze.

Note: despite approval of bereavement leave after the loss of his grandfather to a domestic terrorist attack on Capitol Hill, assisting investigative agent #101. Richard Palient, denied bereavement leave and filed the appropriate request documentation to continue participating in investigations. Filing secretary noted his "extreme rigor and enthusiasm, even in the face of harrowing loss," and also noted the agent's request to take him out for some "parfait."

BEGIN TRANSCRIPT

AGENT BURROUGHS: Commencing investigative interview #22 in case 19:9, chief investigative agent 12-36 Peter Burroughs and assisting investigative agent #101, Richard Palient. Interrogation recipient is Subject #23, Jamie Lafferty. Commencing investigative interview. Can you state your name please, sir?

SUBJECT #23: My name is Jamie. Lafferty.

AGENT BURROUGHS: Jamie, first, I want
you to know that you may speak as
slowly as you need. Do you need a
tissue?

SUBJECT #23: No.

AGENT BURROUGHS: Do you need more
medicine?

SUBJECT #23: Why am I here? Why are
you doing this to me?

AGENT BURROUGHS: Jamie, I want to be
clear on why you have been brought
here today.

SUBJECT #23: Please. I don't know
what's happening.

AGENT BURROUGHS: Jamie, I want to be
clear with you. I want to state what
my expectations are. Then I will tell
you why you are here. Then I will tell
you what I need from you. Then we can
all move forward. Okay?

SUBJECT #23: Are you going to kill me?

AGENT BURROUGHS: Jamie, Jamie, I need
you to trust me. Look at me. Look at
me, Jamie. Can you trust me? I want
what is best for you. Can you help me?
Can you trust me?

AGENT BURROUGHS: Ok. Jamie, listen
closely. Here are my expectations. I
am going to be asking you a series of
questions. I want you to answer every
question I ask you as truthfully, as
honestly, in as much detail, as
possible. Ok? Do you understand?

AGENT BURROUGHS: Okay. Okay then. Now
I will tell you why you are here. You
have been brought here because you
were in possession of something
incredibly, incredibly dangerous. Do
you know what I am talking about?

AGENT BURROUGHS: Okay. You were in
possession of this incredibly
dangerous object, and I need to ask
you a series of questions to ascertain
your involvement and interaction with
this object, in order to understand
what, or how much, was compromised,
and to evaluate what sorts of dangers

372

may result from your interactions. For your own protection.

SUBJECT #23: It hurts to talk.

AGENT BURROUGHS: I need you to try your best.

Video transcription note: Subject #23 nods agreeably. Confirmed visual of subject agreement. Proprietary agent enters the chamber and administers a pre-approved dosage (note: side effects may include drowsiness, inability to operate heavy machinery, hallucinations, regret, pain, echoes of importance…)

AGENT BURROUGHS: Jamie, let's start at the beginning. Can you tell me how you first came into contact with the device?

SUBJECT #23: Someone on the street just gave it to me.

AGENT BURROUGHS: Just gave it to you?

Video transcription note: Subject #23 nods agreeably, although with delayed reaction. Note unusual pupil iteration patterns. Confirmed visual of subject agreement.

AGENT BURROUGHS: Did you know this person?

SUBJECT #23: No.

AGENT BURROUGHS: Can you describe this
person?

SUBJECT #23: All I remember is he was
short. Really short.

AGENT BURROUGHS: About how old did he
look?

SUBJECT #23: I don't know. Thirty or
forty.

AGENT BURROUGHS: Do you know why he
gave it to you?

SUBJECT #23: No.

AGENT BURROUGHS: Was he desperately
trying to give it to you?

SUBJECT #23: No.

AGENT BURROUGHS: Was he relieved in
giving it to you?

SUBJECT #23: It kind of seemed like an
inconvenience to him.

AGENT BURROUGHS: Did he say anything
after giving it to you?

SUBJECT #23: Yes. But I don't
remember.

AGENT BURROUGHS: Did what he said give
you any sense of danger?

SUBJECT #23: No. It was something more
like, I don't know, advice.

AGENT BURROUGHS: What did you do after
he gave the device to you?

SUBJECT #23: I was going to give it to
my girlfriend as a gift.

AGENT BURROUGHS: Why?

SUBJECT #23: Because I thought it was
beautiful.

AGENT BURROUGHS: Did you give it to
your girlfriend?

SUBJECT #23: No.

AGENT BURROUGHS: So what did you do
with it?

SUBJECT #23: I wanted to paint it.

AGENT BURROUGHS: Why did you want to
paint it?

SUBJECT #23: Because I felt like it.

AGENT BURROUGHS: Can you please
elaborate?

SUBJECT #23: What else is there? I just wanted to paint it.

AGENT BURROUGHS: Jamie, I need the entire story.

SUBJECT #23: It's just. Hard to say. I can't describe it. Can I…have some…I'm sorry.

AGENT BURROUGHS: Please continue.

Video transcription note: considerable pause.

SUBJECT #23: Something…primeval erupted in me when I had it with me. It had this eternal geometric simplicity. It felt like the most important thing in the world. It captured everything I've been trying to do.

AGENT BURROUGHS: Trying to do?

SUBJECT #23: I'm an artist.

AGENT BURROUGHS: What kind of artist?

SUBJECT #23: Just an artist.

AGENT BURROUGHS: Can you please elaborate?

SUBJECT #23: I couldn't take my eyes off of it. It's hard to talk.

AGENT BURROUGHS: Please do the best you can.

Transcription note: This is where it gets a little rough. Subject #23 is sobbing, almost hysterical. Whatever gaps there are after interpretation have been filled in with approximate language generated by language software analysis. The following transcription is the best possible interpretation with a calculated 12% chance of error.

SUBJECT #23: Perfection. Beauty incarnate. Geometric perfection. I wanted to capture that. The satisfaction of the perfect circle, perfect sphere. There's something divine about that. I don't know. Something that all artists want. I. I. I wanted to capture something profound. For others to look at. To make sense of their own world, for once. To make things make sense. More than I ever could with words. With images. But I couldn't. I never could. I thought I saw beautiful things that would change people's lives, but I was just seeing shapes and patterns that made no sense. Patterns. Things that make you remember things you don't actually remember. Patterns that make you feel something without a name. That eviscerates your being. Reveal your true nature. What art does.

377

AGENT BURROUGHS: I need you to be very specific. What questions did you ask of it?

SUBJECT #23: I asked about everything. About what the world means. Without art. What does it mean? What beauty is. What makes us feel reverence for an image? What makes us question our being and space.

AGENT BURROUGHS: Do you remember what it told you?

SUBJECT #23: Something stupid. Something with poetry, but also lacking. What art and meaning really are. Not some profound undiscovered planet. Some unobscured mundane thing in the forefront. There is no heaven or hell. What's meaning without art? What's art without meaning? That's the truth behind it all.

AGENT PALIENT: I think we need to call the doctor. He's all loopy.

AGENT BURROUGHS: Maybe from what they gave him. This is all fucked up.

AGENT PALIENT: Should we continue?

AGENT BURROUGHS: Jamie? Can you tell me, word-for-word, what questions you asked?

SUBJECT #23: I can see more clearly
now than I ever have before. Canvases.
That's where we try to capture
meaning. But the universe, it's moving
endlessly, indeterminately. Art and
meaning are not everlasting.
Everything ages with time. Books turn
to dust. Records degrade and shatter.
Canvases are eaten by moths and time.
Art is just a mechanism to stop the
inevitable progression of entropy. It
is destined to fail.

AGENT PALIENT: Let's just get this
over with.

AGENT BURROUGHS: Not yet, Richard,
please, not yet. We have time. Jamie,
can you tell me what you did with the
device?

SUBJECT #23: If I'm going to die
today, can you tell Ophelia I love
her? Can you tell my mother I'm sorry?

AGENT BURROUGHS: Does Ophelia have the
device? Does your mother have the
device?

SUBJECT #23: Was it going to happen to
me, too? Was I going to turn out just
like her? Is it happening already? Am
I going mad?

AGENT PALIENT: I think he's a lost
cause at this point.

SUBJECT #23: It is, isn't it? I'm
going mad just like her. It must be in
me, too. I should have known.
Everything is profoundly and stupidly
different.

AGENT BURROUGHS: Jamie, what did you
do to your mother? Why do you want to
tell her you're sorry?

SUBJECT #23: I know she loves me. Even
though I'm a failure. But I ruined her
life. She'd never admit it to me, but
I know it's true. She would've done
amazing things if I was never born.
That's what I asked it, you know. What
would have happened if I wasn't born.

AGENT BURROUGHS: Does your mother have
the device?

SUBJECT #23: No. She destroyed it.
Threw it out the window.

AGENT PALIENT: Fuck.

AGENT BURROUGHS: Where did this
happen?

SUBJECT #23: At the hospital.

AGENT BURROUGHS: Did you locate it
afterwards?

SUBJECT #23: No. I couldn't find it.

AGENT PALIENT: Welp, back to square one.

AGENT BURROUGHS: Was there anyone else? Did you tell anyone else about it?

SUBJECT #23: No.

AGENT BURROUGHS: Was there anyone else in the room when you brought it to her?

SUBJECT #23: Yes. Someone else. Barely there.

AGENT BURROUGHS: Do you know who he was?

Subject #23: No. Had bandages all over his face.
AGENT PALIENT: I think we're done here, buddy.

AGENT BURROUGHS: No, Richard, please, he's just a kid.

AGENT PALIENT: It's policy.

SUBJECT #23: I thought you were going to help me.

AGENT BURROUGHS: Oh god. Oh god. I'm
so sorry. This is all my fault.

SUBJECT #23: No, please. Don't.

AGENT BURROUGHS: Oh god. What have I
done. What have I done.

AGENT PALIENT: I think he's still
alive.

AGENT BURROUGHS: I need to leave. I
need to get out of here.

AGENT PALIENT: We have to find out who
was at that hospital. We should be
able to get records pretty easily.
I'll send some agents over to
investigate the area. See if they can
find it. She threw it out a fucking
window. Must be out of her goddamn
mind, too. This is all fucked.

AGENT BURROUGHS: I need to leave.

AGENT PALIENT: Calm down, buddy.
Breathe. Remember those breathing
exercises I told you about?
AGENT BURROUGHS: I can't do this
anymore.

AGENT PALIENT: Looks like he's about
to die. Heart rate is slowing. I wish
he'd stop looking at me.

AGENT BURROUGHS: I have to get out of
here.

AGENT PALIENT: Hey, where are you
going?

END TRANSCRIPT

Peter could not catch up to his thoughts. His knee-jerk reaction was to rush to the bathroom to wash the blood off of his face, but deep down he knew he could never wash the blood off of his conscience. The anxiety dominated his body, and his hands were shaking violently.

Hours must have passed before the anxiety subsided. Peter awoke in his office, his lonely office on some lonely floor, without windows—an office that looked just like all the others. He felt drunk, even though he hadn't had a drink in months. He started to understand that his life had fallen apart.

His aimless thoughts were interrupted by a loud and obnoxious knocking at his door. He chose not to get up to answer it. He pretended he wasn't there.

Whoever it was scoffed, then slipped a piece of paper under the door. Peter, lost in the photographs of his wife and children on his desk, couldn't bear to look at them any longer.

The paper was a report, ordered by Richard, on patient records at Saint Emile Memorial Hospital:

CONFIDENTIAL

CASE FILE #19:9

Reporting Agent #18-344: Lisa Horkowitz

Purpose: Classified level 8 clearance, Approval Code #99-B, summary report ordered by reporting agent #101.

Status: Completed

Background: Summary report of patient records at Saint Emile Memorial Hospital, last name Lafferty.

Summary: Investigation of patient records indicate that Mary-Belle Lafferty occupied room 189 for a duration of three days. Further records indicate frequent admissions over the past five years, increasing in frequency and duration as of the past two years. Purpose of admission: monitoring and ongoing treatment for symptoms caused by Huntington's Disease. Visitation records indicate that Jamie Lafferty, son, visited on the date of REDACTED at REDACTED p.m., signing out at REDACTED p.m.

Further investigation of nurse's records indicate that the attending nurse, Bethany O'Keeffe (detained and eliminated as per Nuremberg Status), documented patient belongings upon admission.

Mary-Belle Lafferty was admitted with the following items:

- Hand-written journal
- Lipstick
- Toothbrush
- Worn picture of an infant
- Apartment keys
- Prescriptions for tetrabenazine and haloperidol

Further investigation of patient records indicated another patient was admitted to room 189. Patient's name was REDACTED, admitted REDACTED and discharged on REDACTED. REDACTED was admitted for emergency surgery due to enucleation. Patient records also indicate that REDACTED received numerous and repeated treatments for detoxification and alcohol abuse, along with psychotherapeutic treatment for a variety of issues, namely Post-Traumatic Stress Disorder, Psychosis, Schizophrenia, REDACTED, and suicidal thoughts.

Bethany O'Keeffe's notes revealed that REDACTED was admitted with the following items:

- Wallet with $2 dollars cash
- Sandwich shop punch card
- Picture of a man and two children with cotton candy
- White ball thingy

When he finished reading the report, Peter jumped out of his chair, which he flung into the air and against the pale white concrete wall behind him. Then he proceeded to flip his desk over, stomping on his computer and flinging its disemboweled remains against that same pale white concrete wall.

Peter's violent wrath had a singular cause. He would not find the apparatus and rectify this whole cursed mess if he could not get the redacted name of that patient. He was so close to a resolution, but blocked yet again by some rigid administrative practice without a seemingly reasonable purpose but to complicate, to obfuscate, to make things so more difficult for the sake of being difficult—to redact names, for the sake of redacting.

Carried by a wave of frustration, Peter stormed out of his office, out through the pale white halls with worn blue carpeting, passing by tens of hundreds of portraits of dead white balding men in stale suits, straight to the double elevators.

He went up to the highest possible floor—the 99th floor. A place where no agent was allowed to go. This was the abode of the bigwigs, the fabled Board; the people in charge of it all, whom he had never met, never heard from, never taken orders from. Every case, every project, came to him through a series of overseers, project managers, senior directors, assistant directors, managers, and more supervisors—a seemingly endless chain of command.

Why go up there now? Why risk his career, his life, his soul to confront The Board?

He had reached his breaking point. He had simply had enough. He wanted to confront The Board, to yell and to scream at them, to tell them what big fucking idiots they were, constantly getting in his way, those who approved the Nuremberg Status, those who gave him this case in the first place (by mistake), those who orchestrated the horrible blunders of this company. Those who wasted so many years of his life. Those who were given unlimited leniency for violence, subterfuge, and murder without consequence. He had never questioned it up to this point in his tenure, likely out of a willful ignorance, a foolish hope for something better. For many people these days, bound to a corporate wagon wheel that never stops spinning without really going anywhere, all that keeps them clinging and going on is a desperate hope for something better—which, for most, is never scheduled to arrive.

He also suspected that at least one member of The Board would also likely have the declassified report, with the redacted name that he needed.

The elevator, reaching the seventieth floor, started sputtering and making odd clanging noises. A frightening vibration of clanking and clunking shook under him, as if the elevator's mechanisms hadn't been up to this floor in years. He panicked when he glanced at the laminated elevator inspection paperwork that was dated over a decade ago.

The lights then shut off, leaving him suspended in a frightening yet heavenly state of pitch-black ascension. For a few seconds, Peter wondered whether he had died and started his (unlikely) journey to heaven.

Then the whirring and movement slowed, stumbling to a halt. The doors opened slowly, an isosceles of yellow light breaking through towards Peter.

He wasn't sure what he expected. A massive room of computer screens, a chorus of ringing phones, a gallery of board members sitting around a massive oval table, executives in suits more expensive than his house playing simulated golf—

This was not what he saw. When the elevator doors opened on the 99th floor, Peter was introduced to large, yet vacant, warehouse, lit sparingly by floodlights, its walls and ceiling unfinished, leaving exposed the bare wiring and foundation; an absence of windows, a sense of vacancy and *emptiness reminiscent of the run-down motels Peter would frequent for his sexual escapades*; not some sophisticated office or chamber, but a very empty room.

There was a conference table in the center of the room, with people seated around, looking at each-other, and not a single one moving. They did not acknowledge Peter's arrival or presence. They just went about their mysterious business.

At first, Peter's fear of confrontation left him immobile. But the lack of animation from these Board members gave him some encouragement.

He eased forward, bewildered by a slowing realization that each and every Board member was barely moving. In fact, they weren't moving at all.

He counted twenty in total.

When he edged close enough, he saw why they weren't moving. Their arms, sticking out like crosses, didn't have hands—just empty holes in their suits where hands should be. They were just expensive black suits stuffed with straw, with unshapely straw heads poking out; some with eyes drawn on, others with fake wigs and glasses.

He went to the next floor down, and found a small office with a single desk—labeled "Board Secretary." Another straw person was seated there. This one was dressed in a buttoned up red blazer.

Upset, bewildered, and lost, Peter rushed over to the computer on the desk. This computer was obviously outdated, with an oversized monitor and a single slot for a floppy disk. On the desktop, he discovered a single folder, labeled "UNREDACTED."

This ancient computer had access to every unredacted file in the company database—dating back to the 1960s when the company began storing digital copies.

The first document he found was a letter, written by an apparent "Jamie Lafferty" to his mother, Mary-Belle Lafferty:

Mother,

I'm sorry for the late and undiscussed notice. I have left for Florence. There's a potential commission of my artistic skills to paint portraits of noble visitors from

Peter stood up,, frustrated by the destitute results of his actions. But some distant and forlorn purpose urged him to continue.

It took him less than a minute to find the file he needed. When he pulled it up, he reeled back in disbelief, and wished he was dreaming.

Realizing he was surely awake, he pieced together what had happened that day he lost the device.

He had left the research facility with the device.

In a hurry, wanting to get to the gym before the man he wanted to see would leave the locker room, he rushed out of his office, mindlessly placing the device in his jacket pocket. After the gym, and after…that, he went to see his father.

His brother was there.

His crippled and endlessly suffering brother.

The child klepto.

The redacted name was William Burroughs.

In a demoralized rage, Peter ripped apart the straw secretary and smashed the computer against the wall. He then stormed down to the elevator, went down to the 33rd floor, and ordered the policing agents that had been following his brother for some time now to bring him in, unharmed, for questioning.

Chapter Thirty-Two
My Brother's Keeper

If you listen closely enough to the hum of fluorescent bulbs, you can hear God. I didn't think it was out there, but it's right here. Some definite noise borne beneath vapor. Begging for attention every so often with light flutters and clicks.

How did I end up here? What feeble, so-called choices have escorted me to this room that smells like Pine-sol and sterilized death? What are they keeping me here for? They already have the truth, or at least most of it.

I barely had a chance to turn my life around before two forces of might plucked me from wherever I was wandering and put me here. They didn't say much, but that "Agent Burroughs would like to speak with you." And they asked where the device was. I told them I didn't know. They found it on me almost instantly. Where else can a newly-blind man hide his most prized possessions?

I'd like to imagine that these walls are the whitest walls in the world—not a speck on them. This table feels like metal, like cold and lifeless stainless steel. There must be a two-way mirror in here—the staple of any good interrogation—and there I must be, my reflection in the two-way mirror, stuck in purgatory. *If only I could actually see.*

And this room, clearly, is my purgatory, thought up by some hack of a writer. So unimaginative.

Makes this whole novel shitty, doesn't it? That's the truth I can see now. Our stories are already written. Some of those stories are grand. Most others are god awful—but still *written*. Stories aren't spontaneous. They aren't left up to chance. The words are already on the page, written on the wall, tattooed all over you. Lovely thing not knowing how your story will end. Equally unlovely knowing that your end is inevitable—but terrifyingly dull knowing that your end is *scheduled.*

And I know mine is. I know a lot of things now. That's what total isolation with no eyes and the device does to you. Makes you want to know everything, even the things you've been avoiding asking out of fear, out of a feigning facade of blissful ignorance. But the truth eats at you like that, especially when you know it's there. When you already know the answer. Like a bug in your house you choose to pretend you never saw. Like the sense that someone was following you, knowing wholeheartedly that it is all make believe, but still believing it enough to feel your heart imploding and your chest caving in.

Just think about it for a second, whoever may be reading this god-awful book. Think about the truths about yourself that you don't want to admit are true. Maybe you have doubts about your marriage, about god, about yourself. Maybe you did something awful but are too afraid to admit it. Maybe you are in denial. Not me, not anymore.

But there's still some truths that I refuse to know. (See Chapter 21). I know that my days are numbered. I know how this novel begins—that I am Subject 36 in the prologue, that I will have one final question for the truth box, that afterwards the answer will disrupt me so greatly that I'll slit my own wrists with a #2 pencil (go back and read that prologue, you'll see). My death is timely; it opens and ends the book. That comforts me a little— some sense of order and closure.

I can't change that now. No matter how desperately I fantasize about changing my future trajectory, subverting the whores of destiny and fate. I know with all my stubborn heart that this cannot be changed.

But I'm not afraid of death (certainly not as afraid as Mary-Belle, and I damn well know she is, and that she wishes with all her being not to die so soon). Death is not a truth that scares me anymore. You know you have them, too, those truths you deny to accept. That itching vision, that painful and sudden realization that you bury with dirt and denial, or deliberately choose to distort into the opposite of truth. Those things that, if you simply just accepted them, would shatter everything you are, every- thing you wish to be, everything you want others to see in you. Those truths, those corks in glass bottles—with enough heat and pressure, out pops the truth, and you'll either shatter, bleed to death, or have just enough left to keep drinking whatever life you have left.

But the most painful truth is that those very truths that shatter us are so painfully and pathetically obvious, stabbing at us when we know the daggers are drawn by our own stupid hands. Those truths we admit every day, but choose to ignore every second.

I have a strange feeling Peter is in here with me. Some kind of connection we must have, being brothers and all. I would bet my left eye his arms are crossed, one hand rubbing his mouth with his fingertips, feeling secure behind his window, watching me all alone with myself. He can see me, for all I am. Try my best to make him think I need help, without asking.

Someone opens a door and shuffles in, setting a styrofoam cup in front of me. The smell of styrofoam is stronger than the smell of the coffee. I can tell it's Peter by the way he shuffles—he shuffles when he's nervous, when he's walking into something he is not looking forward to. He sighs, like I've heard before, when I was young—that sigh of disappointment in his younger brother, doing something stupid again, getting himself poison ivy again, chipping his tooth after spin-jumping into the pool and landing smack-jaw onto the concrete edge again.

I wish I had the guts to tell him how I really feel about him. How I know that he despises me, that he sometimes wishes I would just go ahead and die already so he doesn't have to carry the burden of worrying about me anymore. How he detests me for not helping him out enough with Dad. How he has been cursed to carry on the legacy of the Burroughs name (if only he knew Dad was a fraud and his life's work was as meaningless as the piss bottle next to his death bed). How, despite the overwhelming nausea that corrodes him from the inside out when he thinks of me, that he still at least held on to a little bit of love for his pathetic, hallucinating, murderous, drunken, penguin-walking, failure-of-a-soldier little brother.

How I still love him, despite all those truths.

Chapter Thirty-Three
The Trial of Socrates (and the Fateful Hemlock)

CONFIDENTIAL

CASE FILE #19:9

Reporting Agent #12-36: Peter Burroughs

Purpose: Classified level 10 clearance (Nuremberg Status, Approval Code #254ABF792, investigating retrieval of #8-32, modulating intelligence apparatus)

Status: Open

Background: Continued investigation of file #8-32. Subject #36 was apprehended by supporting agents and brought in for interrogation as per Hanberg's Policy #TTT55^^fkf. Subject #36 has been a subject of investigation since the disappearance of #8-32, as is protocol during cases that involve potential threats to corporate welfare and national security, and two agents have been following Subject #36 since RE-DACTED and consistently maintained a proper distance to avoid any suspicion. When the reporting agent had disclosed likelihood that Subject #36 had likely gained access to facilities by stealing Agent #12-36's security access cards while Agent #12-36 was caring for his father in hospice (now deceased). Agent #12-36 can confirm that Subject #36, with whom he shares intimate knowledge of Subject #36's habits and behaviors, has a severe tendency to revert to kleptomaniac behavior in order to satisfy brotherly spite against Agent #12-36. Coupled with Subject #36's debated diagnosis of schizophrenic disorder (likely a psychosomatic by-product of post-traumatic stress disorder), Agent #12-36 came to the conclusion that Subject #36 should be considered a prime suspect in the disappearance of #8-32 and be detained for interview procedures immediately. As was indicated in all previous reports, all investigative avenues have resulted in nada.

Due to a 67% chance of prolonged exposure to #8-32, it is extremely likely that a) Subject #36 may have been exposed long enough to have suffered some high energy radioactive damage and will likely develop some fatal form of cancer within the next 3-5 years and b) has been in possession of #8-32 for a significant amount of time and has likely gathered a troublesome amount of classified information related to national and international security concerns, and, as such, should be treated as a highly dangerous individual and a prime candidate for execution of the Nuremberg Status.

Subject #36 was apprehended after Agent #12-36 and Agent #101's exhaustive interview of Subject #23. Lines of questioning indicated that Subject #36 was present in the same room as Subject #23, having been admitted for emergency surgery due to enucleation. Further investigations and reports indicate that Subject #36 was the original possessor of the device, having attempted to destroy it. However, through a process known as "divine intervention," the device found its way back to Subject #36's room.

Subject #23's intent is currently unknown, but the #8-32 had been obtained by Subject #23's mother (yet to be in custody—current location unknown). Subject #23's mother then proceeded to attempt to destroy the apparatus by sending it through the room's only window. However, the attending nurse, REDACTED, successfully retrieved the apparatus, recognizing it as a cherished belonging of Subject #36, and promptly returned the apparatus. (It is unknown at this time whether REDACTED was aware of 8-32's capabilities.)

When agents were sent to retrieve Subject #36, Subject #36 was found wandering outside a decrepit church. It is likely that, due to his injuries and insufficient acclimation to navigation with severe visual impairment, Subject #36 was completely unaware of his location. He was found in possession of #8-32 and admitted direct involvement in its disappearance.[6]. Current status of #8-32, at the initial timestamp of this report, is *recovered.*

As part of Case File 19:9's research status of "ongoing," protocol demanded that any interviews with Subject #36 be conducted in the presence of Agent #8-32 in order to provide further intensive study of

---

[6] Emphasis added by Agent #12-36.

interaction, query results, and physiological/psychological impacts on possessors. It should also be noted that Subject #36 looked extremely disheveled and malnourished, wearing a pair of sunglasses that he refused to take off. His request to continue wearing said sunglasses was approved to avoid further conflict, despite how ridiculous they looked.

Purpose of interrogation:

1. Determine who else may have been exposed to #8-32
2. Determine nature of interactions and queries between Subject #36 and #8-32
3. Execute Nuremberg Status.

Note: Within the following transcript, violations of Code of Ethics #541abcD have been omitted as Code of Ethics #541abcD policies are null and void per qualifying conditions indicated via Hanberg's Policy #TTT55^^fkf2.

BEGIN TRANSCRIPT

AGENT BURROUGHS: Commencing interrogation #97 in case 19:9, chief investigative agent #12-36 Peter Burroughs and assisting investigative agent #101, Richard Palient. Interrogation recipient is Subject #36, William Burroughs. Please note that I, Agent Burroughs, can confirm that William Burroughs is indeed my blood-related brother. William, say something.

SUBJECT #36: You're not going to ask what happened to my eyes?

AGENT BURROUGHS: I am very concerned about you, William. I'm just trying to do my job.

SUBJECT #36: You've always been married to your job.

AGENT BURROUGHS: I'm also just trying to help you. I don't want you to be harmed.

SUBJECT #36: Don't worry, I'm in perfect shape.

AGENT BURROUGHS: I don't think you understand the seriousness of this situation. The danger you've been exposed to. Do you understand what you had?

SUBJECT #36: I always told myself deep down that you still cared about me.

AGENT BURROUGHS: William, this isn't a therapy session. Do you understand what I do? Why am I here? Why are you here?

SUBJECT #36: Because I had the device and you were looking for it.

AGENT BURROUGHS: Yes, the device. Can you imagine what people could do with that kind of power?

SUBJECT #36: I've started to realize that these days.

AGENT BURROUGHS: I'm going to get right to the point. I need you to tell me who else has interacted with this thing.

SUBJECT #36: Have you?

AGENT BURROUGHS: This is not about me. This is about you.

SUBJECT #36: Why don't you just ask?

AGENT BURROUGHS: Billy, please stop playing games.

SUBJECT #36: I'm sorry. I'm not trying to play games.

AGENT BURROUGHS: You have no idea how deathly worried I am about you, Billy. You look awful. Just fucking awful. We can talk about what happened to you later, when I know you're safe. But I need you to answer some questions that I have to ask you. We need to ask these questions. And you need to answer them honestly. Can I ask you to do that for me, Billy?

SUBJECT #36: I'm sorry.

AGENT BURROUGHS: What are you sorry for?

SUBJECT #36: I don't know exactly. I'm just sorry.

AGENT BURROUGHS: I'm sorry too. It's my fault you're in this position.

SUBJECT #36: Because I stole…

AGENT BURROUGHS: No, no, no. We're not going to talk about that.

SUBJECT #36: Why not?

AGENT BURROUGHS: It doesn't matter.

SUBJECT #36: Shouldn't it, though?

AGENT BURROUGHS: Not today. We need to examine what you know.

SUBJECT #36: Examine?

AGENT BURROUGHS: Find out. I meant find out.

SUBJECT #36: Am I just an experiment to you?

AGENT BURROUGHS: No, Billy. Not to me. You're my brother. But the company does want to know a little bit about

your experiences. Just to understand.
That's all, just to understand what
happened to you.

SUBJECT #36: Is this conversation
being recorded?

AGENT BURROUGHS: Yes, it has to be.

SUBJECT #36: Peter left it at our
Dad's. I stole it.

AGENT BURROUGHS: Are you fuck...Ok,
Billy. That's not what I asked you.

SUBJECT #36: But that's how I got a
hold of it. You left it there. It was
your fault.

AGENT BURROUGHS: That's not true. Let
the reporting record demonstrate that
the subject is clearly falsifying
testimony to agitate the interviewing
agent.

SUBJECT #36: What else do you want to
know?

AGENT BURROUGHS: You don't have to
smile like that. You haven't won.

SUBJECT #36: Sure feels like it. Yeah,
this feels nice.

AGENT BURROUGHS: William, I need you to tell me right now the nature of your interactions with the apparatus.

SUBJECT #36: Do you remember when we were younger, what you told me about those save files on the Mario games we used to play?

AGENT BURROUGHS: What...yes, I do.

SUBJECT #36: Do you remember what you used to tell me?

AGENT BURROUGHS: No.

SUBJECT #36: There were those checkpoints you would reach once you beat a certain level. "Save and Continue." "Do not save and continue." When we were kids, you used to tell me that they meant the opposite. I had to hit "Do not save" to save. So I never saved any of the progress I made.

AGENT BURROUGHS: Are you trying to be poetic right now?

SUBJECT #36: It's a shitty analogy, I know. But it's the best I can come up with to help you understand. How was I supposed to know any better? What reasons would I have to not trust my older brother? I wholeheartedly believed what you told me. But the truth you had told me, that I had

402

accepted as true, was actually
bullshit. Like the truths we live with
that end up being lies. That's what my
life has been like for the past twenty
something years. Living my life
according to some lies that I had been
told or grown to accept because I
trusted them, without ever really
questioning them. And I've been
questioning a lot of things lately.
But getting answers—man, that's heavy.
You'd think that knowing whether or
not there's a god out there somewhere.
Or knowing when you'll die, or what
the meaning of life is. Whether you
have really done those horrible things
in your past. If your father, or your
own brother, actually loves you. If
the person you love will ever love you
back. You know, it's funny. You feel
more alive asking those questions than
you do knowing the answers. I'm no
poet, but that's poetic.

AGENT BURROUGHS: I'm not sure what
you're trying to get at.

SUBJECT #36: Don't say that. Don't
fucking say that. You of all people
should know what I'm talking about.

AGENT BURROUGHS: What are you talking
about?

SUBJECT #36: You're lying to yourself,
Peter. You have this shell of a dead

man's skin hiding who you truly are, and you won't give in and accept it. You choose to ignore it, pretend it will go away. But it won't. Truths that we choose to ignore.

AGENT BURROUGHS: How would you have any idea about me? How would you have a fucking clue? You've been fucking fading away ever since you got back. Selfish fucking prick. Shutting yourself off from the world. From taking care of dad. Boo fucking hoo. That's why your fucking wife left you, because you're a pathetic, slacking piece of shit that doesn't care about anyone else's problems but your own, and doesn't do a goddamn thing about it.

SUBJECT #36: Where the hell have you been? You've never been there for me. An older brother is supposed to guide me. Take care of me. Help me when I need it. You'd rather have me die. You wanted me to die.

AGENT BURROUGHS: What about all the times I've taken you to detox? To the emergency room? Those stupid fucking sleeping pills? I spent an entire weekend trying to get you into rehab for you to change your goddamn mind. I had a fucking panic attack trying to deal with you.

SUBJECT #36: You basically forgot I even existed when you didn't have to watch over me anymore.

AGENT BURROUGHS: And what about dad? You did shit all to help take care of him. I spent months, months having to listen to him fucking howling and dying like some sick animal. Rambling on and on about formulas and realities. I put in my goddamn time and dues, and you did not.

SUBJECT #36: Putting in your dues. You're talking about dad like he was some sort of chore.

AGENT BURROUGHS: You're goddamn right it was.

SUBJECT #36: Speaking about him in the past tense.

AGENT BURROUGHS: That's right, because he's fucking dead.

SUBJECT #36: I know. It's just interesting, that's all.

AGENT BURROUGHS: Interesting? Interesting how?

SUBJECT #36: I don't want to say it anymore.

AGENT BURROUGHS: No, no, fuck no.
You've gotten me all flustered. Now
you have to say it.

SUBJECT #36: I think you know.

AGENT BURROUGHS:[7] I don't know what
you're talking about.

SUBJECT #36: I've found out a lot of
things about the world, Peter. About
me. About you. I've spent a lot of
time with the truth box. It was
addicting, like I couldn't stop asking
it. I asked when Dad would die. Then I
asked how he died. He died right in
front of you. I know I wasn't there.
But you were. He died right next to
you. Right after you gave him his
morphine. And you laid in bed that
night, contemplating it. Did you give
him too much? Did you really give him
too much? Do you want to know how he
died? Do you want to know if you
killed our father?

AGENT BURROUGHS: I didn't mean to.

SUBJECT #36: I know the truth about
that, too.

AGENT BURROUGHS: Billy, you have to
understand. Everything that night was
just going...I had a lot on my mind...

---

[7] Reviewing agent note: notable silence preceding statement.

SUBJECT #36: There's one thing I don't know. I want to ask you right now.

AGENT BURROUGHS: What?

SUBJECT #36: Did you feel relieved? That he was finally dead?

AGENT BURROUGHS: How am I supposed to answer that?[8] I did. I really did.

SUBJECT #36: I did, too. You see that? There's some sort of beauty there. The truth is...you know what, I'm not really sure. I suppose this is a good spot to let the reader figure it all out.

AGENT BURROUGHS: I'm sorry, William. I have to leave the room.

SUBJECT #36: It's ok, Peter. I know it's coming.

AGENT BURROUGHS: What do you mean?

SUBJECT #36: I know. It's ok. I'm ready.

AGENT BURROUGHS: Billy.

---

[8] Reviewing agent note: another considerable pause during recorded speech. Examine further for damage to the record as a potential cause for these gaps.

SUBJECT #36: I know.

AGENT BURROUGHS:[9] You...can ask it whatever you want. I'll be right outside.

SUBJECT #36: That's funny. I don't remember you saying that.[10] I had you for so long. I know this is the last question I get to ask you. You already know what I ask you. What am I going to ask you?

FILE #8-32: You are going to ask me about the baby and her mother.

SUBJECT #36: I am. This is the stupid truth I've known all along. I've known it. I've lived it. I don't really know why I've avoided it all this time. But I guess now's a better time than never, considering the circumstances. Wouldn't you agree?

FILE #8-32: Yes.

SUBJECT #36: Alright, then. Here it is.[11] Did I kill them?

---

[9] Another considerable pause. Is this tape botched?

[10] Reporting agent note: assume the interviewing agent left the room at this point. Significant time gaps occur in between verbal transactions within this transcript; refer to Report #ATJT4433 for exact time frames in between participant utterances.

[11] Reporting agent note: Another, much more considerable silence.

FILE #8-32: No.

SUBJECT #36: No?[12] No. I guess I skimmed that part. Huh. Well. That changes everything.

AGENT BURROUGHS: Richard, no. He's my brother.

SUBJECT #36: This is it, isn't it?

AGENT BURROUGHS: Richard, no. Not now.

ASSISTING AGENT #101: Peter, you know it has to happen.

SUBJECT #36: It's okay, Peter. I knew this was coming.

AGENT BURROUGHS: William. I'm sorry. I'm so sorry.

END TRANSCRIPT

Reporting agent notes: Last known recorded appearance of Assisting Agent #101 Richard Palient. Also last known recorded appearance of Modulating Intelligence Apparatus #8-32. Figure out what the fuck happened in there.

---

[12] Reporting agent note: further considerable pauses. Reporting agent faithfully recommends that this script format be abandoned for a system that can better represent the temporal nuances of human speech.

Chapter Thirty-Four
The Truth is Buried with the Dead

Peter knew that only so many people would have gathered for William's funeral. Beaty, some of the fabled members of his squad. Kirby was there. Dale was there. Jonathan One had died in a freak snowmobile accident. Jonathan Two died from a severe overdose of painkillers.

Peter knew that he had to hand in his resignation that day, no longer able to bear artificial burdens of ineptitude, unable to accept the ruthless and merciless policies and procedures that castrated human life into nothing more than a footnote. He could no longer bear the heaviness of it all.

They required him to sign a nondisclosure agreement, and asked no questions of their own. They had assumed he had been telling the truth—

That William was solely responsible for the disappearance, having stolen Peter's identification and infiltrated the premises, destroying all evidence in his tracks.

That Richard disappeared after murdering William.

That Richard left with the apparatus.

That Richard had been acting senseless and reckless since his grandfather was assassinated.

Peter had filed enough useless reports that would never actually be read; the truth was now buried in bureaucratic graves, coffins made from copy paper and dirt composed of an endless noise of digital communications. Case file #8-32 would never be closed; the file would be open indefinitely, with yet again the same adage: the whereabouts of the apparatus are unknown and investigations are ongoing.

But Peter knew that they would never suspect the truth to be buried so well.

Peter also knew that he could not bear witness to his own brother's cold-blooded murder, despite all the ill memories of their entire brotherhood. Peter knew that he hadn't fired his own firearm for years up until that day, and recognized immediately the euphoric adrenaline sunsetting his patient anxiety—that he had killed a man, like he has done thousands and thousands of times before to a lesser, much more personal, degree. Peter accepted that he was now a murderer. Peter also knew that records could be falsified, camera recordings could be tampered with, and so much truth could be lost in the bureaucratic static, where no one would be the wiser, and a dead man could be buried in a mismarked grave.

Peter knew that the body being buried that day was a lie.

Peter understood that his father was finally dead and gone.

Peter accepted that his brother was gone as well—gone for good, never to be seen again.

Yet, in all this newfound knowledge, Peter felt empty, staring at William's shallow and flat headstone; realizing life's incredible fragility, the shortness of it all, the shame of taking Ada and his children for granted—but, yet again, the unbridled otherness burrowed deeply in his chest, the primeval urge and desire that he'd failed to extinguish—failed to accept—failed to acknowledge and live with as an integral organ to his own self—

Peter and Ada held hands as they adored the abyss of the sky above them. Peter gently pulled away her black veil so he could face her, truthfully, for the first time in ages. She looked dreary, older than Peter remembered in his daydreams. Her eyelids had little browned pits beneath them. Branches of wrinkles stemmed from the corners of her bright blue eyes. She had some gray in her roots. *This is my wife,* Peter sang quietly to himself. *And she is beautiful.* She turned to notice his stoic panic, and rested her hand on his cheek. He burst into tears. She cried as well.

"Ada, I'm..."

"I know," she whispered, smiling, crying, resting her hands on his red cheeks.

He thought she expected him to say he's sorry, for being a terrible father and husband.

She thought his real self was coming out.

They lowered "William" into the embracing bosom of the earth, forever.

They would never find it. *They would never know.*

Why?

Because the truth is buried with the dead.

Epilogue

The truth is, I never thought I would make it here. I can't see a damn thing, but the echoes tell me enough.

"Can you describe it to me?" I ask Mary-Belle.

She sighs, unloading waves of grief and despair. Her son, off on some expedition to Florence, had abandoned her to die, leaving her little choice but to join me on a spur of the moment voyage to some beach in Mexico. It sure was a mystery why she so easily chose to go with me. But she did, and here she is, accompanying me on my trip to nowhere, in search of nothingness.

"It's stunning." She pauses. "The tide breathes, and the clouds recede into an infinite regress outward, towards the gentle curvature of the earth."

And suddenly, I can see it, clear as day.

To my left, Mary-Belle, looking angelic and prepared. To my right, the red-skinned demon Belial, forever following me, leaning back in his lounge chair, his ram-like horns blending into the twisting palm trees; he takes a break from reading this novel, adjusting his reading glasses slightly; hooved feet propped up and crossed, sipping his margarita and sighing at the simple truth of a beautiful sunrise.

www.ingramcontent.com/pod-product-compliance
Lightning Source LLC
Chambersburg PA
CBHW060611300726
48975CB00005B/1523